T0162703

# The Ag Boys

## Edward F. Roberts

iUniverse, Inc.
New York   Bloomington

The Ag Boys

Copyright © 2009 Edward F. Roberts

All rights reserved. No part of this book may be used or reproduced by any means, graphic, electronic, or mechanical, including photocopying, recording, taping or by any information storage retrieval system without the written permission of the publisher except in the case of brief quotations embodied in critical articles and reviews.

This is a work of fiction. All of the characters, names, incidents, organizations, and dialogue in this novel are either the products of the author's imagination or are used fictitiously.

iUniverse books may be ordered through booksellers or by contacting:

iUniverse
1663 Liberty Drive
Bloomington, IN 47403
www.iuniverse.com
1-800-Authors (1-800-288-4677)

Because of the dynamic nature of the Internet, any Web addresses or links contained in this book may have changed since publication and may no longer be valid. The views expressed in this work are solely those of the author and do not necessarily reflect the views of the publisher, and the publisher hereby disclaims any responsibility for them.

ISBN: 978-1-4401-0786-3 (pbk)
ISBN: 978-1-4401-0787-0 (ebk)

Printed in the United States of America

iUniverse rev. date: 3/2/2009

To

Yuki

*A dying bird always looks back towards its nest.*

Old Vietnamese proverb


*Don't ever let the truth interfere with a good bullshit story.*

Old Southern Proverb

# Bolita Sam and Wet Cotton

During the hot summer months, the sun rises gently over the vast expanse of northern Florida pine forests, slowly showing its power as the giant primeval fireball that first brought life to this planet eons ago. The early morning heat of the sun causes the dew that has collected overnight on the leaves of the palmetto bushes and cat briars to evaporate, creating a fine gray mist that looks like some delicate piece of fine lace hanging over the forest floor.

By noon, the delicate mist is gone, and the sun is a giant yellow beast, an unmerciful thing, hanging in the midday sky like an ancient medieval executioner, tormenting every living thing within its reach. The sun beats down on the surfaces of the paved roads, sending up a glimmering sheen of heat that creates dark mirages on the black asphalt surfaces. Dirt roads become elongated ovens when the white limestone sand becomes too hot for the barefoot children who must brave its wrath at midday.

The heat will continue until late afternoon. Then, slowly, but inevitably, storm clouds begin to form on the western horizon. They build slowly in the afternoon sky, unnoticed at first, until they become so large and dark they can no longer be ignored. Looking like a giant ebony blanket being pulled over the land, the black clouds send sharp cracks of thunder and bright flashes of lightning across the afternoon sky. Breezes from the storm clouds cool and stir the air, until the heavy rains fall to the earth in monsoon-like torrents, soaking everything.

By sundown, the rain is gone, and the heat returns, coated with a thick layer of sticky humidity. Clothes cling to the skin, eyeglasses fog up, and the slightest movement brings on a torrent of perspiration.

1

As the short summer night comes on, the air cools, but the humidity remains high. The sinking of the sun brings out the bugs, and the air is alive with the sound of crickets, frogs, whip-poor-wills, and all the other assorted creatures of the night. The sticky heat and the torment of the mosquitoes and yellow flies do not allow a restful sleep for man or beast.

During the dark Florida night, the Florida panthers and black bear prowl the swamps and pinewoods, often with their fur eaten away in patches by ringworms and mange. Deer wander aimlessly, braving even the paved roads, seeking food and attempting to escape the torment of the biting yellow flies that follow them everywhere.

All life twists and turns in its misery, until the dew-drenched break of day, when the cycle begins anew with the gathering of the lace-like mist over the wet vegetation.

I was born in October, when the weather in Florida begins to change for the better. Sometimes, it happens abruptly when an arctic cold front comes roaring across the South preceded by heavy rains. Other times, it is more gradual with the earth slowly cooling like an old skillet taken off the fire. The first sign of the coming of fall is a slow decrease in the humidity. An ever-so-slow cooling then follows the drying of the air, until finally summer is over, and the weather is more comfortable.

People in north Florida greet the cooler days of fall much like their countrymen in the Yankee North greet the coming of spring after a long and cold winter. In Florida, things are reversed; fall is the happy time of year, when everyone breathes with relief that the terrible hot summer is over.

My grandmother told me that there was a white frost on the ground that October morning in 1945 when I was born. It was an early frost, since the weather in north Florida usually doesn't dip below freezing until November or December.

Florida winters are a roller coaster with radical shifts of temperature interspersed with often-violent periods of heavy rain. The large arctic air masses that might have dumped several feet of snow on Chicago or St. Louis are muted in their intensity by the time the jet stream has pushed them to the semitropical Florida peninsula. However, that doesn't mean they have lost all of their chilling bite. When a hard freeze hits, the temperature can drop as low as fifteen degrees, with wind chills going into the single digits. The notion that it never gets cold in Florida is a myth.

The brief cold snaps are made worse by the fact that most Florida homes are not built for cold weather. Only a handful of homes in Union County have what northern people call central heat. Many have tiny redbrick fireplaces and crude cast-iron, wood-burning stoves. Other homes have to rely on electric space heaters or portable kerosene heaters, both of which are dangerous sources of fire, especially when children or pets are involved. When the temperature drops and the air is clear and cold, the volunteer firemen do not sleep well. They toss and turn with an ear turned to the loud siren atop the fire station. When the klaxon sounds, the heart beats faster, and a feeling of dread sweeps the body. By the time the firemen crawl out of bed and respond, the house is only a pile of smoldering charred white pine and twisted tin.

All people can hope for is that everyone got out uninjured. Despite the tragedy, prayers will be said thanking God for no deaths. That's the kind of people they are. Neighbors will collect warm clothing, food, blankets, and pillows. Relatives will take the homeless family in until they can get back on their feet. Soon, mayonnaise jars will spring up in local stores collecting spare change for aid to the family that has lost everything in the fire, except their most important things, family and friends.

The cold snaps are always followed by a nice warming trend, with highs reaching into the mid-seventies during the daytime and lows in the forties at night. The days are picture perfect, warm, and balmy, just right for outdoor activity. It is like a New England Indian summer day that keeps returning all winter. The pleasant warming trend will last until the next arctic cold front comes barreling through, always preceded by heavy rains followed by a hard freeze, again repeating the typical winter cycle.

The coming of spring is always early in north Florida, arriving in late February and early March. It might bring out the pink dogwood blossoms and the wisteria's purple flowers, but everyone knows that this display of nature's beauty only hearkens the return of the sticky, hot days of summer.

Everyone watches for the signs. Easter lilies growing wild in the ditches next to the highway mean that it is warm enough to go without shoes. When the pecan trees bud, it means that there will be no more freezes. When the crepe myrtle sends forth its violet flowers, it tells the old farmer that the watermelons are ripe. The vine-ripe watermelons and the workings of the sweat glands are the final confirmation—for anyone who might need it—that the sticky heat and humidity of the long, hot summer has finally arrived. There will be no relief until late October.

The place God thrust me that cold October morning in 1945 is known in the official records and state maps as Union County, Florida. It is not the Florida of white sandy beaches and luxury hotels. There are no condominiums, dog tracks, or *jai alai* in Union County. This is the other Florida, the noncoastal expanses of deep pine forests and oak scrub. It is the region that sarcastic newspapermen describe as "Baja Georgia." Others have called the inland areas "the Florida poverty strip."

It's really hard to describe Union County. To those driving through, it is just a typical southern, rural, and agricultural county. Its chief industries in 1945 were tobacco farming and naval stores. The term "naval stores" came into being, because the tall masts of eighteenth-century sailing ships were made from evergreen trees, and the sticky sap of the pine tree was used to make the vessels watertight.

Today, the term "naval stores" no longer applies to sailing ships, but rather to the paper products made from pinewood chips, commonly called "pulpwood" and the turpentine obtained by tapping the pine tree's viscous sap, called "pine tar" by the local people.

The naval stores' industry came to Florida in 1929, thanks to a nearly deaf genius named Alfred I. DuPont. Already one of the wealthiest men in the United States, thanks to his family's gunpowder and chemical industry, the sixty-five-year-old Alfred DuPont wasn't a man of leisure. He loved a challenge and was most happy when consumed with matters of business. Mostly estranged from his family in Delaware, the victim of a bad marriage and bitter divorce, Alfred I. DuPont was looking to start over in Florida with the support of his new wife, Jessie Ball-DuPont.

Dupont was shocked when he discovered that two thirds of the three million tons of commercial newsprint used in the United States each year was imported from Canada and the Scandinavian countries. On the long train ride down from his native Delaware, DuPont had seen thousands of acres of pine forests fly past his private railroad car's windows.

All the "experts" politely explained to the handsome millionaire that pine trees are too rich with sap to be turned into paper products. It was believed that southern pine forests were useful only for cheap building materials and turpentine, a product used to thin paint.

All this changed when Alfred I. Dupont came in contact with a Savannah, Georgia, chemist Dr. Charles H. Herty, who maintained that the thick pine tar resin was found mainly in the heartwood of mature pine trees. Herty discovered that trees less than twenty-five years old could be converted into pulp to make paper products. By doing careful research, Dr. Herty discovered that the optimum time to harvest pulpwood trees was when they were fifteen years old.

That was all Alfred I. DuPont needed to know. Along with his brilliant, but eccentric, brother in law, Ed Ball, he began the St. Joe Paper Company. DuPont purchased thousands of acres of pinewood land and built the first paper mill in the panhandle community of St. Joe. The small community had good railroad connections to his vast expanse of woodlands and access to the Gulf of Mexico, where it would be easy to ship his paper products to market.

Much of Union County was destined to become part of the naval stores' industry founded by Alfred I. DuPont. It was estimated that over 80 percent of Union County's 240 square miles of land is covered in pine forests, either in private or corporate hands. The rest was mostly hard scrabble farms, where people try to eke a living out of the sandy loam soil growing cotton, corn, tobacco and raising cattle, chickens, and hogs.

There are four bodies of water important to the basic geography of Union County. The New River forms the eastern boundary of the county, separating it from Bradford County. To call the New River a river is really stretching reality. It is little more of a tiny winding stream, snaking though a wide flood plain of knee-deep grass and cypress swamps. To the south, lies the only slightly larger and more prominent Santa Fe River, which divides Union County from the much larger and urban Alachua County, well known as the home of the University of Florida. To the west is Olustee Creek, a narrow, but fast-flowing, stream banked by nothing but thick cypress swamps and pine forest. It separates Union County from Columbia County, famous in those days as north Florida's vice capitol.

The northern border, separating Union County from Baker County, is nothing but an imaginary line on a map. It cuts razor sharp and straight as an arrow through a vast expanse of mostly uninhabited pine forests. The forth body of water is a small, nondescript lake just to the north of Union County's largest town and capitol seat. It is from this small body of muddy brown water that Lake Butler draws its name.

On the banks of the New River, in the extreme northeastern part of Union County, are the grounds of Florida State Prison. In 1945, it held only about fifteen hundred prisoners and had a guard force of around a hundred men working three shifts.

The Florida State Prison was the only place where the outside world touched Union County. The prison has housed and executed some of the most violent criminals in the United States. Behind its high cyclone-wire fences sits Florida's one and only electric chair. By 1964, it had claimed the lives of 197 convicted capital criminals and had brought worldwide attention to the little community of Raiford, which had the bad or good luck, depending on how you look at it, of being the closest community to the prison.

In 1945, very few people knew where Lake Butler or Union County was, but everyone had heard of Raiford. Lawmen all over the state of Florida told their suspects, "You're going to Raiford, boy." Among law enforcement officers, big city reporters and career criminals, the misnomer "Raiford Prison" was as notorious as Sing Sing, Leavenworth, or Alcatraz.

Other than the random executions, escapes and riots that transpired at the prison, nothing really important or famous has ever happened in Union County. No strategic battles were ever fought on Union County soil. No famous person has been born or has died in Union County. There is not even any real evidence that the county was inhabited by large numbers of pre-Columbian Native American tribes. It was as if God had decreed that this flat, pine-tree-covered little piece of earth would be forever unspoken about beyond its borders, except in the context of electric chairs and steel bars.

To know Union County, a person must be born and raised in Union County. However, ironically, I wasn't born in Union County, and most of the other children and adults I knew as a child were not born there. Union County has no hospital or birthing clinic. Many poor white and black children are born at home with the help of a midwife. However, those who could afford it drove the sixty miles to Jacksonville or Gainesville to have their children in the safety and comfort of a hospital. Therefore, being a member of the economic strata that could afford it, I was born in Alachua General Hospital in Gainesville.

The rules were bent in these cases; a general understanding was in effect. When running for local public office, it was important to be able to put in your campaign literature that you were "born and 'reared' in Union County." Xenophobia is high in small, isolated communities in the Deep South, and outsiders make little headway in social climbing or gaining political power. Even though you might have been born in a hospital in Gainesville or Jacksonville, if your parents were residents of Union County when you were born, you could make the famous claim of having been "born and 'reared' in Union County."

During my preschool years, I spent a lot of time visiting with my paternal grandparents who lived in Worthington Springs. It was a tiny place of only about one hundred voting residents, located in the extreme southwestern part of Union County. Sometimes, it seemed as if this tiny and little-known place on the opposite end of the county balanced the notoriety of Raiford with its famous prison at the other end.

Worthington Springs was perched on a high bluff overlooking the sinister-looking waters of the Santa Fe River. Below the high bluff next to the river laid a freshwater spring that had been turned into a summer tourist destination before the turn of the century. In those days, trains brought heat-exhausted tourists from Gainesville and Jacksonville to refresh themselves in the concrete pool, built to collect the cool waters of the tiny spring. The spring once boasted of a ten-room hotel and a wooden two-story bathhouse, built around the concrete pool to ensure the privacy of ladies, who were required to swim at a separate time than the men.

Early in the twentieth century, there was a series of well-publicized drowning at the spring. This was followed by a series of mysterious fires that destroyed the hotel and bathhouse. This caused the summer tourists to stop coming. By the late 1940s—when I played happily in the front yard of my grandfather's two-story house—the old bathhouse had been nothing but ashes for over forty years, and all signs of the cracked and broken concrete pool were covered with tall stands of dog fennel weeds and thick tangles of thorny vines.

The little town of Worthington Springs had only two white churches, one Baptist and one Methodist; a post office; two grocery stores with gasoline pumps out front; a couple dozen fairly nice-looking houses; and a small cotton gin that was owned by my grandfather, Robert Benjamin Roberts.

My grandfather was a wonderful old man, who was over six feet tall and weighed well in excess of 300 pounds. He was a third-generation Florida cracker and looked the part. He had a full head of snow-white hair and was usually seen wearing khaki pants held up by beige suspenders over an open-necked white shirt. He sometimes wore a coat and tie, but he never wore a belt.

My grandfather's family had moved to Florida from South Carolina sometime after the United States had purchased Florida from Spain in 1821. The family is listed on the 1860 census as owning 450 acres of land, a six-room "dog-trot" house, a barn, and eight slaves. All my family fought for the South during the Civil War, with one of my grandfather's uncles being killed at Petersburg. My great grandfather had ridden with the Second Florida Cavalry, when they repulsed a Union Army invasion of Florida at Olustee Station. After the Civil War, he was active in the Ku Klux Klan, having to hide out for months in the deep pinewoods of Olustee and dodging Yankee cavalry patrols.

My grandfather had been a restless and imaginative youth, who craved the same type of adventure his father had experienced during the Civil War. He left home when he was eighteen years old to travel to Alaska and look for gold. He was very proud of that adventure and loved to tell stories about his days as a gold prospector.

On his white shirt, he proudly wore a solid gold watch with a long, heavy gold chain. On the end of the chain dangled a beautiful gold nugget. It was a large, pear-shaped blob of gold, bigger than a nickel. He had found the nugget in a muddy riverbank in the Alaskan goldfields in the summer of 1901. He could have sold it for a lot of money, but instead, he had it made into part of the gold watch chain. The pleasure he got from telling stories about the gold nugget gave him much more enjoyment than any amount of money he could have made by selling it.

My grandfather had a good understanding of what things were worth. He used to say that it is very important for an old man to have pleasant memories.

Also, my grandfather really didn't need the money. He was a self-made man of considerable worth by Union County standards. Robert Benjamin Roberts had a variety of business interests; he owned large stretches of land, where he had over twenty sharecropper families growing mostly cotton with some tobacco. He also owned and operated a grocery store and a cotton gin in Worthington Springs.

My grandfather's store was the larger of the two stores in Worthington Springs, fully twice the size of the other grocery store. It was a rectangular building, painted white, with green double front doors and a large loading dock in the rear. It had a very steep A-frame roof covered with rusted sheets of tin that made a delightful noise when it rained. The store sold a wide combination of groceries as well as dry goods. You could buy everything from a loaf of bread to a pair of overalls and brogan shoes made from kangaroo skin. There were two gas pumps out front, one for "high test" or ethyl gasoline and the other for the cheaper, low-octane or "regular" gasoline.

My grandfather's store was also the primary social gathering place of Worthington Springs. He had a small office near the main entrance to the store, and it was there that he spent most of his day, sitting before an old rolltop desk, in a well-worn swivel chair, and holding court like a medieval nobleman.

Every day, except Sunday, a small knot of Worthington Springs' citizens would gather at the store, loitering out front, drinking cold drinks, smoking and spitting tobacco, and waiting their turn to go in and ask for a favor.

Next to his old rolltop desk, my grandfather had a large black Diabold safe, where he kept important documents and cash. Many people would come by just to ask him to put something in his safe. It might be a will, a deed, or, often as not, a sum of cash they didn't want to keep at home.

Most of the people hanging around the store wanted to borrow a few dollars. My grandfather was well-known as a soft touch, a real sucker for a sad story; so he often lent out money interest free to those in need, much to the anger of the bank in Lake Butler. However, God help anybody who didn't pay him back. He was known to have a bad temper and little patience with deadbeats.

Grandpa Roberts, or Papa Roberts, as I was officially instructed to call him, was often called upon to display his great skills as a layman's lawyer, a peddler of political influence, arbitrator of disputes, teacher of great knowledge, and giver of vast amounts of free medical advice.

The people in Worthington Springs called my grandfather "Doc Roberts." People claimed that I had a strong family resemblance to him, so they often called me "Little Doc," which made me very happy.

"Doc" Roberts had no medical degree and held no license to practice medicine. He was what people in the South called a "root doctor." His "patients" were a motley collection of ignorant and often very poor white and black folks, who came to him complaining about a variety of minor ailments. Papa Roberts was smart enough to know what was beyond his ability, and, when someone was seriously ill, he would send them, often at his own expense, to a real medical doctor in Gainesville.

Those he did treat, he medicated with a variety of herbs, tonics, poultices, and common sense advice. He was very fond of Castor Oil, BC Powders, Fletcher's Castoria, Syrup of Black Draught, and various other over-the-counter medications. His amateur doctoring was popular with poor people who could not afford to go to a regular doctor. Doc Roberts never charged anybody for his services, but he was constantly cultivating political allies, good friends, and steady customers for his store. His great strength came in the fact that people liked and trusted him and returned his favors by voting like "Mr. Doc" told them to.

Doc Roberts was most famous as the man to see to get rid of warts. When I was four years old, I got warts on my hands, and I was sent by my mother to get them removed.

The hog-jowled old men who loitered outside my grandfather's store said that frogs caused warts. They said that when a frog pissed on your hand, it caused the warts to form. With mock seriousness, they said, "Boy, you better quit playing with them damned frogs." When I went to see my grandfather, I told him I had never had anything to do with any frogs, but, for some reason, that only made him laugh.

My grandfather treated the warts by soaking my hands in a strong vinegar solution and then rubbing them with a chicken bone from a white chicken. He explained that the chicken had to be white; a brown chicken wouldn't work. I never thought to ask him why. The chicken bone came from a glass pickle jar that had been sitting on a shelf under one of the counters in the store. He said that the bones were soaking in alcohol and sugar to give them more power to cure warts. After he rubbed my hands, he wrapped the bone in butcher's paper and tied it with string. He told me to go bury the chicken bone under the back porch stoop, and, when it had rotted away, the warts would be gone.

Actually, a virus transmitted by human contact causes warts. The acid in the vinegar was probably just toxic enough to kill the virus. Warts often disappear spontaneously, with no treatment at all, while at other times they may last for years. However, for most people, they usually go away sooner or later, explaining the need for the mysterious chicken bone. Since no one knew how long it took for a chicken bone to rot, everyone became very patient, and usually the warts disappeared in their own good time.

My grandfather was not a faith healer, calling upon the name of the Lord.

He also avoided the hard-core black magic, like the Negro "bijoux women" used. These mysterious old black women were his biggest competition as a root doctor in Union County. Others shunned them, believing their magic to be un-Christian.

Papa Roberts mostly confined his spells to commonly held local superstitions and folklore. While always professing a deep Christian faith, he did sometimes dwell on the edges of the black arts. He had an instinctive feel for these things. In a lot of cases, if the people think they will get well, they do. A lot of illnesses cure themselves with a little time and patience.

A lot of his "patients" were women who were going through various stages of emotional distress or hormonal deficiencies associated with bad marriages or the time of month. Most of these women he treated with conjures, spells, and good luck charms that were pragmatically effective. Things like a dead chicken's feet, bird's eggs, resurrection ferns, and tobacco twists could become healing tools in the right circumstances. Even such prosaic things as nails and strips of cloth bundled just right and placed in a man's clothing would stop him from drinking. A drop or two of menstrual blood in his food would keep his affections from wandering. However, it was important not to go too far. A black man once killed his wife when he found a used Kotex pad in a pot of collard greens.

My grandfather had on his desk a well-worn volume of hard-to-find wisdom commonly called a "dream book." It had a bright yellow cover and had been used so much it was nearly worn out. My grandfather had fingered the pages of the dream book with his ink-stained hands until you could barely read the wrinkled and worn cover, which read *Aunt Sally's Policy Player's Dream Book*. He always claimed that it had come all the way from New Orleans, but other people claimed they had seen the same book in Tampa and Miami.

He believed firmly that dreams had serious meanings and that they often told the future. He said that many times in the Bible, God had spoken to people through dreams, warning them both of dangers and good things to come. People would often come to my grandfather's store with their dreams, and he would interpret them with the help of *Aunt Sally's Policy Player's Dream Book*.

All this dream interpretation wasn't just ignorant superstition; it also had a very practical application. There was a type of illegal gambling game that went on in Florida in the 1940s and 1950s. In other places, it might be called the "numbers racket" or other such name, but, in Florida, it was given the name "Bolita" or "the Bolita" by the simple country people who played it. The name came from the Spanish word *boleto* or *boleta* for a ticket or receipt. The term also means a small ball or pellet.

"The Bolita" was a simple game of chance that during those pre-Castro days came out of Havana, Cuba. Some people would call it "the Cuba" or just "Cuba" instead of the more familiar term "Bolita." After Castro's rise to power, the game was shifted to Miami. However, the name "the Bolita" and "the Cuba" remained in popular use until the game died out in the 1960s, only to be replaced in the late 1980s by the completely legal and government-run Florida Lottery.

Every Saturday evening right at six o'clock, a small group of broad-shouldered men in expensive suits and off-white Panama hats would gather at a secret location in Havana to play "the Bolita." One hundred small wooden balls, each with a number carefully hand painted on it, were put into a round wire cage, and the cage was rapidly spun by a quick flick of the wrist. When the circular cage began moving, traditionally all the men in the room would yell out "Bolita." Eventually, centrifugal force and gravity would cause one of the small balls to fall through an opening in the outer wall of the circular cage. Once it was outside the cage, the small ball would be slung onto a metal wire ramp. The little ball would roll down the wire ramp until it finally came to a halt and dropped into a small whiskey shot glass.

After the small wooden ball had neatly plunked itself into the shot glass, the man running the wheel would hold up the shot glass, again yelling out the word "Bolita," as he slowly turned in a full circle so that each man in the small group could see which number "fell." The men in the room would then quickly disperse, heading to the nearest pay phone to spread the word across the island of Cuba and to their contacts in Miami and Tampa.

The number that "fell" was transmitted up the Florida peninsula from Miami by a well-organized and highly intricate system, using nothing more technical than an ordinary telephone and word of mouth. Every Bolita ticket salesman, called an "operator," knew who to call each Saturday evening to find out what number "fell." The key word used by Bolita operators was "the price of eggs." This was a code phrase used in case law enforcement officers might tap a phone. In those innocent days, nobody could go to jail for asking about the price of eggs.

The word would get to north Florida between seven and eight o'clock each Saturday night. The news was always received with either resignation or jubilation, depending upon the number on the Bolita ticket you held and the number that "fell" in Havana.

If it was the number you picked that "fell" that Saturday, it paid off sixty-to-one, although the chances of winning were one hundred-to-one. Even at one hundred-to-one, these were much better odds than the modern legal lottery where chances of winning are in the one-to-millions. A ten-cent investment in a Bolita ticket could bring a six-dollar reward. A quarter would give a return of fifteen dollars. A dollar investment would earn sixty dollars, which was more than a week's salary for most working people.

The Bolita was widely played by poor people primarily because it involved very little financial investment. For the price of a Coca-Cola or a loaf of bread, a man or woman could enjoy the possibility of picking up an extra wad of cash. The people who played "the Bolita" couldn't afford to go to expensive dog tracks or *jai alai* and buy two-dollar tickets. They sure couldn't afford an airplane ticket to Las Vegas or Havana, the nearest legal casino gambling.

Since money was always tight, most people picked their Bolita numbers from their dreams. If they hadn't had a particularly vivid dream that week, many would not play. Those who had a well-remembered dream would often bet the maximum of five dollars on a single number based on their dream. If such a large investment paid off, it would bring a return of three hundred dollars, which was a small fortune to pulpwood workers and small-time dirt farmers. The primary source for interpreting these dreams was *Aunt Sally's Policy Player's Dream Book* and the dream-interpreting wisdom of my grandfather, Robert Benjamin "Doc" Roberts.

People would come to my grandfather's store on Saturday morning and say, "Mr. Doc, I dreamed about a snake last night. What do it mean?"

My grandfather, looking much like an experienced doctor diagnosing a serious illness would ask, "What color snake was it?"

The color of the snake was important. A black snake required that you play a higher number than a green or brown snake. A rattlesnake was twenty or thirty-five, and a coral snake was nine or twenty, since a coral snake had white on it. A blue–black indigo snake required that you buy a number in the nineties.

My grandfather used to always say that to dream about anything black required that you play a high number, while white on the other hand meant to play a low number. The larger the white object, the lower the number. For example, to dream of a white elephant required you to play a lower number than a dream about a white dog. The opposite was true of anything black. A black horse required a higher number than a black cat. However, it took an expert like my grandfather to pinpoint the exact number.

Once my grandfather got all the facts of the dream straight, he would usually answer the people from memory, not even having to consult the dream book. Because he had been dealing with dreams for so long, he had memorized most of the information and numbers in the dream book. A red chicken meant sickness, and play number twenty-two or twelve. A black horse meant a cold winter (or a hot summer) and numbers ninety-one to ninety-nine. A white rooster meant more cotton would be produced than usual and numbers two and twelve. He used to tell me that it was good luck to dream about anything to eat. It was bad luck to dream about a dead person. To tell a dream before breakfast would make it come true; to tell a dream after breakfast would keep it from coming true. To share a dream with anyone except the interpreter could make the Bolita numbers invalid.

There were other superstitions he firmly believed in. To count the number of cars in a funeral procession would cause someone in your family to die. Never eat or drink anything in a cemetery. Never point to anything in a cemetery, and never sweep out your house after dark. To see a bird at night was bad luck. To have a wild bird fly into your house meant someone would die soon. Most important of all was to blow on your Bolita ticket immediately after you buy it, and carry it in your right pocket, not your left.

My grandfather never sold Bolita tickets, because it was against the law, and he never broke the law. He was a deacon at Sardis Baptist Church, a position he guarded as if his immortal soul depended upon it, which, for him, it did. He badly needed the respect and friendship of all the church-going folks in this very small and rural county. Politicians, who had to comb the northern Florida pinewoods looking for votes, wanted nothing to do with anything as blatantly illegal as Bolita. My grandfather dealt with influence and power rather than money grabbing. Making a fast buck was worthless if it cost you your reputation and political contacts. My grandfather didn't even buy Bolita tickets; he was way too smart to throw his money away like that. However, his free dream interpretation service told hundreds of other people what numbers to play. This way, he was able to have the best of both worlds.

My mother had a weakness for "the Bolita," and, almost every Saturday morning, she and I would climb into her big Buick sedan and drive out to a place she called Bolita Sam's to buy her tickets. It was from Bolita Sam, an elderly black man, that all the people around Worthington Springs purchased their tickets. Normally, my mother was very racist, always warning me to avoid all contact with black people. However, on Saturday mornings, all of her prejudice disappeared, especially if she had a particularly vivid dream that week and badly wanted a Bolita ticket.

Bolita Sam's small wood-frame house was located well away from the main part of Worthington Springs, on the edge of one of the dark cypress swamps that flanked the Santa Fe River. Few black people lived in Worthington Springs; only a handful lived in small houses down by the railroad tracks. Most blacks lived on sharecropper farms far out in the countryside.

To this day, I'm not really sure how my mother and I got to Bolita Sam's house or exactly where it was located. All I know for sure is that we drove down a twisting assortment of dirt roads that cut through a lot of tall pinewoods before finally arriving at a small house surrounded by a cheap hog-wire fence.

On Saturday mornings, Sam's house was always surrounded by dozens of parked cars and large groups of people, mostly blacks with a smattering of whites, all patiently waiting their turn to go inside and buy their Bolita tickets. As the day wore on, the crowd would get larger as more and more people showed up trying to beat Sam's iron-clad six o'clock deadline.

Bolita Sam would religiously halt the selling of tickets right at six o'clock, no matter how many people were waiting outside. Sam could not run the risk that someone had made a long-distance telephone call to Havana or Miami and learned what number "fell" and was now trying to buy a winning ticket. Such a thing could cost Bolita Sam a lot of money. Sam, like all gamblers, made his money based on the premise that the vast majority of ticket buyers would make the wrong decision and buy losing tickets. When the cage began to spin in Havana, Bolita Sam halted the sale of tickets and closed up shop, telling everyone waiting outside to come back next week.

My mother was a fat and incredibly lazy woman who never moved except when it was absolutely necessary. She used her children as handservants and maids, forcing us to wait on her hand and foot. That was why she always brought me with her to Bolita Sam's. She wasn't about to get out of her car and stand in line with a group of people she considered her inferiors, so she made either me or my older brother do it for her.

She would sit behind the steering wheel of the big Buick, on a hot and humid Saturday morning, counting out a handful of dollar bills and loose change, which she would hand to me with a small slip of paper. The numbers she wanted to play were written on the slip of paper. She would then order me to get out of the car and stand in line until it was my turn to go inside Bolita Sam's house; then, I was to simply hand him the money and the piece of paper, and he would do the rest.

Standing in line is a boring experience for a little boy, so I would always take careful notice of what was going on around me. Because Bolita Sam's house and yard were so interesting, the time seemed to go by fast. There was not a single blade of grass in the yard; it was all white sand that had been neatly raked and swept clean of any dead leaves or litter. The yard had a few scattered azalea bushes and what was known as a "bone yard garden." Animal bones of all types—but mostly jawbones, femurs, and shoulder blades—would be carefully positioned along the fence line and against the side of the house and wired together to form macabre trellises for wisteria, gourd, and honeysuckle vines. The bones also edged the walkway leading to Sam's house. Most of the bones were from old dead mules and milk cows, and a few dog and cat bones were thrown in here and there. The crown jewels in Sam's bone collection were a number of horse and cow heads that decorated the pillars holding up the front porch. It must have taken him years to collect all those bones and arrange them so carefully.

On one side of Bolita Sam's house was a bottle tree. It was, to all outward appearances, just an ordinary crepe myrtle tree except that it appeared to be dead. The tree's branches were devoid of any green leaves moss or any other type of vegetation. On the branches of the tree dangled dozens of blue, green, and red bottles of various shapes and sizes. Most were hung with fishing line, but others were slipped over the ends of the dead branches. The vast majority of the colored bottles looked like old medicine bottles, the kind cough syrup and laxatives came in. There were no soft drink or beer bottles. It appears that whoever decorated the bottle tree chose the bottles very carefully, based on their size, shape, and, most important of all, color. All the bottles were blue, green, or red. The tree had no clear glass or brown bottles.

When the wind blew through the limbs of the bottle tree, the old medicine bottles would rattle against each other and against the dead branches of the tree, making strange noises. The old folks who stood in line outside Bolita Sam's house would often talk to one another about the bottle tree. An elderly woman said that a bottle tree would get rid of ghosts and evil spirits better than anything you could get from a root doctor. Another elderly man said that when he was sick with pneumonia, his family had taken him outside to sleep under the branches of a bottle tree, and it cured him. According to popular folklore, evil spirits and ghosts could be lured out of a house by the sound of the bottles rattling against each other. The spirits would be fooled into thinking the tinkling noises were the bones of dead people they could process; once a spirit entered a blue, green, or red bottle, it could not escape and would be trapped forever or until the bottle was broken. It was very bad luck to break a bottle that had been on a bottle tree. On dark and windy nights, you could hear the spirits moaning from inside their bottles, lamenting that they were trapped forever.

Bolita Sam always looked forward to me coming to see him. The first reason, of course, was that my mother always spent a lot of money on Bolita tickets each week, mostly losing. Also, Bolita Sam liked to tease and play around with me, saying that I was "a combed-down sport in city britches." I had no idea what that phrase meant, but I took it as a compliment.

Bolita Sam was of an average height, but thin as a rail, barely making it to skin and bones status. His skin was a deep, almost purplish, shade of black. His ebony skin hung loosely on his bony flesh, and his veins protruded from beneath his skin. Sam's face was as badly wrinkled as his hands, and his jowls sagged loosely beneath his chin. His eyes had a yellowish tint and were badly bloodshot. He wore thick glasses and had a permanent stoop when he stood up. Sam always wore baggy black suits and large amounts of gold jewelry, including one or more rings on every finger of both bony hands. His hair had been chemically processed so many times it lay as flat and straight as a white man's except for small waves near the ends. Sam's weathered hands and face showed that despite his natty dress and conspicuous display of gold jewelry, this old man had known many hard times and much hard work during his long life.

They say opposites attract, and that was evident in Bolita Sam's small house. His wife was a fat woman, at least 250 pounds, who was light skinned, which folks called a "high-yellow." I remember she had a nasty scar on her neck, almost as if her throat had once been cut. Her real name was Rosetta, but everyone called her Rosy. Every time I saw her, she was sitting quietly in a big rocking chair next to the small kerosene stove that heated the house. In her lap was an old green ledger book, and, in her left hand, she held the short stub of a yellow pencil. Her job was to keep track of how many people had purchased certain ticket numbers. If too many people bought the same number, Sam would have to split the risk with another Bolita operator in Live Oak.

Like Sam, Rosy liked gold jewelry, wearing rings on every finger and at least a dozen or more gold necklaces. She always wore black dresses and what looked like men's shoes. She seldom smiled, but, when she did, several gold teeth were evident. While basically I liked Sam, his wife gave me the creeps. Part of it was that she had what folks around Worthington Springs called an "evil eye." This meant that she had a strange and hard stare that gave folks the willies.

Some people said Sam had met Rosetta while he was living in Tampa. Others said Sam met her while he was working on a shrimp boat in southern Florida. Nobody knew for sure, and Bolita Sam didn't like to talk about his personal business.

Most white people avoided Bolita Sam, except for when they were buying their tickets on Saturday morning. All the deeply religious people around Worthington Springs believed that Bolita Sam and his wife practiced witchcraft. Allegedly, Rosetta could talk to the dead and cast spells. When I was in Bolita Sam's house, I never spoke to his wife and didn't even like to look at her. While Sam liked to talk, his wife almost never said a word. Southerners, both black and white, never like or trust someone who doesn't say much.

Bolita Sam's house was small, but, at the same time, very neat and clean. One of the things I remember about Bolita Sam's house was that he kept pet crows. They weren't in cages; the birds had their wings clipped, so they simply hopped around inside the living room. They would come to rest on whatever piece of furniture they happened to decide to use as a perch. Surprisingly, there was very little bird guano on the furniture or the floor. Even at that early an age, I knew that keeping birds inside was bad luck, and, since all these birds were black, I believed firmly that I was in a place of evil.

Sam also had a dead starling hanging upside down over the front door. The small bird's feet were tied together and hung by a string from an old, rusty nail that had been driven into the wall. Its small body was now dried out and withered by time. The starling's dark feathers, which were once almost iridescent, were now covered with gray spider webs that seemed to bind the dead bird to the wall.

Later, when I told my grandmother about this, she became very upset; she said that witches always kept crows as pets, because crows could carry within their bodies the souls of the dead. The dead starling bird was an old superstition. It was widely believed that a dead starling would keep away the angel of death, but a Christian could lose his soul if he used one. My grandmother carefully explained to me that it was un-Christian to put your faith in anything other than the Lord Jesus Christ.

My grandmother was a perfect example of the selective morality of America in general and the South in particular. The fact that my grandfather's dream book and root doctoring were on the very edges of witchcraft never seemed to concern her. It is the same type of moral thinking that would lead southerners to banish an unwed mother and label the child as a bastard, while fighting a long and bloody war to defend slavery.

A Bolita ticket is a surprisingly innocent-looking object once you get it in your hand. It is a small, professionally printed piece of paper, one inch wide and six inches long. The numbers one to fifty are printed on one side in a long column, and, on the other side, the numbers fifty-one to one hundred are printed. Beside each number was a small black line where Bolita Sam would scribble in pencil the amount of money a person bet on that number. You got one ticket for each number you played. A simple pencil mark initial and a date on the bottom of the ticket made the whole thing official.

Maybe it was just the way things were back then, but nobody associated with the Bolita ever tried to cheat anybody else. When a ticket was a winner, the operators paid off, and no customer would ever dream of trying to alter a losing ticket to make it look like a winner. Such an action could be very hazardous to your health. The pay off, usually less than a hundred dollars, wasn't worth losing your life.

Bolita Sam may have been an elderly black man, and many of his customers were white; however, there were strange situations back in those days when the system of racial segregation simply broke down, and this was one of them. White supremacy might have been the rule everywhere else, but not in Bolita dealings. A vast criminal empire that covered both the state of Florida and

Cuba backed old Bolita Sam. This criminal empire included sheriffs, judges, and even state officials. He didn't have to kiss any white man's ass or put up with any cheating on his Bolita tickets.

As soon as I got my tickets, I would carefully wade through the crowd of people waiting to get into Bolita Sam's house and return to my mother's car. My mother would check each Bolita ticket carefully, before warning me—in what I felt was a terribly loud voice—to make sure I washed my hands as soon as I got home, "since these people often had diseases because of how filthy they lived." I knew that Bolita Sam's house was a clean as any white person's home, but I also knew not to argue with my mother.

When my mother said things like that, it made me cringe. There were black men and women standing only a few feet from her car window, and they must have heard her big mouth. However, they were mostly elderly people, very polite and humble, who didn't want to start any trouble. My mother was a very cruel and inconsiderate woman who had little regard for other people's feelings.

When we returned home to Worthington Springs, my grandmother and my mother would often argue violently about her taking me out to Bolita Sam's house. My grandmother was a church-going Christian woman who opposed all forms of drinking and gambling, and she worried about the effect all this would have on my young mind. She took a special interest in me, and she would often sit and read to me from the Bible and pray about the sinful way my mother lived. When my mother didn't win the Bolita, my grandmother was always happy. The whole thing just left me confused about what was right, what was wrong, and totally bewildered at the strange way grown people acted.

Another of the business interests my grandfather had was a cotton gin. It was a large, rectangular building with a galvanized tin roof and large double doors on all four sides that allowed summer breezes to blow through. On both ends of the building were huge circular fans, mounted over the end doors, which kept the air inside the building moving. Despite all these accommodations to clean air and cool breezes, the inside of the cotton gin was always around ninety to one hundred degrees, thanks to the heat given off by the big machines that ripped the seeds from the strong fibers of the freshly picked white cotton bolls.

My grandfather's store had only a small black and white sign over the front entrance, which most people took little note of. He had got it free from the Coca-Cola Company in exchange for allowing two round, bright red Coca-Cola signs to flank it. My grandfather didn't think any further advertisement was necessary. Anyone with one eye and half sense could simply look at the building and see that it was a grocery store with gasoline pumps out front. If they still couldn't figure it out, the building was covered with colorful tin signs advertising Royal Crown Cola, Bull of the Woods Chewing Tobacco, Martha White Flour, and Merita Bread. All were put up for free by the company named.

Once, a man dropped by and wanted to paint "See Rock City, on Top of Lookout Mountain, Chattanooga, Tennessee" on the building. At first, he said he would put it on the roof. However, after examining the tilt of the roof, the sign painter said he would have to put it on the side of the building. That, my grandfather would not permit. Instead, the sign went on the side of a barn only a few miles down the road.

Unlike the big white store that sat on the main road, my grandfather's cotton gin was only a small building, stuck in an out-of-the-way place beside the railroad tracks. To help drum up business, my grandfather had gone to the trouble and expense of calling down a professional sign painter from Jacksonville. He adorned the building with a massive red and white sign directly over the main entrance that proudly said "R. B. Roberts Dealer in Sea Island Cotton."

In the late 1940s, very few Union County farmers still grew cotton. Most had switched to tobacco because of the boll weevil. My grandfather's cotton gin was not a real moneymaking operation, and the only reason he kept it open was because it was the last cotton gin in Union County, and the small farmers who still grew cotton depended upon him to gin it for them each year. It was only open a few weeks a year, in the early fall, during what was know as the "picking season," as compared to "planting season" in the spring.

On busy days, trucks filled with snow white, Sea Island cotton would line up on the white sand road leading up to the gin. Most of these trucks were just small pickups, but others were large, double-wheeled vehicles. When their turn came, they would pull their trucks under a large tin-roofed shed that jutted from the side of the building.

Using a six-inch-diameter jointed aluminum vacuum pipe, which hung by a rope from the roof of the tin-roofed shed, the muscular black men who worked for my grandfather would suck the cotton out of the backs of the trucks. The large electric vacuum pump and jointed aluminum pipe would deposit the vacuumed cotton into a wire cage just inside the gin building. The wire cage sat on a large black mechanical scale, the kind where you had to place cast-iron weights on a balanced bar in order to get the correct weight.

Cotton was always sold by the pound, and the weight of the cotton determined how much money my grandfather paid the farmers. Later, he would ship the cotton by rail to a wholesaler in Jacksonville, who would buy it from him and give my grandfather a small markup as profit. After all the cotton was vacuumed out of the truck, the owner of the cotton and my grandfather would walk inside the big double doors of the unpainted gin building for the formal weighing in of the cotton.

Every year, just before picking season, the weight inspector from Tallahassee would come around checking to make sure the scale was accurate. The weight inspector was a short, fat man, who always looked like the narrow tie he wore was about to choke him to death. The northern Florida heat and humidity caused him to sweat profusely, staining his white dress shirt and making the tie wilt like a wet noodle. However, despite the heat and discomfort inside the gin, he never got into a hurry, and he never loosened his tie. It was as if the white shirt and black tie were part of his uniform that he couldn't violate.

The weight inspector considered himself a consummate professional, who took pride in his labors. When he said a scale was accurate, you could bet your last dollar it was. He brought with him his own set of brass weights that he carried in a special wooden box with the Great Seal of the State of Florida engraved on top. Each weight was carefully wrapped in a soft red cloth, and he handled them gently, almost reverently, like they were sacred objects. The brass weights were so highly polished they looked like solid gold, and each weight had a serial number and bore the Great Seal of the State of Florida. When he was finished with his tests, the inspector presented my grandfather with an official-looking certificate of accuracy, which also proudly bore the Great Seal of the State of Florida and the signature of the governor. My grandfather always put it in a special glass frame and displayed it next to the scale. It was the final authority that my grandfather's scales were as accurate as humanly possible. The cotton in the wire cage represented a year's hard work for the cotton farmers, and it was important to all concerned that the weight be correct.

The weighing of the cotton took on the seriousness of a murder trial. The farmer and my grandfather would solemnly gather at the scales and carefully place the cast-iron weights on the hanging metal bar of the scale, until the metal point of the bar was sitting right on zero. They would then look down the scale bar and determine the accurate weight. My grandfather knew in advance what the empty wire cage weighed, so when the scales finally balanced, he would subtract the weight of the cage, telling him accurately how much cotton was being sold. Nobody ever complained, because my grandfather—unlike most gin owners—weighed the cotton before the seeds were removed, giving the farmer an edge.

Every morning, my grandfather would make a big show of going down to the small Worthington Springs post office and making a long-distance call to his wholesaler in Jacksonville to find out what the going price of cotton was. He would then loudly announce the price for that particular day, minus his markup of course. The lady who was in charge of the post office and the town's only telephone was well-known as a Bible-believing Christian woman whose word was never to be questioned. My grandfather always had her confirm the price of cotton, and anybody with questions could double-check by talking to her or, if they were still unconvinced, they could also call Jacksonville. However, to the best of my knowledge, nobody ever did.

All these precautions were not unnecessary. My grandfather was also well-known as an honest man, who paid a fair price. However, in Union County, violence was always just below the surface, and men had been killed in disputes over much smaller things than the price of a year's cotton crop.

I enjoyed playing around my grandfather's big store and down at his cotton gin. I enjoyed climbing on top of the big bales of cotton stacked next to the railroad tracks awaiting shipment to Jacksonville. I would often pretend that I was a famous mountain climber reaching the top of Mount Everest.

The big old store was even more fun, because it had all kinds of neat little nooks and crannies to explore. My grandfather was an easy touch. Whenever I wanted an RC Cola, an Eskimo Pie or a Baby Ruth candy bar, I could count on him to give it to me. I always drank an RC Cola, because they seemed bigger and sweeter than a Coke or Pepsi and didn't leave the tell-tale colored ring on my top lip like the strawberry and grape sodas did. I had to be very careful that my mother didn't find out my grandfather had been supplying me with what she called "junk food." I had been given strict orders never to eat anything at the store. This was when I learned one of the most valuable of life's lessons: What mama don't know won't hurt her.

It was at my grandfather's store that I had my first encounter with southern racism. On hot summer days, my favorite getaway from grown people and do-what-I-want-to-do hiding place was sitting in the cool shade under the thick pine floorboards of the loading dock behind the store. I often had a friend and playmate in the person of a little black boy by the name of Mitchell, who was about the same age as I was.

Mitchell and I would often hide together in the quiet darkness under the loading dock, playing in the sand and looking up women's dresses through the wide cracks between the two-by-ten pine boards.

My grandfather's old store didn't really have a formal front door or back door. The people who came to see him used whatever entrance was closest and most convenient to the direction they came from. When it's real hot in Florida, it's best to exert oneself as little as possible. Since the loading dock faced the Negro section of Worthington Springs, most of the women who came that way were black; however, very often white women would also come walking up the steps and across the pine boards, and Mitchell would have the thrill of looking up their dresses. Mitchell used to call women's panties "squirrel covers," because that was what his daddy called them. It would be awhile before either one of us understood why. One of the first things I learned about sex as a child was that white women usually wore white, pink, or blue "squirrel covers," and, during the hot summer, most African American women didn't wear any. Sometimes, I was a very nasty little boy.

Mitchell and I often shared an RC Cola together, because I got them free, and his family was too poor to spend any money on what they called "sodie waters." Also, the big RC Cola bottles always had more carbonated liquid than my little tummy could hold.

That particular day, for some reason, we had come out from under the loading dock and were foolishly sitting on the back steps leading up to the loading dock. I would take a sip from the big RC Cola bottle and then pass it to Mitchell, who would also take a sip and then hand it back. At that exact moment, due to nothing but bad luck and poor timing, my mother suddenly appeared in the back doorway of the store and saw what we were doing. She came outside in a huff and jerked me up by my arm and pulled me into the store. She shook me violently and told me "to never, never, do you hear me, drink after a nigger, ever again." When I asked her why, she tried to slap my head off.

I never had to learn that lesson again. Never ask why! In the South, it just doesn't pay for a child to ask why certain things are done. There are just too many dark and dirty little secrets and unjust social customs for a child to go around asking grown people questions.

My mother told me she never wanted to see me playing with Mitchell again, and she never did; from that day on, Mitchell and I stayed safely hidden under the loading dock. There we shared many RC Colas together. When my mother would come looking for me, we would hide from her not answering her calls, and Mitchell would get a big thrill out of looking up her dress as she strutted back and forth across the loading dock. He once told me my mother didn't wear panties, but I knew she did. In fact, she also wore a big white girdle with built-in garter straps. The reason Mitchell believed she didn't wear any panties was because my mother's legs were so fat they came together about three inches above her knee, really making it impossible for Mitchell to see anything sexual.

Mitchell's father worked for my grandfather, and he had been given the unwelcome responsibility of making sure I never got hurt when I was playing around the cotton gin. The huge steel-toothed, mechanical contraption that pulled the seeds away from the strong cotton fibers filled me with awe. However, for obvious safety reasons, my grandfather had forbidden me to go near it and had given Mitchell's father the power to enforce his edict. If I got too close, he would yell at me, "Little Doc, you stay away from there, you hear?" I never challenged his authority, fearing that it would give my mother the opportunity she wanted to have me banned from the cotton gin. She was convinced that sooner or later, I would get chewed into tiny bits by the sharp steel teeth of the cotton gin, just to aggravate her.

Sometimes, the big barrel-chested black workers would stick my head inside the flexible vacuum pipe. It would suck up my hair making it stand on end. This little game seemed to amuse them greatly. Somehow, my mother found out about this and was horrified, fearing that I would get sucked into the cotton gin and ripped to pieces. It couldn't happen; the suction wasn't that great, and I was already too big a boy to fit through the aluminum pipe. Even if I did get sucked up the pipe, it would only dump me into the big wire cage where the cotton was weighed. However, it gave my mother something to worry about, and she just loved to worry.

After the seeds had been combed out of the white fibers by the steel teeth of the gin, the cotton was forced into a large pressing machine that squeezed the cotton into 500-pound bales that were wrapped in burlap and secured with stapled steel bands. The pressing machine was dangerous, but I had been adequately warned and had enough sense to stay away from it. Despite what my mother thought, I did have a natural sense of self-preservation after all.

My grandfather's black workers used two-wheeled dollies with wooden handles and squat heavy iron wheels to roll the big bales of cotton down to the loading platform next to the railroad tracks. I was amazed at how strong these men were. They were always covered with a thin sheen of sweat that seemed to make their ebony skin shine as if it were illuminated by some inner glow. They moved the 500-pound bales of cotton around with the grace of a ballerina.

Usually, there was a railroad boxcar sitting on the siding next to the loading platform. They maneuvered the big bales onto the boxcar and stacked each bale neatly so the load of cotton wouldn't move while it was being transported to Jacksonville. What this meant to me was that there were always plenty of cotton bales to crawl around and play on.

One day, late in the picking season, I was sitting in my grandfather's small office in the cotton gin when a ragged old pickup truck with its bed filled with cotton pulled up to the shed. A tall black man who wore an open shirt that revealed a muscular upper body drove the old truck. His chest and arms were covered with scar tissue, evidence of the many fistfights, cuttings, and shootouts in which he had been involved. His head was especially badly scarred. You could tell that his eyebrows had been split open more than once, and part of an ear was missing.

It surprised me that my grandfather took such an unusual interest in the black man in the pickup truck. He usually didn't leave the big electric fan in his office until it was absolutely necessary. Normally, one of the black workers had to come and summon him for the cotton weighing. However, this time, my grandfather immediately stopped the paperwork he was doing to stand up and glare out the window. He had a strange look on his face that I had never seen before.

Slowly, he turned away from the window, reached into his desk drawer, and pulled out a blue steel thirty-eight-caliber Smith and Wesson revolver. He silently slipped it into his pocket. My grandfather always wore oversized beige khaki pants that were held up by a pair of wide, tan suspenders. The pants were very baggy, so the pistol just seemed to disappear among the creases and folds of his trousers.

Slowly and deliberately, he walked out under the tin-roofed shed and began to carefully examine the truckload of cotton. The tall black man tried to engage my grandfather in conversation, but he ignored him. This was something my grandfather almost never did. He was by his nature a friendly and loquacious man, who was always looking for an excuse to get into a conversation. He especially liked to talk to black people, who he found laughed at his jokes and stories quicker than whites.

Suddenly, he stuck his arm deep inside the load of cotton as if he was trying to find something hidden in the bottom of the truck bed. After a minute, he withdrew his arm with a hand full of cotton. He looked at the black man with a hard glare and slowly squeezed the cotton. Water began to drip out of the cotton onto the dry, dirty-gray sand under the shed. The black men who worked for my grandfather immediately stepped back and became deathly quiet knowing that trouble was coming.

"You sorry, black-assed bastard," I heard my grandfather growl from my perch on a chair inside his small office.

The black man became belligerent and loud, saying my grandfather had falsely accused him of trying to sell wet cotton, which would weigh more on the scale than dry cotton. The man claimed that one of the men who worked for my grandfather had poured water on his cotton just to make him look bad and that my grandfather was trying to cheat him. My grandfather didn't make any attempt to answer; he just slowly slipped his hand into his pocket where he had put the pistol.

What happen next occurred within the flash of an eye. My grandfather whipped out his pistol and shot the Negro man at almost point-blank range. He doubled over from being hit in the lower stomach, and he was bleeding profusely.

The cotton gin workers, who had discretely retreated when they saw trouble coming, now returned on the run. They scooped up the badly wounded man and threw him into the rear of his own pickup truck. I will never forget the sight of how his blood discolored the white cotton to a bright red that quickly turned brown. There was a lot of confusion as they tried to decide what to do with him. They kept asking my grandfather. He said he didn't care; he just wanted the sorry son of a bitch off his property. Finally, a pair of the black workers decided to drive him to the hospital in Gainesville and asked my grandfather if they could take off work to do so. He quickly gave his permission, but first explained that he wasn't paying "no damned doctor bills" and, if he died on the way, don't bring him back here. They drove off in the wounded man's old ragged pickup truck, and my grandfather returned to his small office and completed his paperwork as if nothing had happened.

Word of the shooting spread like wildfire over the small town of Worthington Springs. Word quickly got to the post office where someone immediately went to the telephone and put in a call to the Sheriff's office in Lake Butler.

"Doc Roberts just shot a nigger down by his cotton gin. Somebody better send the high sheriff down here."

Within an hour, the high sheriff arrived from Lake Butler. He greeted my grandfather like an old friend, not an accused criminal. He and my grandfather retreated into the small office and had a calm and polite conversation behind closed doors. The sheriff shook his head and seemed to fully understand my grandfather's position on the matter.

"I know the son of a bitch well," the sheriff acknowledged. "I've put him in jail for everything from wife beating to making bad moonshine. He will steal anything that ain't red hot and nailed down. He's one of the sorriest gawddamn things that ever shit between two feet. I hope you killed him."

The black man didn't die. I saw him many times after that. He often came by my grandfather's store, and the two of them exchanged a polite banter, talking about the weather and farm prices, but neither of them ever again mentioned wet cotton or guns. He even continued to sell his cotton at my grandfather's gin. However, he never again tried to cheat my grandfather by trying to sell him wet cotton.

My grandfather was never arrested or charged with any crime, although he had shot an unarmed man who was only trying to pull off a minor fraud. However, in Union County, there was no such thing as a minor fraud. People lived too close to the edge. My grandfather used to say they were the kind of people who gnawed right down to the bone. Stealing a hog, selling a sick mule, or cheating in a penny ante poker game could get you killed. It was more than just money; it was a deeply rooted southern thing called "honor." You just couldn't let somebody walk on you and get away with it. If they did, everyone would try it. In Union County, where everybody knew everybody else, word got around. You were in no obligation to back down. Violence was a quick and unpredictable thing in this poor region of the rural South, and a man's honor and reputation were worth more than another man's life.

Contrary to what most people might think, race was not a major part in all this. I believe that my grandfather would have shot him no matter what color he was. I came from a long line of shooters. Nobody in my family can fight very well with either fists or knives. We tend to be a family of slow fat people. So, if you crossed one of us, look out for gunplay.

When I was growing up, I heard all kinds of stories about my grandfather's brother, a short squat man called "Black Enoch Roberts." All I knew about his personnel appearance comes from an old photograph. He had close-set eyes, dark curly hair, and a thick black mustache with mutton chop sideburns. He had been murdered late one night, shot from ambush, while coming out of the poolroom on Main Street in Lake Butler. He had six forty-five-caliber slugs in his chest. Whoever it was had emptied his revolver. They never found out who killed him, and my grandmother said nobody looked real hard.

A year before, Enoch had murdered a man in cold blood in a dispute over a mule. The story was that they were arguing about the price and age of the mule when Black Enoch simply slipped a pistol out of his back pocket, stuck it around the mule's neck, and shot the man in the head. He died instantly. The only witness was an old black man who refused to testify, saying he didn't want to get involved in white folk's business.

A few day's later, the dead man's brother shot Enoch off his horse with a double-barrel shotgun as he was riding toward Raiford. Although he was badly wounded, Black Enoch didn't die. He knew who had shot him, but he would not tell the high sheriff. He said he would handle the matter himself, and that seemed to suit the high sheriff just fine. He realized that this was a no-win situation for him; a blood feud like this was best left alone to work itself out, without the law getting involved.

Later, the feud ended with Black Enoch being murdered on the streets of Lake Butler. His family took no notice and let the matter drop with his killing. My grandmother always said that Black Enoch was a bad man, who would shoot someone like a coward, so it was only fair that someone killed him in a likewise cowardly manner.

My grandmother's family was worse. Her father, Arron Dennis Andrews, had been state representative, and her brother, Will Andrews, was a deputy sheriff. Late one night, while roaring drunk, he killed the sheriff of Bradford County in a hotel room in Jacksonville. At his trial, he claimed that they were both drunk, and he threw the gun on the bed and it just went off. The jury believed him, but the sheriff's family never did. A year later, a black man killed him when he raided a craps game. The black man named Will Moore was the last person hung in the state of Florida before the electric chair went into use. One would think that a deputy who had killed the sheriff would lose his job, guilty of murder or not.

Will's son, Carl Andrews, was even worse than his father. In 1929, he ambushed and nearly killed the postmaster of Raiford. Later, he shot and killed a deaf-mute man, because he didn't return his greeting. While everyone knew that Carl was crazy when he was drunk, this was more than even the people of Union County could tolerate. Carl was given nine years in prison. He wound up at the road prison at Moore Haven, Florida, where he became the dog boy, the person in charge of the bloodhound dogs. During his tenure at this job, he became friends with the sheriff of Polk County.

Together, Carl and the sheriff flew to Puerto Rico in a military aircraft to search for a missing six-year-old girl. They found her, tired and hungry in some of the thickest jungle on the tropical island. Carl and the sheriff returned to Florida and cheers. As soon as they got back, the sheriff began a campaign to get Carl a pardon. Carl wound up getting a special parole and was immediately hired as a deputy sheriff in Polk County in charge of the bloodhounds, where he worked until he retired. The comfortably retired Carl Andrews returned to Union County a local folk hero. He died in 1982.

Seeing my grandfather shoot the black man was like finding out that Santa Claus is a killer. I loved my grandfather and was proud to be his look-alike. I took pride in being called "Little Doc." To know he was capable of that kind of violence really shocked me. However, it taught me an important lesson about my family. They were a violent bunch that would hurt you.

# Slipping Around

My mother and father's lifestyle was an abomination before the Lord. My father was an alcoholic, and my mother had illicit sexual affairs with other men. In a small town like Worthington Springs, there are no secrets. However, my mother went about her everyday business as if nobody on earth knew what was going on.

Every Sunday morning, she would carefully dress me in my little suit and tie and drag me down to the Baptist church. We always sat right next to each other, about halfway back from the front, on the center aisle seat so that everyone could see my mother's fine dresses, jewelry, and hats. My mother spent a small fortune on clothes and jewelry, driving my grandparents to despair over the bills she ran up. They always had to pick up the tab, because my daddy couldn't keep a paying job because of his drinking.

To my mother, it wasn't church; it was a fashion show, and she was the star attraction. She always felt that everyone was looking at her, even when they weren't, so she was determined to always look her best.

Church to me was pure hell. If I so much as breathed too heavily, I would really catch it when I got home. She said my fidgeting made her look like she wasn't a good mother. She was always trying to impress what she called "the quality folks" who went to our church.

Whenever I did something wrong, the way she had of controlling me was to reach over and pinch the hell out of my arm. If it was something minor, like looking out the window, I might get by with a thump on the ear. However, if it was something more serious like reading the Bible story comic books they gave us in Sunday school, eating candy or wiggling too much, that would warrant a real nasty pinch.

I knew that if I got a pinch on my arm during church, I could count on my mother slapping me as hard as she could as soon as we got in the car and were out of sight of all the "quality folks" in church. As she came down on me, she kept saying that people were watching me, and she would not tolerate people talking about my bad behavior in church.

Summers were the worse time. This was long before churches were air-conditioned, and all the windows were wide open; however, I was not allowed to stare out the window upon punishment of having my ear thumped or, if my mother was in a bad mood, then a hunk of my flesh was torn out.

We had small hand fans that were given out free by the funeral home in Lake Butler. Each one was a square piece of stiff cardboard, stapled to a thin strip of wood that acted as a handle. On one side of the stiff cardboard was a colorful picture straight out of the New Testament. Each one showed a blond-haired and blue-eyed Jesus knocking on the door, walking on water, or surrounded by little blond-haired and blue-eyed children and little lambs.

On the back of each fan, the following was carefully printed:

Wilson-Thomas Funeral Home
Corner of Lake and First Street
Lake Butler, Florida
Hyatt 4-6675

I am very sure of what it said, right down to the phone number, because I stared at the fan for an hour each Sunday and memorized each word and number.

For a while, my grandmother rescued me and let me sit next to her in church. She could see the ugly black and blue marks on my upper arm and knew what was going on. However, my mother demanded that I sit next to her, because she said I didn't act right when I sat with my grandparents.

My daddy never came to church on Sunday morning, mostly because he was always hung over from his regular Saturday night drunkenness. My daddy was what my grandfather called a "sawmill Christian."

There used to be a sawmill in Worthington Springs, and, each year, when it got too wet to get into the woods, the sawmill would close down and lay off workers. When that happened, all the laid-off workers would show up in church and sit down on the "moaning bench." That is what folks called the first row of pews just under the pulpit. People sitting on the moaning bench were allowed to address the church, tell everyone their problems, and ask the church to pray for them. When the sawmill started back up, and these people again had jobs and money coming in, that was the end of their church going and the moaning bench was empty.

That was the way my daddy was; he would never be in church except when he had a crisis. Then, he would be down on the moaning bench, singing the blues and asking everybody to pray for him. He was a very weak man, who used religion the same way he used liquor, as a cure-all and an opiate.

One day, Mitchell and I were sitting and talking under the loading dock of my grandfather's store, and he was telling me about the church he went to. What he told me, I couldn't really believe; so I decided I had to go and see for myself.

Mitchell and I talked a long time, working out all the fine details of our high adventure. Years later, when James Bond was doing it, such a thing would have been referred to as a covert operation or a secret agent mission, but, back then, Mitchell and I just called it "slipping around."

We had planned it out in minute detail. Every Sunday night, my daddy went off to get drunk with his friends at the poolroom in Lake City, and my mother used his absence as an opportunity to sneak off and see some man in Lake Butler. I was left at home under the care of my grandmother.

On Sunday evenings, I had gotten in the habit of always going outside and playing under the back porch light. My grandmother was used to this and would not even come outside to check on me until about eight o'clock, when it was time for me to take my bath and get ready to go to bed. This was plenty of time for Mitchell and me to do our "slipping around."

As planned, I went outside about a half hour before dark, slipped out of the yard, and met Mitchell down by the railroad tracks that ran behind my grandfather's cotton gin.

Mitchell led the way, and I followed close behind. We walked on the cross ties, making a game of trying to put our feet on each cross tie and never touch the rock bed in between. We called this "cross-tie walking," and it was a favorite game of young children in the South and probably everywhere else that had railroad tracks.

We had gone maybe a quarter of a mile, when Mitchell and I turned off the railroad tracks onto a wide dirt road that cut straight as an arrow through some very dark pinewoods.

Even though it was now getting dark, what was left of the twilight and the light from the moon and stars reflected off the white sand of the dirt road illuminating our way.

We hadn't walked more than five or ten minutes before we began to hear it, the sound of loud music cutting through the cool darkness of the early evening. Ahead of us, in a clearing in the woods, was a small white clapboard church, not even a third as large as the church my mother and I attended. Its once-bright white paint job was now cracked and peeling. On top of the small white building was a small hand-built cross that had been painted red, but was now faded to a dull pink.

All the doors and windows were wide open because of the warm summer evening. The naked light bulbs inside the church were yellow, because, supposedly, yellow light bulbs didn't attract flying bugs and mosquitoes as bad as white lights.

Between some of the people's feet were smudge pots, small tin cans filled with dampened twigs and leaves set afire. The small fire in the smudge pots was then covered with more wet leaves and damp deer moss that created a thin cloud of white smoke that filled the room and warded off the mosquitoes.

Mitchell and I approached carefully. We finally came to a halt in the shaft of yellow light and smudge-pot smoke that came through the double doors in the front of the church. I stood transfixed next to Mitchell and watched in awed silence at what was going on inside.

The people were dressed nicely, but were not adorned with the suits, fancy dresses, and hats found in the white folk's church. In the front of the church was a small group of women, wearing white dresses, shoes, and wide-brimmed hats; sitting in rocking chairs; and fanning themselves, while lesser members of the congregation paid homage.

Mitchell explained that the women in white were the Queen Mothers, the elder women in the church. They were shown a lot of deference and made most of the important decisions as well as counting the collection money.

The elderly pastor stood behind the homemade pinewood pulpit, leading the singing. Behind him were a small choir and a handful of musicians. They had drums, guitars, and an old upright piano. All we had at the white folk's church was a piano and that damned organ, which always made the place sound like a funeral was going on.

The people were making all kinds of noise, singing, and dancing around. It wasn't the polite, stiff-as-a-board singing like they did in the Baptist church; instead, it was an impassioned display of faith and love of the Lord, like I had never seen before in my life. These people got out of their seats and jumped around, clapped their hands, and yelled out loud anytime they felt like it.

It made me mad; I was a very pissed-off little boy for a few minutes. Why are these people allowed to jump around and have a good time at church and white folks weren't? To me, it was an injustice, something not fair. I bet no little boy was getting pinched in there for looking out the window or wiggling too much.

I wanted to get closer. Mitchell seemed a little worried that we might be seen, so he suggested that we move around to the side and look through the window.

As we moved around to the side of the small church, a problem soon became apparent. Mitchell and I were both too short to see in the windows. If we backed up, all we could see was the ceiling and the very tops of the people's heads. I wanted to see their feet. I wanted to see the dancing. Baptists didn't believe in dancing anywhere on earth, but especially not in church.

Mitchell said, "Let's go over next to the wall, and I'll give you a boost."

Mitchell reached down and made a cup with his hands and told me to put my foot in. With one strong move, Mitchell hoisted me up to the level of the window. I steadied myself by putting my small hands on the window frames.

I found myself only a foot or so away from an elderly black woman who didn't seem to notice me at all. She was totally caught up in the rapture of the Holy Spirit, praising the Lord by singing and clapping her hands.

The drums, guitars, and pianos along with the clapping of the hands all combined to create a glorious noise, a rhythmic chant that echoed off the painted pine boards of the small church and escaped into the now-black woods that surrounded us. It was a rhythm as old as the Book of Psalms. It was a primitive and joyful noise made unto the Lord. It was music to stir the soul; it was religion, as I had never imagined it could be—a magical and wonderful thing. The people would stomp down with one foot in unison and then slide their food across the floor making a magical noise that I swore could make the whole floor vibrate.

One of the men thumbed a "diddle bow," a strong piece of steel wire— the type used to bind hay bales—that was nailed to the roof of the church and then stretched tight to the floor joists. When it was plucked, the entire building became a giant bass fiddle. Years later, I would hear a black musician named Bo Diddly, and his rhythmic guitar playing would remind me of that fateful night.

Neither the elderly black woman sitting in the pinewood church pew a few feet away nor I were paying much attention to each other. If I had been paying attention, I would have taken notice that she had a dip of snuff in her bottom lip.

In those days, poor and elderly people usually had bad teeth because of poor oral hygiene on top of not having money to go to a dentist. They often dipped snuff to control the pain, even in church.

I was looking through the window totally enthralled with what I was seeing, when the old woman suddenly had the need to spit. With one quick move, based on years of experienced practice, she turned toward the window and let one fly. It was a good-sized blob of dark blackish-brown tobacco juice, liberally mixed with an almost equal amount of warm saliva. It flew through the air with the grace and speed of a well-designed aeronautical device. It caught me right between the eyes. I flew backwards, came out of Mitchell's grip, and landed flat on my back. The next thing I knew, I was staring straight up at the night sky.

Suddenly, I saw the head of the elderly black woman sticking out of the church window, bathed in the glow of the yellow lightbulbs and smudge-pot smoke. She was looking straight down at me with wet snuff dripping from her bottom lip.

"Whatcha doing out chear white boy?" she asked.

I didn't try to answer. In the flash of an eye, I was on my feet and running down the dirt road. Behind me, I could still hear the music and singing. I was relieved. It meant that the worshipers in the church had gone about their business and were paying me no mind.

About half way to the railroad track, I finally caught up with Mitchell. We both ran wide open down the dirt road until we reached the railroad track. We paused at the track only long enough to catch our breath.

"What you think?" Mitchell asked almost totally out of breath. "Was I lying to you?"

All I could do was nod my head; I was too winded to talk.

"Got to go home." I finally said. "See you tomorrow."

Just like that, Mitchell and I parted company. I ran most of the way home, getting there, I guessed, just about the time my grandmother usually came out onto the porch to tell me to come inside. However, this night, I didn't see her in the porch light. Sometimes, my grandmother would get all caught up in what she was doing, cooking, sewing, or reading the Bible and forget what time it was. Lucky for me, this was one of those nights.

I walked into the house and was partially blinded by the bright lights in the kitchen. The darkness on the railroad tracks had dilated the pupils of my eyes, and it took me a moment to get used to the hundred-watt bulbs in the kitchen ceiling. Everyone in Worthington Springs believed in a well-lit kitchen. The living room might have smaller wattage bulbs, but the kitchen should always be well lit. The same was true of the bathroom. My grandmother used to say that this was to prevent accidents.

My grandmother was sitting in the kitchen, quietly shelling peas. When she looked up at me, her eyes grew wide in total surprise, and her hand immediately flew up to her mouth, as if she were suppressing a loud scream.

It always scared the hell out of me whenever my grandmother did that. I couldn't figure out what the problem was, until I saw her finger point toward my head.

"My God, son, what happened to your head?"

I never lied to my grandmother. I lied to my mother and father on a regular basis, because it just seemed natural somehow. However, something deep inside me wouldn't allow me to lie to my grandmother.

"A colored woman spit snuff on me," I said.

"Why?" she asked.

I told her, and she became angry that I had slipped off without permission and gave me a good tongue lashing about it.

"Slipping around is a bad habit for a young boy to get into. What if a train ran over you? What if you had got snake bit out there in those woods? What if you had got lost? Don't you ever do that again."

I just stood there with a big wad of snuff spit on my forehead, silently nodding my head and agreeing with everything she said. I always obeyed her, because I believed she was honestly looking out for my best interests. She wanted me to be safe and well. She wasn't just being a hateful bitch like my mother.

"Yes um." I politely and sincerely answered.

"My Lord, boy, what must I do with you? You are something!"

My grandmother just sighed and whispered to herself. "I guess slipping around just comes natural to you; your mama does it all the time."

Gently grasping my hand, she said, "I guess we better wash that snuff off your head before your mother gets home. If she knew you had been spit on by a colored woman, she would want to call the high sheriff and lynch somebody."

She led me into the bathroom and gently cleaned all the smelly snuff off my head. When she was finished, she looked at me and smiled. She then carefully warned me not to say anything about this to my mother.

I totally agreed with her on that point. If my mother knew I had been out slipping around, she would wail the daylights out of me.

My grandmother bent over and kissed me on my freshly washed forehead and whispered something gently into my ear.

"What your mama don't know won't hurt her."

# Of Little Boys and Hookworms

I began my formal education on a sticky hot day in August 1951. That year, Union County's population was a little more than six thousand people. The county's very low population numbers meant that all the county's white school children could comfortably fit into one building. It was, at least to me at the time, a very large building. The one and only school for white children was a double-winged structure with one wing for the elementary grades and the other for the junior and senior high school.

Although we were all in the same building, we seldom saw the high school kids until we got on the school bus in the afternoon. No matter if you were a first grader or a high school senior, in Union County everyone rode home on the same bright yellow school buses.

I remember the school as a big and friendly place; it was full of neat little corners and recesses where a young child could hide and play fantasy games and pretend to be an outlaw on the run from the law or one of Tom Corbitt's space cadets exploring another planet. The exterior of the school was covered with bright red bricks, and the interior walls were wainscoted with a darkly stained pinewood. The whole building had the strong odor of pine oil and the milky white disinfectant they used to clean the toilet bowls and urinals.

In 1951, on hot and muggy days, none of the children in Union County wore shoes to school. We felt that it was uncomfortable and unnecessary. Despite all my mother's threats and bitching about it, when the weather turned warm, I would shed my shoes and go barefooted. The school rule was if you wore shoes to school, you had to keep them on all day. However, if you came to school barefooted, then they had little choice except to allow you to go barefoot. Years later, the Florida legislature would pass a law requiring all public school students to wear shoes, but that time had not yet arrived.

We solved this little "if you wear shoes to school you must keep them on all day" rule problem by taking off our shoes during the morning bus ride and leaving them under our seat. My mother would always make sure I had my shoes on when I left home, and I would always make sure I took them off as soon as I got on the school bus. Remember: What mama don't know won't hurt her.

Our bus driver was a super nice guy named Mr. Robert B. Perrington, but we all called him Mr. Robbie. He had a receding hairline that seemed to be compensated for by an enormous amount of chest hair that stuck up around his collar and his almost-bushy muscular forearms.

Under the rules of proper childhood behavior, it was all right to call grown people by their first name if you put a Mr. or an uncle in front of it.

However, this was only if they were white; we never addressed a black person by any kind of formal title, except if they were family domestic help. Then, you could address them as aunt or uncle. Even small children called all black people John, Sally, Tom, George, or some other first name. I never remember being formally taught this rule of proper behavior. It was just something a young child quickly picked up from watching parents and older children. Today, it seems a shame that even an elderly black man or woman could not have the dignity of being addressed as Mr. or Mrs. even by young white children.

In the afternoons, Mr. Robbie would always stop by the small gasoline station and grocery store he owned and let us buy soft drinks, ice cream, potato chips, candy bars, and other snacks to eat during the ride home. To us kids, this made Mr. Robbie a super nice man. It wasn't until years later that it finally dawned on me that he was picking up a nice little extra piece of change selling candy and drinks from his store to a busload of hungry school children.

I would always buy an RC Cola and a Moon Pie, a large round marshmallow-filled cookie that was absolutely delicious. It was gourmet dining to delight the palate of any young country boy during a long, hot bus ride home.

An RC Cola cost a dime, and a Moon Pie was a nickel. This created elementary school financing problems. I had various relatives and other adults that I could always hit up for spare change. However, when that source of revenue dried up, I would sneak into the kitchen late at night, fix a super-duper peanut butter and jelly sandwich—sometimes with banana slices—and carry it to school with me the next day, hidden in my zip-up notebook. I would eat it as my lunch, so I could then pocket the twenty-five cents my mother gave me to buy a school lunch and spend it that afternoon with wild abandonment at Mr. Robbie's store.

School buses were a fairly new thing for Union County. The first one was purchased in 1940. It was a secondhand bus that was purchased from the much-larger school district in Jacksonville. The hand-painted yellow bus served the entire county until just after World War II, when the county was able to buy six more used buses. Brand new buses were not purchased until the mid-1950s.

During the Great Depression, enrollment in the scattered one-room schools across Union County fell off dramatically. In an effort to stem the tide and keep enrollment up, the school board asked local farmers to voluntarily drive around their area, pick up rural farm children, and bring them to school. Several responded, because they believed in education and wanted their children and their neighbor's children to have an education.

However, others needed more prompting. The school board finally voted to provide each driver with a two-dollar-a-month stipend for gas and wear and tear on their farm truck. This measure prompted other more reluctant farmers to help in getting children to school. On any morning, a person could see local farmers driving large flatbed farm trucks to the nearest school. The children would sit on the back platform with their feet dangling over the side, oblivious to the danger from the big wheels only a few feet away.

One of these drivers was my grandmother's cousin, a man of dubious reputation everyone called "Little Hamp" because of his size. Hamp was famous for being a crazy drunk who had once been shot in the head during a juke joint fight. The problem was that Little Hamp's old Ford farm truck had almost no brake pads of any account. Hamp had devised a method of stopping his near-brakeless truck by swerving back and forth on a dirt road building up soft sand in front of the front wheels that eventually slowed the vehicle enough so that what was left of his break pads could do their job. To Hamp, the trucked worked fine, and he saw no reason to spend hard-earned money on new brake shoes. Hamp argued that any farm child that couldn't hang on to the back of a truck without falling off wasn't much of a farm child.

However, the Union County School Board disagreed. Several times, children had been scattered all over the dirt road as Little Hamp swerved the truck and stomped furiously on his brake petal attempting to stop his old truck. The school board gave Little Hamp an ultimatum; either fix the problem or lose his two-dollar-a-month stipend. Hamp fixed the problem, but not the way the school board figured. Instead of having the brakes fixed, Little Hamp built a wire cage on the back of his truck using scrap wood and leftover chicken wire. He carefully explained to the school board. First off, he had no money to spend on an expensive brake job and that the cage would keep the children from spilling onto the road. Believe it or not, the school board accepted Little Hamp's compromise, although most of the parents did not. They refused to send their children to school until Hamp finally broke down and bought new brake shoes.

Early in the 1951–1952 school year, just when I was getting comfortable settling into the routine of the first grade, we were all marched in silent orderly rows down to the school's auditorium for what was billed as a "very important assembly program."

When we entered the auditorium that morning, we saw several women wearing the freshly starched, immaculately white attire of a nurse. Each had a neat little Red Cross pin on her lapel. They were hovering around an elderly, heavy-set lady that they treated with deference and respect that indicated she was someone very important. As soon as we were seated, our teacher—a harried and overworked woman named Mrs. Myrtle Brown—also joined the group of women hovering around the special lady and paid her respects.

Later, the special lady arose from her seat and came over to see us. I remember she was wearing a navy blue dress with white polka dots, and she had a piece of white lace around her collar. She didn't wear much makeup and didn't smell of the cheap perfume most Union County women wore. She had a kind round face that was covered with a very fine pinkish powder that made her look angelic. She also had a special sparkle in her eyes and a radiant smile that said she was basically a happy person who was at peace with both herself and God. It was a look I would see often in the eyes of my grandmother and many of the other matronly ladies who came into my life as a child and very seldom since.

She told us her name was Mrs. King and that she loved children, and she was very happy that we could came to the program. I could tell from her voice and the look in her eyes that she was one of the safe adults, the kind you could go to with a problem or question without fear of being yelled at or be called stupid. I liked Mrs. King from the very beginning and liked everything I ever learned about her. I would never see her again after that day.

Shortly after we were seated, our principal, Mr. Norman Jones, arose and formally introduced Mrs. King. He told us that she was the widow of Dr. J. W. King, who had been a physician in Union County for many years. Mrs. King was honorary chairwoman of the Public Health Committee of Union County, which was sponsoring this special program just for us. He said that we were about to watch a film, and, afterwards, the nurses would have some very important information for us.

After the lights went off, the projector started and stopped several times, as Mr. Jones tried to work out all the technical problems associated with the old Bell and Howell, 16-millimeter movie projector. After five or six false starts, a large black-and-white image finally flashed onto the screen. The portable silver-colored screen, mounted on a metal stand, was filled with the face of a lady who stared directly into the camera as printed material rolled over her image and an off-camera voice told us that this film was produced by the U.S. Department of Health, with the cooperation of the United States Department of Agriculture. It all seemed very official and very important.

One of the boys sitting directly behind me softly commented under his breath that she was the ugliest white woman he had ever seen. We had all been trained to respect our elders, and this lady looked a little like someone who would live in Union County, so we sat in respectful silence, that is, until she began to speak.

She had an unbelievably high-pitched voice and a strange foreign accent that we had never heard before. It made us all break out in laughter and giggles, until the principal's steel-eyed stare and about a million hushes from every adult in the room, again brought on the respectful silence expected from well-behaved school children.

"Goooo-d eveeen-ing, boys and girls." She began. "My name is Eleanor Roooo-seeee-velt, and I would like to talk to you about hooook-worms."

The way she said the word "hooook-worms," with her high-pitched voice, made my blood run cold. Many times, I had heard teachers and older students discussing hookworms. I had also heard my mother and father argue about them at home. My mother kept telling my father to make us wear shoes or we would all get hookworms, but my father dismissed the whole thing, saying it's too damn hot to wear shoes, and it cost too much money to keep buying shoes for all these "younguns" to wear out.

From what I remember of the twenty-minute film, Mrs. Roosevelt was concerned about what she called "intestinal parasites" in children who lived in the "Deep South."

This was the first time I had my home referred to as the "Deep South." I would hear it again, many times, before I grew up. It came from the lips of Walter Cronkite, Mike Wallace, Huntley-Brinkley, as well as Presidents Eisenhower, Kennedy, and Johnson. They all said it the same way, in an almost baleful manner, like they were talking about some kind of primitive foreign state, not a part of the United States of America.

Walter Cronkite would say, "The Freedom Riders today entered the 'Deep South.'" President Kennedy with his Cape Cod, little rich kid, accent would speak about equal opportunity for all people in the "Deep South." Ironically, it was Martin Luther King who spoke of the South as if it were his home, rather than as some kind of sinister place filled with hooded Klansmen and floating bodies.

Luckily, Mrs. Roosevelt didn't talk for very long, and soon the film was taken over by a professional announcer, who carefully explained to us the serious health emergency caused by the tiny parasite known to those with medical training as ancylostomiasis, better known as hookworms.

Many times in my life, I would be caught up in events that were much larger than me, such as the civil rights movement, the war in Vietnam, and the antiwar movement. However, little did I realize it at the time, but my involvement in events beyond my understanding was beginning here in the first grade; I would be a frontline soldier in Eleanor Roosevelt's war on hookworms.

The man on the screen told us that hookworms are found in tropical and subtropical climates, where the soil is contaminated with human excrement and the population doesn't wear shoes. It sounded to me like he was talking about Union County.

According to the 1950 census, there were over fifty million "unplumbed households" in the United States. The vast majority of these households were located in rural areas of the South and Midwest. People without indoor plumbing used what is commonly referred to as an outhouse or privy. In Union County, they were a common sight, sitting behind the tin-roofed shacks of poor whites and almost all black people.

Hookworm larvae are found almost everywhere in the southern soil. However, the damp ground around outhouses and cesspools is thoroughly infested. These small, almost microscopic larvae easily penetrate human skin primarily through the soles of the feet, but they can also enter the body through soil trapped under the fingernails and between toes and fingers.

Where the hookworm larvae penetrated the skin, an itchy rash appeared, which we called "ground itch." It was "cured," and I use that word loosely, by spraying the bottoms of the feet with a substance that causes a chemical ice to form. This procedure was so painful that most children didn't report the "ground itch" to their parents, preferring to suffer the itch rather than undergo the cure. Untreated, "ground itch" will eventually go away as the hookworm larvae moved further into the body.

By the time the "ground itch" had gone away, the hookworm larvae had traveled through the bloodstream to the lungs. The child then developed symptoms similar to those of a chest cold, except that every time the child coughed or sneezed, the hookworm larvae would enter the mouth and throat by way of the coughed-up mucus. The mucus would then be swallowed, and the larvae would travel down the digestive track, pass through the stomach, and finally settle in the small intestines.

Sometimes, the hookworm larva entered the body and moved directly into the digestive tract, which was the result of children eating food with dirty hands.

My family always insisted on clean hands at the dinner table. However, when I started school, I was totally shocked at the number of my classmates who never washed their hands before eating. Farm children often worked in the fields during the summer and ate their lunches under the shade of a nearby tree. They had nowhere to wash their hands, so they just didn't bother. The practice of eating with unclean hands in the fields carried over into the children's everyday home life. Our teachers spent a lot of time that first year explaining why it was important to wash your hands before you eat.

In the intestines, the hookworm larva develops into the full-grown intestinal parasite. The hookworm attaches itself to the intestine wall by the use of small hooks surrounding its mouth, hence its name. Also, the fully mature hookworm has a characteristic comma shape that to some people looks like a hook.

Thriving on the rich blood found in the small intestine, the mature hookworms produce millions of tiny eggs that pass out of the body through the fecal matter. When this infected waste matter reaches moist, bare soil, the eggs hatch into larva and the hookworm's life cycle begins again.

Except for some anemia and diarrhea, hookworm infestation usually has no symptoms. However, in more advanced stages, the child will begin to display the classic bloated belly that is commonly seen in children in underdeveloped nations. Even in the 1990s, hookworms affected over 700 million children in the poorest parts of the Third World.

Eleanor Roosevelt, who had enjoyed a rich and protected childhood, was horrified when she learned that thousands of children in the United States were infested with intestinal parasites. When her husband became President of the United States, she worked tirelessly setting up programs to screen children for hookworms and to see to it they got the treatment they needed.

The war against intestinal parasites would be waged on two fronts.

The first was to attempt to rid the United States of unsanitary outhouses that spread the infestations of intestinal parasites. As part of the New Deal, the Roosevelt Administration sent out thousands of federally trained and funded "specialists" to oversee the building of new "sanitary privies" across the United States. These new privies would replace the millions of dilapidated, unsanitary outhouses that had become the source of millions of jokes, but were in reality a symbol of the grinding poverty that existed in the rural United States.

The "federal specialists" discovered that many of these rural outhouses were little more than scrap lumber structures seated on top of the ground without even so much as a shallow hole. The waste matter just fell on top of the soil. A hard rain would flood the area, infecting the ground around the outhouse shanties with millions of hookworm larvae. When the pile of offal matter became too high, the lightweight outhouses would be picked up and moved a few feet to a new cleaner location, thereby further spreading the infestation.

Between 1933 and 1945, the federal government oversaw the building of over two million "sanitary privies." Over thirty-five thousand carpenter trainees were put to work building these new outhouses. Those who could afford it paid five dollars cash for a brand-new, ready-to-paint "sanitary privy," safely set on a freshly poured concrete base with a concrete-lined prefabricated cesspit that looked similar to a short section of open-ended culvert pipe. The new privies were all built to federal government specifications, put down in carefully designed blueprints. No deviation from the blueprints was permitted. A special corps of inspectors checked each privy to make sure no cost-cutting measures had been taken that would reduce the privy's sanitation.

In the same spirit of creating jobs and doing good work, thousands of both volunteer and paid health care workers heeded the call of Mrs. Roosevelt and spread out across the United States, screening millions of children for intestinal parasites. Experts were shocked at the results. They had expected the children of black people and poor white sharecroppers to be infected, but they were surprised at the number of middle class and affluent white children who also had intestinal parasites.

In Union County, Dr. and Mrs. King were both great admirers of Franklin and Eleanor Roosevelt, who they had once met in a fancy hotel ballroom in Miami. In 1934, Dr. J. W. King was appointed to be in charge of the program to screen all Union County children for hookworms. Although he was now elderly and in poor health himself, Dr. King personally was constantly out and about, making sure that the federally funded screening program was diligently being carried out. Dr. King was especially adamant that teams of health care workers go into the backwoods of the county and seek out poor children who didn't attend school. He also insisted that as much effort should be given to helping black children as whites.

When Dr. King died in the 1940s, his wife took over control of the program and was reappointed year after year. Although she was also of advanced years and bad health, she worked just as hard as her husband to do all she could to rid Union County of hookworms.

All of Franklin and Eleanor Roosevelt's good works in eliminating unsanitary outhouses and screening children for hookworms were carefully presented in the film. It was the work of Hollywood professionals, but it was way over our first-grade heads. We really didn't understand what it had to do with us, but we had already been trained to glue our eyes anytime visual images were danced before us on a silver screen, even at school.

After the film was over, one of the nurses walked to the center of the auditorium and held up a mayonnaise jar filled with alcohol. Inside was what looked like a small belt or roll of tape. She said it was called a tapeworm, and we might have one inside our bodies right this very minute.

Tapeworms were also found in the rural South. They were not as common as hookworms, but millions of children were still infested with them. There are several spices of tapeworm, but the one most common in the South is *Hymenolepsis nana* or dwarf tapeworm. They were found in the bodies of animals that spend a lot of time lying on wet ground, such as pigs, chickens, and cows.

Tapeworms can also be found in bottom-feeding fish, such as catfish, which often digest human or animal fecal matter that washes into the rivers and streams. During the 1950s, water pollution in Florida was so bad, it was not uncommon to be cleaning a catfish and find small pieces of toilet paper inside its stomach due to the millions of unsanitary cesspools and outhouses that lined the rivers.

Modern catfish are raised on well-managed, sanitary "catfish farms," where the fish hatch and mature in large freshwater ponds and are fed a special catfish food. It was many years before I would eat a farm-raised catfish. When I finally did, I discovered they tasted radically different than the filthy, bottom-feeding things I was fed as a child.

When the flesh of any animal or fish infested with tapeworms is eaten raw or poorly cooked, the tapeworm enters the human body and immediately travels to the lower digestive tract. There, the tapeworm attaches itself to the intestine wall and grows in jointed segments. Tapeworms can obtain a length of several feet and often discard their jointed sections, which are passed out of the body in fecal matter or vomit. One of my most vivid memories of growing up in Union County was when a girl, who had been drinking a soft drink on Mr. Robbie's bus, suddenly began to gag violently and finally vomited up several sections of tapeworm.

The only way to determine if a child has either hookworms or tapeworms is to have a stool sample examined under a microscope. If the child is infected, then the eggs of the hookworm or the jointed segments of the tapeworm will be plainly visible to the trained eye. This rather unpleasant work was done by hundreds of laboratory technicians at the Department of Health in Tallahassee.

Although I was only a first grader, I was a fast learner, and what they wanted us to do absolutely amazed me. Each child was given a small brown glass jar with a stick-on label. On the label, our name and the name of our school were carefully printed in heavy black ink.

Along with the little brown jar, we were given a detailed set of instructions, which were printed on one side and presented in cartoon form on the other side. The cartoon instructions were in case our parents couldn't read. Along with each little brown jar, we were also given a small flat stick that looked much like the kind of stick used to hold a Popsicle, except it was about two inches longer and slightly wider.

Looking at the cartoon directions, I saw that we were supposed to spread a nice, clean newspaper on the floor; have a small bowel movement on the paper; and then, with the stick, ladle the fecal matter into the little brown jar until it was full. Our teachers and the nurses referred to the sticks as "the stool scraper." The girls called them "doo-doo sticks," but the boys immediately christened the little flat pieces of wood, "shit sticks."

That night, my mother took care of all the unpleasant parts of my intestinal parasite screening. Since we had indoor plumbing, my mother was able to fill the jar directly from the toilet bowl. Apparently, the printed instructions were slightly different than those in the cartoons. The newspaper on the floor was intended for people who didn't have indoor plumbing. I think there was also the general assumption that people who couldn't read would automatically have an outhouse.

The next morning, I climbed on the school bus carefully carrying the stool sample in my hand. That particular morning Mr. Robbie's wife, Gladys, was driving the bus, and she seemed unusually nervous about the whole thing. She ordered us to hold the bottles in our hand and not to set them down. Apparently, she was worried about one of the glass jars getting broken, and she didn't want the unpleasant job of having to clean up somebody's hookworm-infested fecal material off the floor of the bus.

That was the first time I got into serious trouble at school. On a dare, I unscrewed the lid of my jar and stuck it under the nose of a girl I had grown to dislike. When we got to school, she told the principal, and I got a "stern talking-to" for what the principal called "utterly disgusting behavior, unbecoming a first grader."

When I finally got to my classroom, the teacher also seemed very nervous. She called us up to her desk, one at a time, to deliver our stool samples. I remember how funny the teacher's desk looked covered with little brown bottles of stool samples.

After turning in our stool samples, there was really nothing to do except wait for the results to get back from Tallahassee, which took about six weeks. There was a lot of speculating going on about who had worms and who didn't have worms. We loved to tease the stuck-up, snooty girls by saying they probably had worms. One girl, the same one from the "stool sample incident" on the bus, started crying and told on me. I was again sent to see the principal who again gave me another good talking-to. He also called my mother.

When I got home, my mother flailed the living daylights out of me with a belt. She didn't whip me, because I teased the little brat girl, but because I caused her embarrassment. She told me that her family was famous for having well-mannered children, and she couldn't understand what happened to me unless I had taken after my father, whose family apparently wasn't nearly as high class. It was nice to know all this family history.

The next day at school, I just happened to see a whole box of "shit sticks" sitting on the teacher's desk. Apparently, the nurses had left them behind in case one of us lost our stool scraper, and we needed a new one. When the teacher wasn't looking, I swiped a couple of the now-notorious sticks off of her desk. I was afraid to take more than two, because I feared that Mrs. Brown would notice they were missing.

About two days later, as we were returning from morning recess, I decided to stop by the water fountain for a drink of water. Especially on hot days, everyone wanted a drink of water, and the line at the fountain was always long. Ahead of me in the water line was the hateful little bitch that had gotten me in so much trouble on the bus. I had decided to leave her alone, but she spoiled it by turning around and sticking out her tongue at me. When she bent over to get a drink of water, I dropped one of the stolen "shit sticks" down the back of her dress.

She didn't know what it was or who had put it down her dress. At first, she was just irritated. She went into the girl's restroom to take it out of her dress. When she saw what someone had put down her dress, she went totally berserk. She came out of the restroom, absolutely crazy, screaming hysterically. It took the teachers about thirty minutes to calm her down and assure her "the stick" was perfectly clean, and there was no way she could get hookworms from a stick.

I would have probably have gotten away with it, if I had not pushed my luck. It happened just before evening recess, when we were in class doing silent artwork. When the teacher wasn't watching, I hissed at her. When she looked over at me, I immediately whipped out another "shit stick," stuck it in my mouth, and sucked on it, much like you would suck on a Popsicle.

Again, she went bananas; except this time; she knew who the culprit was. She pointed at me and started yelling out what I had done, demanding that the teacher do something. Thinking quickly, I immediately took the stick and thrust it deep within my trousers behind my back. It came to rest neatly in the deepest, darkest part of my anal cleavage, where I was reasonably sure Mrs. Brown would never look for it.

However, I had underestimated Mrs. Brown. She was a pro. She immediately grabbed me up by the scuff of my neck and literally dragged me down to the principal's office. She took me into his office and almost threw me on the couch, daring me to move. Nearly hysterical herself, she asked the secretary where the principal was. The secretary said he had just stepped out, but would return shortly. Seizing the moment, I reached into my pants, removed the stick, and pushed it deep under the cushions of the couch as far as I could reach. Just to be on the safe side, I moved over a few feet away from where I had just stuffed the incriminating evidence.

Mr. Jones, the principal of our school, was a short but muscular man, who parted his thinning hair directly in the middle, making him look like something off an old medicine bottle. However, his most distinguishing physical feature was not his hair, but the fact that he was a one-armed man.

He had shot off most of his left forearm while on a hunting trip in 1946. He had been climbing over a wire fence—stupidly carrying his shotgun—when it accidentally fired, blowing off all of his hand and most of his lower arm. After the doctors had finished with him, there was nothing left but a hideous-looking nub of an arm that began about four inches below his elbow.

Mr. Jones had no hang-ups about his misshapen appendage, and he used it as if the hand and forearm were still there. He often wore short-sleeve dress shirts to school, and, when he was talking to you, he would stick that damn nub of an arm right up in your face. We all hated looking at it, and we gave him the nickname "Nubby Jones" or "Old Nubby."

He was a strong man, with a commanding voice, that made everyone absolutely terrified of him. Rumor had it that somewhere in his office he had an electric paddle that had been built by the same man who had designed and built the electric chair out at the state prison. As a first grader, I had no idea what an electric paddle looked like, but it must have been a horrible thing to behold. Since I had been sternly talked to already, I was worried that this offense might bring out the fearsome electric paddle.

Some of the other boys took pride in the fact that "Old Nubby Jones" held no fear for them. These were all tater-fed, raw-boned boys who came from the pulpwood camps and dirt farms of rural Union County. To hear them tell it, their fathers would get all liquored up and beat them so hard that nothing that happened here at school even came close to hurting as much, not even the dreaded electric paddle. They actually bragged about having been beaten with the much-feared electric paddle and having survived the ordeal without crying a single tear.

I didn't know if I could ever be that brave. To tell you the truth, I didn't really want to find out. To me, the electric paddle was a concept too horrible to even think about. It was enough to keep me in line, until I discovered that like the bogey man, the electric paddle was a myth to scare children and make them behave.

When Mr. Jones returned to his office, he listened patiently as Mrs. Brown told him what I had done, and then he became very angry. With his one and only good hand, he seized me by the arm, jerked me out of the seat, and began feeling all over me with his nub of an arm looking for the incriminating "stool sampler." I hated being rubbed on with his damn nub of an arm. When he couldn't find it, he began questioning me, and I protested my innocence with all the tears and charm that a first grader was capable of producing. Slowly, I saw a change come over him as he began to accept my story. Mrs. Brown was adamant that the stick had to be on me somewhere, because she was sure I had done it, just like her little teacher's pet had said I had.

After what was a heated discussion out of my earshot, both Mr. Jones and Mrs. Brown came to the reluctant decision that perhaps a mistake had been made, and, indeed, I had not performed the horrible act of sucking on a stool sample stick. They told me to return to class, and I was elated. I had not only gotten my revenge, but at the same time, I had beaten the rap. However, more importantly, I had learned a valuable lesson; just because adults were bigger and older than me, it didn't mean that they were smarter.

I didn't think about this until years later, but I strongly suspect that the fact that I was the grandson of Robert Benjamin "Doc" Roberts might have had something to do with my lenient treatment. He was a man of considerable political power.

My classmates all wanted to know what had happened in the principal's office and if I had been paddled with the electric paddle. I told them of course I had. The electric paddle hurt terribly, but I took it like a man and had not cried, not once. This little misrepresentation of the truth immediately made me a mega-hero with the other boys.

Several weeks later, the hookworm screening results got back from Tallahassee. I received the call to come to the principal's office. Mr. Jones told me that my stool sample had proven positive for hookworms, but, almost as if he were giving me good news, he said there was no evidence of tapeworms. All this was supposed to be handled with great care, sensitivity, and confidentiality, but when you got the call to go to the principal's office, everyone knew what the deal was. There can be no secrets in a school that small.

Hookworms are treated with a chemical called tetrachloroethylene. I couldn't pronounce it or spell it. All I remember was that it came in the form of a giant red capsule, filled with some kind of syrupy red substance that tasted terrible. I felt like I was swallowing a goose egg covered with red slime. You had to keep taking the pills every day until your stool sample came back clear of hookworm eggs. For me, it took about ten weeks.

Having hookworms meant that every Friday I was called to the principal's office and given another little brown bottle to take home and fill with a fresh stool sample. When Mrs. Brown saw my name on the list of students who had hookworms, she went to the office and demanded that I be given only one stool sample stick, and she even called my mother to make sure that the stick would be "properly disposed of." She also demanded to know in advance when I was to bring back the stool sample. Mr. Jones politely explained to her that since I was given the bottle on Friday afternoon, he would order me to return it on Monday morning. You would think she could figure that out, having a college education and all.

Each Monday morning, Mrs. Brown would meet me at the bus parking area to make sure I took the stool sample directly to the principal's office. She watched me like a hawk. When I asked her why she was there, she said, "To make sure you don't deviate from the designated route and do not do anything disgusting." The thought had never even crossed my mind.

I had once heard her complain to Mr. Jones that I should be sent home until I was "cured." She was worried that I could possibly infect the whole class with hookworms. He assured her that was impossible unless I had a bowel movement in class.

Diarrhea is a common symptom of hookworm infestation, and it appeared to worry Mrs. Brown a lot. She called me up to her desk and told me, very nicely and in a very quiet voice, that whenever I needed to go to the restroom, just to let her know and she would write me a pass. That opened all kinds of new possibilities for misadventure. Since I could go to the toilet anytime I wanted, I spent all kinds of time in the boy's restroom goofing off royal.

Soon, all of us boys who had hookworms began to meet down in the boy's restroom at prearranged times of the day. It became a kind of clubhouse, and we formed a type of elementary school brotherhood, the "hookworm boys."

Some of the older boys, second and third graders, began to bring comic books to read while we were in the restroom. I loved comic books. I had been looking at the Sunday comics even before I started school. Although I couldn't read the words, I could look at the colorful pictures and tell what was going on. Even as a toddler in diapers, I would spread the brightly colored Sunday comics on the floor and examine each panel closely. I loved to look at the colorful little squares and find out what was happening to Dagwood and Blondie, Mickey Mouse, and my favorite Dick Tracy. I would ask my grandmother what this word meant or what that word meant, and, pretty soon, I had a nice little working vocabulary. By the time I started school, I could already read most of the Sunday comics.

However, when you've matured enough to be a first grader with hookworms, you couldn't be seen reading kid's stuff. Any kid who showed up with Bugs Bunny or Daffy Duck was heaped with ridicule. We read macho comics. My favorite was *Blackhawk*. It was about this neat group of guys, who wore leather jackets and flew their own jet airplanes. They were always flying around kicking ass and taking names. I also liked *Terry and the Pirates* (a type of East Asian occidental soldier of fortune with an airplane), Steve Roper (a navy pilot), and Steve Canyon (an air force pilot). I thought the Dragon Lady was a damned good-looking woman and could never understand why Steve Canyon didn't go for her.

While I liked the Blackhawks, the favorite among our group of "hookworm boys" was without a doubt *SGT Rock* and the Combat Happy Joes of Easy Company. It was a great comic book for a future soldier's first grade juvenile mind. Sgt. Rock's platoon shot down German airplanes with M-1 rifles, blew up Nazi tanks with hand grenades, and held off wave after wave of infantry attacks without one single guy in the platoon being killed, wounded, or running out of ammunition.

Years later, in Vietnam, we would still read old *Blackhawk* and *SGT Rock* comic books. The special services used to pass them out to us free. I guess they thought these war comics would improve morale and make us better soldiers. However, comic book stories about a bunch of combat-happy soldiers looked much different in Vietnam than it did in the first grade.

The girls who had hookworms were all ashamed of it. They became very offended and defensive when anyone even mentioned it. However, with us boys, it was almost a badge of honor. I saw no reason to feel ashamed. To me, hookworms were the natural consequence of being a country boy.

My mother was also very embarrassed about the whole thing and made me swear never to mention it to anyone, but especially not to anyone at church or at family gatherings. That year at Thanksgiving dinner, she was absolutely terrified that I would mention it at the dinner table. She promised me the beating of a lifetime if I did. She always told me that nobody in our family had ever had hookworms before me. This was something that I grew to seriously doubt as the years rolled on.

The children, like me, who had hookworms mostly lived in the country and spent their time playing in God's good dirt rather than on city sidewalks. We were generally from poor families and not the type of kids who were academically orientated. Hookworm boys didn't suck up to the teacher, which meant we were all stereotyped by our teachers and the more well-off classmates. The stuck-up assholes in the school tried to use hookworms to put a stigma on us. We were expected to be crude and ignorant, so we were. We lived up to their expectations by tormenting those who had stigmatized us, like the girl that I had harassed with the "shit stick." I had nothing against her personally; it was just that she looked down her nose at me and expected me to be act like a vulgarian, so I did.

Later that same year, I got ringworm and had to have my head shaved. My head bore a large red circle about the size of a fifty-cent piece. Ringworm isn't really a worm, but a circular fungus infection. It is treatable but difficult to cure. My mother got very angry when the school nurse found it and called her. My mother whipped me and accused me of catching ringworm on purpose. She said that nobody in our family ever had ringworm before me. Ringworm, like hookworms, made me some kind of a hero with the guys, although the girls and my teachers tended not to approve.

Once I got out of first grade, things settled down a lot, and I became more or less a good student. I liked school. I was weak in math, a poor speller, and I still don't know where the damned commas are supposed to go. However, I was an excellent and insatiable reader. I really excelled in social studies and geography. There wasn't a country on the globe I couldn't find in a minute. I was an expert on the equator and all the imaginary lines and climate zones of the earth. I knew they grew coffee in Brazil, tea in China, and that rubber comes from Malaya.

When I was in the fourth grade, the Davy Crockett craze hit, and I was way ahead of my time. I had been reading about Davy Crockett, Daniel Boone, and Andrew Jackson for years. I admired Davy Crockett and dreamed of living like him—no parents, no school, and no job— and just travel around and fight Indians while Buddy Ebsen wrote songs about you.

I begged and pleaded until my mother bought me every piece of Davy Crockett junk on the market. I didn't realize it at the time, but I was beginning to define myself, not by what I was, but what I owned. We were all becoming rabid little consumers. It wasn't enough to have a lunch box; it had to be a Davy Crockett lunch box. It wasn't enough to have a coonskin hat; it had to be a Davy Crockett coonskin hat. Later in life, it was not enough just to have an automobile; it had to be a Mercedes-Benz. It wasn't enough to own a watch; it had to be a Rolex. Sunglasses had to be Ray-Bans, and shirts had to be Izods.

# Learning to be Cruel

When I was nine years old, I received my first real firearm, a single-shot, twenty-two caliber rifle. It would replace my trusty Daisy, lever-action, and spring-powered BB gun, which had been my faithful companion since before the first grade. I wasn't actually given the weapon; it was more or less passed down to me by my older brothers, who had both moved up to pump-action, twelve-gauge shotguns.

It was a right of passage. I knew that when my older brothers left home, one of the twelve-gauge shotguns would also be mine. I never thought about the morality or the safety of owning a firearm. It seemed weird to me not to have one. All my heroes in the movies carried guns, and all the great historical figures I read about in school carried weapons. Having a gun just seemed as natural as wearing pants.

I loved wandering in the woods carrying a real gun, although to be perfectly honest, I never shot anything. Instead, I would pretend that I was Davy Crockett defending the Alamo or one of the Texas Rangers chasing dangerous outlaws across the West Texas plains. Hunting was pleasurable to me as a solitary thing. It enabled me to get off by myself. The woods were like the quiet, dark place under the loading dock of my grandfather's store.

Usually, the Florida woods are a hard place to walk because of the heavy underbrush. The palmetto bushes and thick tangles of catbriers can take your hide off one scratch at a time. However, the woods behind my house were laced with plowed firebreaks, cut through the thick underbrush by large Caterpillar tractors pulling heavy plows. These fire breaks were re-cut, usually every two years, and followed the same route over and over again. The rain would erode the plowed-up earth, making it smooth and hard packed. Soon enough, pine needles and leaves had fallen to cover the bottom of the fire break, making them fine, brier-free trails through the woods.

I was twelve years old and in the sixth grade when I went on my first coon hunt. I never liked the killing part of hunting, but I did like the "male-bonding" camaraderie of being on a coon hunt with my older brothers and father. It gave us an opportunity to be together in a natural setting, without the presence of mothers and sisters to monitor our speech and behavior.

Coon hunting is a peculiar southern tradition. Raccoons are edible, but barely so. Back in the 1920s, coon hides could be sold to dealers who used them to make long coats that were the fashion rage on college campuses. However, by the 1950s, the market for coon hides had dried up. I often wondered why we went to so much trouble hunting an inoffensive little creature with hardly enough meat on its bones to warrant the trouble. I could also never understand why coons were only hunted at night, since it seemed to me that it would be just as easy to hunt them in the daytime.

However, I never asked any questions. By this time, I had already learned my lesson about asking questions. I remembered very well the vicious slap my mother had put on me when I asked her why I couldn't share my RC Cola with Mitchell. I was often punished at home for asking questions my mother couldn't or didn't want to answer. The punishment might be anything from a simple scolding right up to a vicious beating, something my mother laid on me with great regularity.

Things were not that much different at school. My teachers were defensive as hell. Never ask them anything about sex or the aspects of religion that were illogical, and never, never, ever question the way things were done. Especially, if that's the way they have been done for generations. Conformity was something that was literally driven into me with both a belt and ridicule. We were not educated to think for ourselves.

I wouldn't learn until many years later that coon hunting, like racial segregation, was a vestige of the long-dead institution of slavery. We often referred to black people as "Coons," but I never understood why. Coon hunting began before the Civil War as a method of training both men and dogs to track down and capture runaway slaves. That's the primary reason why raccoons are hunted at night, because that's when slaves ran away, at night.

The object of a coon hunt is not necessarily to kill the coon, but to "tree the coon." That is, to chase the animal with dogs until it is so exhausted it can't run anymore. Then, it will give up trying to outrun the dogs and climb a tree. If only the dogs were involved in the hunt, the raccoon could just wait them out. Dogs have little patience and would soon wander off. However, as soon as the dog's barking indicated that the coon was up a tree, the hunters would show up with their guns.

I got most of my knowledge about coon hunting at the barbershop on Saturday afternoons. It seemed that coon hunting was a favorite sport of Union County barbers and almost everyone whose hair they cut. While waiting for my haircut, I was forced to endure being force-fed all types of coon hunting lore.

There wasn't much to a coon hunt really. The hunters would go out shortly after dark and find a spot in the woods that was hopefully not "posted" or private land where hunting was prohibited. More than once, a coon hunt had gone sour, because the hounds would go after an old tomcat or somebody's cow, rather than the raccoon they were suppose to be chasing.

The only dog worth a damn in coon hunting was an incredibly ugly beast with floppy ears, skinny legs, and dark bluish-brown spots all over its body. This breed of dog was given the definitely unflattering name of "blue tick coon hound." I suppose it was because the spots on his back looked like ticks after they became gouged with blood.

Usually, the hunters would simply release their dogs and then build a fire and wait until the dogs sniffed out a coon and got on a trail. It was while sitting around the fire that the serious male bonding took place. Even if your daddy or older brothers were along on the hunt, a certain amount of cussing, tobacco chewing, smoking, and sometimes even beer drinking was allowed. Everyone was expected to tell at least one overtly racist or very dirty joke. It was as if all the rules were suspended. We all knew, without being told, that when we returned home and were once again in the presence of our mothers and sisters, such behavior or language would not be tolerated. Our fathers wanted us to grow up polite and well mannered, but, at the same time, they wanted the private assurance that they hadn't raised a sissy boy.

When the dogs finally got on a trail, the woods would echo with the sound of massive amounts of howling and barking. It is amazing how far sound travels in the woods at night. The larger the pack of dogs, the more noise they made, and the easier it was for the hunters to follow the chase. The more coon dogs you had on a hunt, the better.

I knew sorry-ass men in Union County who would let their children go barefooted and hungry, just so they could feed, worm, doctor, and generally support a large pack of coonhounds. These same men would sell their wife's mother's wedding ring to buy a shotgun. That's how important hunting was in Union County.

We never ventured from our fire until it became obvious by the stationary barking and long howling of the dogs that the coon was treed. We would then run through the dark woods, following the sound of the dogs using powerful battery-powered lamps to guide our way. We moved in a hurry, because everyone wanted to be there when the dogs finally got the coon. That was the fun part.

Coons, for some reason, will usually not climb all the way to the top of the tree. They remain on the lowest branch just above the reach of the dogs. Raccoons are curious animals by nature and always appeared to want to see what was happening below them.

At this point, after having treed the coon, it would be an easy matter to simply call off the hunt and go home. Technically, the humans and dogs had won. However, most coon hunters will force the animal out of the tree and let the dogs rip him to pieces. If you don't do this, the dogs will soon lose interest in coon hunting, and, the next time, they will not chase the raccoon with as much vigor. A good coon dog could be ruined by not letting it tear the raccoon apart every now and then. As an old Union County coon hunter used to say, "You've got to let them chew awhile. The worse thing that can happen to a good coon hound is for him to lose the taste for blood."

During the days of slavery, it was just as common to let the dogs attack and maul the runaway slave. It was done for basically the same reason, to keep the dogs interested in the chase. I suppose it also served as some kind of punishment for the slave, to deter future running away. The only difference was that the slave was much too valuable to kill, so the dogs would be pulled off before he was fatally injured. However, the dog bite mark scars on the slave's arms and legs branded him as a runaway. This would lower his value when it came time to sell the slave.

Once we got to the spot where the raccoon was treed, we could have easily shot him out of the tree with a shotgun and threw the dead carcass to the dogs, but that was too easy. Instead, we would shoot around him with our twenty-two-caliber rifles, forcing the animal to leap into the pack of dogs.

What followed was a bitter and violent fight to the death that the dogs always won. It was always better for the dogs to chew on a live coon that had just jumped from a tree, rather than one that had already been killed and thrown to them. The fact that the animal was still alive seemed to give both the dogs and the hunters a lot more pleasure.

Coon hunting gave people who lived in the South a peculiar expression: "You can kill me, but you can't eat me." I personally believe that it was either a runaway slave or a black man about to be lynched who first coined the phrase. It was a last act of defiance before death, a final crying out for justice at the end of an unjust life. "You can kill me, but you can't eat me."

# A Boy Called Rabbit

The one emotion I felt more than any other when I was growing up was fear. The 1950s were the height of the Cold War, and we practiced "duck-and-cover" drills at school, where we would jump up, climb under our desks, and cover our heads with our arms. They showed us a short, black and white movie put out by the Office of Civil Defense. It had an animated turtle telling us that when the atomic bomb was dropped, we would all be safe, if we just remembered to "duck and cover." We were brainwashed to believe and do everything adults said. It never crossed our minds to ask how ducking and covering could possibly protect us from an atomic fireball hotter than the surface of the sun.

Then, there was polio. Several of the kids who went to our school wore the cruel leg braces of polio victims. It was a horrible thing. One day you were a normal kid, running and playing, and the next day, you were in an iron lung, looking at the world through a mirror over your head and writing messages with a pencil held in your teeth. I would just as soon they turned the damn thing off and let me die.

Each spring, the March of Dimes would come around and literally bombard us with images of children in iron lungs, wheelchairs, or hobbling on crutches.

Each spring, the March of Dimes would give us a handful of stiff cardboard cards, with a pathetic picture of some poor kid with polio on it. On the back were empty slots we had to fill with dimes. It took twenty dimes, or two dollars, to fill the card. Any student who didn't fill their card with dimes was singled out by the teachers with shame and scorn. Some even posted our names with a chart showing how many March of Dimes cards we had filled.

The children of well-to-do families filled up card after card, while the poor children were lucky to get one.

In my fifth grade class, there was a tall, dark-haired boy who never filled up a single March of Dimes card. We called him Rabbit. It was one of those weird nicknames that get stuck on a kid when people are too familiar with each other.

Although Rabbit was in the fifth grade, he should have been two years further on. He had been held back twice for not making satisfactory progress. He was probably retarded, but we didn't use that word back then. Even if he wasn't mentally retarded, Rabbit didn't have a chance. He was the first generation of his family to go to school. Both of his parents were dirt poor and illiterate. They couldn't help him with his school work at home, and the bitch teachers either ignored him or made fun of Rabbit's questions and requests for help; so, he just got further and further behind. Rabbit's parents, who had never been in a school, could not give him any motivation to do well or understand his complaints about his teachers being mean to him. They had no idea of what he was going through. They couldn't even read his report card and tell if he was doing well or not.

Unlike poor children of today, Rabbit had not spent his preschool years watching *Sesame Street* and *Barney* the purple dinosaur. He also hadn't had the benefit of a federal Head Start Program. Outside of school, Rabbit's world consisted of a three-room shotgun shack in a remote pulpwood camp at the end of a dirt road three miles from Worthington Springs. His family got their water from a pitcher pump well and used an outhouse that Rabbit's father had built from scrap wood and tin. Rabbit bathed in a galvanized, number 3, washtub sitting on the back porch. When it was cold, he didn't bathe at all. Rabbit's family had no hot water, except what they heated themselves over a fire in the backyard.

His father worked hard cutting pulpwood, and, when the rain made it too wet to get into the woods, he couldn't work, and the only things the family had to eat were small animals such as rabbits, squirrels, and gopher tortoises that they trapped or caught. These small animals, along with some collards and peas they grew in the tiny family garden patch, were their diet.

Rabbit's school lunch always contained an unappetizing mixture of cold potatoes, stale biscuits, and small pieces of greasy fried meat of unknown origin. Some gossiping girls said Rabbit was eating possum in the lunchroom, and others said it was cooter meat. Nobody knew for certain, and nobody bothered to ask. It was crueler just to speculate behind his back. If somebody asked Rabbit what the meat was and he said chicken, it would spoil the little girl's silly whispers and giggles.

I never saw Rabbit wear shoes to school, even on the coldest days of the year, but he always wore two pairs of pants, one on top of the other. This was a common practice among those who worked around pine trees. When you were cutting pulpwood or dipping turpentine, the thick pine tar would get onto your clothes, and it was almost impossible to clean off. Pulpwooders and turpentiners would always wear two pairs of pants; they had one pair of underpants that they washed and tried to keep as clean as possible and another pair of overpants that were so encrusted with pine tar, washing was futile.

Also, wearing two pairs of pants offered some protection against a chain saw's vicious cut. It was seldom that you saw a pulpwooder who had all of his fingers and toes. The chain saws they used in the 1950s did not have all the safety features of the modern machines. They were prone to jump back on you and snap off fingers or toes as they flew out of control through the air. Every year, at least one or two men would be killed in chain saw related accidents in Union County.

Rabbit had dirty yellow teeth and the familiar yellow-brown stains between his fingers that told everyone that although he was only in elementary school, he was already a smoker. One day, a teacher caught him out on the playground, sitting behind a large oak tree quietly smoking a roll-your-own cigarette.

Later, in the principal's office, it was discovered that the cigarette was made up entirely of a substance we called "rabbit tobacco."

When most people think about smoking, they immediately associate it with tobacco. However, in the rural South, there were a variety of plants and tree barks that could be dried in the hot sun and smoked with various degrees of pleasure. All of these plants and tree barks bore the generic name of "rabbit tobacco." The most popular "rabbit tobacco" was the leaves of the grapevine. The second most popular was corn silks mixed in with the dried sucks. The use of "rabbit tobacco" was probably learned from the Native Americans, who smoked a mixture of tree barks called *kinnickinnick* in their ceremonial pipes.

Smoking was popular among poor children, because it killed hunger pains. Old women smoked "rabbit tobacco" and dipped snuff. They claimed the nicotine caused their teeth to stop hurting.

When they could afford it, poor people bought the cheaper, roll-your-own brands of tobacco, which they could expertly fashion into crude little cigarettes, using the thin white papers that you got free with a red can of Prince Albert or a cloth bag full of Bull Durham smoking tobacco.

All of us children had tried "rabbit tobacco" at one time or the other, and it usually left us coughing, gagging, or throwing up. When we learned that our classmate was a regular smoker of the strong "rabbit tobacco," it put us in awe of him, and it gave him prestige and status among us. It also got him his nickname.

Once he discovered that his smoking of "rabbit tobacco" had given him elevated status among us, Rabbit accepted his new nickname with pride, seldom answering to his real name unless it was called by a teacher who was usually about to get on to him about something.

Despite all of his idiosyncrasies, the boys never made fun of Rabbit, at least not to his face. He was head and shoulders taller than the rest of us and would fight at the drop of a hat. Although he was only in elementary school, he was well developed and large boned. His arms, legs, and back were almost solid muscle tissue. I once noticed that the knuckles on his hand were almost as large as a grown man's. His palms were covered with hard calluses, the result of hours swinging an ax or hoe.

He also got a lot of respect from us because of his athletic ability, which was a big thing in Union County. He was able to knock a baseball into the middle of next week. He could outrun and outjump any of us. Everyone wanted Rabbit on their team, and that made him feel good. Rabbit did real well until he walked into a classroom. In the classroom, there were bitch teachers and snooty little girls. He could not beat them up, outrun them, outjump them, or be superior in any way. He was at their mercy. They had no mercy.

The teachers despised a kid like Rabbit. They considered him a troublemaker and a dummy. They let Rabbit know every day, in a hundred different ways, that he was an unwelcome burden on them. He was always being sent to the principal's office where old Nubby Jones would put as many as ten licks on him with a hard wooden paddle. Once, I watched in horror as our teacher brought a yardstick down across his shoulders three times in rapid succession. The last blow was so hard it broke the yardstick with a loud crack. It made me mad, because I knew that they would never do that to him if he came from a well-to-do family. The teachers knew Rabbit's family was poor and illiterate people who wouldn't go down to the school board and complain, so they picked on him.

One day, something very interesting happened that would give me much thought later in life. The teacher was trying to teach us the difference between "peace" and "piece." She called upon Rabbit to make a sentence with the word "peace."

Rabbit replied, "He walked down the road a piece."

Of course, the teacher went ballistic. She rolled her eyes and then verbally sailed into Rabbit, ridiculing his mistake in front of the whole class. Rabbit only stared down at his desk and said nothing. This was the only way he had of dealing with the constant wave of humiliation and scorn that flowed from the authority figure at the head of the class.

However, somehow, I think the joke was on the teacher. Maybe in her world what Rabbit had said was wrong, but in his world, it was perfectly correct. Who made her one of the gods of grammar to say what is right and wrong?

I think it was that day that I began to discover that there was something dark and sinister in the English language. All the rules of good grammar, punctuation, sentence structure, proper and improper nouns, and most of all spelling rules don't really exist to make it easier to communicate. In fact, their objective was to make it more difficult for us to talk, write, and reason with each other.

The rules of "proper English" contain hundreds of little booby traps that are totally illogical. The letters g and h serve no purpose other than to make words difficult to spell. Why is it spelled "tough" instead of the more logical and shorter "tuff"? Wouldn't a child, who has been learning for weeks that the past tense is formed by adding "ed," logically expect that the past tense of "teach" would be "teached" and dig would be "digged," not the illogical "taught" and "dug." Why do we have the letters E, I, and y, although they make the identical sound when we speak, just like C and K? Which is right "cat" or "kat"? Which is correct among the names Edy, Edi, Eddi, Edde, or Eddie? Then, there are the silent letters, the notorious "r" in February and the "p" in pneumonia.

Children are taught that an "s" on the end of a word means that it is plural. It's not with the word "run." Run is plural, and runs is singular as in: The boys run track. The boy runs track.

Slowly, over the years, I began to understand the hidden political agenda in all of this. These illogical little land mines in our language, enforced by English teachers, have an evil purpose. They are designed to separate us by social class, ethnic background, and race. They identify those who are not worthy, those, like Rabbit, who don't belong and will never fit into polite, upper-class society. They tell us immediately who is poor, who is black, who is an immigrant, and, in this case, who is uneducated, poor white trash.

The rules of modern English can be traced back to the Middle Ages, when the rich and pampered nobility never came in contact with the common people. The totally arbitrary rules of grammar, punctuation, and spelling immediately identified a peasant and a trespasser in the court of the rich and privileged. It is the same function served today.

It was like watching a light go out in a lamp. Rabbit slowly surrendered to the cultural imperialism of the New England based English texts we used in class. He simply couldn't grasp the following strange dialog:

"Hi Jane," said Mary, "Will you be ice skating with us this afternoon?"

"Why yes," Jane replied, "Will Robert be joining us?"

"He can't come skating with us," Mary said, "but he can join us later to have a snack."

One day, we were sitting in class doing busy-work exercises out of our English books, when Rabbit whispered over to me.

"What's 'pop'?"

"It's something you do with your bubble gum," I replied.

"No, it ain't," he said. "Look at number seven."

I glanced down the page of my English book, and slowly my eyes fell on question seven. It read as follows:

"Can we go and (by/buy) a bottle of pop?"

"What the hell do they mean by a 'bottle of pop'?"

"Damned if I know," I told Rabbit. "Ask the teacher, that's what she's here for."

Very timidly, Rabbit raised his hand only to get a hard stare from our teacher. However, doing her duty, she called on him.

"What is a 'bottle of pop'?" he asked.

The teacher replied that it was a soft drink such as Coca-Cola or Pepsi.

Rabbit replied, "You mean it's a sodie water?"

This brought a fiery response from the teacher.

"Well, educated, polite people do not use the term 'soda water.'"

"Why not?" Rabbit asked in all sincerity.

That did it; he had asked her a question she couldn't answer. Moreover, he had challenged the way things were done and said. It got him a quick trip to Nubby's office and five hard licks with a board.

The thing that made me mad was that the use of the term "soda water" or "sodie water" was common as dirt in Union County, especially among older people. We never used the term "a bottle of pop" or the word "snack." They weren't teaching us English; they were teaching us a foreign language. We were learning one lesson in school and another when we got home. As a southern friend of mine once said; "I might have a Master's Degree from Harvard, but I got a PhD from my mama and daddy."

Rabbit couldn't talk like they did in the English books—not and go back and live and work in the culture he came from. It was too much to ask of a boy that he give up his parents, his family, and friends—the very fiber of what he was as a human being—just to get a certain grade on a report card and the approval of some bitch of a teacher. It just didn't mean anything important to him.

It was just as hard for Rabbit to learn sentence structure, grammar, nouns, and verbs as it was for me to hit a home run. Rabbit would be judged the rest of his life by what he did in the classroom with pencil and paper. I always thought how unfair it would be if I were to be judged the rest of my life by what I did on a baseball field. Rabbit slowly withdrew from the class, giving up and realizing that this was no place for him.

It's not surprising, I suppose, that during all this, Rabbit unfortunately became a bully. He was so big and strong; he could really hurt somebody in a fight. None of us dared cross him, except for the small group of stuck-up little girls, who he couldn't punch in the face, based on some deep-rooted southern code of chivalry that was so strong it had even been passed on to him. As Rabbit explained it to us, "You can't hit a woman, unless you is married to her."

Rabbit wasn't always a bully. His bullying began, because he never had the twenty-five cents necessary to buy a hot school lunch. Most of us ate the school lunch, because our parents thought it was a good deal. The few students who brought their lunch from home were mostly snooty kids, whose parents didn't think the twenty-five cent school lunches were good enough for their little darlings. When they pulled out their fancy Roy Rogers or Mickey Mouse lunch boxes and ate their homemade cookies and sliced ham sandwiches, it was supposed to put the rest of us to shame. However, with Rabbit, and other kids like Rabbit, it was different.

The rest of the children would sit eating a well-balanced school lunch, which closely followed the four major food groups; breads, dairy products, vegetables, and meats. However, Rabbit would sit in their midst, head and shoulders taller than anybody else at the table, quietly eating his cold potatoes and stale biscuits out of a makeshift lunch pail his mother had fashioned from an old Maxwell House coffee can. Sometimes, one of the other children would give him their milk or offer him some of their lima beans, corn, or cling peaches. Rabbit would always accept. Rabbit once told me that he only had grits and gravy for breakfast each morning, and, by lunch, he was really hungry.

One day, Rabbit's mother had put a slice of raw bacon inside his coffee can lunch pale, instead of the usual piece of greasy mystery meat. Rabbit couldn't eat it raw, so he boldly got up from the table and walked back into the kitchen and asked one of the lunchroom ladies if they could cook it for him.

Rabbit's mother had never been to school. When he told her he ate in a place called the lunchroom and that the other kids ate hot meals, she just assumed that they had a stove, and they would be glad to cook Rabbit's little piece of bacon for him.

The lunchroom lady was nice about the whole thing. She quietly explained to Rabbit that this couldn't be done, but to make up for her inability to cook the little piece of bacon, she gave him a peanut butter cookie. That was the beginning of the trouble.

This was the first time Rabbit had ever tasted a peanut butter cookie, and he loved it. After that, he would go around asking everyone for their peanut butter cookies, wanting to swap one of his cold potatoes for it. However, no one would give up their one and only sweet dessert.

They would say, "Rabbit, you can have my peas, or my carrots, or my milk, even my celery stalk with peanut butter on it, but not my cookie."

However, Rabbit didn't want those things; Rabbit wanted the peanut butter cookie. When he didn't get it, he got mad, and, when Rabbit got mad, everyone else got scared. It was then that Rabbit learned that all he had to do was ball up his big fists, and the peanut butter cookie was his.

From this humble beginning, Rabbit went on to extorting pieces of cake, cling peaches, and ice cream. He finally moved up to taking the lunch money itself, so he could buy soft drinks and candy bars after school.

I would like to say that Rabbit was one of a kind, but that just wasn't true. Rabbit was only a small part of a large group of Union County students born in abject poverty with illiterate parents and teachers who just didn't understand. Faced with constant ridicule and academic failure, their only shred of self-respect was in what they could do with their fists. They made the younger and smaller children's lives pure hell. They lived to fight and beat up somebody smaller and weaker than they were. To deny them anything was to get a black eye or a busted lip.

It always amazed me how the teachers just ignored all this bullying, like it just wasn't happening. Nobody told on the bully; to do so would be a kiss of death. Even our teachers warned us not to be tattletales. Only the prissy little teacher's pet girls were allowed to tell on somebody. It was not a right granted to little boys. If you couldn't fight and stand up for yourself, you just had to take it. There also seemed to be this understanding among parents that bullying was a normal part of childhood. They thought that it somehow taught us to be tough, to fight back, and that way we would grow up mean and manly and not be a sissy boy. What it really taught us was how to be a bully to other people when our time came.

Rabbit dropped out of school as soon as he turned sixteen. He was only in the seventh grade, but, by that time, he was over six feet tall and weighed nearly one hundred eighty pounds. Most of the other kids and all the teachers were glad to see him go. However, I liked Rabbit and personally wished him well.

For some reason, he had never bullied me. It was probably because I had tried to help him with his schoolwork. Also, Rabbit had been one of the older boys with hookworms, who hung out with me down in the boy's restroom.

I always let him read my comic books, because he never had any of his own. Rabbit could read much better than anyone imagined. I think the reason for this was that in the early grades he spent so much time in the boy's restroom reading comic books. I could never check to make sure, but I think Rabbit must have had hookworms every year he was in elementary school.

As expected, he went to work with his father as a pulpwooder, and we all pretty much forgot about him. A little over a year later, we read in the newspaper that Rabbit had been arrested for breaking into a small grocery store near Worthington Springs. He had been seen hanging around the store that afternoon, and the owner suspected him from the very beginning. When the sheriff went to his house, he found all the stolen property stuffed under the floorboards of the family's shotgun shack. Rabbit had not taken any money in the robbery; all he took was the groceries he could carry. Rabbit confessed with no provocation, plead guilty, and was given two years at a road prison for his crime.

People in Union County treated the robbery like it was a major crime wave. Despite all the shootings, cuttings and head busting that went on all the time, property crime of this nature was fairly rare. People in Union County often stole each other's hogs, coon dogs, and watermelons. However, these offenses weren't really considered crimes. However, in a typically weird, Union County way of thinking, they were seen as conflicts between neighbors to be resolved on a personal not a legal level. However, to actually break and enter with property damage was something else.

In the small weekly newspaper in Lake Butler, they printed a detailed list of all the merchandise Rabbit had stolen. It confirmed what I had long suspected. Rabbit wasn't really a thief. He was just hungry for something he didn't have the money to buy. At the top of the list were six boxes of peanut butter cookies. He was just being a bully one more time.

I will never forget Rabbit, and I always remember that society picks its victims very carefully.

# The Man at the Head of the Table

The most powerful person in my life was not my mother, my father, my grandparents, or any of my brothers or sisters. The person who held total domination over me was the man who sat at the head of the table.

The man who sat at the head of the dinner table at our house was the man referred to by others as "my stepfather." He wasn't my "real father." At least, they said he wasn't. He was my mother's second husband. Since my mother had a bad reputation of having extramarital affairs, the man who sat at the head of the dinner table might well have been my "real daddy." As far as I am concerned, he was as good a candidate as anybody else for the job. However, I really didn't know for sure and really didn't care.

It wasn't some type of deep, dark family secret that ate at my guts. In my life, I've met other people obsessed with finding their "true" biological parents, as if they expected to discover they were related to Superman or something. As far as I'm concerned, that trek was a waste of time; one parent is as good as any.

While I was living in Worthington Springs, my mother was married to my "real daddy." Although he sprang from the prominent, and fairly wealthy, family of my gun-wielding grandfather, Doc Roberts, he was a loser. I'm sure my mother just married him for my grandfather's money, because that's why my mother did most everything. Although the marriage lasted nineteen years and produced three sons, there was never really any love between them. He drank heavily, and she ran around with other men, including the man who sat at the head of the dinner table. In 1951, when I was six years old, the whole sham of a marriage collapsed. After years of violent fights and petty bickering, they finally divorced. My mother then turned around and married the man that she had been dating on the side for some time, the man at the head of the table.

My grandfather, Doc Roberts, died only a few years after the divorce, and his wife followed him a short time later. They were both brokenhearted at the way things turned out and terribly disappointed in their son and the trashy and unfaithful woman he had married.

The man everyone introduced to me as "my real daddy" slowly turned into a hopeless alcoholic. In order to support his drinking, he sold my grandfather's cotton gin, general store, and everything else he had inherited, including a good-sized farm and land that would be worth a small fortune today. He went from job to job, from business to business, and wife to wife, drinking and pissing it all away. He was a sloppy, arrogant, and self-consumed drunk, until finally all of the land and money that my grandfather had worked so hard to accumulate was gone. Then, he was finally forced to sober up or starve. He lived out the rest of his life working as a carpenter in the maintenance department of the University of Florida. I was never close to him, but I never held any hard feelings toward him either. He was just somebody in my life.

The only thing I hated about the divorce, which I was really too young to understand, was saying good-bye to my grandfather. I really loved the old man and liked being called "Little Doc" and being compared to him. However, to my great surprise, my so-called "stepfather" also took to calling me "Little Doc," and soon all my new brothers and sisters picked up on it. By the time I was a teenager, the word "Little" had been dropped and I was just "Doc."

My mother's new husband was named Slim Brooks, and I was told by my maternal grandmother, who always looked over me, to call him "Uncle Slim," because he wasn't my "real daddy." Slim was a tall, hulking, and broad-shouldered man with curly black hair rapidly going gray. He had a bad temper that was legendary, with a pair of fists to match. Slim Brooks had no qualms about being on the wrong side of the law. He made and sold illegal whiskey, ran large-scale Bolita operations, and owned several rowdy honky-tonk bars.

To Slim, beating the shit out of somebody was something he did with the regularity and nonchalance that other people display toward going to town to buy groceries. More than once, I had seen him use his fists, and it was an awesome thing to behold. He was never afraid; I don't think he even knew how to be afraid. Before I was grown, I had seen Slim stand up to drawn guns, pulled knives, and men who were so big they looked like walking mountains. I saw him beat men senseless with his fists and with anything else he could get his hands on. He once swung at a man with so much force, it threw his right arm out of socket. Instead of giving up, Slim retreated into a corner and pulled a blackjack out of his pant's pocket with his left hand. When the other guy came at him, Slim kicked him in the balls and then split his head open with the blackjack, leaving the guy a bloody mess lying on the floor. I was there that night and saw it all; one of the things I remember was that the guy pissed in his pants when Slim hit him with the blackjack. Few men who took an ass whipping from Slim, ever came back for another.

Slim rode around Lake Butler in a big, flashy Buick automobile, and he wore a solid-white, snap-brim 5X Stetson hat that cost over sixty dollars. He always wore white dress shirts with an open neck, dress pants, and a narrow black belt. All the people in Union County instantly recognized him, and they always showed him deference and respect. When he went into the grocery store, the manager would come out of his office to personally see if he could help. People acted as if it was an honor to pump his gas or wash his car. Even the high sheriff showed him respect. When he would drive through town, people would get really quiet and slowly point him out, like he was some kind of fearful bogeyman.

I remember the first time I saw Slim, I was about five years old, and I was standing in line at the movie theater in Lake Butler with my older brother, waiting to buy a ticket to see a Gene Autry film. As we stood in the line, there was suddenly a stir in the crowd, as if a movie star or something had just come up. Some of the people were nudging each other and saying, "There's Slim Brooks." I had no idea who he was or that my mother was dating him, but everyone looked at him with a strange mixture of fear, loathing, and reverence. He had stopped at the red light and was just sitting in his big automobile, wearing his trademark white Stetson. Slim was being driven by another man, almost as large as he was. Slim seemed preoccupied with something he was reading in his lap, and he never once glanced up to see me and the rest of the people staring at him. My brother, who was ten years older than me, seemed worried and told me not to say anything about this when we got home.

Everyone didn't like Slim. He had a lot of enemies among the church-going people, because he was the resident gangster and vice lord of Union County. He also had enemies among the lowlife trash he had beaten the shit out of. However, they were all cowards. The Baptist preacher, who often quietly railed against Slim at the deacon's meeting, would engage in fawning servility whenever he met Slim on the street. The sorry drunks that had felt Slim's fists never indicated they held any type of grudge, at least not while Slim was standing there. They might run their mouth when he was gone, but when Slim was around, it was all obsequious flattery.

When my mother married Slim, we moved into a tiny collection of small, one-room cabins that I would later learn was part of an old whorehouse complex during the heady days of World War II. At first, the living was Spartan; we cooked over a portable propane gas stove set up under a shed in the backyard and took our baths under a water hose connected to a shallow well pump. We had no hot water, and, in the winter months, the baths were cold and harsh. However, the worse things I remember were the mosquitoes. In the summer, they descended on us in giant swarms. It was too hot and muggy to cover yourself with a blanket, and we had no screens on the windows. The flying little bastards bit right through the sheets, and we always woke up in the mornings covered with welts and stinging bites. The only relief was alcohol and soaking in a washtub filled with baking soda and water.

However, Slim was a hard worker, and, slowly, the mismatched collection of one-room cabins were combined, and major additions were added. He put screens on the windows and built a nice kitchen and dining room, but, most importantly, he added an indoor bathtub and a hot water heater. By the time I entered high school, the row of cabins had been turned into a very nice, but strange looking, house that was very pleasant to live in. The crowning achievement was an eighty-foot-long, screened-in front porch. The whole structure was painted a dark green color.

The long green house was located directly behind one of the most rowdy honky-tonk bars in north Florida. For years, I went to sleep every night to the lonesome sounds of Webb Pierce, Hank Williams, Faron Young, and, later, the rock and roll beat of Elvis Presley and Little Richard.

On weekends, hundreds of people would crowd into the place, drinking and dancing to the country music and early rock and roll blasting from a big Wurlitzer jukebox. I would often sit for hours on the long green porch staring out at the rowdiness going on just a few yards in front of my house. The rowdy bar was called the Union Tavern, and it was the scene of all kinds of knockdown, drag-out fights; cuttings; and, sometimes, gunplay. Drunks would urinate against the pine trees in front of the bedroom my brother and I shared, and men and women would make love in the parked cars behind the honky-tonk. In the winter months, there were turkey shoots each Saturday with the entire day punctuated by the regular blasts of shotguns going off. My brothers and I would earn extra money by selling boiled peanuts to the crowd of drunks. Even on Sundays, when state law said that the bar must be closed, a steady stream of customers came by to buy liquor from the assorted cases Slim kept on the front porch.

By the time I was thirteen years old, Slim had put me to work tending bar and wiping tables, in total violation of all kinds of state liquor laws. However, like most illegal things Slim was involved in, there was little chance of our getting caught, since the bar was always filled with regular customers. I knew everyone who walked into the place, and, if a stranger did venture by, I would dive under the counter and hide until Slim found out who he was and indicated that it was okay to come out. Not once during my entire growing-up years did a state beverage agent bother to venture into the place, and the small Union County Sheriff's Department had more important things to worry about than what went on at the Union Tavern.

It would be totally incorrect for anyone to think that I was a poor little innocent child forced to do all of this. In fact, I loved working at the Union Tavern. I took naturally to tending bar, since I was curious and a great talker. However, I learned early that it was best to shut up and let the drunks do the talking. I only asked them questions to keep the conversation going.

Slim often became so brazen that he left me and my older brothers in charge while he was away arranging some type of illegal activity, mostly bootlegging liquor, selling Bolita, or running moonshine over to Negro juke joints in dry counties, where liquor could not be legally sold.

After the bar closed at midnight, my older brothers and I would load the trunk and back seat of Slim's big Buick car with cases of whiskey or gallon jugs of pop-skull moonshine we kept hidden out in the woods. Sometimes, Slim would store the five-gallon jugs of moonshine in my bedroom. I would often awake on school days and find large jugs of moonshine sitting next to my bed. I never said anything about it, because Slim had told me not to mention it to my mother. She never came down to my bedroom that was at the far end of the house. Slim always reminded me of our family motto: "What mother don't know won't hurt her."

Slim always bought a Buick automobile, because it had a large trunk. When he would go to a car lot, he would always look at the trunk before he looked at the engine, the tires, or the interior. He could fit at least twenty cases of liquor into the big trunk of a Buick car. He could carry twenty more cases of liquor if he removed the back seat of the car and stacked the whiskey cases behind the front seat. If we really wanted to push it, we could jam twenty-five cases of liquor into a 1959 Buick automobile.

Slim would always warn us to take the state liquor license inventory numbers off the boxes of liquor before we loaded them. That way, if the law caught us, nobody could trace the whiskey back to him. Slim put me in charge of making sure that all the license numbers were removed. As a thirteen-year-old boy, I loved having such an important responsibility. Slim, who was a master of human psychology, recognized my devotion to duty and knew immediately that I would never forget. I would whip out the Barlow pocket knife Slim gave me one Christmas and make an L-shaped cut around the license inventory number and then peel back the outer layer of cardboard, thereby eliminating all traces of the number.

Slim had a bad habit of falling asleep at the wheel when he drove. He had been in several really bad accidents because of falling asleep at the wheel. So, at the urging of everybody concerned, he decided to let my older stepbrothers,

Charlie and Ace, make the late-night liquor runs. At first, Slim went along, letting my oldest brother drive, but later he felt Charlie and Ace could just as easily handle it without him, so he just sent them on their way and went home to sleep.

In those days of racial segregation, black people could not get a legal liquor license. So, they ran illegal juke joints selling bootleg whiskey and moonshine they either made themselves or bought from white suppliers, like Slim. Nobody ever raided or closed down these juke joints, because there existed a tacit understanding between local law enforcement and the juke joint operators. It was a little-known part of the system of racial segregation. Black people might not have been able to ride in the front of the bus or eat at a "whites only" lunch counter, but they were allowed to make a living and juke all night if they wanted to, without any harassment from white lawmen.

To the best of my understanding, a "juke joint" was a place for black folks, and a "honky-tonk" was a place for whites. A honky-tonk would play country music, and a juke joint would play the rhythm and blues and what would later become known as rock and roll. White-owned juke joints had to obey all state liquor laws, including closing at midnight and being closed on Sunday. From what I saw, black-owned juke joints never closed as long as someone wanted a drink.

Although I was only thirteen years old, I begged Slim to let me go on the late-night liquor runs with Charlie and Ace. The idea of riding the roads late at night filled me with excitement and joy beyond most people's understanding. I had seen the Robert Mitchum movie *Thunder Road* about a dozen times and had memorized all the words of the song. To be a "liquor runner" roaring down the road, outrunning the beverage agents, and shooting it out with revenuers was to me the ultimate in high adventure. However, Slim didn't see it that way. He didn't want his boys to have to outrun anybody or have a shoot-out with the law.

It took a long time before Slim would let me go. He was worried that if we got busted, he would have a hell of a hard time explaining it to my mother. I was young and so full of piss and vinegar; I pestered him to let me go until he finally gave in just to shut me up. However, he said we would only deliver red liquor, no moonshine. That way, if we were stopped, we could claim to be delivering whiskey to a bar over in Port St. Joe in which Slim was part owner.

I was overjoyed to be going on a liquor run. I really didn't give a shit about jail, since, at that age, jail was just an obscure concept, not a reality.

Before we left on our first run, Slim sat Charlie, Ace, and me down, and we had a long talk. All three of us boys were there, but I could tell that Slim was talking mostly to me. Slim said that running liquor wasn't like that fucked-up movie we saw at the drive in. He said we should always drive carefully and try to avoid getting stopped. However, if the cops did get behind us, we should just pull over and tell them the lie about the Port St. Joe bar. He said to call him as soon as we could get to a phone, and he would come and bail us out. Slim said he had connections with lawyers, judges, and sheriffs that could take care of most anything short of murder.

Slim said we needed to have at least fifty dollars on us, in case we had to pay someone to drive us home. We would each carry a loaded thirty-eight-caliber revolver in our belts, not to shoot it out with the cops, but for protection in case any of the lowlife scum to whom we were selling whiskey decided to try and cheat or rob us.

We always made our run after midnight on Saturday nights (really Sunday mornings) in order to avoid the "sanctified women" that would be found in any Negro section of town.

"Sanctified women" were more of a pain in the ass than the police. They always looked like they just walked out of church, with long, calf-length dresses; wide-brimmed hats; globs of pancake makeup; and enough dime store costume jewelry to clearly signify their presence. Some of the more virulent "sanctified women" would dress completely in white outfits from head to toe.

Years later, in a sociology class at the University of Florida, I would learn that overeducated and overdignified sociologists—sitting in their book-lined ivory towers on the well-manicured campuses of academia—had discovered through careful research that Black America was a matriarchal society. It is the black women who raise the children, administer the churches, and really run the neighborhoods. It always amazes me how sociologists will spend millions of dollars proving what is totally obvious to any cab driver or neighborhood whiskey runner.

In those days, these "sanctified women" were always looking for white men who came into their neighborhoods. If they spotted a white man driving down one of their streets, they knew immediately that he was delivering whiskey, looking to buy the Bolita, or perhaps seeking a prostitute.

They could have just called the police, but that seemed too simple for them. They would usually start yelling, raising hell, and calling on the name of "Jeeesus" to deliver the wayward white man from his sins. These "sanctified women" had on what the old preacher used to call "the whole armor of God." They were totally fearless. They would come off the sidewalks, swing their pocketbooks or anything else they could get their hands on, yell, holler, quote scripture, sing hymns, and offer prayers. Often, their sisters in the cloth would stand on the sidewalks also singing hymns and clapping their hands, while the sinning trespasser was being verbally harangued by one of these self-appointed avengers of God. Their objective wasn't necessarily to cause physical harm, rather just to embarrass you enough so that you would take your vice and leave their God-fearing Christian neighborhoods.

Our position toward the "sanctified women" was to avoid all contact with them. Charlie and Ace used to say, "Never argue with a crazy person." We knew that the "sanctified women" were never on the streets late at night, especially not on Saturday nights, since they all rose at the crack of dawn to go to church. Except for Wednesday nights, when they might stay late after the prayer meeting, nine o'clock would usually see them all safely in bed, with a Bible on the night table and a pistol under the pillow. To make sure we didn't have an encounter with the "sanctified women," we never left Lake Butler until nearly midnight.

The first load of whiskey we delivered was to a rowdy juke joint near the small village of Lacrosse. The juke was at the end of a long, narrow dirt road directly in the middle of a plowed field. It was impossible to approach the juke by any route except the narrow dirt road. Any vehicle would get stuck up to their axel in the plowed field, and walking over a mile across a plowed field was too much exertion for most white lawmen. The name of the juke was Ruby's Place, because a strange woman known only as Ruby ran it.

The road to Ruby's juke was a dark and spooky place. There were no lights except those given off by our car headlights. We had to snake our way past dozens of old cars, mostly big Buicks and Oldsmobiles, and a handful of dirty pickup trucks. The vehicles were not parked in any type of orderly fashion. They seemed to have just been abandoned wherever the driver felt he was close enough. Since Ruby was expecting us, she had promised to leave us a parking spot near the front door, but she hadn't.

As our big Buick automobile eased up to Ruby's Place, Charlie reached over and turned off the car engine and began telling Ace and me about the first time he came to Ruby's. He said he had to park way back down the road and carry the heavy cases of whiskey a long way into the juke. He said a couple of black men approached him and volunteered to help him carry the heavy cases of whiskey. Charlie mistakenly believed they were sent by Ruby and gave each one of them a case of Old Crow and Early Times. However, as soon as they got their hands on the cases of whiskey, they slipped off into the darkness and were long gone.

"What did you do?" I stupidly asked.

Charlie just glared at me with disgust. "Damn, Doc, what was I supposed to do? Call the police and tell them a couple of niggers had just stolen two cases of bootleg whiskey?"

"Listen," Ace warned me, "no damned nigger touches this shit until we get our money. Do you understand?"

"Sure," I replied.

"You got your pistol?"

"Yeah!"

"You being a young boy and all, one of them might try to take the whiskey. If they do, pull out the pistol and just show it to them. Don't shoot unless you have to. It happened to me once, and all I had to do was fire a warning shot over their heads and they scattered. They may be drunk and stupid bastards, but they all have enough sense to know that a white man will kill um."

Charlie went in first, while Ace and I guarded the car. All around us in the darkness, there were large groups of dark-faced drunken revelers. They were leaning against cars and standing in tight little knots all out in the field and under the tall stands of pine trees that were adjacent to the juke.

I had never learned to fear black people. I wasn't scared that night, and I have seldom been scared since. Later in life, my so-called, white liberal friends would be amazed at my total fearlessness when it came to entering the high-crime and poverty-ridden African American sections of Gainesville and Jacksonville. They would be totally perplexed that I would be so bold as to drive through "those kinds of neighborhoods." I could have told them about how I used to run bootleg whiskey to Ruby's Place, and about how Mitchell and I used to sit under the loading dock or the incident at the cotton gin, but some things white liberals just can't fathom. To these city-bred, college-educated piss ants, all southern white men were Ku Klux Klansmen, and all black people were their pitiful cowering victims, turned into violent and militant revolutionaries by their harsh treatment. White liberals needed to have a good guy, a bad guy, and a victim for their world to make sense. Of course, I knew better, but like Ace used to say, "Never argue with crazy people."

When Charlie came out of the juke, he motioned for me to get out of the vehicle and meet him at the trunk of the Buick. With a quick movement, he threw open the trunk lid, and all three of us grabbed at the cases of whiskey. To my surprise, both Charlie and Ace grabbed two cases, which was really too much for me to carry. Charlie told me he wanted to only make one trip into the juke, because everyone was really drunk and in a bad mood. He said there was blood on the floor where somebody had just been stabbed.

To get into the juke, we had to wind our way through several small knots of wild eyed, drunken black men and loud-mouthed, filthy-talking women. Some cheered us, some tried to engage us in conversation, some moved out of our way, and some just stood there in a drunken haze; however, most were so intoxicated they didn't seem to know we were on the same planet with them.

The inside of Ruby's juke joint was totally dark, except for the lights given off by the Wurlitzer jukebox and the illuminated beer signs around the room; the jukebox was so damned loud, you couldn't hear yourself think. It was turned up all the way, and the vibrations from the big speakers would cause the empty drink glasses to dance around on the tops of the cheap Formica tables. Over the noise of the jukebox, was all the rowdy talk going on between the groups of drunks.

I was told once that all this loud talking was a residue of slavery, when seeing slaves whispering caused white masters concern. Anyway, this was one lesson from slavery they learned very well. All around the room, I could clearly make out every word, even over the blare of the blasting, maximum volume jukebox. It was "mutherfucker dis" and "mutherfucker dat." Damned if it didn't seem to me that they just seemed to love that word. All the women were being called "ho's," and all the men were being called "niggers" and "dudes." The whole place smelled strongly of sweat, stale beer, and piss.

The woman who ran the juke joint was an attractive, light-skinned willowy woman with long shoulder-length hair that seemed to be coated with some type of oily substance that made it sheen. Behind her was a tall hulking man of the type that used to work at my grandfather's cotton gin.

There was never a doubt who was in charge. Ruby reigned over her juke from an elevated barstool at the far end of the counter. She sat directly behind an old cash register, ringing up every purchase. A skinny little black man with a cigarette hanging from his mouth was at her beck and call. He took out one of the bottles of whiskey, held it up to the light given off by a Budweiser sign, and checked it. He nodded his head, telling Ruby that the stuff was good. Without saying a word, she hiked up her dress and removed a wad of sweat-stained bills from her garter strap and proceeded to count out our money. Charlie and Ace watched closely. I couldn't tell how they could possibly know how much money was on the counter, because it was so dark. Finally satisfied, Charlie scooped up the wet money and then shoved it into his shirt pocket.

Ace turned to me and literally yelled into my ear, "Walk in front of me with your hand on your pistol, but don't pull it out unless me and Charlie get into trouble. I'm right behind you. Don't step into that puddle of blood over by the door; it's bad luck."

We walked in a straight line directly toward the car, not looking around and never hesitating, fast and confident in our steps. We didn't run, but we didn't dawdle either. By the time I got to the Buick, I was soaking wet with nervous perspiration. I felt positive that at least one of the drunks would try and take the money out of Charlie's shirt pocket, but none did. The night air felt good after the heat and cigarette smoke of the juke joint. As soon as we were back in the car, Charlie fired up the engine and put the Buick in reverse. We rapidly turned around in the parking area, barely missing several parked cars, before heading back down the dirt road moving at a brisk pace but not driving like we were in a panic. Only after we had pulled out onto the highway did I feel relaxed enough to speak.

"Jesus, what were those people doing all out in the bushes and shit?"

Ace replied calmly and quietly, "They were just niggers, acting like niggers."

He then smiled and said, "Whiskey running exciting enough for you?"

I only laughed and said, "There wasn't anything like this in *Thunder Road*."

"What do a bunch of Hollywood ass wipes know about running whiskey? You got a hell of a lot more likelihood of having your throat cut by one of them damned niggers for the money in your shirt pocket or the case of your whiskey you're carrying than you do in having to outrun the law and shoot it out with G-men. Hell, tonight wasn't nothing; you should be in there on a cold winter night, when all of them are inside the juke joint, with the doors and windows shut."

I could imagine, and a terrible image it was.

"On cold nights, Ruby likes to fire up the old potbellied stove and cook a couple of possums or a gopher. Ruby is a skinny woman, and she gets cold easy. She will get the inside of that juke joint so hot, you feel like you're inside of some kind of damned oven. She will also put on a big pot of chitlins and rice on the stove in the back. She always says that cold weather makes her hungry."

"Do you ever feel sorry for those people?" I asked, getting serious for a moment.

"Not really," Ace replied. "Sometimes, it seems to me that they're the only people left in America having a good time. At least, they are the only people getting any pussy. Slim used to tell me that if you were ever a nigger for one Saturday night, you would never want to be white again."

"You know my Sunday school teacher says we shouldn't call them niggers."

Charlie, who was driving, seemed puzzled by that remark, "Why not?"

"She says it isn't nice, that some black people are God-fearing, honest, and hard working."

"Well hell," Charlie answered, "When I say nigger, I never mean it to include all black-skinned people. The word nigger describes a certain type of colored person, just like 'pecker head' and 'po-white trash' describes a certain type of white person. Anyway, history tends to deal with these little language problems. Used to be, the word 'Yankee' and 'Pirate' was a bad thing to call somebody; now we have baseball teams named after each one of them. What white man a hundred years ago would want to be called an 'Indian' or a 'Brave'? Now it's a badge of honor."

"Do you reckon one day we will have a baseball team called the Niggers?" I asked intrigued by this line of thought.

"Hell yeah," Charlie answered, "and one called the 'Po-White Trash' and the 'Pecker Heads' and probably even the 'Stump-Jumpers' and 'Clod Hoppers.'"

The idea was funny to me, and the conversation helped pass the time as we drove to our next stop. Seeing the big smile on my two older stepbrothers meant that I was being accepted. Charlie and Ace were physically very different, reflecting the messed-up way our family was structured. Ace was tall and dark haired, and Charlie was redheaded and chunky. I looked like a cross between them, a chubby boy with dark brown hair.

I leaned over and turned the radio on. There was nothing but static, meaning that WAPE in Jacksonville had signed off for the night with the traditional playing of "Dixie." I began fishing the dial looking to find another station. In those days, the southern night was filled with music from clear-channel radio stations broadcasting from Memphis, New Orleans, and Nashville. All the large clear-channel, 100,000-watt stations had only three call letters instead of the usual four. The most popular to us was, of course, the Grand Ole Opry out of Nashville. After a lot of looking and fine-tuning, I finally located the WSM signal and settled back to listen to Webb Pierce singing "There Stands the Glass" on the *Ernest Tubb Record Shop Show*. The broadcast tower was a long way from northern Florida, but, on a clear night with a slight chill in the air, we could pick it up clear as a bell.

Music was a big part of our lives back then. In those days, you never saw musicians in movies and very seldom on television. It was a big deal when Elvis and Bo Diddly appeared on *The Ed Sullivan Show*. My teacher couldn't understand how they could possibly allow such a thing as that to be on television. Ace, Charlie, and I loved rock and roll. We listened to country music a lot, and it wasn't like we didn't like it, but we were of the new generation, rock and rollers to the bone.

The weird thing was when we were listening to the clear-channel, late-night rock and roll stations, we couldn't tell which entertainer was black and which was white. We would often argue about it as we rode over the rural roads connecting the scattered juke joints. We all three pretty much agreed that Jerry Lee Lewis was probably black and that Buddy Holly was definitely white, but we couldn't make up our mind about Wynonie Harris, Frankie Ford, or Eddie Cochran. Even though we knew they were black, we loved

T-Bone Walker, The Platters, and most of all Little Richard and Chuck Berry.

I have never felt that rock and roll music has ever been given the credit it deserves as a hero of the civil rights movement. To teenage white boys living in the South during the 1950s, the idea of going to school with a "nigger" was too horrible to think about; however, to go to school with Chuck Berry, Little Richard, or Fats Domino wouldn't just be all right, it would be a thrill. I think the first time a lot of young people seriously questioned racial segregation or white supremacy was listening to rock and roll music on the radio late at night.

Later that night, we hit two more juke joints in and around High Spring and Alachua. They were all either way out in the sticks or in the middle of the poorest and most run-down part of town. It seemed that each one was louder and more rowdy than the last, if that was possible. Each time, we were paid in small bills that were pulled soaking wet with sweat from between some fat woman's titties or out of some man's nasty socks or pant's pocket. Charlie was always bitching about how black folks were always wadding up their money and sticking it in strange places. He said that once he had to wait until a man sat down on the floor and took off both shoes in order to get enough money to pay him for his whiskey.

Between the widely placed stops, we continued to talk.

"Do you think integration will work out?" I asked Charlie and Ace.

We drove for a long time, everybody thinking quietly to himself, before someone answered me.

"I don't really know, but I doubt it," Ace finally said. "White folks and niggers got a lot in common, but they also got a lot of differences. You take that damned juke joint back there; you know white people will never tolerate that type of noise and rowdiness in their neighborhood. For integration to work, either black people will have to become white people or the other way around, and I just don't think that will happen. Black people are just too damned loud and party-happy to get along with white people. They just make too much damned noise. They talk too loud and can't listen to music until it is turned up just as loud as it will go. Also, we both got our own special tastes in music, how we dress, what our houses look like, even how we conduct our church services. Niggers just live too sloppy. They throw paper and trash everywhere and paint their houses all kinds of weird colors like pink and purple."

I didn't reply. I didn't realize it at the time, but I would spend the rest of my life trying to figure out if they were right or not. Charlie, Ace, and I talked about integration in the same way we talked about the end of the world. We knew it would happen some day, but we figured that day would be a long time off.

Our last juke joint was on the north side of Lake City in a run-down part of town. With that delivery, we only had two cases of Ancient Age left. Charlie had given me a wad of the money to keep. I tried to straighten it out, laying it on the dashboard of the car to dry it. Charlie wasn't really crazy about the idea. He was afraid the money would blow out the window. He told me to put it in my shirt pocket, and quit bitching about how wet and nasty it was.

"Hell boy, you outta be happy," Ace laughed and said, "as horny as you are; it smells just like nigger titty."

Our last delivery was in a poorly lit Negro section of town, somewhere on the outskirts of Live Oak, Florida. By then, it was almost four o'clock in the morning, and all the radio stations had signed off the air except for one over in Louisiana that only had preaching on it. Charlie ordered me to turn it off. He wasn't in any mood to hear somebody yelling at the top of his lungs about the fires of hell.

In these impoverished Negro sections of town, the roads were usually dirt without sidewalks. Most of the time, the city had not even bothered to put up stop signs or red lights. The street signs were nothing but little square concrete markers about four feet high with the name of the street written on two sides. When one of the concrete markers was hit by an automobile, nothing was left but an iron reinforcing rod sticking out of a small square of broken concrete. Lucky for us, the streets had numbers, and, when and if we found a concrete marker with a number visible, we could simply count streets to find the one we were looking for. That night, Charlie had to shine the headlights on the marker, and Ace had to get out of the car and stomp down some weeds to see the number. It said Fifth Street. We only had to count four streets further on to find the one we were looking for.

Our delivery point that night was on a long and narrow dirt road that was flanked on both sides by rows of ramshackle wooden houses. The cheap clapboard houses were set so close together a person could hardly have room enough to walk between them. They all had tilting front porches, rotting steps with boards missing, peeling paint, and rusty tin roofs. Each house looked almost identical, except for a small number painted over the front door.

The neighborhood was typically dark with no streetlights, and all we had to go by was a street and house number. We weren't even sure we were on the right street. Ace believed the streets ran up the other direction, and, instead of being on 9th Street, we might be on 2nd Street. Charlie wouldn't hear it; we were all now very sleepy and wanted this thing to be over with so we could go home.

Our orders from Slim were to leave the liquor in the front room of house number 25, on South 9th Street, which was owned by a well-known local Negro "house bootlegger." The term "house bootlegger" meant that he sold liquor by the drink out of his home to friends and neighbors instead of going to all the bother of operating a juke joint. This type of operation was also called a "bump house," because the shot of liquor gave you a jolt or bump. It was strictly a takeout operation; drink your shot of liquor, and then be on your way.

I had once met the old man who owned the house we were looking for when he had his nephew drive him over to the Union Tavern to see Slim. The poor old man looked like he was nearly dead. He was almost blind and could barely walk. Slim always had a soft heart and agreed to provide him liquor to sell in order to supplement his pitiful little Social Security check. The old man understood that we would have to bring the liquor over late at night. He told Slim he couldn't stand late hours anymore, but they worked out an arrangement. We knew he would be asleep when we got there, but we agreed to drop off the liquor in his living room, and, in return, we would find the money for the whiskey inside a ceramic vase on a shelf near the front door.

My brothers were nervous about the whole situation, because the road came to a dead end at a wire fence surrounding an old junkyard. If the police got in behind us, we would be trapped on the narrow dirt road with no place to run. At the end of the narrow dirt road was just enough room to turn a car around before hitting the wire fence surrounding the junkyard. Charlie insisted that we turn around first, so we would be pointing in the right direction should something happen. It was a good idea that we had learned trying to get away from Ruby's juke.

We quickly turned around down by the junkyard and then began riding slowly up the narrow dirt road with our headlights on low beam. We finally located a house that looked as if the number over the door might be 25. Or was it 75? Or maybe 15? We couldn't be sure. Charlie cursed himself for not bringing a flashlight.

After talking it over for some time, we decided to take a chance and go ahead and try to deliver the whiskey. We were worried that the longer we sat on this damned dirt road the more likely that someone would either call the police or, worse yet, thinking we were thieves, come out of their house shooting at us.

Quickly, we came up with a plan. Charlie would sit behind the wheel of the Buick with the engine running and the lights off so as not to attract attention. Ace and I would carry in the two cases of Ancient Age liquor.

However, we all had this worried feeling that we had already attracted attention, and everyone in the small houses was peering at us from the darkness on the other side to the small glass window frames.

"Doc," Charlie whispered, "Let's get this over with, and get the hell out of here." My mouth was dry as old cotton, so I only nodded as Ace and I climbed out of the Buick.

Ace opened the trunk, and I grabbed a large case of Ancient Age whiskey in fifth bottles. Ace got the second case of Ancient Age in pint bottles and closed the trunk lid with his elbow. Holding the case of whiskey in my arms, I spun around only to discover that I couldn't see a damned thing. I realized, really too late, that I had lost my sense of direction on the dark street and couldn't be sure if the house in front of me was the right one. Or was it the one next door?

"Hurry up, damn it," Ace commanded.

I knew the door would not be locked; it was not because this was the late 1950s and people still slept with their doors unlocked, but because Negro row houses like these didn't even have locks on the doors. It really didn't make much sense to lock the front door when all you had to do to get inside was to open a window or simply pull off one of the sideboards of the house with a claw hammer. These people depended upon their neighbors to watch their houses when they were away. That was when people were seldom gone for very long and still had neighbors.

I carried the box of Ancient Age up the steep front porch steps, and, balancing the case of liquor on my knee, I turned the worn old doorknob and pushed the door open with my foot. I walked inside and was looking around for a place to set down the whiskey, when suddenly a single 75-watt naked light bulb in the ceiling came on. As soon as it did, I knew immediately I was in the wrong house.

There were pictures of Jesus everywhere—Jesus with the little children, Jesus with the disciples, Jesus knocking on the door, Jesus walking on the water, Jesus healing the sick, Jesus delivering the sermon on the mount, Jesus standing before Pontius Pilot, Jesus carrying the cross, Jesus hanging on the cross, Jesus rising from the dead, and Jesus ascending into heaven. The whole life of Jesus was on those walls in bright colors, enclosed within cheap plastic frames. There was also a huge family Bible lying on the coffee table in front of a ragged couch that was covered with an old bed sheet. Above the old couch was a huge Mexican-made tapestry of the Last Supper.

*Oh shit*, I thought to myself. *This is the wrong place for a white boy to be carrying a case of whiskey.*

It was then I saw her; she was an extremely muscular Negro woman, wearing a pink nightgown with her hair up in huge blue curlers. In her hand was a broom, which she held like a baseball bat, business end up. Before I could say or do anything, she was on me. She swung the broom like Babe Ruth in Yankee Stadium and hit me square across the shoulders.

"Git outta cheer wid dat thing," she yelled.

I tried to say, "Excuse me. I'm sorry. I'm in the wrong house. I'll leave right away. Please forgive me." However, she didn't want to hear it. She just kept flailing at me with that damned broom handle and yelling, "Git outta cheer wid dat." I went out the front door and onto the rickety wooden front porch with her right behind me, screaming and swinging the broom handle. I looked down and saw Ace standing there with a look of absolute terror on his face.

He started yelling, "Doc, don't drop the whiskey; don't drop the whiskey."

One of the great accomplishments of my life was getting off that damned ragged front porch and down those old wooden steps while being hit with a broom handle, swung by a totally hysterical woman—who was constantly calling on the name of "Jeeeesus"—without dropping the case of Ancient Age!

Ace and I both climbed into the front seat of the Buick; each of us was holding a case of liquor in our laps. Mine felt like it was glued to my hands. I couldn't see too well, but the cardboard case must have had my fingerprints deeply imprinted into the sides.

The woman was on the porch screaming over and over for the "po-leeece," when Charlie gunned the car, and we hauled ass out of there. We drove at breakneck speed, running red lights and stop signs, until we were safely out of town and back on Highway 90 in route back to Union County.

The worse part was the long drive back to Lake Butler. I was dreading what Slim would say and do when we told him why we hadn't delivered the whiskey. We stopped once in Lake City and had a cup of coffee and a hamburger in an all-night drive-in called the Bronco. Ace had Charlie do the driving after we left the Bronco, and we rolled back into Union County just as it was cracking daylight.

What happened when we got home was why, despite all his faults, I truly loved and admired the man they called my "stepfather." Slim got very angry, very quickly, but he never stayed that way. My brothers and I took a long and hard cussing out. If Slim called us dumb ass once, he must have called us dumb ass a million times. However, by the time he had finished yelling and cussing, the whole thing somehow had gotten very funny to him, especially when he saw the bruises on my back where the woman had beat the shit out of me. While Slim might have been crooked, he was not twisted. He took no pleasure in hurting anyone, although he had almost no hesitation to do so.

That same Sunday afternoon, Slim and the three of us made a special trip over to Live Oak to give the old man his two cases of liquor. We timed our arrival to be around seven o'clock when we knew the sanctified women would be at their evening church services. He seemed so happy to see us. He was worried sick, because he woke up Sunday morning, and his liquor wasn't in his living room. Without his little bootlegging business, he really wouldn't have enough money to buy his arthritis medicine and still pay for rent and groceries.

The next weekend, he sent us out again, this time over to a group of well-known Negro juke joints in and around Alachua and High Springs and back to the old man's house in Live Oak. This time, we did it right. We delivered the load of whiskey around two in the morning, returned home to Slim, and handed over the money, completely proud of ourselves.

All in all, I really think Slim was one of the most decent men I ever met, even though he broke all the rules. Slim sold illegal whiskey, but he never cheated or did anyone wrong. Slim would beat the shit out of somebody one weekend and then lend him twenty dollars the next. Slim had a violent temper, but he never held a grudge. He was also the best father any kid ever had. He often ranted and preached, but he was always willing to forgive a mistake. Slim had no pettiness or psychological hang-ups. He also had no shame or deep, dark secrets. There was nothing he was trying to hide, to live down, or forget. Everybody in Union county knew everything there was to know about Slim, and he just didn't give a shit.

To understand Slim, you had to understand where he came from. He had been born in 1913, in a squalid shotgun shack community next to a large sawmill just east of Lake City, Florida. The miserable rows of three-room houses were called Watertown, because of the swampy roads that existed between the rows of run-down houses.

These painted clapboard houses with rusty tin roofs were called "shotgun shacks," because the front door lined up with the back door, and people used to say that you could shot a shotgun through the front door and the pellets would fly out the back door without hitting wood. This was where the impoverished sawmill workers lived, as long as they didn't quit their jobs or fail to pay their rent to the owner of the sawmill. They had no running water or electricity, and everyone had to use a community outhouse.

Slim's father was killed in 1925 when the leather belt propelling a three-foot-diameter circular saw he operated broke and flew back, hitting him in the head. He was killed instantly. With no breadwinner in the house and with five younger brothers and sisters, Slim was forced to stop attending the small one-room Watertown school, after having just reached the sixth grade. He reported to work at the sawmill at the ripe old age of twelve. If he had not immediately gone to work at the sawmill, not only would the family be without income, but also the company goons who took care of such matters would have evicted them from their row house.

Because he was so young and inexperienced, Slim was forced to take the lowest-paying job at the sawmill, loading pulpwood on railroad cars for seventy-five cents a day. His father had earned a dollar and a quarter a day, operating the big circular saws; it was a job he had labored over thirty years to earn.

Slim worked six years at the sawmill until he was eighteen years old. By that time, his younger brothers were old enough to take his place at the railroad spur loading pulpwood, freeing Slim to leave home. With everything he owned tied in an old blanket he threw over his shoulder, Slim left Watertown and started hitchhiking down Highway 441, destination Miami, where he hoped to ship out on a banana boat for Cuba. Instead, a truck driver who was smuggling bootleg hooch to Tampa picked him up. He and Slim swapped life histories, and he took a liking to the young boy and promised to help him find a job in Tampa's Ybor City.

The truck driver kept his word, and Slim went to work for a well-known bootlegger in Tampa, who found good use for the hard muscles on the young boy from the north Florida backwoods.

Two years after Slim left his job at the sawmill, President Franklin D. Roosevelt signed legislation repealing the 18th Amendment, ending the nation's failed experiment with Prohibition. However, the noble experiment did not end everywhere. While legal booze might have flowed in Los Angles and New York, through most of the rural South, counties decided to continue Prohibition by banning the legal sale of alcoholic beverages. These counties were said to be "dry." The ironic thing about living in a "dry" county was that there was a good possibility it was right next door to a "wet" county, where the selling of whiskey was perfectly legal.

To anyone lucky enough to get a legal liquor license, there was a tremendous opportunity to make a fortune. Not only could you do a thriving liquor business in the "wet" county, where the legal bar was located, but also by supplying bootleggers and black juke joints in the "dry" counties that almost always surrounded each "wet" county. Even as late as 1997, Florida had several rural "dry" counties.

Slim had started out working for a salary, delivering illegal whiskey all over central Florida. Compared to loading pulpwood at Watertown for seventy-five cents a day, the four dollars he made unloading liquor trucks seemed like a fortune. Later, he worked for a percentage of the profits and then finally branched out to begin his own bootleg operation, becoming a full-fledged member of the Dixie Mafia.

The Dixie Mafia was a loose confederation of assorted peoples of all races, religions, and cultures who supplied illegal whiskey, prostitution, and gambling all over the South. The Dixie Mafia could be found almost everywhere, but it was most powerful in towns that had large military bases.

Where there were a lot of single men, there was always a good market for illegal whiskey, gambling, and prostitution. Some cities—such as Phenix City, Alabama; across the Chattahoochee River from Fort Benning, and Biloxi, Mississippi, near Keesler Air Force Base, and Fayetteville, North Carolina, the home of Fort Bragg—were known to be controlled by the Dixie Mafia, much like Chicago was controlled by Al Capone's mob back in the 1920s.

The Dixie Mafia was powerful in north Florida because of all the naval bases in and around Jacksonville. While it wasn't as powerful as it was in other places like Phenix City and Fayetteville, it was well-known that many north Florida sheriffs and judges were on the Dixie Mafia's payroll.

Unlike its northern counterpart, the Dixie Mafia had no romantic old-world ritual or secret codes. No matter if you were white, black, Cuban, Haitian or southern "cracker," everyone was more or less equal when it came to supplying whiskey, gambling, or prostitution. Like most things in the South, proper behavior in the Dixie Mafia was clearly understood and just plain common sense. There were no "Godfathers" or power struggles, primarily because of the distances involved. The Dixie Mafia wasn't jammed into New Your City or Chicago, but, instead, it was spread all over the South. It was a live and let-live organization. Everyone more or less had their territory and stayed in it. Lawmen were bribed, and no violence was tolerated unless it was absolutely necessary. The most violent place was Tampa, where they had the notorious "cigar wars" between rival Ybor City gangs.

Slim always had one thing going for him, despite his fearsome reputation for a bad temper and lightning-fast fists, he was also a likable guy; he was full of good bullshit stories, and he was honest and fair. He treated everyone with respect; hired people he really didn't need, because he knew they needed the job; and was overly generous with anyone in need. All those who worked for Slim were fiercely loyal, and his customers, who honestly liked him, were willing to bankroll him with money and political connections to help him get a legal liquor license.

In 1940, Slim took the money he made bootlegging in Tampa and moved with his family to Union County, buying up five acres of land on Highway 100 near the New River. Slim choose Union County, because it had less than one thousand registered voters. With the help of friends and relatives already living in Union County, they circulated a petition and quickly got one hundred signatures, calling for a wet–dry election.

Under the constitution of the State of Florida, each county could decide by a plebiscite, if it wanted to allow the sale of alcoholic beverages. All that was needed to have the election was 10 percent of the registered voters signing a petition. As Slim used to say later, "Finding a hundred drunks in Union County was not a problem." The wet–dry election was held in May of 1940, and the wet forces won by a narrow, very narrow, margin. Only three votes separated the two sides. Using friends in Tallahassee who had been silent partners in his bootleg operations and members of the Dixie Mafia, Slim was able to get himself a legal liquor license in Union County.

During the summer of 1940, Slim oversaw the building of the Union Tavern, which he hoped would be one of the finest honky-tonk bars in north Florida. He drove all the way to Savannah to buy an antique bar complete with a brass footrail and cast-iron, bolted-down-style bar stools from an old Prohibition-era speakeasy scheduled to be torn down. He hired special carpenters to tear it apart and bring it back to Union County in pieces by truck and then resemble it. The Union Tavern also had a large dance floor and a secret back room to store the "extra whiskey" that he bootlegged to neighboring dry counties and where illegal poker games were held on slow weeknights.

The coming of World War II was as much a blessing to Slim as it was a curse to the rest of the world; his business boomed as thousands of soldiers stationed at nearby Camp Blanding flooded out on weekends with their pockets bursting with money. Slim added on five small cabins that he staffed with what were know as "victory girls," because they were so good for the morale of the troops.

By 1945, he owned five other bars and a large jukebox and pinball machine company. He had a forty-five-foot yacht, which he kept tied up to a private dock on the St. John's River, next to a bar he owned in Clay County. He lived in a six-bedroom mansion in Lake City and proudly bought his wife her own Cadillac. Slim put all of his brothers and sisters to work for him, and he bought his aging mother a nice home with a live-in caretaker.

One of Slim's big problems was that he didn't know how to relax and enjoy his wealth. He had come a long way from loading pulpwood in Watertown, but he was burning the candle at both ends, running from early in the morning to after midnight each night, and managing his honky-tonks and pinball machine business. It all came to a screeching halt shortly after midnight in 1950, when he fell asleep at the wheel of his wife's Cadillac going into the ditch and flipping the car at least a half dozen times. Slim survived the wreck but with terrible injuries. His wife, however, was dead. He was left with three children, two boys and a girl. Sometime shortly after the accident or maybe before, nobody knows for sure, he began to secretly date a married woman from Worthington Springs, my mother.

Slim married my mother, and it was the beginning of all his misfortunes. Only three months later, the IRS brought charges against him for income tax evasion. Slim, with his sixth-grade education, had somehow totally messed up his tax returns. In reality, he never filed any tax returns. He had about as much illegal income as he did legal, and he hadn't bothered to declare the legal stuff, much less his illegal earnings. He had hired professional accountants to manage his affairs, but they tended to be men who drank too much and who Slim knew were down-and-out and needed work. It was a long, drawn-out affair—as most IRS matters usually are—and, when it was over, he had escaped prison but was ruined. He had to sell his nice home in Lake City to pay legal bills; the IRS had seized his yacht, his pinball and jukebox business, his Cadillac, and everything else they could get their hands on.

He had only managed to save the Union Tavern with the five small whorehouse cabins in back. I guess the IRS wanted to leave him some way of earning a living so they could come back and seize it later.

A good lawyer or decent accountant could probably have avoided all of these problems for Slim. However, with only a sixth-grade education, he just didn't know anything. These poor, ignorant boys from the sawmill at Watertown never had any idea that the federal government could just come in and take everything a man had worked hard all his life to earn.

For the rest of his life, Slim would have an IRS judgment against him for one hundred and eighty-five thousand dollars. He could not have anything in his own name, not even a car. His family, which he had supported with his hard labor at the sawmill at Watertown, and with a good job after he made a lot of money, now rallied to his side helping Slim to buy whatever he needed.

However, Slim might have been down, but he wasn't out. He was a tough man. Within a few years, by hook and crook, he had gotten back on his feet, creating a nice home out of the four cabins and building a successful moonshine–bootleg operation out of the Union Tavern. However, he never returned to his former glory. The IRS kept an eye on him and wouldn't allow that.

Slim worked day and night to support us. Despite the fact that he had very little education, Slim managed to keep seven children, including my handicapped little sister who had cerebral palsy, well fed, housed, and clothed.

Our family was a mixture of his children by his first wife, my two brothers, and my crippled half sister who had been born two years after he married my mother. I never played the silly game of "stepbrother and stepsister." All these people lived in the house with me. We ate together, slept together, played together, tended bar, and ran bootleg liquor together. I considered them all my brothers and sisters, with no stupid-ass "steps" thrown in. Brother and sister, in the final analysis, were my choice, and, if I wanted them to be my brothers and sisters, then they damn sure were. The same applied to Slim; if I wanted him to be "my daddy," then damn it, he was.

Slim seemed to have an instinctive knowledge of what it took to be a good father, especially with the five boys in the house. Although my two sisters were clearly his favorites, he was always fair and understanding with us boys. The way he treated my brother and me after our ill-fated bootleg trip showed that underneath all his gangster toughness and violent behavior he was really a gentle and understanding man.

The best thing Slim ever did for me was keep my mother under control. There were times when I thought she was as crazy as a bed bug.

My mother came from what people would call today "genteel poverty." Her family was certainly not rich, but they had a lot more than most of their neighbors. Her father had been an eccentric, but fairly well-to-do man who farmed 150 acres and worked for the State Road Department. My mother's family was all a decent Christian group of people that valued hard work, honesty, and clean living. Her mother, my maternal grandmother, was the finest person I ever met.

My mother had an amazing ability to see only what she wanted to see and to pretend that things were not what they were. She had somehow developed the strange notion we were not a poor, white trash, bootlegger–moonshiner family that lived in a former whorehouse behind a rowdy honky-tonk bar, but rather high-quality, respectable folks. She never failed to insist that we go to church on Sunday, and she paid meticulous attention to how we dressed for school.

My mother always wore the finest clothes with lots of jewelry. All of this was her armor; she honestly believed that the diamond rings on her fingers and her big hat and fancy dresses kept people from seeing the real her that was under all that junk. We got regular lectures on what types of children we were supposed to play with at school. She always told us to only associate with children from high-quality families, and never play with "trash." During my entire life, I always totally ignored my mother's advice, and I never once regretted it.

My mother's father had died of a stroke in 1935, and, immediately afterwards, she turned into a wild and rebellious daughter. My grandmother, a saintly and gentle Christian woman, was unable to control her daughter without the firm hand of a father. She spent many nights in tearful prayer begging the God she so firmly believed in to do something about her daughter.

My mother married my so-called "real daddy" much too young, although he already had a bad reputation for being a heavy drinker. My grandmother visited with us on a regular basis and tried to teach me right and wrong, even as my mother was taking me to Bolita Sam's place every Saturday. When my mother divorced my "real daddy" and married Slim, moving us into an old whorehouse behind a honky-tonk bar, my grandmother was driven to tears. She was terribly ashamed of how her youngest daughter had turned out. She tried to correct things by doing whatever she could for her grandchildren.

I spent almost every summer and school holiday visiting with my grandmother in her small house. She lived next door to my aunt, whose husband had died very young, leaving her a small trailer park. I loved that trailer park and my grandmother's little wood-frame house on the edge of it. I lived just to visit my grandmother and get away from the bitch that was my mother. My grandmother became my mentor and guiding light, taking me under her wing and making sure that I was instilled with proper Christian values, despite the moral cesspool in which I lived. Without her love and guidance, I really don't know what I would have turned into.

My grandmother died peacefully in her sleep on a beautiful spring day in March 1958. I was then thirteen years old and had just began to tend bar and think about delivering whiskey for Slim.

# Baby Boomers and Hog Chitlins

I was a member of what became known as the "baby boom generation." I never understood for certain why they called us that. Some people said it was because there was a huge surge in births following the return of servicemen at the end of World War II. Others claim the name "baby boomers" refers to the fact that we were the first generation born after the dropping of the atomic bomb. I suppose it really isn't important; a name is just a name. All I know is that we jam-packed maternity wards all over the country. Later, we would overcrowd the public schools and, still later, fill the colleges and universities of America. I suppose when we get old, we will jam nursing homes and cemeteries.

When I was growing up, the "baby boom generation" had a bad reputation, especially in rural and very provincial Union County. We were always being accused by our elders of being self-indulgent, lazy, and generally a bunch of spoiled-rotten little bastards. Later, we would become long-haired, dope-smoking, draft-dodging, and unpatriotic spoiled-rotten bastards.

Almost all the adults I knew during my formative years were veterans of World War II and the Great Depression. Generally, as a group, they held all of us young people in great disdain. Part of it was no doubt due to the fact that we were better educated and were able to see the world through the one-eyed monster that was television. This gave us some form of sophisticated superiority over our elders that they sensed and resented.

I really didn't understand it at the time, but I think now, looking back, that they were really jealous of us. They envied our nice clothes, our radios, our televisions, our drive-in movies, our fancy hot-rod cars, and our full bellies. However, most of all, I think they envied the fact that we seemed to be enjoying our childhood, while theirs was nothing but Depression-era hard times and wartime deprivations.

I knew from a very young age that I didn't have to work as hard as my elders, because they were constantly reminding me of that fact. If I listened to one story about how hard it used to be during the Great Depression, how they had to plow a mule from sunup to sundown and walk ten miles to school and had nothing to eat but sowbelly and turnips, I must have listened to ten thousand. These stories came from my parents, my ministers, my schoolteachers, but most of all from the grown men who hung out at the barbershop.

Waiting your turn to get a haircut was an insufferable experience for a young person. In Union County, young people were supposed to be seen and not heard. When you were at the barbershop, you just sat there and endured anywhere from thirty minutes to an hour of being badgered and harangued about how terrible it was when they were young and how good we had it now.

The fact that we had enough leisure time to watch television and listen to rock and roll music seemed to really gnaw at the guts of grown people. This was only made worse by the fact that we didn't seem to feel guilty about not having to work hard and suffer through all the hard times they endured. I somehow got the feeling that they felt we were reaping the rewards of their sacrifices and handwork, without being properly grateful, and they resented it. We didn't seem (at least to them) to fully appreciate what they had done in World War II or the nice things we had that they couldn't afford during the Great Depression. They seemed to think that we took too many things for granted and that they had somehow committed a serious mistake by working hard to end the Depression and winning World War II for such an unappreciative bunch of spoiled-brat young people.

I really didn't understand what they wanted from me. It wasn't my fault the stock market crashed or that the Japanese had bombed Pearl Harbor or that Hitler had risen to power in Germany. However, the adults seemed to behave toward us young people as if we did it all personally.

Their negative attitudes later created what would become known as the "generation gap." It was a schism between our two generations that would never be resolved until the 1990s, when millions of old hippies suddenly became conservative Republicans.

Somehow, I always felt trapped between those two worlds, and I never really belonged to either one of them. My youth and education kept me out of my parent's conservative world of hard-working, Depression-era white people, bound to home and the soil with traditional values. My southern accent and rural upbringing meant that I was never really part of the upwardly mobile, hip, with-it California counterculture, although I tried to be.

My best knowledge of the hard times and shortages of the war years came from the stories told by Slim. Slim, like most southern men I knew, was a great storyteller and had a wonderful sense of humor. His favorite place to tell stories was at the dinner table when he was like a medieval warlord holding court. No one was allowed to leave the table when he was talking, and very few times did anyone want to.

Slim loved to invite company to dinner. They were sometimes his regular customers and friends, but the best stories came when one of his brothers or sisters came over. They had a way of remembering the good times and lambasting the bad that was, to me at least, excellent entertainment. I always wondered what type of writer Slim would have become if only he had been able to get a decent education. I also wondered how many others there were out there in run-down farms and shotgun shacks capable of telling great stories that could change the world.

The Great Depression and his bitter childhood were something Slim never stopped talking about. He feared that this new modern world, without hard times and bread lines, would make us all soft and weak.

Slim had a yearly ritual in which the whole family participated. It was supposed to make us children appreciative of all the sacrifices and hard times he had experienced during his childhood.

Every fall, after the first white frost, Slim would proclaim at the breakfast table that it was "hog-killing weather." We all knew what that meant. The next Saturday, we would arise well before daylight and ride over to Slim's uncle's farm in northern Columbia County for a yearly ritual as old as the South itself.

We called the sixty-year-old man who greeted us when we drove up to the farm as "Uncle Rob." I never saw him when he wasn't in bib overalls, cotton work shirt, and old-fashioned brogan shoes. He wore a wide-brimmed felt hat that was heavily stained with perspiration from his nearly bald head. Uncle Rob had the typical "redneck" farmer's tan. As a result of hours spent outdoors under the hot Florida sun, from his eyes down, his skin was as red as a strawberry. From the eyes up, where his wide-brimmed felt hat offered protection, his skin was a creamy white. There was an almost perfect, V-shaped red mark on his upper chest and throat where his shirt gaped open exposing him to the blistering hot sun. The classic "redneck" has become a part of our vocabulary to describe white, working-class southern people. He had massive large arms, and shaking hands with him was like putting your hands in steel vice that was covered with large, rock-hard calluses.

His wife, Aunt Pink, was a matronly mass of misshapen flesh in tiny black shoes and a faded blue and white dress. She never went outdoors without her split bonnet, and she took great pains to keep her long gray hair pinned back in a tight, round bun. She never wore any kind of makeup or perfume, not even on Sunday when she went to the Primitive Baptist Church. Every day of her life, she read her Bible and prayed to the God she firmly believed in.

Uncle Rob and Aunt Pink had electric lights, but no telephone or radio. They had never even seen a television, except in store windows in Lake City. It was something Uncle Rob and Aunt Pink could not abide. They were afraid that they would waste time watching television when there were more important things to be done. Back them, as a smart-mouthed teenage boy, I considered them backward, ignorant, and foolish. Today, as a middle-aged man, I'm not so sure.

Uncle Rob and Aunt Pink's farm was almost in Georgia; it was located on the very edge of the Osceola National Forest. It was almost a stereotypical Florida cracker dirt farm. Nothing was painted, including the family's clapboard "dogtrot" house. A split-rail fence that Abraham Lincoln would have been proud to build surrounded the place.

On the split-rail fence were planted thick tangles of gourd vines, which old southern folklore says will repel poisonous snakes. The gourd is a strong crawling plant related to the pumpkin, squash, and cucumber. It grows best along fence lines in bright sunlight. The yellowish-colored gourd itself is not good to eat, but it has a thick and hard rind that can be cut with a saw and put to various uses, including making a water dipper or a birdhouse.

In the front yard of Uncle Rob's house were two twenty-five-foot-high cypress poles; each had three, six-foot-long crossbeams on which were hung rows of bird houses made from gourds that were originally yellow but had been bleached white in the hot sun. Each gourd was the nest of a family of purple martins that Uncle Rob swore would eat their own weight in mosquitoes every day.

The house and yard were always neat as a pin, with well-tended gardenia and azalea bushes. The front porch posts were covered with thick tangles of wisteria vines. Aunt Pink scrubbed the front porch every other day with a special scrubber made from a rectangular piece of cypress with holes drilled in it to hold rows of corncobs. The whole homemade contraption was attached to a long pole, and it looked much like a modern push broom, except that the corncobs replaced the bristles. Uncle Rob used to say that nothing would scrub down a wood floor better than lye soap and corncobs.

Although Uncle Rob and Aunt Pink had electric lights, there were still old-fashioned kerosene lamps sitting around, just in case. In the middle of the living room was an upright, cast-iron wood-burning stove that sat on a special bed of old bricks carefully laid on the floor. The living room was decorated with little framed pictures of family members. A large family Bible sat on a special shelf beside the front door. The house was quietly functional, without any unnecessary display of wealth or conspicuous consumption.

The farm was just as neat and orderly as the house. Uncle Rob despised the idea of a man who didn't take care of his tools and animals. Every tool and piece of farm equipment had a designated storage place where it always sat neatly cleaned, oiled, and put away.

Uncle Rob and Aunt Pink both arose before the crack of dawn and worked steady until dark. They ate all three home-cooked meals together, and they were bathed and in bed before nine o'clock. They grew corn, truck crops, and sugar cane, and they had a two-acre tobacco allotment. Uncle Rob also raised cows, which roamed free in the wooded pastureland behind the farm. His pigs and hogs rooted in the black mud in their small pen about two hundred yards from the house. Turkey gobblers, chickens, and African Guinea hens roamed at will across the farm grounds.

The entire family would gather at Uncle Rob's farm three times a year. These gatherings took place in the summer, when it was time to crop the tobacco; at hog-killing time; and later in the winter, when it was time to grind the sugar cane.

Uncle Rob had a cane-grinding mill, which was a strange-looking contraption that was little more than a series of gears that turned two large rollers that squeezed the juice out of the long stalks of sugar cane. A long pole that was pulled around in a circle by an old swaybacked, mule powered the cane mill. The freshly cut sugar cane was squeezed by the mill into juice, which was later boiled down to syrup in a huge cast-iron pot.

For most of their lives, Uncle Rob and Aunt Pink made do with a pitcher pump well in the backyard; however, a few years before, their four grown children all pitched in and put in a modern electric well pump with a ninety-gallon, glass-lined water tank. They ran galvanized pipe into the house and installed a modern indoor toilet, as well as a new sink with faucets in the kitchen. The next year, they used part of the tobacco money to run underground pipes out to the barns, the cane mill, and the pig pens. Thanks to a fifty-foot length of green water hose, Uncle Rob and Aunt Pink never had to carry water again.

Uncle Rob raised black and white Poland–China hogs that, despite their name, are a Native American breed. He always kept two sows and a boar for breeding stock, but he butchered all the others each fall except for the shoats, which is kind of like a teenage hog that has been weaned but has not grown to full size.

The hog killing was done in a small clearing well removed from the house, near the hog pens. Killing hogs was nasty work, and Uncle Rob insisted that everyone work hard to keep the area clean.

Hog killings had to be done at the crack of dawn on a bitterly cold morning, because of the real danger that killing hogs in warm weather would allow parasites and bacteria to take root in the pork meat.

Slim always insisted that the boys actually participate in killing the hogs; the girls were excused. The girls would all run into the house and make a big show of covering their ears until the shots were fired, and the animals had stopped squealing. Hogs make a lot of noise when they die. Either shooting the animal in the head with a twenty-two-caliber rifle or hitting the hog in the head with an axe did the killing. Uncle Rob preferred to kill hogs with an axe, because he said the small twenty-two-caliber rounds didn't kill the hogs fast enough. Sometimes, it might take two or three shots before the animal finally fell over dead.

As soon as the hog was dead—and often before—the big animal's throat was cut, and the hog was hung up by his hind legs so all the blood could drain out. The blood was collected in a dishpan to make a breakfast dish called "hog's-head cheese."

The centerpiece of the hog butchering was a large cast-iron scalding kettle, under which a roaring fire was built to heat the water until it was boiling like a witch's cauldron. The carcass was dipped into the pot of boiling water using a special portable A-frame brace with a block-and-tackle rope system that was hung from the strong cross beam of the A-frame. The hot water made the hair easy to remove by simply rubbing the outside of the carcass with a dull-bladed knife. While the hog was still hanging up, it was eviscerated, and the internal organs were collected in a washtub. Southern people who butcher their own hogs are always poor, and, with hogs, the old adage of "waste not, want not" surely applies. No part of a hog would go uneaten except for maybe the hair, eyeballs, and hoofs, and even these could be ground up to make dog food.

After the hair was removed and the hog gutted, the carcass was moved to a series of long cypress wood tables built between two oak trees. Underneath one table were a small brass spigot and a water hose. It was here that the meat was cut up, and the chitterlings or "chitlins" were cleaned.

Hog killings could be a lot of fun. It was almost like a family reunion. It was nice to see all your aunts, uncles, and cousins, especially the ones your own age. Living out in the country, we didn't have any neighborhood children to play with, and we often got very lonely for kids our own age.

It was always beautiful early on the cold winter mornings. There was never a cloud in the sky, and the air was as crisp and cold as it ever gets in Florida. The frost-covered grass would snap and crunch under your feet when you walked on it, and the air always had the delightful smell of smoke. I remember most how cold our hands would get and how nice and warm it was standing around the warm fire built under the scalding pot. It was a sentimental time, especially for the old folks. They just couldn't resist telling stories about how it used to be when they were young and killing hogs. I came from a rich oral tradition, dating back to the Viking Skoals and their Norse sagas of Oden and Thor. We were not writers, because English really wasn't our native language. The junk they taught us in school was the language of English noblemen and kings, the court aristocracy, not down-to-earth common people like us.

Hog killings were usually over by nine or ten o'clock in the mornings. After the animal was cut up, the better pieces of meat—the hams, the shoulders, and the butts—would be taken to Uncle Rob's pine log smokehouse and hung up. There, they would remain under close watch until the thick smoke coming from an oakwood fire, covered with wet leaves and a piece of tin, had done its job and the meat was cured.

The lesser parts of the hog were ground up and made into sausage. The brains would be eaten with scrambled eggs, and the jowls, feet, and backbone would be used to season turnips and rice. The underbelly would become bacon, and the thick skin was cut up and put into a heated pot and rendered into lard. The small children fished out the "cracklins," the greasy pork rinds left over when the fat was extracted. It was a well-known fact that too many cracklins would give you a terrible bellyache, so the old folks were always warning us young people not to eat too many cracklins. Aunt Pink would mix the cracklins into her corn bread batter and bake cracklin corn bread that was delicious with cane syrup and collard greens.

However, there was one part of hog killing we all dreaded. When we drove to Uncle Rob's house in the predawn darkness of hog-killing day, Slim would always bring along in the trunk of the Buick a large, Number 3 washtub. It was an old custom for everyone to be given a small part of the pork meat as a reward for helping out with the hog killings. We all knew that Uncle Rob and Aunt Pink were poor, and the slaughtered hogs would be the biggest part of their winter diet, so most relatives would only take a couple of links of sausage. To refuse to take anything would hurt their feelings, so the secret was to take something but not too much. Slim's cousin, an ignorant shit, came to the hog killings once and asked for a ham. This made Slim mad; when no one was looking, he took him off to one side and cussed him out for being a greedy son of a bitch. His cousin immediately changed his mind and asked for two pig's feet instead.

Slim would always proudly make a big show of taking part of the chitterlings, primarily because he knew nobody else wanted them. However, probably just as important, he did this because he knew they would run us children crazy.

However, before we could take the chitterlings home, they had to be cleaned, and that had to be done before they cooled off. When the guts fell out of the slaughtered hog, steam would rise off of them in the cold morning air, almost as if they were coming out of a boiling pot of water. We had to immediately drag the big washtub of chitterlings over to the long table, stretch them out, and begin the laborious and unpleasant task of cleaning them.

As soon as the hog dies, its natural immune system shuts down, and the bacteria in the hog's bowel track, which occurs naturally and helps the animal digest its food, begins to go out of control and spread all over the animal's body. Immediately cutting the animal's throat and draining out the blood help slow down the spread of the bacteria through the bloodstream. The hog could not be gutted until after the hair was removed, because of an old superstition that said that if the hair ever touches the meat, especially the internal organs, it would cause it to taste bad.

When killing hogs, it's important to move in a hurry, to get the hair off as soon as possible, and get the guts out of the carcass before the bacteria can spread. That is why the colder the weather, the better. Cold weather expands the amount of time you have to get the dead hog scalded, scraped, gutted, and cleaned before the bacteria can spread.

When cleaning the chitterlings on the long table, you have to work both fast and careful, because the intestine is where the bacteria originated in the fecal matter and undigested food. Another superstition, or maybe it's just good folk logic, said that if the bowels are not giving off steam in the cold morning air, then it was already too late to start cleaning the chitterlings. If the chitterlings had cooled off, then enough time had passed for the bacteria to have already spread from the undigested food and waste to the walls of the intestine, thereby making the chitterlings unfit to eat.

What I hated most about cleaning chitterlings was that on a bitter cold morning, we had to use the water hose to wash the excrement and undigested food out of the hog's bowel track. The cold water would make your hands numb, and you had to keep warming them by the fire. Uncle Rob would never build a fire too close to the tables where the chitterlings were cleaned, because the heat from the fire would warm up the chitterlings.

We fussed and complained about the cold; however, since we knew we would have to eat these damn things later on—cold or no cold—we always did a very complete job of washing them over and over again, until not a speck of waste matter or food was visible. Slim once cracked that we were so lazy, we probably wish we could clean chitlins in the washing machine.

As soon as we got home from the hog killings, Slim would put on a huge pot of water, add a little salt, and begin cooking the chitterlings. They had to boil a long time to make sure that any bacteria inside the digestive track missed by the cleaning were good and dead. Chitterlings also are tough. The longer they cook the more tender they become. This isn't really saying much, since even chitterlings that have been cooked to death still feel like a piece of shoe leather in your mouth. Slim always included the pig's stomach as a part of the chitterlings, which added extra time to the cooking.

Nothing on God's green earth smells as bad as chitterlings cooking on the stove. I had heard stories of rats and roaches leaving the house because of the smell and of turkey buzzards leaving the county during hog-killing week, because they didn't want to smell the chitlins cooking. All of us would stay outside as much as possible, simply because the odor inside the house would literally make you wretch.

Sometimes, my mother would take pity on us. She knew a way of cooking chitterlings where they were cut into short sections and dipped into a batter and fried. They didn't stink as bad when cooked this way, and they damn sure tasted better. Some other people also cooked chitterlings with vinegar, which they claimed reduced the smell and improved the flavor.

In our house, eating was more than just taking in nourishment; it was a semireligious ritual. Nobody, on pain of a belt on the ass, ever complained about what we had to eat or for that matter even asked, "What's for supper?" I had done so one time, and, as a result, I was given a stern lecture on how unappreciative and spoiled rotten I was and how I should have been around during the Great Depression; then, I would know what hard times were. Then, I wouldn't ask such damn stupid questions. Slim always said, "Whatever it is, you're going to eat it and like it." His rule was "eat it or wear it." When he had finished his ranting and raising hell about such a simple little question, I was sorry I ever brought it up.

On the days when we ate the chitterlings, my mother would also prepare what Slim called "hard times food." She would cook up a large pot of pigtail and rice to be eaten with fresh collard greens. Collard greens were another thing that was only eaten after a frost. The collard plants are tough and bitter until a hard frost settles on them, making them sweet and tender. Collards always taste better when you throw in a large piece of pork fat to season it with. My mother would also serve thinly sliced and deep-fried sweet potatoes that Slim called "Hoover steaks," since that was the nearest thing they had to beef during the Great Depression.

Most religions on earth have some form of dietary code, food that isn't to be consumed under any circumstances. Jew and Muslims will not eat pork or shellfish. The Hindus and Buddhists will not eat meat. Southern people seem proud of the fact that they have no dietary code and will eat absolutely anything and then brag about it. Southerners eat gophers, ground hogs, raccoons, possums, frog legs, squirrels, rabbits, rattlesnakes, and every part of a hog except the teeth, hooves, eyeballs, and hair.

Eating these foods that outsiders usually find totally repugnant is almost a sacred ritual in the South; it is a way Southern whites have of reminding themselves of their history and heritage. They didn't start eating chitterlings, hog brains, possums, and coons on large plantations with magnolia-scented mansions. They started eating these foods on the southern frontier in small cabins where times were hard and food was scarce.

The antebellum South with its beautiful Southern belles in fancy hooped skirts, mint juleps, and refined Southern gentlemen was mostly a minstrel-show myth. Very few southerners lived the lifestyle of Scarlet O'Hara, and it is almost a fraud to depict it as a reality. It is much like stereotyping all of the United States by the lifestyles of Beverly Hills and Park Avenue. However, it is a well-cherished myth, which is instilled into the southern psyche by the writings of Margaret Mitchell and the music of Stephen Foster.

In reality, most of the South before the Civil War, and for generations afterwards, was a wilderness as primitive and desolate a place as existed in the so-called Wild West. Only a small group of wealthy planters in the tidewater regions of Virginia and South Carolina or in the "black belt" Mississippi Delta lived on huge plantations with hundreds of slaves and a Greek revival mansion.

In the remote regions of the Southern Frontier, cotton was not king. There, the farmers grew corn and vegetables, and they bred hogs, which they drove to market in large herds. In reality, the lowly razorback hog and the cracker farm homestead are much more realistic symbols of the South than Tara and Twelve Oaks.

Before the Civil War, only one out of every four southerners owned any slaves, and over half of these owned fewer than five. According to the 1860 census, half of all white southern farm families tilled less than one hundred acres of land. Yet, these poor, hog-raising dirt farmers made up the bulk of the Confederate Army. Stubborn, clannish and proud, they were ready for war, not to preserve slavery or even to secede from the Union, but to prove their manhood just as their ancestors had done before the walls of Rome.

Southern whites appear to revel in hard times. Southerners seem proud of the fact that their women wore homespun dresses during the Civil War, and they will tell you, with a great deal of pride, how they ate hand-caught catfish and hog chitterlings during the Great Depression.

Surviving hard times has become part of southern folklore and a type of civil religion. Every New Year's Day—the same day Hank Williams Sr. died of a combination of alcoholism and drug abuse—southerners, by tradition, and to ward off bad luck, eat collard greens, black-eyed peas, and the salty fat meat of a hog's jowl. Just like the Jews at Passover, who eat unleavened bread and bitter herbs to remind them of their slavery in Egypt and their flight to freedom, southerners eat the least desirable piece of meat from a hog's body and hard-time winter vegetables to remind themselves who they are and where they came from.

The hog killings had a strange effect on me that is hard to explain. I was both repulsed and attracted to it. It did, I think, what Slim wanted it to do. The hog killings gave me a deep sense of family and heritage. It told all of us young people who we were and where we came from. It also told us what we believed in and what our values were.

# The Great Evil Thing

The great evil thing of my generation was, of course, television. It had invaded Union County in 1952, when a small radio station in Jacksonville began broadcasting grainy black and white images of Howdy Dowdy across the north Florida pinewoods.

Slowly, with a deep reservation reserved for any type of new technology, the more prosperous citizens of Union County began to buy television sets and festoon their rooftops with the bug-eyed contraption's aluminum antennas. These aluminum monstrosities proclaimed for all to see that the residents of the house below were proud owners of a television set. By the time I was in the third grade, our class was divided between those who had television and those who didn't have television. By the time I reached the fifth grade, the majority had a television. By the time I reached the seventh grade, only a handful of kids, all from very fundamentalist religious families, didn't have TVs. By the time I reached the ninth grade, even they had caved in and bought a television. Ooops.

To me, television was a blessing from God. This magic wooden box with the silver letters Philco on the front brought to me—amidst all the poverty, ignorance, and provincialism in my life—pale gray images from far off and wonderful places called New York and Los Angeles. It introduced me to new people who did not speak with a southern accent or babble for hours about coon hunting, tobacco farming, and how hard things were when they were my age.

I soon began to bond with the characters I saw on television, more than I did with my own parents and the other adults in my life. The television seemed to know in advance what I wanted and how I felt. It never passed judgment on me, criticized my hair or my dress, or felt I was a sorry good-for-nothing just because I had not plowed a mule during the 1930s or stormed ashore on D-Day. Television released me from the prison that was my hometown; it enlightened me that there was indeed another world out there, full of all kinds of wonderful things. It told me about Broadway, Hollywood, London, Paris, and Rome. It also drove a wedge between the generations, forever separating me from my parents.

Television introduced me to the mysteries of sex. I believe my first sexual longings came from watching Annette Funicello on *The Mickey Mouse Club.* However, what had been only repressed emotions in the mid-1950s became raging hormones by 1960, when Dick Clark's *American Bandstand* drove me mad with sexual passion and a rebellious spirit to break free and see the world. Television was condemned by almost every adult authority figure in my life. My teachers said it would make young people grow up not knowing how to read. My minister said it would lead young people astray from the word of God. Local farmers said it would make us all lazy and shiftless. Secretly, deep within my soul, I knew what they were saying was probably true. Television would probably be the ruin of America or at least the America they lived in, because I could already feel its effects. The one-eyed thing that sat so innocently in my living room was having a fundamental change in the way I saw the world. It was also having a fundamental change in the way I saw my parents. It showed me black people, not just as the drunken pulpwood workers that hung around the colored juke joints, but as singers, comedians, and dancers. I realized that Sammy Davis Jr. and Mahalia Jackson carried within them a human dignity and goodness that my vain and arrogant mother just didn't have. I began to see the racism, provincialism, and ignorance in my elders for what it was, a terribly evil thing.

Slowly, I began to feel different. I just didn't care if television would be the ruin of America. Maybe, that would be what was best. If it was the ruin of America, then I quietly decided that I would be ruined with it, and I would enjoy every minute of it.

Anything was better than living my entire life like the vast majority of grown people I knew. Except for their military service, they never traveled anywhere and never even wanted to. They never experienced new things or ever wanted to do so. In fact, new things tended to scare them. They were never excited about the future. They never pondered the mysteries of the cosmos or wondered what was on the backside of the moon. However, worst of all, they never asked any fundamental questions about the morality and the purpose of their lives. Everything to them was measured in dollars and cents. Materialism was their god and the litmus test by which they judged everything. If it put a dollar in your pocket, then it was good; if it caused you to give up one single worldly possession, then it was bad. They never had any concept of living in harmony with nature or the world around them. It was as if they were possessed by the same demon that occupied the mind of Ty Cobb, the need to over and over again prove one's racial, economic, and masculine superiority.

I also knew that it was true that rock and roll music drove young people mad with sexual feelings and rebellion in a way that Roy Acuff and Ernest Tubb never could. The gyrating hips of Elvis and the sexual innuendo of Chuck Berry were magical. The simple fact that it was not my parent's music was enough to make me love it.

Rock and roll made me think of a beautiful, but unfortunately, far-away place called California. Although I had never been there, I knew it was a magical place, full of motorcycles, hot rods, beautiful tanned blond girls, and all-night beach parties. In California, I could escape from this cheap imitation of Tobacco Road, with its hookworms, hog chitterlings, and rowdy honky-tonks to surf the wild waves with movie stars.

In 1960, all this was coming to a head. The Vietnam War and the Peace Movement lay ahead, and I would deal with them in time. However, right now, I had a more serious problem. I was fifteen years old and still a virgin. I couldn't stand it. I was as horny as a two-peckered billy goat and couldn't think about anything but sex. Looking back now, I know it was probably as much curiosity as it was blind lust. It would be a decade before *Playboy* would show pubic hair and *Hustler* would not leave anything to the imagination. I had no idea how the sex act was performed or even what a woman's genitalia looked like, other than the dark and fleeting shadows I had seen under my grandfather's loading dock.

Dating a girl was a problem, since the vast majority of Union County teenagers lived on farms and rode old yellow buses to school each day. This was a time when most of our mothers didn't work, and they were always home. There were no motels in Union County, and the ones out of town would never rent to someone our age. So, the only place a pair of teenagers could have sex was on a lonely dirt road, deep in the pinewoods, on a Friday or Saturday night date. For that most forbidden, and most pleasurable, of illicit activities, you needed an automobile. By 1960, the year I entered the ninth grade, the automobile problem was well on the way to solving itself. Being fifteen years old entitled me to a restricted driver's license, which I got with little problem.

Sitting behind a polished oak desk inside the courthouse, I took a simple written test, paid the three-dollar fee, and it was mine. I could drive during daylight hours, if I had a licensed driver over the age of twenty-one in the car with me. It was only the first step, but it was an important first step. All I had to do now was practice my driving skills, wait patiently for one year, and then I could take the driving test and get my operator's license. With my operator's license, the keys to the kingdom of sexual experience would be in my hand.

However, with driving, like most everything else, Union County was not like other places. It was a farm community, and most of us had been driving tractors or farm truck since we were old enough to reach the clutch and gas pedal. Almost everyone could drive an old stick shift pickup truck by the time they were twelve. The sheriff understood how boys had to help out on the farm, and, if you had your restricted driver's license, then you could count on the sheriff not hassling you about driving after dark or without somebody over twenty-one in the car with you. If you were caught burning rubber or speeding, all they did was haul you home in the back of the sheriff's car and talk to your parents. You could bet your sweet ass you were totally grounded after that. Usually, the highway patrolman assigned to Union County went along, but sometimes we got an asshole that would write you a ticket. When that happened, you had to go before the judge, and he would pull your license.

However, we were all perfectly willing to take the risk. Nobody wanted to be a chicken shit. The risks were all just a part of the fun of growing up; it made the whole thing more exciting. If there wasn't some kind of danger involved, what good was it?

Some guys were even so bold as to leave Union County and venture over to Starke or Lake City. Starke was particularly dangerous, since it was well-known that Union County boys were not liked over there. It was an old feud going back a long time to before Union County was even created. All I knew was that if you drove around in Starke with a Union County tag on your car, you were just asking for trouble from both the police and the local teenage tough guys. The cops said we only came over to Starke to start trouble; the local teenage boys claimed we were over there trying to take their girls. Most of the time, both was right.

Lake City was something else. It was a regular Sodom and Gomorrah, where everyone was welcome. There were all kinds of really neat drive-in restaurants with names like the Kit-Kat, the Bronco, and the Magnolia. There were motorcycles in Lake City and poolrooms that allowed in minors; there were even some bars just north of town that would let us drink beer, but, best of all, Lake City had whorehouses. They were thinly disguised pseudo-bars built along Highway 441 and US-90 that catered to truck drivers. The two most famous whorehouses were called the Railroad Crossing, located on Highway 441 just north of town, and Lake Lona on US-90 between Lake City and Live Oak on the Suwannee County line.

We had stumbled into the Railroad Crossing late one Saturday night when a group of us Union County boys were out carousing. We had seen the small red Budweiser sign from Highway 441 and figured we might get some beer. Usually, little small and isolated places out in the country didn't check IDs as close as places in town.

When we went inside, the first thing I noticed was it didn't smell like a regular bar. There was none of that spilt beer smell you usually find in such a place. Also, there was only one man behind a makeshift bar and half a dozen girls; each one was wearing a cheap-looking outfit, much like what the girls who worked with the carnival wear. The place had about half a dozen barstools, and, instead of tables, there were couches against the wall where you could sit and talk with a girl. It looked more like some trashy woman's living room than a bar. We walked nervously up to the bar and ordered a beer. The man behind the counter growled, "No beer."

"Whiskey?"

"No whiskey."

"What you got?" we asked.

"Pussy and Coca-Cola!"

Of course, shortly thereafter, he ran us out. Not only were we under age, but, also more importantly, we were also broke. No money, no pussy.

I would soon learn that there was a lot more to finding a girlfriend in Union County than just having the use of an automobile. The idiosyncrasies of rural Union County society, and the backward provincialism of the area, made it a place where Hugh Hefner couldn't get laid.

The 1950s—the decade we were just coming out of, and in reality were still in—was a very structured and conservative period of time. Eisenhower was in the White House, and the World War II and Great Depression generations were firmly in charge of everything, and God knows they were a bunch of tight asses.

One of the hardest things about finding a girlfriend was the dating hierarchy that existed at Union County High School. At the top of the dating pecking order were the girls everyone dreamed about; the cheerleaders, the band majorettes, and the homecoming queen. However, these girls were not fools. They were really beautiful, and they knew it. They used their beauty as a well-honed tool to get the men they wanted, and the men they wanted were the football heroes and the good-looking studs with nice cars, who they believed would make perfect husbands and fathers.

These girls knew how the game was played. The key to getting the man they wanted was the maintenance of their virginity until after marriage. It was very important to never have what everyone back then called "a reputation" (that is, a reputation of not being a "nice girl"). To have one illicit fling or to go "too far" just once was enough to put a Union County girl's future in serious jeopardy. In a community this small, there were no secrets.

Because I knew how these beautiful dream girls were, I was not really all that envious of these big-time football heroes and their beautiful girlfriends. If they wanted to have sex with one of these girls, they would have to marry her first. These guys would not explore the mysteries of sex for a long time to come, and I was in kind of a hurry. I wasn't exactly looking for a girl who was a slut, but, at the same time, I wasn't exactly looking for a sexually deferred, long-term Billy Graham and her parents approved relationship either.

However, I did envy the football players for one thing: their football jackets. Players who lettered in football were presented with a beautiful gold jacket with a bright purple trim. The gold jacket was adorned with a large, eight-inch-high purple letter U with gold trim. It stood, of course, for Union County High School. I never knew for certain why purple and gold were chosen as the school colors, but, when they were put together, they made one hell of a nice-looking jacket.

The golden jacket was given only to varsity football players who had played enough quarters during the season to letter. Players who sat on the bench too much didn't get one.

In Union County, football was king, and all other sports had to pay homage. Basketball players, the baseball team, and track and field athletes were all given only a white knit sweater adorned with the standard purple and gold letter. Compared to the beautiful gold football jacket, it looked absolutely pitiful. The same white sweater was also presented to the cheerleaders and the girl's basketball team, who wore it with pride. However, to boys, it was an affront, an insult; it was saying your sport isn't as important as football.

Most male athletes refused to wear the white sweater, deciding instead to sew their basketball, baseball, or track and field letter on one of their denim or leather jackets. This caused trouble with the school principal and the coaches who just didn't seem to understand that a sweater wasn't the same as a jacket. They were raised in the 1930s and 1940s, when having a school sweater was a really cool thing. They just didn't seem to understand that we were raised on James Dean in *Rebel Without a Cause* and Marlon Brando in *The Wild Ones*; and damn it, they didn't wear no sissy-looking white sweater; they wore a jacket.

Sometime around 1958, an unknown football player did what was at the time the unthinkable. On a particularly chilly north Florida winter morning, he let his girlfriend wear his golden football jacket. For someone who wasn't authorized to wear the golden football jacket, it was really a sacrilege! However, this inept athlete had inadvertently stumbled onto one of the great secrets of teenage romance during the Eisenhower years.

Before the day was out, every girlfriend of every football player had talked their sweethearts into letting them wear their gold football jacket. What was discovered, by sheer accident, was that no matter how dumb or ugly you were, some fairly good-looking girl would be willing to walk around school with you, arm in arm, just for the privilege of wearing your football jacket.

The main problem I had with all of this golden jacket nonsense was that I was not a football player and never would be. I had given it a try, playing junior varsity football in the eighth grade, but I just didn't like it. The blocking, the tackling, the running, the sweating, and the whole hundred yards made me sick, literally. Every time some big linebacker would plow into me, I would get off the ground feeling like I was about to puke my guts out. I didn't like being hit, and I really didn't like having to hit other people. To me, the whole silly game was a lot of unnecessary pain and suffering. My negative attitude was not lost on the coach, who felt he was punishing me by making me sit on the bench during a game. It didn't bother me a bit. I didn't like getting hit in a game anymore than I liked getting hit in practice.

When my junior varsity season was over, they presented us with a lousy purple and gold t-shirt. That's all we got for three stinking months of sit ups, push ups, wind sprints, and having the living holy hell knocked out of us on a regular basis.

Despite the pain, I was prepared to stick it out another season in order to play varsity football and hopefully get one of those coveted gold jackets. However, the next year, on the second day of practice in pads, I received a jarring blow from behind that tore the muscles in my right leg away from the bone and left me with an injury that still bothers me to this day. The only good thing about the injury was that it mercifully ended my football-playing career forever. After that, I totally lost all interest in football in particular and sports in general.

However, all was not lost. Not playing football might eliminate any chance I had of getting a gold jacket and dating the homecoming queen, but there were still plenty of relatively pretty girls in high school. All I had to do was find one.

If I were a straight A student, I might have had a chance with some of the brainy girls in the Beta Club; but, you guessed it, I was not a straight A student. I had tried the band in the seventh grade, but I couldn't carry a tune in a bucket. The Science Club girls were fairly cute, but they would not date a boy who didn't know how to use a slide rule, and I didn't even know how to crank one up. For a while, I dated a girl in the Library Club, but she was always reading a book, and, when I tried to talk to her, she would shush me. My idea of a good time was not watching a girl read a book.

One by one, my options vanished before my eyes. Finally, I had reached a point where the only girls left were the loners; they were the strange, owlish-looking girls that didn't seem to belong to anything and one last group: the Future Homemakers of America, better known as the FHA.

I knew from the very beginning that most of these FHA girls tended to be fairly plain-looking girls; they were not too pretty, but not ugly either, and they were a little on the plump side, because they did a lot of cooking. However, they were passable; as a respectable date, they would do.

To get a date with an FHA girl, you had to know where they were coming from. FHA girls were very home and family orientated. They believed that the most important things in life were a good home-cooked meal and the proper raising of children. They actually enjoyed doing needlepoint and sewing their own clothes.

FHA girls knew all the rules. For example, the proper length of a dress worn to church was two inches below the knee; for a date, it could be shorter, but not too much shorter. Colored socks were never worn with saddle shoes, deviled eggs must always be served chilled, and only poor white trash would put dark meat in the chicken salad. A black dress is not worn in the daytime, except for a funeral. A white dress is not worn at night, except for a wedding. While these girls might not be overly sexy and beautiful, they would, in the long run, probably make a fairly good—if not a little plain and chubby—wife and mother. The biggest problem with dating an FHA girl was that they were the sister organization of the FFA, the terrible and much-feared Future Farmers of America.

Every spring, the two groups held a joint FFA–FHA banquet and prom; it was the primo social event of the season. During the school year, there were various other little social gathering, such as a special back-to-school party, Thanksgiving dinner, a Christmas party, an Easter party, and parties held after each home football game.

The FFA and FHA also had a special "pep bus" that took members of the two groups to away football games. I was told that a lot of necking took place on the back seats of the FFA–FHA "pep bus." However, the school was so full of rumors and lies pertaining to sexual activity, I tended to doubt just how much making out actually occurred on the "pep bus." I also seriously doubted if the chaperones, especially Miss Kitty Epperson, the FHA sponsor, would sit by and let that happen. Anyway, FHA girls just weren't the make-out type.

During the summer, before tobacco-picking season began, FFA and FHA members could go to special summer camps for two weeks. The two camps were located on a remote lake near Tallahassee. The boys' camp was on one side of the lake, and the girls' camp was on the other; however, to put it mildly, there wasn't any kind of no-man's land between the two camps, and the possibility of hanky-panky going on was definitely there. Even without the possibility of sex, there was swimming, dancing, and all the other usual summer camp activities. Everyone really looked forward to going to camp each summer.

All of these joint FFA–FHA activities were characterized by loads of free food, lovingly prepared by the FHA girls under the close supervision of Miss Epperson. To FHA girls, cooking was everything. Miss Epperson had taught them and their overweight mothers that food equals love. To present food was the same as presenting love; to refuse food was to refuse love. They were not the type to understand that boys sometimes wanted sex along with their pecan pies and fried chicken.

Everything the FHA girls cooked was filled with too much butter, sugar, and animal fats. Tragically, these young people would follow the eating patterns they learned as children and teenagers throughout their lives until their ever-enlarging bellies led them to heart attacks, strokes, and early graves. Both the FFA and FHA chapters had a hard and fast rule that all of their activities were closed to nonmembers. No exceptions were ever made. It was just another of the many ways the school had of telling us to always stay with our own kind. It was a lesson we learned often and early growing up in Union County. Since the FFA and the FHA did so many things together, FHA girls generally found it advantageous to date only FFA boys. In the early 1960s, Union County was a teenage social desert, without a lot of things for young people to do. To ask an FHA girl to pass up the spring banquet and prom, the Thanksgiving dinner, the Christmas party, summer camp, and all the other social activities just because her boyfriend was not a member of the FFA was asking a lot.

Looking at my situation analytically, I finally decided that if I were to have any chance of dating a future homemaker, I would have to join the FFA.

It is really hard to explain all of this to a young person today. They look at you as if 1960 was part of the Old Stone Age. It seems like a million years ago and a faraway place. In 1960, pot was still something you put a plant in, Coke was still a soft drink, and a joint was a cheap bar where black folks got drunk. This was before the birth control pill brought on the sexual revolution, and the Vietnam War and the hippie-yippie movement caused us to doubt and challenge all of our values. In 1960, we never challenged anything. Our values and beliefs were rock hard. That was the way thing were, and we supposed at the time that was the way things would always be.

# The Blue Corduroy Jacket

The idea of being a farmer made me sick to my stomach. Every summer, I was sentenced to the tobacco fields of Union County to work picking the damnable weed in order to earn enough money to buy my school clothes. I utterly detested everything to do with agriculture and certainly had no intention of ever becoming a farmer. Furthermore, I wasn't even interested in the academic or philosophical side of the profession. I really didn't care if 8-8-8 fertilizer was better than 10-10-10 fertilizer, if hybrid seeds were better than regular seeds, or if you should disk before you break new ground or the other way around.

However, if I didn't join some kind of high school club and get in tight with some group, I might be forced to remain dateless and celibate until after high school, which, in my mind, at that particular time, were forever and a day. After carefully pondering the issue for some time, I decided that I should join the FFA no matter if I liked it or not.

I had received my football-playing, career-ending injury on the second day of practice, which began two weeks before the beginning of the new school year. It worked out really well, because it gave me a week to think it over and plan my next move, while I was waiting for my leg to mend. By the first day of school, I had decided on my course of action. On that first day, I walked boldly into the front office and asked for a class schedule change form. Within five minutes, thanks to the careful guidance of the school secretary, it was all done. I had signed up to take vocational agriculture second and third periods, the only two periods freshmen were allowed to take it. In order to make room in my schedule for Ag class, I dropped physical science and physical education. After spending a week nursing a painful football injury,

I was more than anxious to give up any form of athletic activity as soon as possible.

This simple administrative procedure was in reality an act of great courage on my part. My revulsion to farming was not the primary reason for my great anxiety about taking vocational agriculture; by signing up for the two-hour block of vocational agriculture, I was at the same time applying for membership in the dreaded FFA.

The FFA was the nearest thing we had in Union County to an urban (or perhaps in this particular case rural) street gang. Teachers measured their classes as either good or bad, by the number of FFA boys enrolled. FFA members or "Ag boys" as they were more commonly known were notorious for their disruptive behavior in the classroom and their vast amounts of tobacco and alcohol use.

Their signature bad conduct activity was the use of chewing tobacco and snuff in class, right under the eyes of the teacher. Every Ag boy was a master at going long periods of time with tobacco juice in his mouth without spitting. When they finally did spit, they could hide the activity so well that a teacher could be standing only a few feet away and never notice. It was such a brazen act of defiance to school authority that it filled the other students with awe. The ultimate challenge was to answer a question posed in class or work a math problem on the chalkboard with either a dip of snuff in your lip or a chew of tobacco in your mouth. The Ag boys staked out their territory with the copious amounts of tobacco juice they left behind. They would spit into trashcans, desk drawers, behind bookcases, in file cabinets, and between the pages of library and textbooks. It was a sign to all those enrolled in Union County High School that the Ag boys had been there, and they would be back.

Members of the FFA wore a dark blue corduroy jacket, adorned with a large golden-yellow FFA crest or great seal, as it was officially known, stitched on the back. On top of the FFA great seal, running across the shoulders, was the word "Florida" sewn in large golden-yellow letters. Under the great seal were the words "Union County" in the same large golden-yellow letters. The similarity between the layout of the FFA jacket and the denim and leather "colors" worn by California motorcycle gangs, such as the Hell's Angels, was not lost on the members of the FFA. Next to the gold football jacket, it was the most coveted piece of wearing apparel in the school, ranking way above the pitiful white sweater in prestige.

On the front of the jacket was a smaller FFA crest, neatly stitched over the left breast. On the right breast, parallel with the small great seal, each member had his name stitched using the same bright golden-yellow thread that adorned the rear of the jacket. If an Ag boy held a position in the FFA chapter—for example, president, vice president, or secretary— it was also listed under his name, again in golden-yellow letters.

The FFA member's name was just above the spot on his jacket where he wore his medals, little globs of bronze, hanging on the end of a brightly colored ribbon, affixed to the jacket with a carefully concealed safety pin. These small medals were handed out at the end of a long series of agricultural competitions in which the local FFA chapter was constantly engaged. There were so many of them, it was almost impossible for someone to remain in the chapter for any length of time without having numerous decorations hanging proudly from the right breast of his jacket.

The Ag boys formed teams and judged corn, hogs, chickens, turnips, cows, horses, beans, fertilizers, and even the soil itself. Ribbons were handed out for first, second, third, and fourth place, with maybe five or six more given for honorable mention. Just to make sure nobody would have to walk around school bare chested, they had special medals awarded just for being on the judging team. The net result of all this judging was a bunch of country boys, who were normally too dumb to count rocks, walking around school with a chest full of small bronze medals, making them look like some kind of agricultural General MacArthur.

Besides the possibility of getting a date, and maybe even a steady relationship with one of the FHA girls, there were also a lot of other nonromantic benefits in being a member of the FFA and taking vocational agriculture. The first was that Ag class had absolutely no academic challenges whatsoever. It was a joke; nobody could flunk vocational agriculture if they tried. Knuckle-headed boys with nothing but Ds and Fs in every other class in the school got an A in agriculture. Another advantage was that you took agriculture two class periods a day, which was nothing but a lot of very nice goof-off time.

If you took agriculture, you were exempt from physical education and all science classes, excluding tenth-grade general biology that was required, because it had a carefully hidden sex education curriculum buried deep within it. While you were learning how all those single-celled organisms, plants, and animals were reproducing, you were also secretly learning how humans did it. It taught us the facts of life without anybody getting upset.

Generally speaking, taking two hours of vocational agriculture each day greatly relieved us from what we felt was a lot of unnecessary mental exertion.

The FFA headquarters was a small building located across Highway 121 from Union County High School, which everyone referred to as the Ag building. The Ag building was divided into two main parts. The front part was the classroom, which also included the Ag teacher's small office. The rear of the building was a large open area that was part garage, part woodworking shop, and a general tool and equipment storage area. The big room had several band saws, circular saws, table saws, a complete set of automotive tools, a hydraulic jack, welding equipment, and dozens of other pieces of expensive mechanical equipment that nobody ever touched, much less learned how to use. Generally speaking, the big room looked and smelled like a typical grease-monkey hangout, except that every piece of equipment looked brand new and was shining clean.

The agriculture teacher was a stoop-shouldered, pale little man we called Mr. Clemmons. His first name was Clarence, but the only way we knew that was because it was printed in the yearbook one year. Nobody dared call him Clarence, because he hated the name. He was really pissed off that it had been printed by accident in the yearbook, and, after a bitter protest by Mr. Clemmons to the principal, he was thereafter listed only as one "C. Clemmons" in the yearbook. However, the damage had already been done. The word was out. His first name was passed down from one year's class to the next, almost like a generation-to-generation thing. We all fully understood that we would have a real good laugh behind his back, but that nobody would dare call him by his first name to his face.

Mr. Clemmons had thinning red hair that was already streaked with gray, even though he appeared to be only about forty years old. He had pale, almost yellowish-looking skin that would get a bright crimson when he got angry. It was almost as if Mr. Clemmons had a built-in anger barometer; you could actually measure how pissed off he was just by looking at his face. It would begin with the veins in his neck bulging out, and then it would slowly spread up his head, finally climaxing with the large vein in the middle of his forehead busting forth like a purple river in a sea of flush-red flesh. He was famous for wearing the same clothes every day; he wore a white, open-necked shirt and pleated khaki trousers, with soft-soled loafers. In his right shirt pocket, there was always an open pack of nonfiltered Camel cigarettes and a box of Eli Witt brand wooden matches that rattled as he walked. Mr. Clemmons was well-known for having the worse-smelling breath in the school. People, who had been closer to him than I ever wanted to, said his breath smelled like a mixture of old cigarette smoke and sour milk. He also sweated a lot and usually had the strong odor of old underarm perspiration about him. His white shirt was often sweat stained and dingy around the neck. Mr. Clemmons was one of those people who never washed the back of his neck. Sometimes, when we were really bored, we would make a contest out of counting his blackheads. He was so out of shape that just moderate exercise, such as walking around the Ag building, would leave him panting for breath and dripping wet with perspiration.

Mr. Clemmons was a two-pack-a-day smoker, who was always seeking some excuse to go into his private office so he could grab a Camel. Technically, he wasn't supposed to smoke in front of students, although he often did, but he only smoked when we were outdoors, far away from the school grounds, where no other teacher could see him doing it. While he was around the Ag building, he would never light up until he was safely inside of his office with the door closed. God help anybody who walked into Mr. Clemmons' office without knocking first and giving him time to extinguish his cigarette. If you did knock and make him put out his cigarette, you had better have a damn good reason for doing so, like the building is on fire or something like that.

All this smoking caused a strange situation to develop around the Ag building. Mr. Clemmons was always trying to get away from us, so he could get into his office and sneak a smoke. At the same time, the main objective of the Ag boys was to get away from Mr. Clemmons long enough to also smoke a cigarettes. It was, in reality, a rather silly exercise in crisscrossing with us avoiding him and him avoiding us.

If he caught us smoking on the school grounds, he was bound by his teaching contract, and some kind of weird bond between professional educators, to report us to the principal for disciplinary action. However, he never caught us, because he never tried to catch us.

The Ag boys were always smoking at school and not just around the Ag building. Ag boys smoked in the restroom, in the auditorium, behind the lunchroom, and anywhere and everywhere we could do it and not get caught. Every boy who wore the blue corduroy FFA jacket reeked of stale cigarette smoke. If you didn't smoke when you joined the FFA chapter, you would almost be forced to light up soon afterwards. The peer pressure to smoke in the FFA was unbelievably strong.

The favorite brands were Winstons or Marlboros, real men's smokes. We all wanted to be like the Marlboro man we saw on television. Those Ag boys, who were just starting out smoking, usually choose Salems, because of the light menthol taste. They would always later switch to Winstons or Marlboros, because the Ag boys considered Salems to be a girl's cigarette. Some of the Ag boys had been smoking since early childhood, and they chose unfiltered Camels. They were looked upon as the toughest of the tough, because they had developed enough tolerance to handle the rough smoke of the unfiltered Camels.

The agriculture building was an old World War II vintage, cinder-block building, which was painted white and trimmed with green doors and window frames. A large blue sign stood in front of the Ag building with the great seal carefully hand painted on it. Beneath the great seal were printed the words "Union County Chapter, Future Farmers of America." There was a sidewalk that ran from the street crossing to the main entrance of the Ag building. The area around the sidewalk was landscaped with azalea bushes, and the grass was always neatly trimmed.

The front entrance of the Ag building was a single wooden door that opened into a narrow vestibule that led into the classroom area. Anyone going or coming into the classroom from the direction of the school had to walk directly in front of Mr. Clemmons' small office. From inside his office, Mr. Clemmons could stare out the window and see someone coming from the moment they left the main entrance of the school until they reached his office. That was more than enough time to extinguish a cigarette and prepare a proper reception.

A narrow dirt and gravel driveway ran from the highway, parallel to the sidewalk eventually curving around the Ag building where it dead-ended in a large circular parking area. It was here that the Ag trucks were parked under an open-sided pole barn shed directly behind the Ag building. Opposite the pole barn were the green double doors leading into the shop area of the Ag building. A single 100-watt yellow bug light was positioned over the two double doors, and a small water spigot was at the far corner of the building.

Anyone approaching the Ag building from any other direction than the sidewalk or the gravel driveway would have to pass through about one hundred feet of typical Florida pinewoods, filled with all types of cutting briars and tangling vines. What all this meant in plain, simple talk was that the Ag building was so totally isolated from the rest of the school, it was almost impossible for anyone to sneak up and catch us doing anything wrong.

Shortly after I started taking vocational agriculture, I was called into Mr. Clemmons office to sign some papers and found it to be just like I expected it to be. It matched Mr. Clemmons' personality perfectly. It contained only his cluttered gray metal desk, two gray metal folding chairs, a wooden bookcase, and two gray metal file cabinets. Large stacks of back issues of *Progressive Farmer* magazines were scattered around everywhere; they were stacked on the floor and on the dusty and cluttered shelves of the bookcase and piled on top of the file cabinets and on the floor behind the desk.

The chapter had a subscription to *Progressive Farmer* that dated back beyond the memory of anyone, including Mr. Clemmons. Every month, the magazine arrived, but nobody ever bothered to properly catalog it or neatly stack the magazine on the shelves in any kind of logical order. So, they just piled up, laying around everywhere, stacks and stacks of *Progressive Farmer* magazine; some dated back to World War II.

Mr. Clemmons spent almost the entire school day in his office, sitting in a straight-back wooden chair, chain smoking cigarettes, and pouring over the paperwork he felt was more aggravation than it was worth. The large ash tray on his desk was always filled to overflowing with twisted cigarette butts and stale ashes. The ceiling tiles and walls in his office were stained a dark brown and were sticky to the touch, a mute testimony to what the unfiltered Camel cigarettes were doing to his lungs. He never opened the windows, and he had no fan or air-conditioning in the office. The air was always stale, smelling like the inside of an old inner tube that had been filled with cigarette smoke. The only decoration in the office was a large wall calendar, which was given away free by a major chemical fertilizer company. On the calendar was an oversized, color photograph of a tobacco plant in full, midsummer bloom.

Adjoining Mr. Clemmons' office was the classroom. This room was in stark contrast to the Spartan office. It was well-designed and laid out with great care. There were no desks, only wooden tables assembled in a rectangle. Mr. Clemmons' predecessor had set it up during the final days of World War II, so he could not take any credit for how nice the classroom looked. At one end of the room was a hand-carved and colorfully painted, four-foot-high relief image of the great seal of the FFA. Official FFA folklore said the great seal had been carved and painted by a talented inmate serving a life sentence at the state prison. The classroom was filled with varnished wooden shelves, stuffed to overflowing with every type of trophy and award one could imagine. The classroom's walls were covered with one plaque after another, bestowing honors on the Union County FFA chapter for everything from outstanding chicken judging to soil conservation and timber harvesting. We soon learned that this space wasn't really a classroom; it was more like a shrine, a holy place, the *sanctum sanctorum*, where we were taught to worship the gods of American agriculture and pat ourselves on the back for a job well done.

A close examination of the numerous plaques and trophies would reveal that most were awards handed out to members of the FFA chapter by other members of the FFA chapter or awards given to our chapter from other chapters or the national organization. The FFA spent an inordinate amount of time and money honoring itself for fairly minor achievements.

However, such talk was heresy, and no one dared to point this out, either to the other FFA members or the community at large. In a rural area like Union County, the teaching of vocational agriculture was considered of supreme importance. Despite Mr. Clemmons' dorky appearance, he wielded a considerable amount of political power, and no politician or school administrator dared find fault with the workings of the FFA.

Although we hardly ever learned anything in Ag class, except smoking and goofing off, Mr. Clemmons covered his tracks well. In his desk drawer was a professionally printed curriculum guide, given to all Ag teachers by the national office of the FFA. It explained in detail all the exciting and interesting things students were learning in vocational agriculture. According to the curriculum guide, we were supposed to receive six to eight hours a week of formal classroom lectures by Mr. Clemmons on the methods of modern agriculture, timber harvesting, and soil conversation. On Mr. Clemmons' desk was a well-worn grade book, into which he scribbled in pencil the records of all the mythical academic work we were supposed to be doing. I knew he never graded any tests, because we never took any. Yet, the grade book showed numerous lists of high-test scores, which were phantom grades on phantom tests, that nobody ever took.

Everything the FFA stood for was symbolized by the great seal that adorned everything even remotely associated with the FFA. It was on our blue corduroy jackets front and back, on the metal sign outside of the Ag building, and on almost every vehicle and mechanized piece of farm equipment we owned. It was even on the spiral ring notebooks and writing tablets we carried to class. They even went so far as to give us little great seal lapel pins to wear on our dress clothes when we went to church.

The great seal of the FFA is comprised of several elements, the first of which is a large golden-yellow circle surrounded with oversized, absolutely perfect kernels of yellow corn. This golden-yellow circle of corn represents America's common agricultural heritage. According to FFA orthodoxy, as published in the FFA handbook, corn is a plant native to the United States (actually it was first grown in Mexico), and it is grown in all of our states. Once, during an orientation meeting for new members, when the great seal was being explained, I questioned Mr. Clemmons about whether or not corn is really grown in our two newest states. Somehow, I just couldn't imagine corn growing on the beaches of Hawaii or the frozen tundra of Alaska.

It was then I learned that Mr. Clemmons didn't like to answer questions in general, and he especially didn't like to answer questions to which he didn't know the answer. My question about Alaska and Hawaii got me called into his smelly little office where he let me know, in no uncertain terms, that he would not tolerate a "smart-ass" in "his" Ag class. If the FFA handbook said that corn grew in all the states, it damn sure wasn't my place to question it. He promised me that the next time I pulled a stunt like that, he would have me out of the chapter. In the direct center of the great seal was a bright red rising sun, which symbolized progress in agriculture and the confidence that all FFA members have in the future. In the foreground is a plowed field on which sat an old-fashioned plow, the type pulled by a mule. The plow was the symbol of the tillage of the soil. To me, the plow was the symbol of backbreaking labor in the unmerciful heat of the Florida summer. Sitting on the plow was an owl, the symbol of wisdom and knowledge. Atop the large circle of corn kernels was an American eagle to remind all members that the FFA was a national organization. Printed in large black letters on the great seal were the words "Vocational Agriculture" in an arch around the plow and the rising sun. Slightly above center was the large black letters "FFA." We were taught that the great seal was as sacred to members of the FFA as the American flag, the Bible, and our sister's virginity.

The only time we went into the classroom was when the FFA chapter held one of its poorly attended monthly business meetings or one of its mandatory general meetings; these meetings were held on an irregular basis to swear in new officers, present another metal or trophy, or when Mr. Clemmons wanted to chew us out about something.

The tables in the classroom were positioned to form a rectangle, with a wooden teacher's desk on a raised dais at each end of the rectangle, much like you would see in a corporate boardroom. You just didn't come into the classroom and have a seat. There was a pecking order to the whole thing. Seniors got the first choice of seats, followed by juniors, and then sophomores. Freshmen were usually forced to stand up behind the seated upperclassmen. Every meeting reminded us of our status in life, as well as that eternal message of Union County High School. Stay in your place, with your own kind, and wait your turn.

Officers had special positions and symbols of their rank carefully positioned within the classroom. The president of the chapter sat at the head of the rectangle of tables, behind one of the two desks. Before him, sitting on the desk, was a small hand-carved and carefully painted wooden plaque. On the plaque was the rising sun from the great seal, the symbol of rank for the president of the FFA chapter, as well as the hope that all FFA members have in the future. The president also sat directly beneath the four-foot-high great seal that hung on the wall behind his desk. It was yet another sign of his vaulted position within the chapter.

On the opposite end of the rectangle of tables facing the president, but not on a raised dais, was the desk of the vice president. His symbol was a small plaque with a plow, also from the great seal, that represented the tillage of the soil. The reporter was stationed by his symbol, a small American flag, which told everyone that the FFA was dedicated to American ideals and good citizenship. The treasurer sat before a small statue of George Washington. He was supposed to take charge of all financial receipts and disbursements, just as our first president had maintained his farm accounts before the Revolutionary War.

Of course, all this symbolism was just a bunch of bullshit. How could a bunch of rowdy pseudo-farm boys who spit tobacco juice into their textbooks respect American values and good citizenship? The guy we elected treasurer couldn't pass basic math even if he was allowed to cheat off somebody else's paper. Mr. Clemmons did all the paperwork dealing with money and only called the treasurer in to sign the requisitions. Usually, by the second semester,

Mr. Clemmons had learned to forge his signature and didn't even bother to call him in anymore.

The secretary was stationed next to the symbol of his post, the ear of corn. His duties were to keep an accurate record of all our meetings and correspond with other secretaries wherever corn was grown and the future farmers met. In reality, we usually had a girl from the future homemakers come over and record our meeting and write any letters we might have to send out. Mr. Clemmons couldn't spell at all, and the poor guy we elected secretary could only write with a pencil so he could erase.

Finally, we had Mr. Clemmons, whose position was advisor; his symbol was the owl, representing his great wisdom and age. It should have been a pack of Camel cigarettes and a jackass.

All the officers had special seats in the overcrowded classroom. The reporter and the secretary flanked the president, proudly sitting with their symbols of rank before them, at the head of the rectangle of tables. The treasurer and advisor likewise flanked the vice president at the other end of the rectangle of tables. The sentinel, whose symbol was a carved relief showing a pair of male Caucasian hands clasped together in an eternal handshake, stood by the door. His duty was to see that the door was only opened to friends of the FFA and to safeguard all the trophies, symbols of office, and other semisacred paraphernalia that filled the room.

Despite the official protocol stated in the FFA handbook that said the advisor sat next to the vice president, Mr. Clemmons usually sat next to the president so he could tell him what to do. He bumped the treasurer down to the end of the table next to the vice president, who never did anything anyway and took his seat. Mr. Clemmons always sat close to the girl from the FHA chapter who came to our meeting to act as unofficial reporter. He liked to keep an eye on what she was writing down to make sure she didn't record anything controversial.

The FFA had a special ceremony for almost all official occasions; we had a special oath we quoted at each meeting:

"To practice brotherhood, honor rural opportunities and responsibilities, and develop those qualities of leadership, which a future farmer should posses."

We always opened and closed our meetings with the pledge to the flag and the saying of the Lord's Prayer. These meetings were usually kept short with us rushing through the prayers and ceremonies, since everyone in the room, including Mr. Clemmons, was having a nicotine fit.

To understand what went on at the Ag building, one must first understand the peculiar nature of Union County High School. It was a large one-story building that was built like a giant squared-off letter U, with the two open ends facing, almost reverently, toward the football field in the distance. The building was made of red Georgia brick, put together by the hardworking men of the Works Progress Administration during the Great Depression.

The school was built with a floor plan obviously meant for a school in the cold north. The school had a large boiler that was housed in a separate ante building positioned between the two wings. Most of the year, it just sat there, and it made a great place to sneak a smoke, when the teachers were cracking down on smoking in the boy's restroom, which was our usual spot. Each classroom had large, cast-iron radiators, through which New York style steam heat flowed during the few weeks each year when the weather was cold enough to fire up the big boiler. Each classroom also had a separate cloak room, so we could hang up our heavy winter garments, except that nobody ever wore heavy winter clothing in Florida. Therefore, the cloak room provided another good place to sneak a smoke. During most of the school year, when it was typically hot and muggy, the classrooms were roasting. There was no air-conditioning and poor ventilation, and the only fans were the ones the teachers bought and paid for themselves.

One wing of the school was for the elementary grades. The other held the junior high and high school classes. Between the two wings was the auditorium, which was large enough to hold all the students in the school at one time, which wasn't really very large, since there were never more than three hundred and sixty students enrolled at Union County High School during the 1950s and 1960s. There were only fifty-five members of my graduating class in 1964, which was at the time the largest graduating class in school history.

Directly beside the high school wing was the school's large, redbrick gymnasium. It was the pride of the county, since most surrounding counties still played basketball in old wooden gymnasiums that looked like old barns. Behind the gymnasium was a small white clapboard building we called the "lunchroom." It was the only part of the school made of wood. It could only hold about one-third of the students at one time, so we ate in relays, with the elementary students going first.

Although it held grades one through twelve, this whole U-shaped complex and assorted outbuildings were called Union County High School, which consisted of the Ag building, the band building, the gymnasium, and the lunchroom. Union County is funny that way. We were the smallest county in the state of Florida in both population and land area. And, to be truthful, we were a little embarrassed that all of our students could be educated in one U-shaped school building. We didn't want to be known as Union County General School or any kind of stupid name like that. The teams we played on the football field called themselves such and such high school, so we called ourselves Union County High School. If this was technically or legally incorrect, it never really crossed our minds. It was just the way we did it.

Between the ends of the two wings of the school and the football field was a large open area where nothing but grass grew. It served as a practice field for the football team, the elementary student's playground, and the parking area for the well-attended home football games. Looking out the library window or from the back steps of the lunchroom the wooden bleachers of the football stadium looked like some type of old-time sailing ship gliding into port across a wide green sea. The school sat at the intersection of Highway 121, which ran east and west, and Lake Street, which ran north and south. Lake Street ran from the small lake on the other side of town all the way down past the school and the football field to finally dead end at a post-World War II housing development we called "Sprinkle Field."

The school was located south of Lake Butler on the very outskirts of the small town. Except for Sprinkle Field there were no housing areas close by. To the east of the school was a small dairy farm; to the west of the school was nothing but a couple of hay barns, some woods, and Dukes Cemetery. To the south, beyond the football field and Sprinkle Field housing area, there was nothing but deep pinewoods that ran uninterrupted all the way to Gainesville, sixty miles away. To the north of the school, beyond the Ag building, there was a small strip of woods that evolved into an area of older, Victorian-style homes. This two-block area was known only as South Lake Street. It was on South Lake Street that the houses of the wealthiest and most politically powerful people in Union County were located.

One of the more modest homes in this neighborhood was the white, two-story home of Dr. and Mrs. J. W. King. To the older people of Union County, Dr. King's home was almost as important as if a president had lived there. Mrs. King had been the very nice lady I remembered from that day in the first grade when we were being screened for hookworms. Older people kept telling me that I was lucky to have been able to meet Mrs. King, but it was a shame that Dr. King had died before I was born.

Since Mrs. King's death in 1958, the house had not been lived in. However, it was not run down and did not look abandoned. Dr. King's sons made sure it was kept up. The house was painted every two years, and a Negro man was hired as caretaker to keep the grass mowed and the hedges trimmed. He and his wife, who kept the inside of the house clean, lived in a small apartment above the small garage in the rear of the house. My mother always said that it was nice that people loved and respected their parents enough that they would keep the house up after their deaths as a memorial. Slim, ever cynical, said it was a damned shame that some people had so much money they could afford to keep up an old house that nobody lived in.

From Dr. King's home, Lake Street continued north, where it intersected with Main Street. I suppose from that point on, it was really North Lake Street; yet, I never heard anyone call it that. Lake Butler just wasn't big enough.

It was at the intersection of Main and Lake Street that the courthouse stood, with the small jail and sheriff's office directly behind it. The courthouse took up an entire city block, and it was the legal and social center of Lake Butler. Surrounding the courthouse and running both directions down Main Street was the main business district. It consisted of half a dozen assorted garages and gasoline stations and five churches; two Baptist, one Methodist, one Church of Christ, and one Pentecostal. Union County did not have a Catholic church, and I never knew a single Catholic while I was growing up there. There were also no Episcopalian, Presbyterian, or Unitarian churches in Union County. Some of the kids at school said that Catholics weren't allowed in Union county, because they worshiped idols and did everything the pope in Rome told them to do. This meant they weren't really Americans. All this anti-Catholic rhetoric became more visceral as the 1960 presidential election heated up. Union county was solidly behind the Texan Lyndon B. Johnson. The notion of a Roman Catholic getting the Democratic nomination was anathema in the small town.

Main Street also consisted of the town's one and only bank, two drug stores, a pool room, a movie theater, two bars, two barber shops, two grocery stores, and one auto parts store. That was it, the entire cosmopolitan heart of Lake Butler. All the rest of the small town was private homes, cemeteries, and a couple of small ten-acre farms.

Lake Street ran only three blocks past the courthouse through a nice middle-class neighborhood; past the City Hall, where the county's two fire trucks were parked; and all the way down to a small park and skating rink on the banks of the muddy body of nearly stagnant black water, after which the town of Lake Butler was named.

In the rear of the Ag building were parked two Ford pickup trucks, each painted with the official FFA blue with the great seal neatly stenciled on each door. The two trucks were the most important pieces of equipment in the FFA inventory. Both trucks had the high, wooden-slat sideboards needed when cattle were transported to the stock market in Gainesville.

We would always pile into the rear of the trucks to be driven down to the Ag barns. The rules of the chapter said that a junior or senior with a proper Florida operator's license could only drive the Ag trucks. However, the unofficial rules said only officers drove the trucks, and only seniors sat in the front seats. Another unofficial rule was that whenever somebody had to get out to open a gate, it was always a freshman. If no freshman was in the truck, then a sophomore or junior did it.

The blue FFA trucks would pull out onto Highway 121 and go about a hundred yards before the vehicles, loaded with Ag boys, took a hard right turn onto Lake Street, headed south toward Sprinkle Field, and passed directly beside the gymnasium and the big grassy field, until they came to a narrow dirt road running behind the home side bleachers of the football field. Turning right at the ticket booth, the Ag trucks would take a short, but bumpy, ride down the soft dirt road until they finally arrived at the real *sanctum sanctorum* of the FFA. It was the place every Ag boy considered heaven on earth or at least as near to it as you could get and still be at school; they were the famous, or perhaps notorious would be a better word, Ag barns.

The area we called the Ag barns was actually a collection of plowed fields, small chicken houses, pigpens, and a medium-sized cow pasture. The nearest thing we had to a barn was a rectangular, cinder-block building with a bright red roof. This was where all the chapter's farm tools, seeds, fertilizers, and pesticides were stored. It was painted the familiar FFA blue with the great seal of the FFA stenciled on both of its big double doors. Next to it was a long, tin-roofed pole barn shed under which was parked all of the FFA's harrows, disks, sprayers, seeders, and plows. Everything needed to get a field ready for planting, cultivating, and harvesting was parked under the long, open-sided pole barn shed.

Each piece of equipment was painted the familiar FFA blue, except for the chapter's Farmall tractor. It was left red, the color it bore when it left the factory. It was one of those persistent quirks we lived with every day of our lives. A Farmall tractor just wouldn't be a Farmall tractor if it was painted anything other than red. Nobody questioned this; to do so would bring icy stares. Again, it was part of the hidden curriculum of Union County High School: Some things are the way they are, just because they have always been that way. Never ask why.

Every piece of farming equipment under the shed was in perfect condition, clean as a whistle, well-oiled, and carefully maintained.

The great thing about the FFA was that we always had three or four times as many boys available for work at the Ag barns as there were things that needed doing. Some work had to be done, and everybody knew it; so, everybody pitched in, did it as quickly as possible, and got it over with. All the animals had to be fed daily and if necessary vaccinated, castrated, wormed, or dipped.

In the spring, there was disking, plowing, and planting. That was followed later by the laying down of the appropriate amounts of fertilizers and pesticides. If there was one thing the FFA and Mr. Clemmons believed in, it was to always put down enough chemical fertilizer and pesticides. The fields would have to be cultivated all summer, and, in the fall, the corn crop would be harvested. The chapter always grew corn, because it was easy to grow, and the chapter used it for animal feed.

We had in the chapter a hard-core group of Ag boys who were really serious about becoming farmers. They were actually proud that they knew how to change the oil in a tractor, plow straight furrows, put down fertilizer, spray pesticides, and treat screw worm infestations in dairy cows. We were supposed to stand around and watch them do all this interesting and fun stuff, so we would know how to do it later when we became farmers. Somehow, we always wound up sitting on our ass under the trees smoking cigarettes and bullshitting, while they did all the work. Other times, out of sheer boredom more than anything else, we would oil down one of the sets of disk blades or sweep out the shed. Even with all our goofing off, we always had everything at the Ag barns looking neat and clean. No piece of equipment was allowed to remain dirty or neglected, no fieldwork was left undone, and no animals were unattended, not with this many teenage boys hanging around.

Mr. Clemmons always wanted the Ag boys out of the Ag building as soon as possible, because their hanging around interfered with his smoking. Unless there was some serious thing that needed doing around the Ag building, he would give out a list of chores to do and send everyone to the Ag barns. Usually, the list said the same thing each day. Feed the cows, feed the chickens, slop the hogs, check the oil in the tractor, and things like that; it was a general list of farm chores that never took more than thirty minutes to complete. Since everyone took Ag for two hours at a time, there was plenty of good goof-off time. Nobody was in any hurry to get back to the Ag building, because we knew it would seriously piss off Mr. Clemmons if the Ag boys came back early and messed up his smoking.

Mr. Clemmons only came down to the Ag barns one or two times a week to conduct a brief inspection to make sure the work was getting done. To the best of my knowledge, no other teacher had ever been to the Ag barns. Sometimes, the principal would come down, but it was always a special occasion, like the birth of a new calf or something like that. However, usually, we were almost always by ourselves.

The Ag barns were so remote from the rest of the school, it was almost impossible for anyone to sneak up and catch somebody doing something wrong. Even a lazy, half-awake lookout could very easily spot someone approaching on foot across the large grassy area between the football field and the school. If they came by vehicle, they would have to come up Lake Street and take a hard right at the fee booth at the end of the football field, giving us plenty of time to put out our cigarettes and look busy. To approach the Ag barns any other way would mean walking over plowed fields or going through a cow pasture and dodging a mean-looking Brahma bull.

The Ag barns were freedom personified. To some of the Ag boys, it was the first time in their life without adult supervision. They could actually be themselves for once, and freedom can be a heady thing. At the Ag barns, everyone was free to smoke cigarettes, dip snuff, chew Red Man tobacco, scratch their balls, release noxious flatulence, cuss, and just generally be teenage good-old boys during the golden age of rock and roll. It was a wonderful experience, sort of a farm-boy heaven.

The Ag barns were held in such reverence, no student of Union County High School who wasn't an Ag boy was not allowed to go anywhere near this sacred place on penalty of an ass whipping. Also, no freshman was allowed to go to the Ag barns until after he had been officially initiated and accepted into the chapter. Until then, they were expected to stay busy up at the Ag building, washing the trucks and cleaning and oiling the equipment in the shop area.

The green hands were warned not to venture too close to Mr. Clemmons' office or disturb him with any noise while we were in the classroom. Green hands only went into the classroom on the direct orders of an upperclassman to polish or dust the trophies and plaques or sweep up. Sometimes, just to fuck with us, the upperclassmen would order us to read an article in one of the old editions of *Progressive Farmer* magazine.

Looking back over the years, I realize now that the guys in Ag class never kidded themselves. They were really smarter than anyone knew. They all carried within their souls a knowledge and certainty about the future that would have been extremely fighting, if they had ever let their guard down. They knew they would never go to college and never have a high-paying executive position. They would never be doctors, lawyers, accountants, or college professors.

They would stumble through high school with Cs and Ds, if they were lucky. Then, they would find some low-paying blue collar job, get married and have kids, get divorced, get married again, have more kids, and generally try to scratch out a living, doing the best they can, and hoping to give their children more than they had, but not really counting on it. They would only produce a new generation of kids just like themselves, losers from the very beginning.

There wasn't anything they could really do to change this scenario; it really wasn't their fault; they just weren't born smart, gifted, or talented. They had known it since the first grade, and, by high school, they had grown to accept it and pretend to revel in it. All the smoking, cussing, farting, crude language, and phony macho behavior were just feeble attempts to deal with this terrible certainty about the future in the only way they knew how to deal with it: just not give a shit.

However, despite all this, these boys would grow up to become the type of men who had built America and would continue to build it in the future. They would grow up to be the men who had the dirty fingernails, soiled jeans, and sweaty shirts. Their busted knuckles and grimy hands would make the world of the young urban professional possible. They were the people who poured the concrete and hammered the nails. They would build houses they could not afford to live in. They would dig the swimming pools and install the Jacuzzis for others to enjoy. Even in 1960, down at the Ag barns, they already knew it, but, for right now, they were rulers of their own kingdom.

Vocational agriculture was in many ways an exclusive little club, an elite brotherhood of the future have-nots. The Ag boys knew who they wanted in their chapter, and they also knew who they didn't want. This was their world; it smelled like a fresh fart and ancient sweat, and it was covered with tobacco spit and cow shit, but it was theirs and gawddamnit, right or wrong, they were going to keep it theirs. They didn't have much in this world, and later they would have less; however, right now, they did have this.

To keep the FFA the organization it was, it was absolutely imperative that no intellectual geeks, nerds, crybabies, teacher suck assess, or tattletales ever wore the blue corduroy FFA jacket. One little crybaby jerk-off could forever spoil this great thing the Ag boys had going. The guys who wore the blue corduroy jacket had to be above reproach. They had to be guys you could absolutely count on never to tell on another FFA member or tolerate someone who did. This was their honor code, and they lived by it. They also enforced it.

The FFA had ways of running those who were unfit out of the chapter, but it was better if these people never got into the chapter in the first place. The method of weeding out the unworthy came during the fourth week of the new school year; that was initiation week, when the Ag boys would decide if the new candidates for membership in the FFA were worthy to wear the blue corduroy jacket.

People wanting to join the FFA and take vocational agriculture were called green hands. They began attending Ag class the first day of school, but they were in a kind of uncertain twilight zone until after initiation week. Even though their class schedule said they were taking vocational agriculture, they were not really in the program until they had passed through initiation week and had been accepted into the chapter.

No matter if the green hands knew it or not, they were also under very close scrutiny. Because Union County High School was so small and everybody knew almost everybody else; they knew some of the green hands were not going to fit in based just on their reputation around school. These guys were approached in private and told to drop out of FFA or else. The smart ones got the message right away and would immediately go down to the principal's office and change their schedule, dropping vocational agriculture for science and physical education. If they didn't, the Ag boys would just beat the living shit out of them at the earliest opportunity; it was just as simple as that. I only saw it happen once, and it wasn't a pretty sight.

There was this one kid who had signed up for vocational agriculture the same year I was a freshman. He had a bad reputation for a being a straight A student, and, worse yet, he was a known member of the Science Club in the seventh and eighth grade. He was one of those nonconformist, beatnik types that we would encounter in greater numbers as the 1960s wore on. He was not from Union County; he had moved here three years ago from Houston, Texas. His parents worked for a big petroleum company, putting a natural gas pipeline through the county. He had gone to a large, racially mixed high school in Houston and imagined himself to be some kind of big city boy, who was smarter and worldlier than the rest of us hicks. He wasn't a snitch or anything like that, and, later on, he probably made a great antiwar protester; it was just that he wasn't what the Ag boys wanted in their chapter.

The seniors, who were experienced in these matters, felt like he was joining the FFA just to prove something. He wanted to establish that anyone could be a member of the FFA, not just tobacco-spitting country boys. He was always talking about being a lawyer someday and spouting off at the mouth about rights and freedoms and other obscure legal matters that the Ag boys just didn't understand or believe in.

This attitude on his part really bothered the Ag boys a lot, because it seemed frighteningly similar to racial integration, which was what Martin Luther King was trying to do. The Ag boys were not about to be forced to associate with and accept someone they didn't want to have around. By running this kid out of the chapter, it would almost be like defeating the integrationists.

Only the four senior officers of the FFA—the president, the vice president, the secretary, and the sentinel—were allowed to make the decision to run somebody out of the chapter. However, the ordinary members of the chapter had the right to approach the officers about any green hand they didn't like or were suspicious of. Mr. Clemmons probably had a hand in all this, but nobody knew how much. It was one of the many things we just didn't talk about.

There was never any open discussion of the matter. When the decision was made to blackball somebody, most of the members didn't know anything about it until it was already over. It was kind of like something that was just understood without question; some people just didn't fit into the FFA program, and they had to go. The Ag boys imagined that they were like the Marine Corps or West Point; they had their standards.

On the second day of school, the four FFA officers pulled the kid over in the hallway and told him to drop out of vocational agriculture, or else, but this kid was a belligerent little smart ass. He laughed and told the four FFA officers to go take a flying leap and that he had certain constitutional rights, and he knew what those rights were and that no bunch of senior thugs were going to infringe on his right to take any class he wanted. What arrogance! He was bravely going where no geek had gone before. The FFA officers who spoke to him couldn't believe what they were hearing. They really didn't know what to do; nobody had ever defied them like this before, so they just turned around and walked off.

The little shit actually thought he had won and the next day bragged to some girls about how he had told off the four FFA officers. His bragging was soon all over the school, and every chapter officer wanted to fight him then and there. However, this kid refused to fight, saying he didn't believe in violence and that it took a bigger and braver man to just walk away. In Union County, that kind of thinking can make your life miserable. Some of the other green hands actually felt sorry for the little nerd and tried to reason with him, telling him he was just too small to challenge the seniors, and they would kill him. "They wouldn't dare hit me," he kept saying. "My father would sue this damn school and have the FFA chapter closed down."

The next day, the kid from Texas showed up for Ag class cocky and unafraid. Nobody spoke to him, especially the other green hands; he was a walking heat wave. Sometimes, trouble is just like shit; if you get too close, it can rub off on you.

He was sitting alone in the empty classroom, pretending to read a ten-year-old edition of *Progressive Farmer*, when Mr. Clemmons casually walked into the room. The stoop-shouldered little Ag teacher asked him almost casually if he intended to drop out of the FFA chapter. The answer was an emphatic no. Mr. Clemmons said nothing; he made no effort to argue with him. He simply told him to get into the Ag truck and go with the four officers down to the Ag barns. If the kid had any brains at all, he would have remembered that green hands were never allowed to go to the Ag barns until after initiation week and smelled something funny. If that didn't tip him off, then the fact that none of the other Ag boys except the officers, who he had so badly pissed off, were going to the Ag barns with him should have told him something. I really wanted to warn him not to go, but what was the use? He never listened to anybody anyway. I never really figured out if he was just too naive to be real or if he just couldn't bring himself to believe that they would actually mess him up.

When they got him to the Ag barns, the four officers took turns whipping his ass. He came back a bloody mess. Most of the blows he took were in the stomach and kidney area. His abdomen was badly swollen and a mass of ugly dark bruises. He also had a nasty-looking split lip, and one eye was cut open and swollen shut. The officers had really made an example out of him.

The official story was that he tried to drive the tractor without permission, fell off, and was dragged a considerable distance before one of the older boys could rescue him.

The stupid kid went right home and told his parents what had really happened, even though he had been warned that if he told anybody, he would have to fight every senior in the FFA. His parents complained bitterly, contacted the principal and the school board, and finally called in the sheriff who refused to get involved, saying it was a school matter. All their protesting went nowhere. It was his word against the four officers. Mr. Clemmons stated that the kid had told him that very afternoon that he had fallen off the tractor.

His parents were just about as weird as he was. His father was a short, thin man, and his mother was a tall blond woman. The father had an advanced degree in chemistry, and he worked for the petroleum company analyzing soil and water samples. Both of them had been born and raised in California, and, to hear them talk, that made them next to God himself in importance. Everyone believed they were strange. They tended to wear a lot of black clothes, and the mother could often be seen wearing a beret around town. She claimed to be a poet and an artist, but everybody said her paintings looked like shit, and nobody could understand her poetry, which had cuss words in it. She once told me that the family only came to Florida to get out of Texas, a place she thoroughly hated. She said that they intended to move on to Miami, as soon as the pipeline was built that far, and hoped to eventually get back to California. I could never understand people who moved to Florida and then bitched because it is not like where they came from. If it was so damned much better where they came from, why didn't they stay their ass there?

They often came out to the school taking an active interest in their son's education. They tended to complain a lot about how things were at school and seemed to have a messianic complex, like they were white missionaries sent here to convert the savage heathens. I kind of liked the kid from Texas, because he had been to Disneyland. He once invited me to come home with him, and his parents seemed real happy that their son finally had a friend. The entire family was friendly, at least to me, and seemed like nice people who were just badly out of place. I sensed that they were very book-smart people, who just didn't have any common sense. They certainly didn't understand how Union County was and didn't seem to want to learn. To their way of thinking, Union County would have to change to suit them, not the other way around.

The superintendent of schools and the Union County School Board refused to take any action on the matter and declared it over and done with. The parents made a big show of contacting a lawyer and were talking about a lawsuit. However, in private, the lawyers said it was basically just a schoolyard fight, the kind that happens every day, and they didn't want to handle the case. Once the kid realized that the legal system he so proudly believed in was not going to do anything to help him, he decided finally to shut up. The formerly loud-mouthed little know-it-all urged his parents to just let the matter drop.

A week later, his parents withdrew him from Union County High School and enrolled him in a private school for gifted students in Gainesville. His mother drove him the sixty miles to Gainesville every school day and picked him up every afternoon. After he got his driver's license, they bought him a car so he could drive himself. We never saw him much after that. His parents wouldn't allow him to go to any teenage social events or football games in Lake Butler unless they were with him. About a year later, his father managed to get a transfer back to Texas, and he was gone for good.

Up to that point, I had always thought of Mr. Clemmons as just another dumb-ass schoolteacher. However, the ass-whipping that kid took down at the Ag barns showed that he knew full well what was going on in the FFA chapter and either didn't care or personally approved of it. The word around the FFA chapter was that Mr. Clemmons had ordered the kid to be beaten up. I really don't know if that is true or not, and I can't prove it either way, but it sure wouldn't surprise me.

The fourth week of school was known as initiation week; it was when every club on campus, including the FFA, initiated their new members. It was always the four days prior to the first home football game. To most students at Union County High School, initiation week was just four days of fun and games, but, to the Ag boys, initiation week was a test of their fitness to belong to such a valuable and special organization as the FFA.

All the green hands had been ordered to report to the Ag building classroom at seven o'clock Monday night, the first day of initiation week, to begin their initiation ritual or, as the Ag boys called it, "the initiation ordeal."

# Green Hands and Testicles

We had been prepared for initiation week since the first day of school by listening to the older FFA members recounting the horrors of what they had been through. We heard stories of green hands being taken to the agriculture inspection station and being thrown into the tick-dipping trough. They told us we would have to eat a dog turd. We were told that our colon would be probed with a mechanic's grease gun and screwworm medicine injected inside our ass. The trouble with all these stories was not knowing what was the truth and what was just some bullshit meant to scare the hell out of you.

I recalled that when we went to get our football physical, all the varsity players told us they were going to stick a square hypodermic needle in our left testicle in order to get a sperm sample. Some of the guys actually believed it. Others didn't, but were still nervous, because they were young, and this was their first physical of any kind, and they really didn't know for sure.

My macho self-image would not allow me to be afraid whatever was going to happen; they had survived it, and so would I. I kept telling myself that all those stories were just a bunch of nonsense; they could never get away with filling our colon with screwworm medicine or throwing us into the tick-dip trough. However, then, I remembered the smart-ass little kid from Texas; he had not believed that they would beat the living shit out of him either, but they had.

Swallowing my fear, that first Monday of initiation week, I sheepishly reported to the Ag building at seven o'clock to be tested to determine if I was fit to wear the famous blue corduroy jacket of the FFA.

The first night's meeting began deceptively calm and boring. Mr.

Clemmons oversaw the program in the Ag building's classroom and made a long, drawn-out speech about the importance of agriculture to the American economy and how important it was that we carry on this most valuable of all-American vocations. After a round of solemn rituals, including the pledge to the flag and the swearing in of the green hands, Mr. Clemmons carefully explained the significance of the great seal and all the other FFA regalia. The meeting was closed with the official FFA prayer. The whole thing had lasted almost an hour.

I had never been so relieved in all my life. Walking toward the door, I seriously believed that all that was going to happen would be to have to sit through a lot of boring ceremonial nonsense. Just as I approached the door of the classroom, the president of the FFA chapter arose and instructed the green hands to go to the rear of the Ag building and wait until Mr. Clemmons had departed the area.

The president of the FFA chapter was a long, tall, and lanky boy with flaming red hair and freckles. We all called him "Specks," because of his large brownish-red freckles. The vice president was a huge mass of tight muscle with no brain thrown in. His real name was Ernest, but we all called him "Frog." Why? I never really found out. Frog was nineteen years old, because he had to repeat the first and fifth grade. He was at least six feet tall and weighed over two hundred pounds. He had been right tackle on the football team until his grades got so low he became ineligible to play. Frog often spoke with an awkward stutter, but he could whip anybody in the school, and we all knew it.

Basically, Specks was the brains of the chapter, and Frog was the muscle. They worked together like a hand in a glove. Nobody crossed them. In 1960, in Union County High School, if you weren't afraid of anything else, you were afraid of Specks and Frog.

Almost every boy in the FFA chapter had some type of silly nickname. However, we never used the term "nickname." It just didn't sound manly enough to suit us; we called a guy's nickname his "handle." It was something to be proud of; it meant that you were accepted, and it meant you were a "good-old boy." Nobody ever inquired how people got their "handle." It was considered bad form to do so. Guys had "handles" such as Moon Pie, Cornbread, Hound Dog, and Peanut Butter, which probably reflected their likes and dislikes in life, especially food and hunting. Many of the names rhymed with their last names, such as Polly Parrish, Biscuit Brannon, or Cornhole Carter. You weren't given your handle when you joined the FFA; this wasn't Harvard after all. Most of the guys had acquired their nicknames in the elementary grades and still wore them proudly. We even called one slow-witted boy Bugger Nose Butch Bowers, because he went through most of his elementary years with his finger up his nose.

After the end of the official meeting in the classroom, Specks ordered all the green hands to assemble behind the Ag building. The area behind the Ag building was totally isolated from the rest of the school, and what went on there couldn't be seen from the road that ran in front of the Ag building or Lake Street. This was where the two blue Ag trucks were parked under the small pole-barn shed. The entire area was illuminated only by the glow of a single hundred-watt yellow bug lightbulb, perched over the double doors in the rear of the Ag building.

Specks didn't mince words. He told us in no uncertain terms that all the mumbo-jumbo we just sat through didn't mean that we were members of the FFA. The officers would have to approve of each applicant, and, if we didn't pass muster over the next four days, we could all kiss the FFA good-bye. He told us that each night we would assemble at this spot promptly at seven o'clock to perform those tasks directed to us by the FFA officers. Anyone who failed to be here on time or did not show up was automatically dropped from membership in FFA and could no longer take vocational agriculture. He also said that any green hand who didn't want to continue with the initiation process could drop out simply by requesting permission from one of the four officers or Mr. Clemmons. However, by dropping out, you forever forgo the right to be a member of the FFA.

From somewhere behind us, Frog bellowed, "Turn around." In his right hand was a small bucket that smelled strongly of paint and turpentine. Actually, it was a green stain allegedly mixed up using a secret formula that had been passed down through the generations to be used especially for the initiation of green hands. Frog ordered each one of us to step forward and stick our hands into the stain up to our wrists. Under no circumstances were we to remove the stain in any manner before Thursday night, the official end of initiation week. The green stain on our hands would signify to all who saw us that we were candidates to be members of the FFA. The green stain was no surprise to me. I had more or less expected to be forced to stick our hands in some type of green stain, because all of us had seen last year's green hands walking around campus with their hands stained a pale green. However, the next command totally took us by surprise. "DDDDrop yorrr paaants," Frog commanded in his stuttering, nervous speech. Slowly, with a look of incongruity, we unfastened our belts and let our trousers slip down to our knees. "Drawers too," Speck's ordered, taking over from Frog. Slowly, we slid our underwear down to our knees. We were completely bewildered by this unexpected development and had absolutely no idea what was coming next.

Standing there, I realized that there is something about nudity that robs a person of all their human dignity. It also drains a person of all their strength and will to resist. To be naked is to be powerless. After initiation week, I never looked at a *Playboy* magazine the same way again. I could almost feel the nakedness of the women and the terrible feeling of vulnerability and powerlessness that went with it. We were ordered to look straight ahead and not move. We just stood there like idiots, with our pants down around our knees, staring into the inky black darkness of the woods behind the Ag building. I couldn't see what was going on behind us, but I could definitely smell it. It was an odor familiar to my football-playing days. It was a noxious, jelly-like salve, purchased by the gallon by the Athletic Department; it was used to treat pulled muscles, sprained ankles, and torn ligaments.

The jelly-like salve had the commercial name of Heat Balm, and, the second it touched your skin, you were in a type of semiagony. The sadistic balm burned and stung like fire when it was applied to hard muscle tissue, but the pain was manageable. However, should it touch the sensitive area of the penis, anus or testicles, the pain was almost unbearable. No one could endure it without screaming in agony.

With a gloved hand, Frog and Specks masterfully wiped huge handfuls of the Heat Balm on our buttocks and testicles and made sure it was applied to the sensitive anal tissue. Within seconds, we were all on the ground, rolling around on the dirt and gravel driveway behind the Ag building and withering in pain. Some of the green hands wiped loose sand on their burning flesh; others sought out the water spigot and tried to flush the oil-based ointment off their flesh with water. Nothing worked.

While all this was going on, the small group of seniors who had followed us to the rear of the Ag building was cracking up with laughter. They were almost gleeful in their enjoyment of what was going on. One of their perks as members of the senior class was the right to observe green hands being chemically tortured, and they loved it.

Without realizing it at the time, we were fulfilling an ancient southern ritual brought over from Europe by the earliest of our ancestors. It was part of the "cult of cruelty" that was supposed to turn weak young boys into tough men and ferocious warriors. In the dark and misty reaches of pre-Christian Europe, in the tribal communities of the seminomadic Celtic people, there was no room for weaklings. Everyone had to be tough and merciless. When these people migrated to America and began their slave-holding plantations in the frontier South, the same truths applied. Weakness and gentleness could not be tolerated when dealing with either Negro slaves or the painted Indian warriors just beyond the pale of white settlement. It was absolutely imperative that young southern white men be capable of unspeakable acts of cruelty and barbarism and at least pretend that they actually enjoyed it.

Years later, I would see pictures of Negroes who had been lynched and castrated, hanging in the dark night air from the limbs of a moss-draped oak tree. A gleeful crowd would surround the dangling dead bodies looking white faces, illuminated in the primitive glow of an ancient photoflash. They posed with the corpse much like a hunter poses with the carcass of a deer.

Later in life, I often stared hard into those smiling faces and twinkling eyes. I was wondering if I could see myself. By that time, I had survived my childhood and had been to Vietnam. I knew the depths of my own depravity, but it is hard to see the evil within yourself; you can see it easier reflected in others. As I looked at the faces in the photograph, I knew full well I had seen them many times before in the eyes of my parents; my teachers; my classmates; American soldiers on a drunken, whoring, three-day pass in Saigon; and behind the Ag building the first night of initiation week.

I got home shortly after nine o'clock and immediately showered. However, the water was little relief from my agony. It felt like my testicles were burning off. It was impossible to sleep that night. I kept getting up and taking a shower over and over again, provoking a heated discussion with my mother. She wanted to know what was wrong, but I couldn't break the FFA code of silence. Just before daylight, the burning ceased enough so I finally drifted off to sleep. It was a brief and fitful rest that came to an abrupt end when my alarm clock went off.

That day at school was pure hell. To try and sit still and pay attention in class with your ass literally on fire were super-human feats. Many of the green hands didn't come to school that day, and I watched in silence as one of them at a time asked to go to the office and call home sick. Finally, around third period, I decided to join them. I called my mother and lied, saying that I had diarrhea.

The seniors were tying to keep a close eye on us to see if any of us would wash out or break the code of silence. They were not happy that so many of us were going home sick. They were afraid that the teachers would get suspicious or that one of the green hand's parents would call the principal and complain. After the incident with the little kid from Texas, Mr. Clemmons was nervous and had warned the seniors not to go too far.

As I was sitting on the concrete steps in the front of the school waiting for my mother, a couple of the seniors, along with Specks and Frog, came around the corner. They glared down at me in disgust.

"You wimping out," Specks said.

"Nope," I lied, "doctor's appointment."

"For what?" he laughed. "To get that damn Heat Balm off your ass?"

I didn't think it was funny. I was still burning, although the pain was now more of a dull ache than excruciating misery. Before they left, Frog looked at me with what might have been pity in his eyes, but I couldn't tell for sure. Specks spoke softly, almost in a whisper.

"You know you really don't have to take this shit; all you have to do is come see us and say you've had enough. It's really easy. Later on, you'll have to sign a letter of resignation in Mr. Clemmons' office, but just your say-so will stop the pain."

I honestly think he was trying to help me, but I rejected his advice. I wasn't about to wimp out now. Hundreds of other boys had gone through the FFA initiation and survived, so would I. That was what I told myself. I had bought into the bullshit. No pain no gain. Winners never quit; quitters never win. First in football and now with this, I was really a believer; they had me brainwashed. Yet, despite it all, deep inside, I still had my doubts. The doubts would come out of my intellect, my logic, and my common sense, something that was more of a hindrance than a help. I would have to shove the doubts back in and suppress the thinking part of me in favor of the overwhelming desire of every teenager to fit in, to be part of the group.

I sat there on the steps for a long time watching them walk off. Did I really need that damn blue corduroy jacket to find a girlfriend? I really had no interest in agriculture, so why was I joining this stupid-ass club? Why was I putting up with all this bullshit? It took me almost the rest of my life to figure all this out; to decide in my own mind why I somehow needed to make it through that stupid FFA initiation? In the long run, one thing was obvious; it really had nothing to do with sex or agriculture. It had to do with whether or not I was worthy. I had already been a failure at football, and my grades were nothing to brag about. Deep within myself, I was afraid of failure, of not being as good as everybody else. I had to prove to myself that I was as tough as the guys who had gone through all this last year.

In the early fall of 1960, nobody in Union County believed in the equality of the human species, at least no white people did. I couldn't speak for the nonwhite citizens of Union County, because I had so little contact with them. When I did have contact with them, we sure didn't talk about whether or not all men were created equal.

I had a Sunday school teacher who once told me that equality meant that on Judgment Day, we would all be judged equally and fairly by God. She said it had nothing to do with this world, and it certainly didn't have anything to do with the relationship between the races. She said that God had made colored people and white people different for a reason. It was to keep us apart. Skin color was God's way of saying don't have anything to do with these people. She taught us that the Bible preached "like kind after like kind." Race mixing was a sin in the eyes of God.

Even if we were not thoroughly indoctrinated against it, equality was totally illogical in Union County. Only two miles down the road from the Ag building was the "Colored School." It was officially know as the Union County Consolidated School, but we all simply referred to it as the "Colored School." It was where the Negro children of Union County sat in segregated and overcrowded classrooms, trying to get a "separate but equal" education.

The Ag boys were often called upon to go down to the "Colored School," delivering textbooks, desks, and athletic equipment. The "colored children" (that was the polite term we used at the time) had everything we had, just as soon as we wore it out. After the white students had used a certain textbook for a number of years and it was replaced by a new textbook, the Ag boys were summoned to load the old textbooks into the back of one of the blue Ag trucks and carry them down to the "Colored School." The same policy was followed for anything else we no longer had any use for, such as desks, library books, bookshelves, football uniforms, and even old basketball and baseball equipment.

When we discovered that a certain textbook was scheduled to be sent to the "Colored School" the next year, we would write "Nigger" or "Jungle Bunny" in large block letters inside the pages. We always wrote in ink, so the black children couldn't erase it. To some, that wasn't enough; they would put chewing tobacco spit, bubble gum, and sometimes even urine or human excrement between the pages.

The people who did this said it was their way of protesting integration and telling that "gawddamned Martin Luther 'Coon' what we thought of him." It was our way of supporting Governor Faubas in Arkansas and racial segregation in Alabama. Some of the guys said by doing this, "damned niggers" would learn to stay in their place.

However, I really think it was more fundamental than that. It always seemed to me that in Union County, nothing was fun unless it hurt somebody or held them up for embarrassment and humiliation. It really made no difference if we were hunting coons, going to a cockfight, or writing "Nigger" in a textbook; the purpose was the same. It was our way of having fun.

My first trip down to the "Colored School" came shortly after the school purchased a new riding lawn mower. Mr. Clemmons told us to load the old push mower onto the back of one of the Ag trucks, and take it down to the Colored School. At the last minute, he decided to go with us.

The principal of the Colored School was an elderly man with snow-white hair and several gold teeth. He wore a dirty white shirt and wrinkled black pants that were shiny with wear and age. His black skin was badly wrinkled, but it had a deep ebony sheen to it that almost glowed in the bright Florida sunshine. I remember how the Negro schoolteachers, all of whom were women, were dressed like they were on their way to church on Sunday morning. They had on high heels, stockings, and modest below-the-knee dresses. The black children were quiet and well behaved. The teachers were also respectful and polite; yet, anybody with any perception at all could detect the vast amount of resentment just below the surface. To look into those small eyes was to behold a vast amount of repressed anger.

I will never forget the look of quiet, suppressed embarrassment on the faces of the Negro children, as Mr. Clemmons made one of his long, drawn-out speeches explaining to the assembled group of children how lucky they were to be getting this fine "new" lawn mower. The elderly black principal stood up and groveled, thanking Mr. Clemmons over and over for this "fine new lawn mower." Mr. Clemmons just ate it up; he glowed in the presence of such flattery. I now knew why he came along. He loved having these people grovel at his feet. He loved having a respectful captive audience to listen to his bullshit. All in all, it was a pathetic sight.

On the way back to the Ag building, we were given a lecture from Mr. Clemmons on how to deal with "colored people."

"Now, those are good niggers," he lamented. "If all the niggers were like them, then everything would be all right. You see they don't want to integrate, they are happy right where they are."

African American people were a total enigma to us. We honestly didn't understand what the civil rights movement was all about. We didn't understand why they wanted to go to school with us, when we didn't want to go to school with them. It was illogical to us. Why would somebody want to be someplace they weren't wanted? It was like the stupid little kid from Texas. What the hell was wrong with him? The civil rights movement was more than just something we were opposed to; it was something totally incomprehensible, and it was something we just couldn't fathom, like the size of Jupiter or the concept of light-years.

We really didn't understand women either. We loved women. We loved our mothers, our sisters, our aunts, our grandmothers, and our girlfriends. However, there was one thing that separated us from women. Women were weak and sensitive. They needed protecting, and that made them inferior.

When I played football, anytime we dropped a pass, fumbled the football or missed a tackle, the coach would bellow like an old bull, "You guys play like a bunch of little girls."

The worse thing you could call someone on the football team was "a little girl." It was a term we used over and over. The coach would say, you run "like a little girl;" you block "like a little girl;" and you tackle "like a little girl." One of the football coach's favorite training techniques was to force a boy to drop his pants exposing his genitals to prove he wasn't "a little girl." Even as stupid as most of us were, after awhile, the message got through; the worse thing on earth was to be a female, "a little girl."

Male supremacy, like racial supremacy, wasn't necessarily taught to us; it was something that was just pointed out, much like a teacher might point out a certain star in the Milky Way. We were always admonished to "act like you've got two between your legs."

Bravery was associated with testicles. When someone wanted to pay you a compliment, he would say, "That guy's got balls." We all knew that girls didn't have balls, so that automatically made them inferior. Of course, we all knew, almost instinctively, that "having balls" was not just a physical thing; it was also a matter of attitude, what the military called "guts" or "intestinal fortitude."

Men obtained their supremacy over women, black people, Asians, Indians, integrationist nigger lovers, or anyone else we were taught to hate and fear through strength. Strength showed you had balls, and strength was displayed through cruelty. Boys were superior to girls, whites were superior to blacks, and some white boys were superior to other white boys. That was the belief system we lived under. The most important thing in life was not to be among the weaker class. We ignored what it said in the Declaration of Independence, the Constitution, and even the Bible. All these lofty documents were all just bullshit compared to what our fathers and peers taught us. It was a higher law. It was the law of nature that took precedence over everything else. It was the law of male bonding and white supremacy.

Anything weak or sensitive was an anathema to us. I spent my whole childhood and adolescence pretending that I wasn't afraid, spurning any type of sensitivity and always putting on a boisterous display of strength. Once during that first week of school, two of the Ag boys caught a gopher tortoise behind the Ag building. I voluntarily stepped forward and stomped it to death with the heel of my boot, just to prove to the other Ag boys that I was as tough as they were. One of our favorite expressions was, "He would pull the eyeballs out of a puppy dog's head."

There were some boys in our school who were weak, sensitive, or afraid. These things we could not be tolerated. These things made them "girl like" and inferior; they served no purpose for the Ag boys other than to be their victims. To us, weakness and cruelty went together like bread and butter. The weak, the sensitive, and the afraid were the ones the Ag boys spit chewing tobacco juice on, popped with wet towels in the gym, and bullied in the hallway.

One of the Ag boy's favorite tricks to gain status as a tough guy was to walk up to a kid they knew would never fight back and say, "I hear you been saying you want to whip my ass." This was no fun unless it was done in front of a crowd of other kids; the more other Ag boys in the crowd, the better.

The terrified little kid would protest strongly and stammer with cold terror in his eyes that he had never uttered such a terrible statement. The blue-jacketed bully would respond by pushing him backwards a couple of times to show who was in charge. Then, he would end the confrontation by issuing a stern warning that he had better watch his mouth and that anytime he wanted to fight, just to let you know.

Of course, all this was just bullshit. Everyone knew deep down inside their souls that the guy in the blue jacket was really a coward and that the only reason he picked on the kid was because you knew he was afraid and would not fight. He never said he wanted to whip anybody's ass, and, if he had offered to fight, the bully would have found some way to get out of it. However, it never happened that way, because they chose their victims carefully. That way, the bully could walk away from the confrontation with a jaunty strut, knowing that he had indeed increased his reputation for being a real badass. Ironically, this meant there was far less likelihood of him ever actually having to fight someone. Once everyone knew you would actually fight, nobody ever tried to bully you.

The Ag boys carried their cruelty into the classroom. I had seen certain teachers, almost always female and mostly substitutes, actually begin to cry in class because of the disruptions of the Ag boys. They farted in class, threw spit balls, smart mouthed, talked back, and threatened to beat up any student who complained or told on them.

That night, I summoned up all my strength to return to the Ag building for the second night of initiation. My mother dropped me off at the curb, and I walked the half a block to the Ag building. As I walked up the gravel driveway that bent behind the Ag building, I noted that the sun was already going down. I chanced a glance at my watch and noted it was only a little before seven o'clock, but it was almost dark already. Fall seemed to be coming early; it felt like only a few days ago we were in the intense heat of Florida summer, and the sun stayed in the sky until eight or nine o'clock.

The air was already beginning to take on that slightly damp, fall chill that told us that winter would soon be upon us.

I remember that for the first time that school year, I had put on a long-sleeved cotton shirt. I always wore it out over my jeans, open down the front, showing off my bright white t-shirt. My jeans were chosen with much care; they were always Levi's and had one-inch, turned-up cuffs that rode just over the laces of my white sneakers. Some of the Ag boys wore high-topped cowboy boots; we called them cockroach killers, because of their pointed toes that allowed you to get the little buggers when they ran into a corner. I liked the pull on Wellington work boots and usually wore them to school every other day. In the summer, we wore nothing but t-shirts, which were always white. We never wore colored t-shirts or t-shirts with logos or advertisements. That day had not yet come.

When the weather turned nippy, we put on cotton work shirts, usually plaid but sometimes with vertical stripes. Those who had them wore either their gold football jacket or the blue corduroy FFA colors. Since I had neither, I wore a bate James Dean style windbreaker. I wanted a motorcycle leather jacket, but my parents refused to let me buy one with my tobacco money. They claimed it would make me look too much like a hoodlum. Hell, that was the whole idea.

I was a greaser or punk, back when the word punk didn't mean a queer like it does today. That meant that I had long hair and combed it in an Elvis Presley pompadour with a ducktail. I kept it under control with vast quantities of Vitalis that gave my hair that particular odor that the girls seemed to like. It was all right to have a flattop or GI buzz cut, but those who played football usually wore them. Compared to what was to come, our hair was fairly short. However, to our parents—who always wore the familiar over-forty, white sidewall, every two weeks, store-bought haircuts—our hair was way too long.

When I rounded the corner of the Ag building, I saw the other green hands standing sheepishly, hands in their pockets, waiting for the seniors to show up to begin our second night of torment. We knew from talking to some of the other boys that we were in for another dose of the Heat Balm, and, to be truthful, I didn't think I could stand it. This was not like Monday night when we were all a little cocky, bolstering up each other's courage with brave talk. On Tuesday night, we were all glum and introspective; we knew what we were in for and were all asking ourselves the same question. Can we hack it?

Specks, Frog, and the other seniors came out the back door of the Ag building in a huff. Specks' eyes were alive with anger.

"You fucking bunch of little pussies," he growled.

Specks flew into a verbal assault on us for being weaklings and cowards. He kept saying "little pussies" over and over again.

At first, I really didn't notice why he was so all fired up, but, then suddenly, it dawned on me. Five of the previous night's green hands were absent. They had approached Mr. Clemmons one at a time during the school day and told him they wanted out.

One of the green hands' mothers had brow beat him, until he told her about the Heat Balm, and she was furious. She called Mr. Clemmons and cussed him out over the telephone. As soon as he hung up, Mr. Clemmons called in the officers and gave them pure hell. He accused Specks of not being in control of things and not instilling enough fear into our hearts so we wouldn't go snitching to our mothers about how bad we had been treated.

Specks was fired up after the chewing out. He spent the whole afternoon stewing in his own frustration, thinking what he was going to say to us, much like a politician rehearsing an important campaign speech. When Specks finally addressed us that evening, he was well prepared.

He paced back and forth, cussing and spitting. He preached to us like he was our daddy or something. He began by saying that the FFA was one of the great organizations of all time, and it should be our pleasure to be in it. He also explained to us, again, that if we ever dropped out, we could never come back.

"Furthermore," Specks screamed, "One of you miserable fuckers has ratted about the Heat Balm. Only a little pussy would even try to drop out, and only a low-down, ass wipe little pussy would go tell his mother about what went on at FFA meetings. Each one of you has sworn to withhold the secrets of the FFA. If you don't want to be in our organization, just say so, but, gawddamnit, don't go home crying to you fucking mama. I promise each one of you that the little motherfucker who told on us today will have the shit beat out of him before this week is out. I personally will stomp his ass into the ground right through the concrete floor of the school, at the earliest opportunity."

After Specks finished his rant, we got on with the initiation. It really wasn't too bad, at least not as bad as I thought it would be listening to him cuss and rave on. They painted our other hand green, and, of course, we got another dose of the Heat Balm. However, this time, they kept it on our buttocks and lower backs and avoided the genitals. It burnt at first, but then slowly the pain went away. It wasn't any worse than having it smeared on your sore muscles during football practice. Obviously, everybody didn't agree with me, because the next morning, three more green hands decided they no longer wanted to be part of the FFA.

Wednesday night, it was raining, so we expected things to be short, and they were. However, there was one surprise. We were all startled to see the familiar bucket of green paint sitting at the feet of the four FFA officers. We all wondered what else there was to paint, since both our hands were already green. My bet was that they would put some paint on our nose or ears or something like that to further humiliate us. However, I was wrong.

"Drop your damned pants," Specks yelled out.

Slowly, we undid our pants and let our jeans slide down our legs until they were neatly bunched around our ankles.

"Drawers too," Frog bellowed.

We stood in terror as we finally realized what they were going to paint.

With one or two masterful strokes of the brush, we now had green testicles to go with our green hands. I was thankful they hadn't chosen to paint our penis.

Specks stood before the group of inductees and almost proudly announced that already eight of the original twenty inductees had dropped out. He promised us that tomorrow night the officers and upperclassmen of the FFA intended to separate the men from the boys. He told us to be here at seven o'clock sharp, nobody late. The Wednesday night festivities were finished with another dose of the Heat Balm. It was smeared all over our buttocks, legs, armpits, and anuses. In only a few seconds, we were again in horrible pain.

Tradition dictated that the fourth week of the school year, the four days before the first home football game, was to be the official time for all club initiations. All the initiations must be completed before Friday morning, because the football coach didn't want the team distracted by any silliness on the eve of the first home game. By Friday morning, all signs of the initiations were to be gone, and a mood of absolute seriousness and school spirit was to descend upon the campus. All the clubs strictly enforced the rule, even the FFA. Nobody wanted to be blamed for the football team losing their first home game. Such an onus would be too much to bear in this football-obsessed little community.

You really didn't feel silly running around the school with your hands painted green, simply because everyone else was also doing something equally ridiculous. The girls in the Science Club had to come to school each day with their hair rolled around test tubes. The Science Club members had to wear a foul-smelling chemical poultice around their necks. Beta Club inductees had to attend school that week with their noses painted blue. Members of the FHA came dressed like Minnie Pearl.

Only the stoic and scholarly Library Club failed to have some form of initiation humiliation. The school librarian, Mrs. Doric, was known to be a woman of few smiles, who really didn't approve of any type of nonsense. Checking out a book was too serious a responsibility to be entrusted to those prone to childish pranks.

I had heard all kinds of stories that week from older boys about what was going to happen to us the final night of the FFA initiations. I tried to write them off as exaggerations. However, after what I had already experienced, I was beginning to have second thoughts. Two more freshmen that day notified Specks that they would not be at the initiation Thursday evening. They all protested that their parents made them quit and that they really wanted to go on. Specks simply looked at them with disgust and told them to go get a class change form from Mr. Clemmons and to wash the paint off their hands with mineral spirits, since he didn't want the rest of the school to think such "little girls" were candidates to be members of the FFA.

All that week, when we met at the Ag building, only the seniors and FFA officers had been present. It was a perk of their rank and status that they could be present every day of the initiations. However, that didn't mean that the rest of the FFA members, the juniors and sophomores, were going to be left out. They made that week a living hell for the green hands.

During initiation week, all the green hands came to fear and hate the sight of the familiar blue corduroy FFA jacket. The more human among them would come up behind us and knock our books out of our hands, and then they would go away laughing. The more sadistic would give us a fresh kick in the butt when we reached down to pick them up. Sometimes, a particularly brutish bunch of juniors would give you a sharp slap in the testicles with the back of an open hand. That cruel blow would always make you double up in agony. By the time you recovered, the upperclassmen would be long gone, and you would probably be late to class.

If you left your textbooks unattended for a second, you would return to find them covered with tobacco spit. The books might also have bubble gum and spit inside the pages. Somehow, the upperclassmen managed to get the combination for all of the green hand's hall and gym lockers. I opened my hall locker one day and found a fresh, damp pile of cow shit sitting on top of my notebooks. Other boys, who took physical education or went out for sports, opened their gym lockers to find that someone had covered their gym clothes with urine or had put human excrement inside their gym shoes and jock straps.

All of this went totally unnoticed by the teachers and the principal who seemed to accept it as a normal part of the school year. Unless something got totally out of hand, they generally didn't interfere. The school was overflowing with all kinds of silly nonsense that week.

A girl was found tied to a chair in the biology lab. Someone had removed the small glass soap containers over the wash basins in the boy's restroom and replaced the yellow hand washing soap with urine. Just enough soap was left in the container to make it lather up as usual, but, then, you detected the odor, and, for the rest of the day, your hands smelled like piss.

Someone had brought a box of fudge to the FFA class laced with laxatives and required each freshmen girl to eat a piece. By noon, dozens of terrified girls were asking to go to the restroom. The sight of all these girls, dressed like Minnie Pearl, walking briskly down the hall created a tidal wave of snickers and laughter throughout the school. When they got to the girl's restroom, they discovered that all the rolls of toilet paper had been removed, soaked in water and bleach, and then carefully replaced on their rollers. The girls had no choice but to wipe their ass with the contaminated rolls of paper. Most of the time when you saw a freshman FHA girl dressed like Minnie Pearl, she had a noticeable odor of bleach about her that lingered for several seconds after she passed.

After the word got out, you would see Minnie Pearl look-alikes scurrying down the hall with handfuls of notebook paper. Boys would yell for them to make sure they didn't wipe with their homework.

In the band room restroom, the toilet seats were covered with wet shoe polish. In the gym, the toilet seats were covered with the terrible Heat Balm. All in all, it was a bad week to have a bowel movement.

On Thursday night, as ordered, promptly at seven o'clock, we assembled in the growing twilight in the rear of the Ag building. Unlike the other nights, the entire membership of the chapter was on hand, minus of course Mr. Clemmons. It was a sea of blue corduroy jackets. The sophomores, who had undergone this same ritual only one year ago, seemed particularly eager to see us suffer.

The whole thing began with a ridiculous kangaroo court held in the classroom. Specks sat proudly under the great seal, dispensing justice to those green hands accused of wrongdoing; in other words, all of us. I was found guilty of farting in front of the great seal of the FFA. Another boy was accused of sexually fondling the owl. Another was convicted of doing something disgusting with an ear of corn.

After we had all been legally found guilty of some serious crime, we were sentenced to undergo the rites of initiation. At this point, two of the boys decided they didn't want to continue and asked Specks if they could withdraw. They were refused. The sentinel, who stood by the door, proclaimed that they had come too far and knew too many of the deepest secrets of the FFA to withdraw.

The truth was the chapter needed a certain number of freshmen to join each year to replace the graduating seniors, and that was the number of terrified freshmen still standing in the classroom. We had started the school year with twenty-one green hands, and now there were only ten left. This worried Mr. Clemmons; so he ordered Specks and Frog not to let anyone else drop out. This little bit of truth might have given me hope, except that I didn't know it. If I had known, I might have assumed that since they needed us to keep the enrollment of the chapter at an even level, maybe the rest of the evening would be a lark or at least not as bad as I thought it would be. If I did think that, I would have been dead wrong.

Specks then ordered the green hands to strip buck naked, not a stitch of clothes on; we even had to remove our wristwatches. We were told to fold our clothes neatly and stack them in an orderly manner on the desk in front of the great seal, like some type of grotesque offerings to the gods of vocational agriculture. Frog said that this was so we could easily find them once we got back. This made me feel a little better; at least they intended to let us live to retrieve our clothes. I had no idea at the time that I would not see my clothes again that night.

We went outside, and all ten of the green hands piled into the back of the paneled Ag truck. It had high wooden slat side panels that would give us some privacy in our nakedness. The kangaroo court in the Ag building had taken long enough, so it was now completely dark, and, as long as we didn't stand up and remained squatted down in the back of the truck, nobody should be able to see us.

The high top, wooden side panels on the sides of the truck bed were normally used to hold in the hogs and cows that were being transported to the livestock market in Gainesville. They could be easily removed by sliding them up and out of the special recesses built into the truck bed. Mr. Clemmons liked to leave the side panels on the truck all the time, because the trucks were used on a daily basis to transport the Ag boys down to the barns, and he didn't want any of us falling out of the back of the truck and getting killed. As he used to say, "That would mean a whole lot of extra paperwork for me to fill out." We didn't realize it at the time, but the high side panels had a more sinister purpose than just to give us some privacy and hold in cows on the way to the stock market. They were intended to deflect lit cigarette butts thrown back on us from the three seniors sitting in the front of the truck.

The first one came flying in shortly after we had pulled out onto the road that ran in front of the school. It had a high arch trajectory and landed on the right shoulder of one of the boys near the back tailgate. However, the evil thing wasn't finished doing its damage yet. It rolled off his shoulder and fell directly on the calf of my right leg. It then bounced onto the top of another boy's foot, before finally coming to rest on the floor of the truck, where another green hand stepped back on it, finally crushing out the burning cigarette with his bare foot. Each green hand touched by the burning cigarette let out a sharp cry of pain, followed by a barrage of profane curses and oaths.

We were hunched down in the back of the truck so tightly that we could barely move. There was nowhere to go to flee the burning missiles coming from the front cab, short of leaping out of the moving truck. When the second cigarette came flying at us from the front cab, we all panicked and started jumping around like crazy. That only made it worse. Our erratic movements batted the hot cigarette all over the place, burning more people than it would have if we just let it fall naturally. We quickly learned to watch for the trajectory of the glowing hot missile and try to deflect it with the backs of our hands. If it landed on the floor, we tried not to move, but let the boy nearest the butt pick it up and push it out through the cracks in the wooden side panels.

The three seniors sitting in the cab of the truck continued to barrage us with cigarette butts all evening. Some of them we were able to deflect; others we could not. Before the evening was very old, each green hand had a half dozen or more stinging cigarette burns. The worst part came when the second Ag truck, filled with smoking upperclassmen, pulled up next to us when we stopped for a red light. They pelted us with dozens of lit cigarettes at one time. It was impossible to dodge them all, and every one of us came out of the altercation badly burned.

We were so busy dodging cigarette butts that we paid little attention to where we were going. When the cigarette butt barrage ceased long enough to let us look around, we could see that we were approaching Union County's one and only skating rink that sat beside the muddy lake from which the town of Lake Butler took its name.

The Lakeside skating rink was the major teenage hangout on the weekends, but it was usually closed on school nights. We were really surprised to see it lit up on a Thursday night. It was a well-publicized fact that the skating rink was available for private parties on weeknights, and, apparently, the FFA chapter had rented it for the last night of initiation week.

The pickup truck backed up as close as it could get to the open double doors at the front entrance of the skating rink. We were ordered to run inside despite our nudity. Completely naked, we piled out of the truck rushing up the sidewalk into the large building, hopefully before any passing motorist could see us. Clutching my green testicles, I sprinted into the building, stubbing my little toe on the threshold of the front door as I entered the building. I tried to immediately squat behind the door to hide my nakedness and wait for the throbbing pain in my foot to go away, but Frog grabbed my arm and jerked me like a wet rag doll from my hiding place and pushed me onto the skating rink floor.

I hardly took notice at the time, but as soon as the green hands got out of the rear of the Ag truck, a group of sophomores took their place in the back of the vehicle, and then the truck quickly sped off. Each of the sophomores in the back of the truck was wearing coveralls and rubber boots. Three of them were holding shovels.

Inside the skating rink, Specks quickly took control of the situation ordering us to line up and pick out a pair of roller skates our size, from the rows of skate shoes that were neatly stacked behind the rental counter. When several boys complained that they couldn't skate, Specks and Frog smiled a sadistic little smile, and the rest of the Ag boys snickered.

Specks told us that before we could become members of the FFA, we would have to prove our fitness by skating three times around the skating rink completely naked from the ankles up.

I had never been on roller skates before in my life, although I was a regular hanger-outer down at the skating rink. The skating rink was a strange type of place. Every Friday and Saturday night, almost every teenager in Lake Butler would be there. However, very few of them would actually be skating. The rest, like myself, more or less just hung out there simply because there was absolutely no other place in Union County for a teenager to go. They had bleachers on both sides of the skating rink floor, where people could sit and watch the other people skate. They sold the usual array of soft drinks, hot dogs, potato chips, and candy in a small concession stand next to where you rented your skates. The skating rink charged a dollar entrance fee, even to those who didn't skate; the people who ran the skating rink were making money even off the fairly large group of teenagers, like me, who just hung out.

To those of us who didn't skate, there was still plenty to do. They had pinball machines, a large Wurlitzer jukebox, and the concession stand. We would always sneak outside to have a smoke, and somebody usually had a half pint bottle of Early Times or Old Crow whiskey. The ultimate dream of every boy going to the skating rink was to find a girl and convince her to take a walk out onto the city dock.

It might seem like everything in Union County is shaped like a squared-off U, but that wasn't really accurate. However, the two most important places for us, the high school and the city dock, both were. The dock ran out almost a hundred feet into the inky darkness over the lake water. It then ran another hundred yards parallel to the shore before turning back toward a small beach created by dumping white sand on top of the jet-black lake mud. The three-sided square dock formed a fairly shallow swimming area, which allowed parents to keep an eye out for alligators and water moccasins, which often invaded the swimming area inside the dock.

The swimming area had its share of critics. The water was so dark and black you couldn't see six inches underwater, and the floor of the lake was nothing but swampy ooze that was disgusting when you stepped on it. Many people refused to let their children swim in the lake, fearing not only alligators and water moccasins, but also ear and eye infections from the muddy water.

However, to the teenage population of Union County hanging out at the skating rink on Friday and Saturday nights, the dock was a perfect make-out place. There were wooden benches on the dock, and, if you were lucky, maybe you could get in a little smooching. Maybe, if you were really lucky, you could get a titty feel or maybe even get your finger wet.

In order to discourage this type of immoral sexual interaction among the youth of Union County, the Lake Butler City Council passed an ordinance closing the dock after dark. The law was applauded by the guardians of public morality, until somebody realized there was really no way to close a dock. It didn't exactly have a front door that you could padlock, and the no trespassing signs were totally ignored. The high sheriff with his one lone deputy gave the city council firm notice that they weren't about to spend every Friday and Saturday night patrolling the dock. The sheriff's office had too many drunk drivers and barroom brawls for that. The Florida highway patrolman assigned to Union County said his job was to catch speeders, not guard the city dock.

Eventually, the city council hired a part-time city policeman, who only worked on Friday and Saturday nights. However, the man they hired was over sixty years old and a lazy cuss. He almost never got out of his car, which was a 1955 Ford six-cylinder sedan, painted black with a kind of generic police badge on the side. The slow-moving vehicle didn't even have a radio and siren.

The city council also installed a series of powerful spotlights that lit up the area around the dock, but, for some reason, they kept getting busted out.

Eventually, the city council had to cut back the city policeman's hours, because of a short fall in tax revenue caused by a busted water pipe. They couldn't pay him for two nights a week and still fix the broken pipe, unless they raised taxes. After a lengthy debate, where the only quick decision made was not to raise taxes, the council decided to cut back the policeman's hours, having him work only one night a week. Faced with a 50 percent loss in salary, the policeman flat refused to work the reduced hours. After a heated argument, he got mad and quit. The city council tried to hire someone else, but it is kind of hard to find a good, one-night-a-week police officer. The next guy they hired must have been seventy-five years old, if he was of drinking age. He kept dozing off while sitting in the police car. One night, while he was sleeping, someone made off with all four of the police car's hubcaps. After a heart-to-heart talk with the city council members, he resigned, citing poor health. The next guy was fired, because he came to work drunk one Saturday night and drove the police car into a pine tree and smashed out the right front headlight. In 1960, the post of city policeman had gone begging for over two years. The black Ford police car sat behind the fire station rusting away, with all four tires flat and the front headlight still unrepaired. Faced with the reality that guarding the sexual morals of Union County's youth was going to cost more money than they had to spend, the guardians of decency on the city council sort of gave up and stopped worrying about it.

The fact that I didn't know how to skate was a closely guarded secret. I never admitted it, and I wasn't about to go out and try to learn to skate, falling down over and over, with all my friends watching and laughing. Living out in the country the way I did, there wasn't anyplace to learn in private. It's pretty hard to learn to skate on a dirt road. Most of the other teenage boys in Union County, and especially those in the FFA, were in the same shape as me, not knowing but never admitting it.

However, tonight I had to skate. A group of seniors pushed me onto the floor where I immediately fell down with a hard thud. Once I stood up, I was slapped with a wooden paddle and chased around the rink until I fell down again. I would get up, only to get swatted again, causing me to fall down again. One freshman, a large boy for his age, got tired of this treatment and began throwing punches. He was immediately pounced upon by a half-dozen seniors who were much larger and tougher than he was. They made an example of him, so none of the rest of us would get the same idea. The poor guy was beaten to a pulp and was left lying limp as a wet dish rag on the skating rink floor.

We didn't see him again for the rest of the night. In fact, we didn't see him until Tuesday of the next week. We saw him standing outside the principal's office. He had two black eyes and a split lip. However, unlike the kid from Texas, he had steadfastly refused to tell his parents, the principal, or anybody else what had really happened.

He claimed that he had only fallen off of a tractor. His parents had talked to the little snitch from Texas' parents, and they didn't believe the tractor story. They were church-going folks who would not tolerate a rebellious and untruthful son. They decided to withdraw him from school and send him someplace where he could get a proper education and learn traditional Christian values, especially, "Honor thy father and thy mother."

A group of the Ag boys showed up and talked to him for only a few minutes in the hallway. He said that his parents were sending him to a Christian school someplace up in north Georgia. All the Ag boys slapped him on the back and congratulated him for keeping his mouth shut. They told him he was a real stand-up guy. He came back to Union County High School at the beginning of our sophomore year and was immediately made a member of the FFA. The next year, he was vice president. It was his honor for keeping his mouth shut. No member of the sacred fraternity of Ag boys ever wore his blue corduroy jacket with more pride.

All during the time we were in the skating rink, the seniors seemed distracted by something. After the fight, they stopped hitting us with the paddles, so all I had to worry about was making my three laps around the skating rink. Even without being hit, I must have fallen down a dozen or more times. Every time I fell down, I instantly put down my hands to break by fall, and soon the palms of my hands were covered with ugly, bloody splinters from the cheap wooden floor of the skating rink. Finally, I had, through trial and much error, finally finished my third circle around the rink.

After our ordeal on skates ended, the seniors allowed us to sit down to remove our skating shoes and rest. I used this valuable time to get myself a drink of water and go to the restroom and try to pull some of the splinters out of my hands and buttocks.

I felt miserable. I now had big purple bruises on top of my cigarette burns. I was tired, and, with the sweat drying on my body, I suddenly began to feel cold. I also had a growing sense of rage and frustration. I had enough of this nonsense, and I wanted to go home. However, the worst part was not knowing what to expect next; it was the uncertainty that really chewed at my guts.

Our rest was interrupted by the sound of a truck horn blowing outside the skating rink. Again, Specks took control and ordered us to line up by the door. He explained that as soon as he gave the word, the trucks would pull out and begin to drive away. Our mission was to run out of the skating rink as fast as we could and go and catch the truck before it reached the end of the road. Specks said that anyone who failed to catch the truck would be left behind naked at the skating rink. Since the idea of being left naked at the closed skating rink didn't seem like fun, we all lined up at the door determined to be the first one in the truck.

Specks' shrill cry went out, and we all flew through the double doors of the skating rink and ran as fast as we could to catch the blue Ag truck as it began to slowly roll forward and move down the road that led away from the skating rink, back toward town. The truck was not moving very fast, but, at the same time, we were all running barefooted on a paved road; every step was pure agony. The truck could have easily pulled off and left us, but it seemed that the driver was going just fast enough to stay just beyond our grasp. As the truck neared the first intersection, it continued to slow until the first green hand finally reached the back bumper of the truck and propelled himself inside, rolling head first into the back of the truck with his bare white legs flying in the air.

I caught up with the truck just before it reached the stop sign. I put my hands on the tailgate, placed one foot on the rear bumper, and, with all my strength, hurled myself into the back of the truck. I landed on my back, near the wooden sideboards on the passenger side. As soon as I landed, another green hand came flying over the top of the tailgate, followed by another, and then another. I rolled over on all fours to crawl toward the front of the truck to make room for the other guys.

It was then I first noticed it; the bottom of the truck was covered with something very cold, damp, and slippery. As soon as the stench assaulted my nose, there was no doubt about what it was although it was dark as pitch in the back of the truck, and I couldn't see anything.

"Pig shit!" I screamed. "They have filled the back of the truck with stinking pig shit."

All around me, the other green hands were gagging and gasping for air. We had all took a flying leap into a truck full of pig shit. The truck took a hard right turn, and the soupy mixture rolled to one side of the truck, only to return to the center when the truck straightened out. The truck then took a hard left, and the pig shit sloshed in the other direction. It was impossible for us to keep our balance, and we kept sliding down into the slippery, noxious-smelling liquid. We were soon covered from head to foot in the dark, brownish-black pig shit.

Located less than half a mile from the Union County High School was Dukes Cemetery. You could actually see the redbrick high school from the front gate of the cemetery. But to see it, you had to look across the two acres of plowed fields in which the FFA planted corn each spring. The entrance to the cemetery was directly parallel to the Ag barns and the football field, as the crow flies, across the open fields that were at this time of year overgrown with high weeds mixed in with old corn stalks.

It was the final resting place for some of Union County's most distinguished citizens. Dukes Cemetery was the largest and most prestigious cemetery in Union County. However, when it was begun, sometime after the turn of the century, it was little more than a pauper's burying ground. For the first twenty years of its existence, most people were buried in Dukes Cemetery without markers or coffins. A few graves did have markers, but they were little more than old cypress boards, onto which had been crudely carved the name and other vital information about the deceased.

As the Ag truck careened through the streets of Lake Butler, we were so busy trying to keep our footing in the back of the truck that we again took no notice of where we were going. We were surprised when the Ag truck pulled into Dukes Cemetery and drove down the narrow dirt road that dissected the four acres of well-tended graves. The blue Ag trucks came to an abrupt halt in a cloud of white dust near the center of the cemetery.

We didn't have to be told to get out; by now, we knew the drill very well. It was dark in the cemetery, and the air, which had hinted at fall at the beginning of the evening, was now very damp and cold.

As usual, Specks gave the orders; however, this time, because we were in the cemetery, he whispered what he expected us to do. He told us that a quarter had been put on the top of ten of the tombstones and that we would not be allowed to leave until we had found every one of them.

We groaned when we heard what was expected of us. Specks growled under his breath and said for us to get busy so we could get out of here.

It was dark as pitch as we scattered through the cemetery seeking the elusive quarters. All we could do was grope blindly, run our hands slowly over the top of each tombstone, and feel for the elusive quarters. Some of the guys used this precious time out of the sight of the upperclassmen to scrape some of the pig shit off of their bodies using dead leaves and handfuls of grass. To me, it seemed like an exercise in futility, because, sooner or later, we would all have to again get back into the rear of the pig-shit-filled Ag truck.

I had a sneaking suspicion that there were no quarters on the tombstones and that when the seniors got tired of watching us make fools out of ourselves, they would call us back to the truck. The way things were going, it would take us all night to locate the damn ten quarters in this sea of granite tombstones. I voiced my feeling to a small group of green hands nearby, and they agreed. We decided to find a dark corner of the cemetery and drop out of this idiot's scavenger hunt.

Near where we were standing was the family plot of Dr. J. W. King. He was the first full-time physician in Union County. He had moved here from Georgia sometime before the beginning of World War I. Dr. King had parlayed the small amount of money he made delivering babies and treating various ailments into a small fortune by wise investments in land, a cotton gin, and turpentine still. He was also very active in politics, although he had never held public office. When he died, sometime in the 1940s, every high-ranking politician in Florida and most of Georgia attended his funeral. I had heard the old folks say that even the governor of Florida had been there.

Although Dr. King was supposed to have been a simple man despite his wealth, his children and the local townspeople had made sure that his cemetery plot reflected his distinguished position in the community. His grave plot was marked by a twelve-foot-high obelisk, carved from pink marble, and transported to Union County by train, from the deep mountain quarries of his native north Georgia. At the foot of the obelisk were two regular-sized, squat upright head markers, marking the final resting place of Dr. King and his wife. The plot contained several blank headstones, made from the same pink marble, for his children and grandchildren, should they choose to be buried in the family plot.

We naturally gravitated toward the King plot, because its pink marble obelisk was the tallest marker in the cemetery, and, even in the dead of night with no moon, the light of the stars reflected off the pale marble, making it almost glow. We decided that this was the best place to hide out.

Dr. King's plot was shielded from view by a low growth of boxwood plants, and it was far enough away from where the upperclassmen were lounging around the parked Ag truck that they could not see or hear us. However, because they had stupidly left the parking lights on in the Ag truck and the big-mouthed bastards made so much noise, we could easily keep an eye on them.

Each of us found a nice, comfortable, but cold, headstone and had a seat. I think I was sitting on top of Mrs. King's headstone, but, it was so dark, I couldn't be sure. I though back to when I was in the first grade, and Mrs. King had smiled at me the day they showed us the film about hookworms. She was a very nice, kind lady, and I suddenly realized that she probably wouldn't appreciate a naked teenage boy covered with pig shit sitting on her grave. I knew I should have gotten up and moved, but I was just too damn tired. Anyway, whatever disrespect there was had already taken place, and I figured that it now made little difference how long I sat on her tombstone. I only hoped that wherever Mrs. King was, she would understand and forgive me.

We whispered as we spoke, trying to decide how to extradite ourselves from this situation. Shortly after the whispered conversation began, one of the green hands remarked that he felt something funny on his ass. He stood up and rubbed the top of the tombstone but couldn't find anything. At that point, he reached behind his back and pulled loose a quarter that had been stuck to his right buttock, held firmly in place by the now dried and encrusted pig shit. The rest of us then began to feel around first on our buttocks and then on the tops of the tombstones looking for quarters. Right away, we found another quarter on a ledge around the base of Dr. King's grave. I think it had originally been on top of the headstone, but he had knocked it off when we sat down.

"So, they did put quarters on top of the tombstones!" I whispered.

It seemed logical when I thought about it; they would put the quarters in the oldest part of the cemetery, in the largest plot, near the grave of the county's leading citizen. I guess they did it that way so they could easily find their ten quarters, should we fail to do so. Two dollars and fifty cents was a princely sum in 1960, when a quarter would buy you a large RC Cola, a Baby Ruth candy bar, and a pack of gum. A quarter and a dime would buy you a pack of cigarettes.

I tried to guess what time it was. It was hard to tell, since, when you're cold and miserable, time seems to go slower than usual, and this night had not been a barrel of laughs. I figured it must be between nine and ten o'clock. I wished I had my watch, but it was sitting on the desk in the Ag building with my clothes.

I could tell that the events in the cemetery were not that much fun for the upperclassmen hanging around the truck. It was too dark for them to see what we were doing, and, apparently, a bunch of naked guys running around a cemetery wasn't as funny looking as they thought it would be. Also, the guys at the truck were starting to respond to the cold. They all had their blue corduroy jackets on with the collars turned up. We could hear the truck engine running, which indicated they probably had the heater on and were taking turns warming themselves in the cab.

After about fifteen more minutes of us groping around in the dark, we had found all ten of the quarters. They were all on top of tombstones in and around Dr. King's burial plot. Once we had discovered where the first ones were located, then the rest were fairly easy to find. We could have ended the whole cemetery thing early by announcing our find, but we had quietly decided among ourselves that that bunch of bastards up at the truck would never see these ten quarters. We had an odd sense of pride in having found the money, and, with nothing more than pure revenge as a motive, we buried them in the soft soil in the rear of Dr. King's tombstone. We vowed to return at the first opportunity to retrieve our loot. The ten quarters would buy each of us a cold drink and candy bar when this was all over.

Finally, two long horn blasts and Frog's bellowing voice summoned us back to the truck. One of the hardest things I have ever had to do was crawl back into the rear of that shit-filled truck. The worst part was not the smell; we had kind of gotten used to that and the gooey feeling of the excrement on our bodies, but God Almighty, that pig shit felt like ice water when you stepped into it.

As the Ag truck pulled out of the cemetery, we were all grouchy and irritable. When one of the green hands slipped in the noxious goo in the bottom of the truck, he got up cussing and accusing the rest of us of pushing him. The only thing that prevented a fight from breaking out was that the truck made a sharp and violent turn to the right that sent all of us all sprawling into the soupy excrement.

At this point, the only thing that kept us going mentally and physically was the sure knowledge that they would now probably take us back to the Ag building to get our clothes, and all this would be over.

When the truck turned out of the dirt cemetery road and started driving away from the school back toward town, we were all totally bewildered as to its destination, not to mention being completely crestfallen that we were not going back to the Ag building.

In a few minutes, the blue Ag truck was speeding down a totally deserted main street. No business in Lake Butler stayed open past nine o'clock at night, except the poolroom, the skating rink (on weekends only), and the town's three rowdy bars. Most stores and gas stations closed their doors before six. The old adage about a town rolling up the sidewalks at dusk truly applied to Lake Butler. Not even the pool room was open after eleven, and the bars, by law, had to close at midnight, but most closed earlier on weeknights when business was usually slow.

For the life of me, I couldn't figure out where we were going this late on a weeknight. My only educated guess was that they were going to take us down to the lake to wash off the pig shit in the muddy black water before going back to school. However, the thought of going into that black alligator-filled water filled me with horror.

One of the green hands mentioned that they had just built new outdoor shower stalls in the small park by the lake.

"Do they have hot water?" somebody asked.

"Hell no! All you're supposed to do is wash the mud off of you after you come out of the lake. Nobody needs hot water in the summer."

"Jesus! We'll freeze our balls off."

Before this lame conversation could go any further, it became obvious that our destination was not the showers down by the lake, but someplace entirely different. The Ag truck made a hard right and turned into the Pure Oil station on Main Street, just across the street from the courthouse.

We all knew this place very well. A man named Harry Stanton who had been president of the FFA chapter in 1953 owned it. He was a strong supporter of the FFA, and there was no doubt in my mind that he had given permission for the use of his station for whatever they were going to do to us.

The Pure Oil station had a unique service for its customers: a high-pressure wash on a concrete slab behind the garage. It was for the use of the big pulpwood trucks that flooded into town every afternoon to fill their gas tanks. There were a lot of these pulpwood trucks in Union County, and their tanks held a lot of gas; so all the stations vied for their business.

Usually the soil in this part of Florida is a gray sandy loam, except around the thick cypress swamps, low ground hollows, creek bottoms, and ponds. There, the soil can become a black, syrupy mud that would stick to anything it touched. When the syrupy mud dried, it would become hard as a brick. The big trucks hauling pulpwood out of the swamps would often become covered with the thick mud, especially around the wheels and undercarriage. If it wasn't washed off on a regular basis, the mud would dry and cake up, throwing the wheels out of balance and causing the expensive truck tires to wear out prematurely. If the wheels were not put back into alignment, they could eventually damage the rear axle and transmission. A regular water hose could do little to release the mud especially after it had dried and was caked on. To get it off, you needed special equipment, a lot of water under very high pressure.

Adding the high-pressure truck wash to his station was a smart business move for Harry Stanton. It ensured that almost every mud-covered pulpwood truck in Union County would gas up at his station, since every fill-up allowed the truck driver the free use of the truck-washing equipment.

As soon as I saw that the Ag trucks were pulling into the Pure Oil station, I immediately knew how the Ag boys intended to get the pig shit off of our bodies and out of the Ag truck. I was in tremendous fear of what was going to happen. I had often watched the muscular black men who loaded and drove the big pulpwood trucks wash their vehicles. Even these strong men needed both hands and all their strength to control the big gray water hoses. I had often seen them lose their footing and get knocked off their feet by the pressure of the water.

As soon as the truck rolled to a stop, we all began to stand up in the back of the truck, yelling for help and threatening all kinds of things if they dared hit us with the high-pressure water. Our protest was cut short by a tremendous blast of ice-cold water that had so much force, it knocked all of us off our feet and pinned one boy to the back of the truck. It felt as if a thousand ice-cold needles were being driven into my flesh. I felt helpless and thought the torment of the cold water would never end.

That was it. I had had it. I had been burned with cigarettes, hit with paddles, smeared with pig shit, and burned with the noxious Heat Balm, but now this was too much. There were houses within close running distance from the station, and we weren't that far to the courthouse and the county jail. I knew someone would be on duty at the jail, so I had decided to try and leap out of the truck and make a run for it.

As I climbed up on the wooden sideboards of the truck, I immediately saw that the truck was surrounded by upperclassmen that were not about to let anyone go anywhere. We were badly outnumbered by boys four year older and much larger than we were. How could a group of boys, barely finished with puberty, gang fight a larger group of fully mature juniors and seniors?

Despite the difference in our sizes, the small group of green hands was united. Like me, they felt they had been pushed beyond further endurance. No matter what happened, we weren't going to take any more. We began to violently cuss out the upperclassmen, spewing forth all our anger in a caustic display of animal aggression. Their threats to beat our ass were ignored. After what we had already been through, an ass whipping seemed like nothing.

I crawled up on the top of the sideboards and stood defiantly with my bare feet between the wooden slats. I had totally forgotten about being naked. It seemed as if I had been forced back into some kind of primitive boy warrior state. This week's suffering had forced me to become my primeval self, with all the trapping of civilized living driven from my conscious psyche by the Heat Balm, cigarette butts, wooden paddles, pig shit, and ice-cold water. I cussed both Specks and Frog for everything I was worth; every cuss word, vile oath, and obscene threat I had ever heard in my life came out of my mouth. I called Specks a "goddamned, afterbirth-eating, cow-fucking, shit-eating Siberian son of a bitch." It was the best cussing out I could think of at the time. I told all of the Ag boys gathered below me that they couldn't keep the truck guarded all night, and if we were not immediately taken back to the Ag building to get our clothes, we would jump out and run for it regardless of the consequences.

At this point, Specks stepped forward and almost calmly told me to watch my language and stop making so much noise before somebody in one of the nearby houses called the sheriff.

"I don't give a shit who they call!" I screamed. "I don't give a good goddamn whether or not I'm blackballed out of the FFA or not; you can take your goddamned blue corduroy jacket and wipe your fucking ass with it."

Several of the other green hands rallied to my cause, saying they also wanted to quit. One boy was crying hysterically, and another was shivering so violently with the cold, I thought he might be having a seizure.

The upperclassmen began responding to our threats with a chant of "pussy boys, pussy boys."

Finally, Specks and Frog could not tolerate any more. They were afraid that some of the people who lived nearby would call the sheriff about the noise, and that would blow the whole deal. They both disappeared for a few minutes and then reappeared. Frog was carrying an old broom handle, and Specks had a two-foot-long oak limb in his hand.

"Shut up, damn it!" Specks screamed, waving his oak limb at us. "I've had it; now goddamn it, I mean shut up."

"Fuck you," I screamed defiantly.

With that, Specks flew into the back of the truck and came down on me with the oak limb. I instantly threw up my arm to block the blow, but the oak limb caught me square across the arm and shoulder. I went down into the wet bottom of the truck, doing my feeble best to ward off any further blows. I knew immediately that I had suffered some serious damage to my arm and shoulder, but I wasn't about to give them the pleasure of crying.

Specks was like a wild man. There was panic in his eyes. He seemed to sense that this thing had gotten out of control and that only brute force could get us back in line. The blow he had delivered to me made the rest of the green hands back up and quit yelling and cussing. One guy was still shaking violently from the cold, but the only real sound was the soft whimpers of the one kid crying in the bottom of the truck.

His sobs seemed to drive Specks wild with rage. He forgot all about my defiance and directed all his anger at the crying kid lying in the bottom of the truck. Specks, without really realizing it, had reverted back to the old standard bully's tradition. He was picking on the weakest and most vulnerable among the group. Those of us who had been cussing him out just a few minutes before were being totally ignored by the club-wielding FFA president. We hadn't made him near as angry with our open defiance and profanity as the little kid who was sobbing.

"Shut up, you little pussy bastard!"

The kid only continued to cry.

"Shut up, goddamn it!" Specks screamed, raising the oak limb over his head.

The kid didn't stop crying.

Specks berated him over and over, threatening to brain him with the club, but the whimpering only got worse. Finally, in disgust, Specks lowered the club and ordered the trucks to get moving.

The crying kid in the bottom of the truck was named Sidney Martin, and, personally, I was surprised that he had gotten this far without breaking. His father had been the county agricultural agent for a short time before resigning to become a salesman for a large chemical fertilizer company. Sidney didn't come from a family of farmers. His mother was a heavyset woman who worked part time as a music teacher. She had raised her one and only child to play the piano and be a little gentleman. He was polite and well mannered; his grades were good enough to get him an invitation to join the Beta Club. Sidney didn't smoke, didn't chew, and never got into trouble.

Sidney's father, Larry Martin, was a macho-type guy, who constantly boasted about his college football career at Mississippi State University. People who knew Larry Martin well remembered his football career as fairly lackluster, with him spending most of his time warming the bench. No matter who was right about his football-playing days, Larry Martin had managed to receive a Bachelor's degree in Agriculture that opened for him several career opportunities that required little or no physical exertion. Since his graduation, the once-handsome and athletic football player had turned into a cigar-chewing, hog-jowled lard-ass, full of loudmouth bluster and brag. He was well-known in Union County as a tremendous glutton, who consumed vast amounts of fried chicken and corn bread.

Larry Martin was worried about his only son. The boy had taken after his mother's side of the family, becoming a roly-poly teenager, who was more interested in music and science than sports and agriculture. Although he was already fifteen, Sidney showed no signs of puberty and was too girlish looking to suit his father.

Larry Martin was worried most about what effect his overprotective wife was having on Sidney. Larry worried that Sidney might be becoming a mama's boy and that his son needed to spend more time with boys his own age. He wanted to do something to turn his son into a real man he could be proud of.

Sidney knew full well he gave his father little to brag about. Larry Martin communicated to Sidney every day in some subtle way about how disappointed he was in him. It created in Sidney a guilt that he could not bare. He would do anything to win his father's approval, even joining the FFA. Sidney saw the FFA as a way to finally make his father proud of him and prove his masculinity, while, at the same time, helping his father's business. Larry Martin's livelihood depended upon his ability to get local farmers to purchase his chemical fertilizers, pesticides, and herbicides. He hoped that having a son in the FFA could help him land lucrative sales contracts from local farmers. The overweight fertilizer salesman had no idea when he pressured his son to join the FFA what kind of hell he was putting his polite and sensitive child through.

Sidney Martin was not considered to be FFA material by upperclassmen. His grades were too high, his conduct was too good, and, worst of all, he didn't look like one of the Ag boys. His hands were soft, his muscles were flabby, he wore glasses, and his hips were slightly wider than his shoulders.

Sidney would have been hounded out of the FFA long before initiation week, except for one very important thing. Mr. Clemmons wanted Sidney Martin in the chapter. Sidney's father had solicited Mr. Clemmons' friendship with free trips to agricultural conventions in such exotic places as Des Moines, St. Paul, and Kansas City. They once went to a convention in Nashville, where Mr. Clemmons fulfilled his lifelong dream of seeing the Grand Old Opry. That night, they got to watch both Minnie Pearl and Roy Acuff perform live and in person on the stage of the Ryman Auditorium. Mr. Clemmons returned to Lake Butler the proud owner of autographed pictures of Minnie Pearl and Roy Acuff. For weeks after he got back, Mr. Clemmons couldn't talk about anything else and still brings it up in conversations whenever he can.

Mr. Clemmons had reciprocated by introducing Sidney's father to every local farmer he knew, allowing him to put up advertisements at FFA events, and making sure that the FFA chapter purchased all of its fertilizers, herbicides, and pesticides from Larry Martin's company. On those rare occasions when Mr. Clemmons did teach a class, he hardly ever talked about anything except the pressing need for more pesticides, herbicides, and fertilizers in modern agriculture. Sometimes, listening to him, I wondered if we were going to be farmers or chemists.

Another important thing was that Sidney Martin was the first literate kid to apply for membership in the FFA in years. Mr. Clemmons had use for such a bright young man. He felt Sidney would be a good candidate for reporter or treasurer, taking some, if not all, of the hated paperwork off Mr. Clemmons' hands. The other Ag boys resented the fact that this little chubby kid was being given special treatment. Mr. Clemmons treated Sidney like he was an already-initiated member of the chapter, giving him access to the chapter's minutes and financial reports. He even went so far as to give Sidney and his father a personal tour of the Ag barns, showing off all the farm equipment, animals, and the vast stockpiles of fertilizers, pesticides, and herbicides stored in the cinder block building. To the Ag boys, this was sacrilege.

On the first day of initiation week, Sidney Martin was hit in the balls so many times that, when he got home, his testicles were so badly swollen his father had to take him to the hospital. The next day, Sidney stayed home from school, and his father called Mr. Clemmons to complain. A furious Mr. Clemmons called Specks and Frog into his office and told them that the next person who hit Sidney in the balls was out of the chapter and on his shit list.

This put a bad taste in everybody's mouth, especially Specks and Frog. The fat little fuck had snitched on the upperclassmen that hit him in the balls. It became more obvious that Sidney Martin was getting special treatment, because of who his father was, when he was excused from the Heat Balm treatment by order of Mr. Clemmons, who claimed Sidney had a sensitive skin condition. However, not even his big-shit father could help Sidney dodge the last night.

Sidney Martin was one of those types of kid that cried easily. If he fell down during physical education class, he would cry. If he got a bad grade on a test, he would cry. If one of the judges criticized his science project, he would cry. If he bumped his head on something, he would cry. It drove the rest of us crazy.

We hated a damned crybaby worse than anything on earth. We could tolerate a boy with bad breath or a boy who farted too much and never took a bath. We could even tolerate Bugger Nose Butch Bowers who was always picking his nose, but a crybaby was just too much. Ag boys don't cry, never, no matter what. That was one of the things that made us special; we weren't a bunch of whining crybabies. We had all been told the story about the Ag boy who had gotten two of his fingers bitten off by one of the old sows down at the Ag barns, but didn't cry. It had happened sometime either in the late 1940s or early 1950s, but nobody knew for sure. Also, nobody seemed to remember what the kid's name was. However, by 1960, the story had become a part of FFA folklore, being passed down from year to year. With legends like that, how in the hell could an organization that prided itself on being tough possibly explain a Sidney Martin within its ranks? Yet, we had this political situation between his father and Mr. Clemmons.

Early in the year, Specks and Frog had pulled Sidney off to one side and talked to him privately. They told him they wanted him to make it into the FFA, but the first time he started crying, he was out. The green hands had also talked to Sidney. We started off trying to be nice; we told him that if he ever started crying, it would only make it harder on the rest of us to hang tough. Sidney protested that he couldn't help himself; he was a sensitive kid, and the tears just seemed to come automatically. This was not what we wanted to hear, and, real quick, we just got very plain and simple with him. We told Sidney point blank that his big-shot daddy wasn't dick shit to us and that we would not be embarrassed by any of this crying crap. We promised him that the first time he started crying, we would all beat the shit out of him. Even Sidney's father had given him a pep talk about how to be a real man and not cry. Sidney had promised all of us that no matter what happened, he wouldn't start crying.

To his credit, Sidney had hung tough all week. He had endured the cigarette burns, the skating rink, the pig shit, and the cemetery, but now his chubby little spirit had just given out. The cold blast of icy water that knocked him off his feet and onto the hard floor of the truck was just too much. He now lay at our feet, curled into a little ball, crying hysterically. Specks was furious at the sight.

"Ag boys don't cry, you little pussy," he screamed at the soaking-wet fat figure of a boy at his feet.

Specks called Sidney every cuss word and dirty name he could think of trying to make him mad, to shut him up, but nothing worked. He just lay there, looking purely pitiful, with huge tears rolling down his chubby cheeks.

Disgusted, specks ordered us to move out. As the truck pulled away from the Pure Oil station, I noticed we were driving slower than usual. They were taking seriously my threat to jump off the truck and run. I thought for sure we would now return to the Ag building, since we were finally clean of the pig shit. My heart sank like lead, when the trucks passed the Ag building rolling on beyond the gymnasium toward the Ag barns behind the distant football field.

The Ag barns were remote and out of yelling distance from any homes. I cursed myself for not taking my chance when we were in the middle of town, close to the courthouse and jail.

As we turned at the ticket booth onto the dirt road that ran behind the bleachers, I could see ahead that the entire membership of the FFA was assembled at the Ag barns. This was the first time since the mock kangaroo court at the Ag building that I had seen the whole membership gathered together in one place.

Undergoing all the misery of the night, it was hard for the green hands to appreciate all the careful planning that had gone into making this night a living hell for us. We didn't realize it at the time, but the whole thing had been carefully laid out so that one group would keep us busy at one place, while another group was getting things ready somewhere else. Only the seniors had been with us all evening. They drove the trucks and generally dished out the punishment under the close direction of Specks and Frog. While we were making fools of ourselves at the skating rink, the sophomores had been given the thankless job of shoveling the pig shit into the back of the Ag trucks. The whole episode down at the cemetery was only to give the juniors time to close up the skating rink and get things ready at the truck wash. The big question now was: What was everyone doing while we were at the truck wash?

As the truck slowly rolled up to the Ag barns, we were silent. No one spoke. Yelling and cussing now would do no good, for there was no one within earshot to hear us. Even Sidney had stopped his whimpering. The Ag truck rolled to a gentle stop, and we all quietly piled out of the back. After we were all out, the truck was slowly driven around the cinder block building and parked behind the pole-barn shed under a stand of pine trees. A select group of sophomores, under senior supervision, had spent the whole evening at the Ag barns preparing for what was to be the climax of the evening.

All the assembled Ag boys stood in silence, like some kind of angry lynch mob, watching us approach. Each face bore a sadistic smirk of a smile. Cigarettes dangled rakishly from the corners of their mouths as each one tried to assume some kind of Humphrey Bogart pose. Many of their jaws were extended with large globs of chewing tobacco, as if on cue from an invisible director just off stage, they would carefully turn and spit in a manner that was threatening and sinister. Every one of the Ag boys was proudly wearing his blue corduroy jacket, carefully decorated with their tiny bronze medals. This was to be a very special occasion.

The scene at the Ag barns had a surreal element about it. A bonfire was blazing behind the pole barn, and the flames cast an eerie red glow on the tops of the pine trees and on the faces of the young men in their blue jackets.

Directly in front of the cinder block building—used to store the large bags of fertilizer and herbicides—sat a device we called the branding barrel, and the sight of it filled me with absolute terror.

It was a crude, homemade device fashioned from half of a fifty-five-gallon oil drum that was mounted on four legs made by welding pieces of angle iron together to form a stand. It was filled with charcoal and fired by a liquid petroleum gas burner. It also had a hand-cranked blower that, when turned rapidly, could raise the temperature of the charcoal to a point where it could make a piece of metal cherry red hot in a matter of minutes. The branding barrel was an easily portable device that could easily be loaded onto the back of one of the Ag trucks. It was only used twice a year: in the spring, when the FFA chapter made extra money by hauling the device out to rural cow pastures to brand the newly born calves, and, in the fall, when it was an important part of initiation week.

The sight of the branding barrel filled each green hand with total agony. My mouth was so dry, I couldn't spit if I had to on a dare. It was one of those times in my life when I was frightened to the point of feeling like I was having difficulty breathing. My fears were real; if there was one thing I had learned that night, it was that these bastards were capable of anything.

As soon as we climbed out of the Ag truck, I could tell that the whimpering little Sidney was to be their target. These sadistic sons of bitches could almost smell fear; they knew who was weak and who was about to crack. They knew who would be their best victim, and Sidney was it.

A group of seniors moved the branding barrel to the center of the dirt road and began to fire it up. As the coals in the branding barrel began to heat up and glow red, four burly seniors grabbed Sidney Martin and put him in a painful double-arm lock. With his hands pinned sadistically behind him, almost up to his shoulder blades, and with only the tips of his toes touching the ground, they paraded him in front of the assembled Ag boys. Specks stepped forward and began to rail against Sidney, telling everyone how he had started crying at the truck wash.

While he was pacing back and fourth ranting and raving like a tent preacher, Specks kept an eagle eye on the branding barrel, carefully watching the glowing coals out of the corner of his eye. Specks finally nodded his head, a silent signal to Frog, indicating that the charcoal was now hot enough to stick in the two metal branding irons. Frog grabbed the wooden handles of the two branding irons and buried the metal ends deep within the hot coals in the barrel. A strong-armed sophomore began to furiously crank the handle on the blower. In only a few minutes, the hand-cranked blower would raise the temperature of the branding irons until the curved end of the branding irons were glowing red hot.

Meanwhile, Specks continued to berate Sidney, recounting to the members who hadn't been at the truck wash how he had turned into a bawling bag of blubber. He cussed Sidney and told him that now he would have to pay for his sins.

Sidney begged for mercy; he whined and groveled, just like the upperclassmen wanted him to. Sidney apologized for crying and offered to do anything in order to be spared whatever it was they had planned for him. He was like a small child begging his abusive parents not to beat him anymore. The rest of us stood mute. We knew that if we made a single sound, we would be their next victim.

I looked into the assembled Ag boys' eyes, and they were sparkling in the red glow given off by the branding barrel. They looked like some kind of wild animals about to eat their prey, but wanted to play with it first. I could see no mercy, tolerance, understanding, empathy, or pity in their eyes. They each had a smug sense of pleasure about what they were doing. The more Sidney cried and begged for mercy, the more they enjoyed it. They took Sidney and spread-eagled him over an old oil drum that had been half buried in the soft ground of the dirt road, directly in front of the branding barrel. They carefully positioned Sidney so that he was facing away from the branding barrel, but was yet close enough to feel its heat. Ropes were affixed to Sidney's arms and legs and then looped around nearby trees. The ropes were then tightened and secured firmly.

Sidney looked like some type of giant distorted frog on the dissecting table of a mad scientist. His large white buttocks protruded into the air, reflecting the red glow of the charcoal in the branding barrel. His green testicles dangled between his fleshy white thighs, flattened against the cold sides of the half-buried oil drum. I had seen illustrations in history books of people being tortured during the Spanish Inquisition, and the sight of poor Sidney hog-tied over the barrel made me think of that terrible period of history.

Specks ordered the rest of us to turn away from the sight of Sidney and the branding barrel. The remaining eight of us were carefully lined up in the soft white sand of the dirt road and ordered to kneel and put our hands behind our heads and interlock our fingers. I had seen old World War II movies where the Nazis forced people to assume this same position just before they shot them in the back of the head.

I later learned that in years past, the Ag boys had actually tied up green hands during this part of the initiation, and I often wondered why they didn't do the same to us. The most logical explanation was that they had already had to beat up one boy at the skating rink, and the rebellion at the truck wash was still on their minds. They might have figured, probably correctly, that if they tried to tie us, they would have to beat the shit out of all of us.

Specks warned us that under no circumstances were we to turn our heads around and try to see what was happening. Anyone who did would suffer the consequences. Specks never said what the consequences were, so we each let our imaginations run wild.

I could hear Sidney crying hysterically behind me and pitifully begging to be released from the ropes that were holding him. He said over and over that he wanted no further part of the FFA and would resign first thing in the morning, if they would only turn him loose. This plea brought howls of laughter from the gang of assembled Ag boys who had gathered in close around the branding barrel to make sure they got a good view of what was happening. Several of them started spitting tobacco juice on Sidney's large white buttocks, and a couple flipped lit cigarettes at his restrained and helpless body.

Specks withdrew the red-hot branding iron from the barrel where it had been heating and waved it under Sidney's nose. To further make his point, Specks spit on the crimson branding iron, and the saliva sizzled so loudly, we could hear it over where we were kneeled in the sand. Sidney was now so terrified that he let out a huge fart and screamed that he might have a bowel movement. The assembled throng of blue-jacket-clad Ag boys began to jump up and down howling with laughter. Several were so excited, they began doing a demonic little dance around the branding barrel.

Specks slowly stepped behind Sidney, who was now begging and crying with all his might, no longer to be set free, but just for Specks not to brand him with the hot iron.

"Please don't! Oh my God, please don't!"

Despite my fear, kneeling there in the sand with my hands behind my head, my mind was racing ninety miles an hour, trying to figure all this out. I was not about to let these sons of bitches brand me, not without one hell of a fight first. I eyed a small piece of pine limb a few feet away and wondered if I could get to it before they were on me. I knew I wouldn't have a chance, but so help me God, I would lay a couple of them out before I went down.

However, at the same time, my logical mind kept telling me that they have got to be bluffing. For God's sake, they can't get away with branding somebody, could they? A burn that bad would have to have medical attention and would leave a horrible scar. Untreated, it could get badly infected. Wouldn't it? A person who had been branded would have to be taken to the hospital; there would be questions, an investigation, and criminal charges. Mr. Clemmons would get fired; wouldn't he? They could never claim that the burn on Sidney's ass had been caused by him falling off a tractor.

Then, there was that damned code of silence. Suppose nobody talked. Sidney would probably lie and say he burned himself by accident, and so would most of the other green hands. They wouldn't say anything.

No matter what logical, intelligent thoughts raced through my brain, it all came back to one thing: This was still Union County. It was an ignorant, backward area in the darkest bowels of the Old South. I could never forget that my grandfather had shot a man in cold blood for trying to sell him wet cotton, and nobody had done anything about it. In Union County, you could get killed over a political election, a poker game, or a round of nine-ball pool with five dollars riding on the shot.

They lynch people down here and then have their pictures taken with the dangling corpse. They lynch Negroes for being "uppity," and they lynch white people for supporting integration. They had killed a woman in Alabama for riding down the road with a black man in the front seat of her car. They had brutally beaten and murdered a thirteen-year-old black boy in Mississippi for asking a white woman for a date. Black men had been castrated for simply looking at a white woman. My daddy once said they flogged a man over in Levy County, because he allowed his black hired hands to use the front door of his house. If they can lynch, castrate and flog people for something as innocent as that, then they could brand somebody on the ass for crying at an FFA initiation and get away with it.

What none of the green hands had noticed during Sidney's torment was a small ice chest sitting innocently just a few feet from the branding barrel. Who could have taken notice of such a simple thing as an ice chest, with all of this horror going on around us?

As Specks brought the red-hot branding iron closer and closer to Sidney's naked buttocks, Frog carefully retrieved a small triangular piece of ice from the chest. The red-hot branding iron was less than a quarter of an inch from Sidney's buttocks, and he could feel the heat closing in.

"You ready for this you fat little motherfucker?" Sidney whispered to Sidney with a sadistic curl on his lip.

"I'm going to give you something to cry about, you sorry little ass-wipe bastard."

Sidney had almost stopped crying. He was now in so much terror that all he could do was pant for breath. His bladder had failed him, and a small puddle of bright-yellow urine had run down the side of the branding barrel and collected in the bright-white sand at the bottom of the branding barrel.

The Ag boys had begun to chant in unison, "Do it. Do it. Do it."

Just as the red-hot iron was less than a hair's length from Sidney's butt, and Specks was yelling, "Here it comes, here it comes;" Frog suddenly thrust the triangular piece of ice deep between Sidney's buttocks, tight against the tender sphincter muscles of his anus.

I will never forget that scream. It was so loud it echoed wildly off the concrete wall of the cinder block building and seemed to literally bounce for long seconds off the sides of the pine trees surrounding the Ag barns. Nobody thought for a minute that it was a fake scream. It was real; it was blood curdling. In his state of hysteria, Sidney couldn't tell one type of pain from another. He really believed that they had branded him and reacted, as the Ag boys knew he would. I froze in pure terror at the terrible sound coming from behind me. The hairs on the back of my neck stood straight up, and chill bumps covered my body.

"Okay, who's next?" Specks said, as if he were giving haircuts.

I don't remember who ran first, me or one of the other green hands;

however, it was probably me, since I knew that next to Sidney I had caused Specks the most aggravation that night. In a flash, I undid my hands from behind my head and came up from my kneeling position like an Olympic sprinter. Within a fraction of a second, my only feelings were of my bare feet digging into the soft sand of the dirt road. From the corner of my eye, I could see the wooden bleachers of the football field flying past me. The ticket booth at the end of the dirt road came closer and closer as I ran wide open. No one was in front of me, but the labored sound of heavy breathing told me that the other green hands were right behind me. What I didn't know was where the Ag boys were, and I wasn't about to turn around and look.

There was elation in my running. It felt good. All night, I had felt like a captive, and now I felt free and liberated from some unspeakable prison of torment. My body was filled with adrenaline. There was no pain and no fatigue, just the urge to run and run and run some more, to go and keep on going, until I was a long way away from here.

Since I had stopped playing football, I had ceased to exercise and let my body go. The cigarettes I smoked didn't help either. I had started smoking in the eighth grade, so I would be used to them by the time I joined the FFA as a freshman. That way, I wouldn't embarrass myself by gagging or coughing when one of the Ag boys offered me a smoke. Right now, I sincerely wished that I had never seen a cigarette, since I needed every molecule of oxygen I could pump into my lungs.

By the time I reached the end of the dirt road, my stamina was finally expended, and I had to stop and get a breath. One by one, as if they were taking their cue from me, the other green hands slowly came to a running halt.

If pure physical exhaustion had not prompted us to stop running by the time we reached the ticket booth, the hard asphalt and rock pavement of Lake Street would have. The dirt road had been soft white sand ideal for running barefoot, but nobody's feet were tough enough to run on a hard road.

Panic gripped me; I immediately had the trapped feeling all over again. Surely, the Ag boys were right behind me. I turned and looked back toward the Ag barns and was surprised to see that the road was empty. They were still down by the branding barrel with poor Sidney.

"Should we go back and rescue him?" one of the green hands asked between labored breaths.

"Hell no!" another commented between gasps for air, "We're going to be lucky to rescue ourselves. Whatever they were going to do to Sidney, they have already done it."

From our vantage point at the end of the road, I could see the blue-jacketed upperclassmen begin to pile into the back of the Ag truck; in a few minutes; they would be on us.

Unknown to us, we had been saved from being immediately pursued, by an obscure order from Mr. Clemmons issued several years ago. He always worried that the sparks from the charcoal in the branding barrel would set off the gasoline fumes from the Ag trucks. He had decreed that whenever the branding barrel was fired up, the trucks were to be parked beyond the pole shed, far enough away from the branding barrel so that there was no danger of fire.

The area around the Ag barns was covered with the dried pine needles that could catch fire easily, so the only safe place to set up the branding barrel was directly in the middle of the dirt road in front of the cinder block building. In other words, when the branding barrel was fired up, it blocked the road so they couldn't get the trucks out from behind the pole barn.

They had to turn off the propane gas and disconnect the tank before they could even think about moving the branding barrel. Even then, it was too hot to be handled, so Specks just kicked it over, and Frog wet the whole thing down with a water hose. Only after a thorough dousing with water was the hot branding barrel cool enough for them to drag it out of the road.

Also, they had foolishly put the fifty-five-gallon oil drum, where they had tied poor old Sidney, directly in the middle of the dirt road. Before they could come chasing after us in the truck, they had to untie Sidney and move the barrel. All of this, the branding barrel, and moving Sidney had given us the precious time to get away. By the time we reached the end of the dirt road, they had almost finished clearing away all the obstructions and were beginning to pile into the Ag trucks. Of course, we had no way of knowing what was going on back at the Ag barns; all we could think about was getting out of there.

"Where do we go now?" somebody asked.

One of the green hands suggested that we try and hide in the woods across the street. The woods of northern Florida are not a hospitable place for naked boys. Not only was the floor of the forest covered with a thick growth of palmetto bushes, and about ten different varieties of briars and thorny vines, but, worst of all, it was the natural habitat of fleas, ticks, mosquitoes, red bugs, black widow spiders, and, most importantly, the eastern diamondback rattlesnake.

"We can't run into those damned woods," I yelled.

"Well maybe we could just run a little ways into the woods and then squat down and hide," the kid fired back.

This created in my head the horrible image of me squatting down over a huge diamondback rattlesnake. The woods were not an option, but we had to go somewhere and quick.

About two hundred yards down the road from the football field was Lake Butler's newest residential area. It had no official name, but most everyone called it Sprinkle Field, after an old army airfield that existed just east of Lake Butler during World War II.

The homes in Sprinkle Field were all small and modest, but at the same time very neat and well kept up. The homes were always freshly painted, and the yards were carefully landscaped with azaleas, wisteria, gardenias, geranium, and rose beds. This small neighborhood of less than a dozen homes had been started shortly after the end of World War II by returning veterans. They used their low-interest, Veterans Administration mortgages to build modest homes on cheap lots sold by one of Dr. King's sons.

Many of these veterans took advantage of their GI Bill and attended the University of Florida in Gainesville, only sixty miles away. A few of the veterans became doctors and lawyers, but most majored either in agriculture or education. The guys who became doctors and lawyers soon made enough money so they could move out of Sprinkle Field into a more upscale neighborhood. Most of the guys who majored in agriculture eventually purchased farms or got positions with fertilizer companies or either the state or federal government. However, almost all of those who majored in education returned to Union County to find jobs teaching at their old high school. These college-trained schoolteachers never left their small homes in Sprinkle Field. Therefore, Sprinkle Field was where most of our teachers lived. It was where Mr. Clemmons lived, and it was to Sprinkle Field that we decided to flee from the horrors of the FFA initiation.

Moving as fast as we could, we crossed the hard pavement of Lake Street and then ran along the steep ditch bank the hundred yards or so to the paved road leading into the small Sprinkle Field subdivision. As soon as we reached the road, without saying a word to each other, we split up and scattered trying to find a safe hiding place among the houses.

At the time we split up, I turned back and took one last look toward the football field. I saw the Ag truck filled with upperclassmen stopped at the ticket booth where the dirt road met Lake Street. They could obviously see us running into the subdivision, but, for some reason, they didn't turn onto Lake Street and chase us. I could only surmise that they were debating among themselves whether or not to follow us into Sprinkle Field.

In the meantime, I had other worries. Messing around in somebody's yard in Union County could be a dangerous thing. Only fifteen miles away from the Sprinkle Field subdivision was the Florida State Prison. Behind the chain-link fences of the prison were confined the most dangerous criminals in the state, if not the nation. There were escapes on a regular basis. Most were minimum-security trusties who just walked off from a work detail, but sometimes really dangerous felons managed to wiggle out of the more secure parts of the institution.

Only a year before, four desperate convicts had broken into a house on the outside of town. The owner of the house was my sixth grade school teacher, Mrs. Doris Ricard, and her husband, David. Luckily, they were not at home at the time the convicts entered their house. The Sheriff's Department estimated that the convicts were lost in the woods and had just stumbled onto the house. It was around nine o'clock in the morning, and, since they didn't see a car, they figured the house was empty. They had been in the woods all night following the run of the New River swamp. As soon as they got into the house, they took off their wet prison clothes and took a bath. They found clean clothes in David Ricard's closet and changed into something dry and warm, if not a perfect fit. They raided the refrigerator and ate everything they could find, including a large bag of shelled pecans that Mrs. Ricard had spent an entire day picking out for a fruitcake.

David Ricard was an avid hunter, and the escaped convicts quickly armed themselves from his collection of shotguns and sports rifles.

Since she taught school, Mrs. Ricard never came home before three o'clock in the afternoon. However, David was a mechanic at his own garage in town. Like most Union County citizens, he was a creature of habit, following the same routine day after day. He always came home at noon to eat a cold lunch his wife had prepared the night before and left in the refrigerator. After eating his lunch, David would take a thirty-minute nap on the couch. The garage usually stayed open only until five o'clock, but, sometimes, he had to stay as late as seven or eight o'clock to finish up work he had promised to have ready. The brief nap always left David refreshed for the afternoon's work at the garage. However, David would not eat lunch this day, and he wouldn't take his nap either.

When David Ricard's pickup truck pulled into the dirt drive to his house, he didn't immediately get out of the truck. David Ricard had been living in that house with his wife for over twenty years. Something way down deep inside his almost prehistoric sense of familiarity and survival instinct told him something was wrong. It took him a few minutes to figure it out, but finally he realized that his old hound dog didn't rush out to the truck to greet him like he usually did. The old dog was a gentle beast that wouldn't hurt anybody; he was hardly a watchdog. The convicts had locked him in a storage shed in the backyard just to be on the safe side.

David Ricard just sat there in the truck, staring out over the steering wheel. His stomach was slowly turning into a large knot of fear. It was a strange kind of fear, the worst kind of fear, when you're afraid, but your not exactly sure of what.

David Ricard was famous all over Union County as one of the best wild turkey hunters around. A wild turkey is a hard animal to hunt, because the bird is extremely cautious and spooks very easily. The hunter has to be able to sit absolutely motionless for long periods of time, scanning the thick Florida underbrush for the telltale red throat of a wild turkey gobbler. The slightest sound or movement will scare the bird off, and, once a turkey is spooked, it might never come back that way again. Although he was over forty years old, David Ricard still didn't need glasses. He had the eyes that could spot a wild turkey a hundred yards off on a cold and foggy morning.

He just sat there staring straight ahead, not really knowing what he was looking for. His ears were strained for any sound; it was so quiet in his front yard he could clearly hear the noise of the wind in the top most branches of the pine trees; the snapping of a twig would have sounded like a clap of thunder. His eyes were fixed on the front of the house. His eyes darted back and forth between the front door and the two windows that flanked it. His peripheral vision took in the flowerbeds and stands of pine trees around the house.

After sitting motionless for about five minutes in the truck, David's razor-sharp eyes finally saw something. It was a movement so slight that any other man but David Ricard would never have noticed it. A front window curtain had moved only a fraction of an inch as one of the convicts peered outside to see what David was doing.

The convicts were planning on taking David hostage as soon as he came in the house and using his truck to make their getaway. However, David Ricard was too much of a turkey hunter to be taken off guard like that. It was a game of eyeball to eyeball, and the convicts had blinked. If he had to, David Ricard had the self-discipline to sit motionless in his truck all afternoon, and almost no other person would have the attention span and eagle eyes needed to spot that ever-so-slight movement of the front window curtain.

Moving almost in slow motion, his left foot quietly depressed the clutch, and his right hand effortlessly pushed the gearshift into reverse. Without the slightest tremble or shake in his hand, David turned on the ignition and slowly let up on the clutch. Without his right foot even touching the accelerator, the truck began moving slowly in reverse, inching its way back up the driveway. David tried to steer the truck by looking into the rearview mirror not daring to turn his head away from the front window. Then, he saw it! It was a sight he would never forget as long as he lived. His front door flew open, and one of the escaped convicts was standing there drawing a bead on him with one of his own shotguns.

David floored the accelerator pedal, and the truck flew down the driveway in reverse. The shotgun exploded, and the windshield of the truck was splattered with a neat pattern of number four, bird shot pellets. The convict must have been a city boy, since David had at least four boxes of double OO buckshot in his gun cabinet. If the convict had fired David's thirty-thirty Winchester lever action, he would now be dead. The steel-jacketed, thirty-caliber bullet with thirty grains of gunpowder would have went straight through the windshield directly into David's head or chest. However, the number four birdshot that he used for turkey hunting never even broke the glass.

David Ricard drove at breakneck speed to the sheriff's office, and, in a matter of moments, the house was surrounded by heavily armed deputies, highway patrolmen, and correctional officers who were already in the area with their bloodhound dogs looking for the four men. The convicts made no attempt to flee. They had no place to run. They had spent two days and nights sloshing through the New River swamp fighting mosquitoes, bugs, and water moccasins. They weren't about to run back in there.

Expecting to have to rush the house, the sheriff brought up a bulldozer to give them cover. Luckily, someone had the brains to think of having the prison chaplain call David Ricard's house and talk to the men on the telephone. It worked; one at a time, they came out with their hands raised.

After they had eaten almost everything in Mrs. Ricard's refrigerator, the four convicts had washed and neatly stacked the dishes and sweep the floor. They had even replaced David's shotgun in his gun cabinet. Before they surrendered, they had politely taken off David Richard's clothes and put back on their dirty, wet prison clothes. Mrs. Ricard was amazed at how little mess they made.

Everybody kind of felt sorry for them. They were young white boys, who had taken a wrong turn in life somewhere and now had made it all that much worse. They had exchanged two days and nights of freedom in the New River swamp for many more years behind bars. The next Sunday, our preacher prayed for them.

Although Lake Butler had very little property crime, people still locked their doors and kept loaded guns close at hand. I bore that in mind as I sulked through the mostly dark homes of Sprinkle Field, looking for a place to hide. It filled me with anxiety to think how these people would react to the sight of a naked boy with green hands and testicles running around in their yards.

At the first yard I tried to enter, a waist-high, chain-link fence and a very loud dog repulsed me. The next house had no fence, and I slipped silently around the house into the backyard.

The adrenaline in my system had long since worn off, and extreme fatigue was beginning to grip my body. I was covered with sweat, but, at the same time, I felt a chill. All I wanted was a place to sit down and catch my breath. I stopped in the middle of the yard, bent over, and put my hands on my knees, gasping for air. The fatigue settled over me like a cold, wet blanket. It felt like all the blood was being drained from my arms and legs. I was on the verge of collapse I simply couldn't run anymore.

All the dogs in the neighborhood were barking like crazy, apparently some of the other green hands had also run afoul of the canine yard beasts. As the dogs' barking grew louder, one at a time, lights were coming on in bedrooms throughout Sprinkle Field.

I wondered if my panting for air was so loud the people in the house I was standing behind could hear it. Suddenly, I was bathed in a pool of light. Someone had flipped on a back porch light, and I was caught dead in the center of the incandescent glow of a naked one-hundred-watt bulb. I was temporarily blinded by its fury. I tried to run, but my body would not respond. I felt faint, as if I was on the verge of a heart attack.

Slowly, my blurred vision returned, and I was horrified at what I saw. Standing in the back porch doorway was Miss Irma Doric, the school's militantly, no-nonsense librarian. Probably the most horrible thing that could happen to a teenage boy is to be seen absolutely naked by one of his female schoolteachers. I though that after all I had been through this week, all of my sexual modesty was gone, but now I realized it was not. She was absolutely stone-faced, showing no surprise or shock at the appearance of a naked teenage boy with green hands and testicles standing in her backyard. I felt like I was four years old. She slowly turned around, went back in the house, and closed the door.

Miss Doric was one of the most unusual women I had ever met. She was the stereotypical, old-maid schoolteacher in every way. She had dedicated her life to the education of children and making sure that that none of them ever had any fun. She managed the Union County High School library like a medieval monk must have managed the holy relics. She hated students who moved the books around and got them out of order. When anybody dared check out a book, when it was returned, she would examine it like Sherlock Holmes to make sure that no damage had been done to the precious manuscript of learning while it was out from under her tutelage. She especially hated me, because I was a known library gum chewer, which was something she could not tolerate; she also though I spent too much time looking at the naked pygmy women in the *National Geographic* magazines. She had the power to ban anyone from the library, and I had been banned many times.

Miss Doric had taught English to both my mother and the parents of most of the other students who populated Union County High School in 1960.

Born in Andalusia, Alabama, Irma Doric had graduated from Bessie Tift

College for Women in Forsyth, Georgia, Class of 1928. She was recruited to teach English in Union County and was able to maintain her position during the Depression, despite the fact that the hard times forced many of her students, especially the boys, to drop out to help support their families.

The day after Pearl Harbor, Miss Doric resigned her teaching position and enlisted in the Women's Army Corps. She took a liking to the discipline and structure of military life. She was commissioned an officer and eventually rose to the rank of captain, commanding a basic training company at Fort Benning, Georgia. She eventually was sent overseas, serving as a finance officer with the occupation forces in North Africa, Italy, France, and eventually Germany.

In 1946, she returned to Florida and used her GI Bill educational benefits to attend classes at the University of Florida only one year after the institution went coed. Irma Doric received a Master's degree in Library Science, and, in 1948, she opened the Union County High School library, the first library in the county. Since that day, she has been Union County's one and only librarian, and the library became her kingdom upon which no one trespassed.

Miss Doric was a good gardener, and the backyard of her home in Sprinkle Field contained some of the most beautiful plants and flowers in Lake Butler. Since I felt that I could not run anymore, I decided to try and find a place to hide.

The azalea is one of the favorite ornamental plants in the South. It is a strong, fast-growing, flowering plant that is both drought and freeze resistant. It loves the sandy, acidic soil of the Florida peninsula, and, each spring, it rewards its owner with a lavish cascade of delicate pink blossoms that most southerners find beautiful.

When the azalea bush reaches a certain size, its limbs and foliage create a large, round leafy ball. Within the deep recesses of this vast green ball, under the leaves and branches, lies a cool, dark place, which is the heart of the plant.

I first noticed it when I was a little boy playing in my grandmother's backyard. During the summer, at midday, when the sun was hot and the humidity was oppressive, the dogs would retreat under the dark foliage of the azalea bushes. One day, I decided to follow them. I got down on my hands and knees and crawled through the small hole that the dogs had made, and I discovered a nice, dark, and cool little hiding place a few feet from my grandmother's back porch steps. The azalea bush became an important part of the fantasy world in which I retreated in my childhood. Unlike most boys my age, sports always bored me; so I would always pretend that I was Hopalong Cassidy or Roy Rodgers and that I was hiding from the bad guys in a secret cave somewhere in the mountains of the Old West. I would often hide from by brothers and sisters by ducking around the corner and then vanishing under the nearest azalea bush. I was invisible under the thick foliage, and they had no idea where I had disappeared.

Fleeing from the wrath of the Ag boys, those old memories suddenly came flooding back to me, and I looked around Miss Doric's well-trimmed yard, hoping to spot an azalea bush that could conceal my now much-larger body.

The azalea bush is a fairly slow-growing shrub. The ones in my grandmother's yard might have been anywhere from fifty to one hundred years old. The ones in Sprinkle field had been planted sometime after World War II and were simply not large enough to give me adequate cover. However, they would have to do, because they were the only hiding place available.

The first bush I chose, I had to abandon because of a vicious red ant nest. The second was really too small, but I thought I could get away with it by curling up into the fetal position.

When I played this game when I was a kid, it was always on a hot summer day, not a cold and damp fall night. The ground under the bush was clammy and cold, and I felt that I was crawling into my own grave. The dew had already fallen, and, as I crawled under the bush, I was showered with tiny drops of cold water.

On the other side of the street, two of the other green hands had come up with the same idea, and, like me, they were having trouble finding a plant large enough to hide themselves. They were in the backyard of Mr. Edward Rippinger, the only full-time employee of the Lake Butler Volunteer Fire Department. Mr. Rippinger was a tall, very nice-looking, sandy-haired man who had returned from World War II a genuine hero. He had parachuted into France with the 82nd Airborne Division in the early morning hours of D-Day. Later, he would win the Purple Heart and the Bronze Star fighting in Holland.

When he returned from the war, Mr. Rippinger was given the job of fire chief. It was an important position; the two small fire trucks parked behind the small Lake Butler City Hall building were the only firefighting equipment in Union County. When the sheriff's office received an emergency fire call, a large air-raid siren would wail, producing enough noise to be heard all over town. The town's volunteer firemen would come on the run, grabbing and putting on their equipment as they hurried to the fire station. Two loud blasts meant that the fire was somewhere in the county; one long blast meant it was in town.

It was his job to see that all the firefighting equipment was maintained properly. If he found one speck of dirt on the fire truck, he would be on somebody's ass about it. He also conducted the investigations after the fire and made out all the insurance forms. If arson was suspected, he would work with the sheriff's office and the state fire marshal to help catch the culprits. It was Mr. Rippenger's thankless job to convince the volunteer fire fighters to stick around after the fire was put out and help clean up the mess. People, who were very willing to do their civic duty in putting out a fire, would often balk at the mundane tasks of postfire cleanup.

However, Mr. Rippinger was a former army sergeant and a leader of men. He was always very strict, insisting that all the hoses and equipment had to be collected, wiped off, and stored properly on the trucks. He always made sure the fire trucks were gassed up after every fire and returned to the station with everything properly squared away.

Mr. Rippinger had been watching television when he heard the strange commotion outside his kitchen window. Somebody was definitely in his backyard. If the noise didn't tip him off, the fact that every dog in the neighborhood was barking like crazy certainly confirmed it. He told his wife to call the sheriff's office, while he went into the bedroom to retrieve his U.S. Army-issued, Colt forty-five automatic pistol, which he kept in the dresser drawer next to his bed.

The pistol was a war souvenir brought back from the army. It had been presented to him as a gift by his commanding officer after he had won the Bronze Star. He loved that gun, and, twice a week, religiously, he would field strip the weapon and carefully clean and oil each working part. About once a month, he would go out in the woods and fire off a box of forty-five shells. Mr. Rippinger believed that it was not good for a firearm to go too long without being fired.

Mr. Rippinger loved to show off the pistol. In many ways, he was more proud of it than he was of his Purple Heart and Bronze Star. As he used to say, "A Bronze Star and a dime will get you a cup of coffee, but that pistol is worth something." He once visited my fourth grade classroom and told us about the D-Day invasion and the war in Europe. We had all watched John Wayne movies and honestly believed that war was like a football game. In the movies, only the bad guys get killed, and the good guys always win. Mr. Rippinger told us it wasn't always like that, and, many times, innocent people got hurt. I always liked Mr. Rippinger, because he was one of the few World War II veterans who talked to us honestly about what a war was really like.

The climax of his talk was when he invited one of the students to blindfold him. As we watched in awed silence, the blindfolded Mr. Rippinger completely disassembled the pistol and put it back together again, without a second's hesitation.

After retrieving the automatic pistol from the bedroom, Mr. Rippinger slowly walked to the hall closet and took out the large five-cell flashlight that he used to investigate darkened fire scenes. He next walked into the kitchen and stood silently by the back door listening for a repeat of the noise he had heard earlier. He did not turn on the kitchen light or flick on the back porch light; he was still too much of a soldier to give away his positron to the enemy. He slowly opened the back door and stood silently in the dark staring out through the screen door. He could plainly hear movement in the bushes near his back steps. He pulled back the slide of the automatic and chambered a brass forty-five-caliber shell into the barrel. He made as much noise as possible, because he wanted whoever was out there to know he was armed.

The sound of the chambered round caused the movement in the bushes to halt. This filled Rippinger with dread. If it was an animal of some kind, it would probably continue to move around or run away. The fact that it froze at the sound of the weapon told him that whatever was in the bushes was probably human.

Assuming the combat crouch he had been taught in basic training, he pushed open the screen door, crossed the back porch, and quickly moved down the steps and out into the backyard. He was a very brave man, perfectly willing to take a life to defend his family. He had killed during the war, and he was perfectly willing to do it again. He flicked on his flashlight and pointed the beam directly into the shrubs beside his back porch steps. All he saw was green foliage. He bent low to get a better look to see if something was under the bush. The high-powered beam of the flashlight revealed a set of shiny white buttocks with one large green testicle sticking out from between two chalky thighs.

Mr. Rippinger was a regular visitor to the high school and vigorously supported all of the school's athletic and extracurricular programs. He often lectured students on fire safety, and, for a while, he helped coach junior varsity football. He knew about the green hands and all the shenanigans that went on during initiation week. He also knew immediately that whoever was in the bushes was not an escaped convict or dangerous criminal bent on murder and mayhem. What he didn't know was how many green hands were in his bushes. He decided the best way to find out was to have a little fun of his own.

He lowered the pistol, pointed it straight down at the ground, and quickly squeezed off three shots into the soft earth at his feet.

Bam! Bam! Bam!

The three shots cut through the cool fall air like a steel saw blade hitting a tree. They caused me to break out in chill bumps from the top of my head to the bottoms of my feet. My heart began pounding as I tried to guess which of the green hands had paid a horrible price for this night's foolishness. Were they dead or simply wounded? Would I be the next to die?

Mr. Rippenger's gunshots caused the boy in the bushes to scream and leap out of the bushes with their hands over their heads, begging for the unknown gunman to spare his life. A close look revealed that one of the young men had pissed all over himself.

To his rear, Mr. Rippinger heard more noises and turned to see two more dirt-caked figures with green hands and testicles emerge from behind his wife's gardenia bushes. He could hardly contain himself; it was the funniest sight he had ever seen in his life. The only thing that made him control his laughter was the fact that he was not at all sure why these naked young men were in his backyard.

He turned toward the back porch door and yelled for his wife to bring out three large towels. He only wanted the towels to cover the boy's private parts, but inadvertently didn't tell his wife why he wanted the towels. From the darkened guest bedroom, where she had taken refuge from the unknown danger outside, Mrs. Rippinger could only assume that someone was shot, and the towels were needed to control the bleeding. She leaped to her feet, ran to the bathroom closet, and grabbed every towel in sight.

She ran through the darkened kitchen, flipped on the back porch light, flew through the screen door, and then stopped dead in her tracks. Right in front of her directly in the glare of the back porch light she could see her husband, gun still in hand, calmly talking with three naked teenage boys with their hands and testicles painted green.

Mrs. Rippinger was a decent Christian woman who had not missed a single day of church or Sunday school in over a decade. She had never seen any male naked except her husband and her son and then only when he was a small child. The sight of three naked teenage boys in her backyard was more than she could handle. She dropped the towels on the back porch and then retreated back into her darkened kitchen.

Later that night, the neighbors reported hearing heated words coming from the Rippinger house. This was something very unusual for the Rippingers, who were famous for being very happily married and never fighting. She told her husband, in no uncertain terms, that she did not appreciate him not warning her that there were three naked boys in her backyard. She worried what the neighbors would think and what her reputation would be down at the Baptist church. Could she continue to teach Sunday school after this?

Somehow, her husband didn't seem to share her anxiety, and he slowly drifted off to sleep with his wife still bitching at him.

# The Baptism of Harry Byrd

They say when a person is dying their life flashes before their eyes. As I lay under the azalea bush, terribly uncomfortable and chilled to the bone, I tried to think about other, more pleasant things. My mind turned to thoughts of early childhood and the good times I had with my grandmother. Years later, in Vietnam, I would do the same thing; let my mind take me away to another place and time, where things were better. Maybe it was the chill night air or maybe it was the need to put the ant bites, the burns, the abrasions, the bruises, the splinters, and the cold and damp dirt out of my mind, but some very strange thoughts began to come into my head.

In the far distance, I heard the plaintive wail of a siren. I knew that meant that Sheriff Brannon was on his way to Sprinkle Field. There is something about a siren that always causes me anxiety. When I was a little boy, I would spend holidays and summer vacations at my aunt's house on Waldo Road in Gainesville. Every Saturday, we would go shopping at the F. W. Woolworth's store in downtown Gainesville. While we were shopping, if either my aunt or my grandmother heard a siren, they would immediately go to a payphone and call my aunt's house to make sure everything was all right.

When I was in elementary school, I would hear the siren blow down at the volunteer fire department and get scared, wondering if it was my house on fire. There was so much anxiety about the siren that Mr. Rippinger began a system to tell people where the fire was located. He would make one very long blast if the fire was in town and two shorter blasts if the fire was out of town.

Lake Butler was a quiet little place to grow up, and the people, especially the older people, didn't like unnecessary siren blowing. We never blew it on New Year's Eve or the Fourth of July or any other time when it wasn't an emergency. A siren just simply frightened people too much. My grandmother once told me a strange tale of how the first siren came to Union County. It was sometime just before the beginning of World War I; my grandmother always thought it was 1913, because that was the year my mother was born, but, in her old age, she couldn't be sure.

This was before Union County existed as a political entity, when it was still part of Bradford County. Lake Butler was an isolated little community situated along the railroad tracks connecting Jacksonville with Gainesville. The town was small with only about four hundred people. Almost all the white people lived within sight of the tall oak trees in the town square. The small black population of Lake Butler lived in rigid segregation just beyond the railroad tracks in their own squalid section of town.

Lake Butler's only law enforcement officer was the constable, who was referred to as the "town marshal." I never really figured out why he was called "the marshal" rather than constable. The only logical explanation was the popular, ten-cent western story magazines that almost everyone in Lake Butler read for entertainment. Having a town marshal just sounded better and more western than having a town constable. The town of Lake Butler was too small to afford to pay the marshal a salary, so he was paid by the arrest; he was given two dollars for each person arrested, with a maximum of ten dollars a month. This really wasn't a bad salary for what was basically a part-time job.

What the marshal was primarily expected to do was keep the Negro population under control. Usually, the marshal only worked on Friday and Saturday nights. During the week, everyone was too tired from work and too broke to do much hell-raising. The marshal almost never arrested a white person, although they would get just as drunk and rowdy as the Negroes. If the marshal threw too many white people in jail, he would anger both them and their relatives and probably lose his job. The final result of all this was that drunk whites got a ride home, whereas Negroes, who were not allowed to vote and thus had no political power, were thrown into jail at a rate of two dollars each.

Those days, just before the start of World War I, were the tail end of an era my grandmother called "the horse and buggy days." The automobile was around, but most people didn't own one. Almost all the roads were unpaved, and the mule and wagon were still the most common, and reliable, method of travel. The only paved road, in what would later become Union County, was four blocks of Main Street in Lake Butler that fronted the oak-shaded town square. It had been covered with red bricks, brought down from Georgia by train, and laid in place using convict chain-gang labor.

Only two people in Lake Butler owned an automobile: Dr. King, who was always being called out in the middle of the night to deliver babies, and the town marshal, a man of dubious reputation named Harry Byrd. It was Marshal Harry Byrd who brought the first siren to Lake Butler. With only two automobiles in the whole county, and with only one paved road, one might wonder why Marshal Harry Byrd felt the need to have a siren.

Every other year, when the Florida Legislature met, Harry Byrd would put on his one and only dress suit and take the train to Tallahassee. He told everyone he had important, and confidential, business with the state legislature, but most people knew the truth. When the legislature was in session, the whorehouses in Tallahassee brought up white women from Miami and Tampa to service the politicians. Harry would check into one of Tallahassee's cheaper hotels, hang out in the lobby, bum drinks in the saloons, and sample the sexual vices of Florida's capitol.

It was during one of these trips that Harry Byrd met a lobbyist representing a New York company that made sirens. He was in Tallahassee trying to talk the legislature into requiring them on all automobiles driven by police officers. Representatives from Tampa and Miami were sponsoring the "siren bill" as it was called, but it was not likely to pass, because of opposition from small north Florida counties. While a siren might be needed in the crowded streets of places like Miami, Tampa or Jacksonville, there was really no use for them in small, rural counties with few paved roads.

Harry Byrd was fascinated by the device and talked the lobbyist into giving him one for free. Harry was a well-known raconteur and chronic liar; he told the lobbyist that he was a high sheriff and close personal friends with the governor and a lot of other politicians. It is hard to believe that the lobbyist really believed that this potbellied, balding Florida cracker, with dirty fingernails and bad breath, could be a high sheriff with political connections. Anyway, the lobbyist promised Harry that he would ship him a siren as soon as he returned to New York.

Harry Byrd was able to afford these trips to Tallahassee, because he had built up several lucrative auxiliary careers besides being the Lake Butler town marshal. He was also a small-time dirt farmer growing corn and cotton on his puny forty-acre farm just outside Lake Butler. Harry Byrd was also a prolific moonshiner. While his wife and children were given the laborious job of working his small farm, Harry Byrd spent most of his time making and drinking his own illegal wares. On weekends, he could be found in the Negro section of town, either peddling his moonshine or arresting people who drank too much of it.

The two dollars Harry made for each arrest was not all profit; he was expected to use part of that sum to feed the prisoners and maintain the jail. The Lake Butler town council felt that Harry should be able to clear about ninety cents profit for each arrest. However, Harry cleared almost a dollar and a half. He did this by feeding the prisoners nothing but grits and gray, twice a day, and forcing his wife and daughters to cook the food and bring it to the jail.

The town jail was a small, redbrick building with a strangely rounded roof. It consisted of absolutely nothing but two tiny cells. There was no office, kitchen, or anything else, just two jail cells. The two cells had nothing inside but a bucket for a toilet and a bed made from pine boards. There were no blankets, pillows, or heat in the cells. All these things cost money and would come out of the two dollars Harry Byrd made for each arrest. Heavy doors made of crossed iron slats secured the cells. During the winter, cold winds blew in between the iron slats, and, in the summer, the mosquitoes and fleas were unbearable.

No one stayed at night to guard or tend the prisoners. Once he locked them up, Harry just went home to his family. One particularly cold night, an elderly Negro prisoner died of exposure in one of the unheated cells. After that, the town council ordered Harry Byrd to both heat the cells and provide blankets or stop making arrests when the temperature dropped below forty degrees. Harry was not about to spend good money on firewood and blankets, and, since he didn't own a thermometer, he just stopped making arrests from late November until the first of March, unless it was something very serious like a white man getting robbed or a killing. All this made the marshal angry, not just because it reduced his income, but what Harry Byrd really couldn't understand about the whole deal was why someone would make such a fuss over one old dead nigger.

People used to say that Harry Byrd also made money for his trips to Tallahassee by starving his wife and children. Harry came from a long line of poor white trash and had inherited the small farm from his wife's father, who was Harry Byrd's mother's brother. Back then, and to a great extent even now, marrying your cousin was not considered any big deal.

Harry's wife was a thin, longsuffering woman with four children, two girls and two boys. They lived in a small clapboard farmhouse with rotten roof shingles and sagging floor joists. His wife made her own lye soap and washed the family's clothes in a large number three washtub on the back porch. The older boys worked the fields, planting in the spring, cultivating in the hot summer, and picking in the fall. In their spare time, they trapped possums, coons, and other small animals to eat.

The girls helped their mother by making soap and working a small truck patch garden adjacent to the house. Because of their efforts, the family had green vegetables on the table. Luckily for the family, Harry was gone most of the time returning only to sleep, eat, beat the children, and demand sex from his wife. Besides doing all the farm work, the family also had to feed the prisoners and keep the jail cells as clean and orderly as possible. Every day, you could see Harry Byrd's wife and oldest daughter walking barefoot down the dirt road to the jail and carrying a bucket of grits and gravy to feed the prisoners. People gossiped about what a sorry excuse for a man Harry Byrd was and wondered why he couldn't at least give them a ride in his automobile. Harry defended himself by saying that he did give them rides to town when it was raining, but it just cost too much gasoline to go and get them every day.

Harry's children never attended church and seldom showed up in school. The children were always barefoot and dressed like beggars. All the children had head lice and ringworms. They would have been much worse off if folks hadn't taken pity on them. Every few days, one of the better-off women in Lake Butler would drop off a load of washing or mending for Harry's wife to do on the side to make extra money. At the same time, they would usually deliver a pecan pie, a pound cake, a mess of collard greens, or some clothes that they claimed their children had outgrown. Harry's wife would smile and accept the gifts; she was poor, and every little bit helped. Everyone in Lake Butler said it was a shame and disgrace that white children had to live like that.

The small redbrick jail was located on the far end of Main Street out of sight behind an old warehouse that sat beside the railroad tracks. Across the railroad tracks from the jail was the small section of Lake Butler where the black population lived. Polite people called the few acres of run-down shacks "The Quarters," others used the more commonly heard name of "Nigger Town."

Harry Byrd would spend hours riding through the narrow dirt street of "The Quarters" wearing a dirty pair of khaki work pants, a sweat-stained white shirt, and scuffed brown brogans. He called this outfit his "uniform." He carried his revolver in a black cross-draw holster that rode high on a worn Sam Browne belt that strained to hold in Harry's ever-growing belly. His badge was literally a tin shield with the word "Marshal" scratched on it with a nail.

It was late one Friday afternoon when the express agent down at the train depot notified Harry Byrd that the package he had been expecting had arrived. It took all day Saturday for the town's blacksmith, who doubled as a sometime auto mechanic, to install it on the wide running board of Harry's secondhand, 1909 Model T Ford automobile.

The vehicle was Harry's pride and joy; unlike everything else he owned, Harry kept his automobile washed and running good. He had purchased it a little more than a year ago for a hundred and ten dollars, which was a small fortune in those days.

The siren was not electrically powered. To make it work, a person had to sit on the passenger side of the vehicle and turn a hand crank. The siren was designed for a large city where they had two officers in the police cars. The blacksmith had tried to mount the siren on the driver's side, but because of the way the crank was positioned, and the high front bumper of the Model T, it had to be positioned on the passenger side to operate properly. This was a serious problem. Harry Byrd was the only lawman within a twenty-five-mile radius of Lake Butler, and he couldn't drive his automobile and operate the siren at the same time. It was a terrible thing to have a fine new piece of equipment and not be able to use it. Harry Byrd was like a little boy who had received a new bicycle for Christmas and couldn't ride it. It was just a little after ten o'clock on Saturday night when the marshal finally thought up a solution for his problem.

Earlier in the day, he had arrested an elderly Negro alcoholic that everyone called "Uncle Amos." He was, as the marshal liked to say, "a regular" down at the small jail. Harry drove down to the jail and found Uncle Amos asleep in the small cell, shivering from the cold. It was early March, and Harry Byrd had just resumed making arrests after taking the three coldest winter months off. Sometimes, jail prisoner's families would bring them a blanket and extra food, but Uncle Amos lived out of town on a sharecropper's farm and had no kinfolk to look after him.

Harry rousted Uncle Amos from his sleep and told him he could go home if he helped him do something. Although Uncle Amos was very cold and craving a drink of moonshine, he hesitated, telling the marshal he might as well spend the night in jail since he was already there. This made Harry Byrd furious; he would normally have pistol-whipped the old Negro, but that would not solve his problem, and he didn't want anybody else dying in his jail. After much bickering back and forth, Uncle Amos finally agreed, but only after Harry promised to sell him a quart of moonshine on credit and give him a ride home. Everyone knew to sell anything to Uncle Amos on credit was the same as giving it to him free, since Uncle Amos had never paid back a financial debt in his life.

The two men got into the marshal's car, and Harry Byrd showed Uncle Amos how to crank the handle on the siren. When he tried it, the elderly black man was shocked by the noise. The high-pitched wail could be heard at least a mile away. In those days, people were not used to loud noises. A barking dog, a clap of thunder, or a shotgun blast was about as noisy as things got around Lake Butler, Florida.

The marshal cranked up his car and drove off from the jail with the siren wailing at full blast. He drove down Main Street twice, circled the town square, and then drove back down Main Street heading into The Quarters.

Harry wanted to see what effect the siren would have on the Negroes, so he circled The Quarters three times before heading out of town to take Uncle Amos home. Once he had cleared the city limits, the wail of the siren slowed and then finally stopped. Uncle Amos complained that his arm was getting tired from turning the crank, and, since they were out of town, Harry decided that to continue blowing it was a waste. Anyway, he was so proud of his new piece of equipment, he certainly didn't want to wear it out.

One of the first people who heard the wail of the marshal's siren was Reverend Rastus Slaughter, who lived in the parsonage of the First Baptist Church on Main Street. Reverend Slaughter had lived his whole life studying the Book of Revelations and reading everything he could about the Second Coming, the final judgment, and the end of the world.

My grandmother always scoffed at such people. Why, with so much work to be done, would a person want to waste all their time worrying about the end of the world? It particularly irked her how happy these people got when they started talking about the end of the world. It was almost like they were so miserable here on earth, they were really looking forward to it. What a miserable way to live. If the world is going to end, then let it end! Why worry about something you have absolutely no control over?

Reverend Slaughter considered people who scoffed to be poor lost souls or ignorant fools who refused to see the truth. Reverend Slaughter firmly believed that such things as the electric light and the airplane were proof positive that man had transgressed into God's domain. The reverend was particularly upset with the airplane. If God had intended man to fly, he would have given him wings like a bird. For us to transgress into the heavens, God's domain, in these winged contraptions smacked of the Tower of Babel.

Reverend Slaughter also disliked the electric light. He felt it was an unnatural thing; light without fire went against God's plan. He believed it would ruin the youth of America by allowing them to stay up late at night reading books and playing cards. He feared that grown-ups would no longer be able to work in the daytime after they had spent the night partying and loitering with friends under the hellish glow of the electric light.

Reverend Slaughter was a true believer in the "rapture," the notion that one day the whole world would be suddenly depopulated of born-again Christians, who would arise and meet the Lord Jesus Christ in the air. Under no circumstances, he urged his congregation, would Jesus return to earth; we will go to meet him in the air. Some people believed that Jesus would return to earth, but Reverend Slaughter knew these people were seriously misguided, if not under the influence of an evil force.

Reverend Slaughter knew all the sure-fire signs of the rapture: wars and rumors of wars, floods and droughts, tornadoes and hurricanes, and the increasing wickedness of men.

Like most fundamentalist Christians, Reverend Slaughter believed that the return of Jesus could be any day now. The appearance of Halley's Comet and the sinking of the Titanic were all positive signs that indeed the time for the rapture was at hand. Reverend Slaughter had taught that the Second Coming would likely be at night, since Christ had warned that he would come like a thief in the night.

When Reverend Slaughter heard the wail of the siren on Harry Byrd's car, he sat straight up in bed. He had never heard such a noise in all of his forty-four years on earth. It could only mean one thing. He immediately ordered his wife to get dressed and prepare to meet Jesus. He told his children that the noise that had awakened them from their sleep was the sacred trumpet of the Angel Gabriel announcing the immediate return of Christ.

After dressing in his Sunday best, Reverend Slaughter went to the small barn behind the parsonage and saddled up his horse. Waving a kerosene lantern, he rode through the town of Lake Butler, Paul Revere fashion, summoning the people to gather in the town square to meet Jesus. He warned everyone to be properly dressed and bring their children. Anyone who had not been shaken out of their slumber by the siren or the reverend's yelling from horseback was finally roused from their sleep by Reverend Slaughter pounding on their door. He literally went door to door getting everyone up.

The normally quiet and peaceful Dr. J. W. King greeted the reverend at the door with a fireplace poker, threatening to bust his head if he pounded on the door one more time.

"Don't you realize," the reverend shouted, "It's the end of the world. Jesus has returned."

"Hogwash," Dr. King screamed. "All you're doing is running around scaring people to death. I'll see you in the morning, after the world ends."

Undaunted by the hardworking doctor's unbelief and need for a good night's sleep, the reverend continued going door to door, periodically dismounting from his horse to pound on a door summon the faithful to the town square to meet Jesus. Within only a short period of time, the entire population of Lake Butler, minus reprobates like Dr. King and a few other people who were too drunk on this Saturday night to get out of bed, had gathered at the town square. No Negroes were in the gathering. Reverend Slaughter had not crossed over the railroad tracks to notify the black population that they too could meet Jesus. However, many of the white people had live-in Negro domestic help. They begged for and received permission to go get their relatives. The news actually spread faster in the Negro part of town than it did in the white section, since the houses in The Quarters were so close together.

After a short period of time, terrified blacks were also beginning to gather at the town square, but they kept a respectful distance from the whites. When Jesus came again, he would find a segregated Lake Butler to greet him. The young wife of Dr. King let her curiosity override her husband's skepticism. She decided to get dressed and walk to the town square and see what all the fuss was about. The doctor who had been treating patients all day was tired. He again scoffed and said for her to go if she wanted to, but he was going back to sleep. When Mrs. King got to the town square, she estimated that about three hundred people had gathered under the big live Oak trees.

Most of the white people were dressed in their Sunday finest and were carrying kerosene lanterns. Almost all the Negro women were wearing the traditional white gowns they wore to church each Sunday. Some of the Negro men had on Sunday suits, but most came in the bib overalls they wore in the fields.

Dr. King had grown up in a very liberal Advent Christian denomination that didn't approve of all the extremist nonsense found among some other congregations. Basically, he believed that the world ended when you died. At least, it ended for you. The world might go on for thousands of more years, but, when they put you in the ground, then you would go home to heaven. Dr. King and his family often antagonized the fundamentalists, like Reverend Slaughter, because he also believed in salvation by grace, the notion that some people who never went to church or were baptized would still go to heaven simply because God would have mercy on them, like the good thief on the cross. The fundamentalists firmly believed that any unbaptized soul was doomed to the fires of hell and that salvation by grace was a bold lie spread by the Catholic Church. The God they worshiped only loved those who had been baptized. His rule was harder than stone and could never be broken.

In those days, there were no buildings in the town square, only a large open space filled with live Oak trees and grass. It was a neat and well-tended area that was a favorite site for picnics and band concerts during the spring and fall. It was also where the politicians came to speak around election time. There was talk that the local chapter of the United Daughter's of the Confederacy would erect a statue to the confederate dead, but, so far, nothing had come of it.

By the time Harry Byrd had returned to town from taking Uncle Amos home, Reverend Slaughter had gotten the gathering organized, arranging the colored people on one side and white people on the other. There was a great amount of hymn singing, praying, speaking in tongues, and praising of the Lord going on when Harry Byrd drove up in his automobile. When the fat marshal was told that everyone in town had heard the horn of Gabriel and that the end of time was about to happen, he was filled with terror. He had not lived a good Christian life, and his sins were well-known both to him and everyone else in the small town.

Besides his moonshining, drinking, and whoring in Tallahassee, there was an even worse side to Harry Byrd. One year, while Dr. King was treating Harry's children for rickets, he discovered that the oldest daughter also had gonorrhea. Since the doctor had often treated Harry for the same social disease, it didn't take a genius to figure out what had happened. Dr. King became very angry and cussed Harry out threatening to go to the high sheriff in Starke if it ever happened again. Harry cried and took on like a typically repentant hypocrite, saying he was ashamed. He blamed the whole sorry affair on alcohol and the fact that his wife no longer enjoyed sex. He promised the doctor that from now on when he had the urging, he would go see a colored woman he knew down in The Quarters. Dr. King, who treated everyone in Lake Butler, black and white, knew that the "colored woman" Harry Byrd referred to was only sixteen years old and mentally slow.

After that incident, the doctor drove his automobile out to the Byrd farm on a regular basis, checking the girls and looking for any sign of social disease or sexual molestation. He also checked Harry's wife to make sure he hadn't been beating on her. When Dr. King examined the women, he forced Harry Byrd to stand in the yard or drive to Lake Butler. When he protested, the angry doctor threatened to see him on the damn chain-gang if he didn't kill his sorry-ass first. Dr. King was the only man in Lake Butler who had no fear of Harry Byrd.

When Harry Byrd heard about the rapture, he leaped out of his car, fell on his knees, and began calling on the name of the Lord for salvation. He cried, wailed, and gnashed his teeth. With his big bare hands, he pulled giant handfuls of grass from the town square and threw them into the air. Reverend Slaughter kneeled to pray with the repentant marshal.

During the course of this exchange, the terrible secret was revealed. Harry Byrd had not heard Gabriel's horn, clear evidence that he was not one of the chosen. When further questioned, it was learned that he had never been baptized. A cold chill of pure terror ran through the crowd; here was their worst nightmare come true, an unbaptized sinner about to meet a just God.

"Baptize me, please God baptize me," Harry cried with tears streaming down his cheeks.

"Nobody can be baptized once the rapture begins. The trumpet has already sounded; it is too late, my brother," the minister told the prostrate sinner.

The marshal slowly rose from his kneeling, repentant position; pulled out his revolver as he moved upward; and pointed the deadly weapon directly into the belly of Reverend Slaughter.

Marshall Byrd screamed, "Damn it, if you don't baptize me right now, I'll blow your guts out. So help me God, I will."

Reverend Slaughter was sure that the end of the world was coming within the hour, but, at the same time, the barrel of the revolver was too real to be ignored. In typical Baptist doublethink, the reverend decided and then proclaimed to the crowd, "Who am I to say who can and cannot be baptized!"

Seeing his Christian duty clear, he told the marshal that he would gladly baptize him, but the church was in darkness, and there was no water in the concrete pool behind the pulpit where baptisms were held.

Shoving the gun deeper into the preacher's belly, the marshal reminded him of the existence of the nearby lake, after whom the town of Lake Butler was named. Pointing to his automobile, he ordered the good reverend to get in.

With the whole town following on foot, the preacher and the marshal drove slowly down the small dirt road leading from the town square to the lake.

Together they formed a torch-lit parade. The collected white citizens fell in behind the marshal's automobile, holding their glass-faced kerosene lanterns high on forked sticks to better light the way.

Some Negroes also had lanterns, but most of them carried flaming torches made from snarled pine knots, what folks called "fat lightered." These pine knots were found in the woods around old dead pine trees. They were filled with hardened pine tar that had settled in the lower parts of the tree once it had fallen. When set afire, the pine tar dripped out like large flaming gobs of fat, hence the name "fat lightered." The fat-lightered knots put out a lot of light and burned for a reasonably long time, but, most importantly, they were free to anyone who would go out in the woods and find them. Kerosene costs money.

The procession must have been a strange sight, moving down the narrow dirt road that was flanked and overhung with large oak trees thick with Spanish moss. From the town square to the lake, the narrow dirt road snaked through an area that was nothing but hard woodlands with swampy palmetto undergrowth. It came to a stop in a small clearing where fishermen launched their boats and put out catfish lines.

Harry Byrd parked the automobile as close to the dark waters of the lake as he could. The headlights illuminated the dark black waters, reflecting off the red eyes of two big alligators only a few feet offshore. Fearing that leaving the lights on would kill his car battery, Harry Byrd waved his pistol in the air and ordered the gathered citizens to gather brush and build bonfires for illumination.

It took the huge crowd only a few minutes to find enough dead limbs and pinecones to make a large bonfire. After the brush had been piled just right, one of the Negroes stepped up and tossed his pine knot torch into the dry pinecones. Within a few minutes, the flames were spreading and growing. People began to fall down in prayer as the heat of the fire reminded them of what was in store for the poor lost souls. The flames reflected off the dark waters of the lake and cast strange shadows in the moss-draped trees.

It was a Druid-like gathering, this strange mixture of Negroes and white people under the big oak trees next to the lake. It harkened back to both pre-Christian Europe and preslavery Africa.

In those times, before the coming of Catholic missionaries to the dark woods above the Rhine River and the slave ships off the windward coast of Africa, the ancestors of both these people danced naked around roaring fires to welcome the summer solstice.

Within each one of them was a deep-rooted desire to return to their pagan roots. That night, they were close to being once again wild and free creatures of nature, worshiping the spirits of the forest and the old gods of their ancestors.

Thousands of years of brow beating and intimidation by Bible-thumping preachers and bloated popes had failed to drive it out of them. They longed to once again worship nature outdoors, in the greatest of all cathedrals, instead of within the claustrophobic stained-glass prison of a church, where the air is always stale, and the spirit is depressed by long, boring sermons and meaningless ritual.

That night, under the jet-black sky, in the light of the growing fire, they could see in each other's eyes the reflection of a time long gone. The thing that most of them found in the roaring flames of the bonfire was not the fires of hell but something of the loins as well as the spirit.

With the flames leaping into the air, Reverend Slaughter spoke to the crowd and said it was now time for the baptism service to begin. Even with the end of the world only a few minutes off, this old-time Baptist preacher could not resist the urge to preach at least one more sermon. He strutted back and forth in front of the crowd, quoting by heart from the book of Daniel about the significance of the horn of Gabriel. He spoke of heaven and the joys waiting there and of hell and the torments within that horrible place.

"Amen, let's get on with it," Harry Byrd impatiently called out. Reverend Slaughter ignored Harry's hint and continued to preach. The longer he went on, the angrier Harry became. The marshal began fingering his revolver. He was suspicious that Reverend Slaughter was stalling, hoping that the rapture would come before he was baptized. *That Bible-thumping bastard would love to see me in hell*, Harry thought to himself.

Finally, he could take no more and grabbed the preacher's arm and thrust the revolver deep within his ribs.

"Gawddamn it, let's go," he bellowed.

The preacher refused to move until Harry had holstered his revolver. The argument was heated, with Harry Byrd threatening to shoot the preacher on the spot. However, this time, Reverend Slaughter stood his ground. He was not about to baptize a man at gunpoint. Finally, the angry marshal slid the revolver into his cross-draw holster and meekly waited for the reverend to complete his sermon.

A Southern Baptist baptism is a simple procedure. The Protestant teaching of John Calvin was a bitter protest against the ornate costumes and formal ceremonies of the Church of Rome. Calvin, whose teaching made up the fundamental core of all Southern Baptist belief, stressed simplicity in all things. All religious costume, statuary, and pageantry were banned. Biblical teachings replaced the pope's authority. Any ceremony that survived the Protestant Reformation was basic, down to earth, and completely grounded in scripture. There would be no robes, rosary beads, golden candlesticks, incense, or saints in the Southern Baptist faith. These people's religion was just like their lives, plain and simple: simple preaching, simple praying, simple singing, and simple doctrine. Some things were right, and other things were wrong. There was no room for error or debate. The Bible said it, they believed it, and that settled it. There could be no honest difference of opinion, no tolerance of others beliefs, since their beliefs were wrong. There was only one way, one correct teaching. You were either in or out, lost or saved. These people might pick up a live rattlesnake during their worship or drink poison, but they would never bow down to a statue, don a vestment, or honor any authority other than *The Holy Bible* and their own conscience.

It was almost midnight when Reverend Slaughter finally led Harry Byrd down to the dark lake waters. After a brief pause, the preacher summoned up his courage and waded into the cold water. With each step, he could feel the dark brown mud closing around his best pair of shoes, slowly oozing through the soles and laces soaking his socks and feet. The cold water rose slowly up the reverend's pant legs, ruining forever his best pair of dress pants. Finally, the water reached the preacher's crotch and soaked his suit coat.

Harry Byrd could care less about his attire. His old brown brogans had been in the mud and water around his moonshine still hundreds of times. His khaki pants were so worn and stained that the lake water would make little or no difference.

The two men stopped in hip-deep water, and Reverend Slaughter positioned himself to perform this most sacred of Christian ceremonies. Although he had done hundreds of baptisms, each one held special significance to him. It was his reason for living, his mission on earth, and the reason he became a minister. It was his direct contact with God. It was God's work.

Baptists belief firmly in total submersion; they scorned any faith, like the Methodists, who only sprinkled water over the head. My daddy use to call himself a "dunked or be damned Baptist." Part of the ceremony involved a handkerchief that was held in the right hand palm of the person to be baptized. When he began to descend into the water, the right hand was raised, and the handkerchief would cover the mouth and nose keeping the water out. Reverend Slaughter quietly asked Harry Byrd if he had a handkerchief. "Sure," Harry replied, reaching into his back pocket. Harry Byrd pulled out a piece of old red bandana cloth that had probably never been washed in its existence. It was covered with spit, dried snot, tobacco juice, and oil from the crankcase of his automobile. The reverend whispered for him to hold it in his right hand and prepare to cover his mouth and nose with it. Harry simply nodded, not seeming to mind putting the filthy rag over his mouth and nose.

Following a time-honored tradition, which went back to the River Jordan and John the Baptist, the reverend put his left hand in the middle of the marshal's back and raised his right hand toward the heavens. He uttered a brief prayer asking Almighty God to grant his saving grace to this poor lost sinner. He then turned to face Harry Byrd and asked him in a voice loud enough for all to hear, "Do you accept the Lord Jesus Christ as your personal savior?"

"I do," Harry answered in a weak whisper.

"Therefore, in obedience to the Great Command, I hereby baptize you in the name of the Father, the Son, and the Holy Ghost."

The reverend reached down, took the marshal's right hand, and raised the dirty red rag to cover his face. With his left hand in the small of Harry Byrd's back for support, Reverend Slaughter began to slowly lower Harry Byrd into the water.

At the last minute, Harry thought about his holstered pistol. It had cost him thirty-eight dollars, and he didn't want to get it wet. With his free left hand, Harry reached across his belly and pulled out the weapon. Just as the marshal's head went under the water, his left hand flew skyward, holding the dark blue Smith and Wesson revolver toward the night sky. All of his body went under the water except for the left forearm and hand, which held the pistol high and dry.

Reverend Slaughter was furious that Harry Byrd would desecrate the baptism ceremony by drawing his gun. The pistol protruding from the black lake water filled him with rage. He decided that he had been intimidated by the foul-smelling lawman long enough. With a smooth move, he simply withdrew his hand from the small of Harry Byrd's back and let him drop into the gooey mud in the bottom of the lake.

As Harry felt himself losing his balance, he squeezed the trigger of his pistol, firing a shot into the air. The bullet missed the reverend's head by inches. Harry Byrd didn't know how to swim and panicked when he felt the reverend's hand move. As he descended the two or three feet to the bottom of the lake, Harry Byrd began to flail his arms and legs wildly, stirring up the mud and entwining himself in all kinds of aquatic weeds. Finally, he regained his footing and arose from the water, covered from head to foot with brown mud and weeds, looking like some kind of strange form of swamp monster.

With his nose and mouth full of water, Harry began gasping for air and violently spitting out lake water and pieces of the weeds he had swallowed. Suddenly, he noticed a strange feeling between his legs; it was probably just a string of aquatic weeds, but, in Harry's mind, it was either a water moccasin or one of the big alligators. He began to jump up and down and scream at the top or his voice.

Suddenly, without warning, Harry Byrd began firing his revolver wildly. The bullets flew over the heads of the crowd, causing everyone to hit the ground or run panic-stricken into the swampy woods. Reverend Slaughter dove for cover, flying into the dark water and furiously swimming the few feet to shore. As he crawled out of the water, Reverend Slaughter could see Harry spinning around like a top in the water, stomping his feet, screaming, and firing his revolver wildly. Convinced that Harry intended to kill him for letting him drop into the lake, Reverend Slaughter fled into the woods and took refuge behind a large pine tree stump.

Harry Byrd continued to fire his pistol until all his ammunition was gone. Even with his bullets spent, the marshal continued to stomp and scream attempting to scare off the nonexistent water moccasin or alligator he believed was at his heels. Finally, the portly marshal ran from the water like a marine storming a beachhead and collapsed on the shore only a few feet from his automobile. For a long time, he just laid there, not moving. Some people thought he had suffered a heart attack and was dead. Only an occasional moan and groan told folks he was still alive.

Slowly, the chill in the air began to bring Harry Byrd back to life. He arose from the cold dirt standing on his knees and looking around like a dog that had just woken up from a long sleep. Finally, he slowly rose to his feet, raised his hands toward the heavens, and yelled, "Praise the Lord! I'm saved!"

"Praise the Lord, I say, praise the Lord!"

Reverend Slaughter emerged from behind the tree stump repeating Harry's words, admonishing the crowd to "Praise the Lord!"

The crowd slowly arose from their hiding places, at first only muttering the words under their breath, and then, with the encouragement of Reverend Slaughter, they began shouting over and over, louder and louder, "Praise the Lord. Praise the Lord!"

Soon, the crowd had gathered around the penitent Marshal, lying on hands and offering individual prayers. Soon, the whole crowd was singing and clapping, enraptured with the Holy Spirit and joyous over the salvation of this one miserable soul from the fires of hell.

Several other people approached Reverend Slaughter asking to be baptized. Although going back into the cold lake water was not what he wanted to do, this was really a Baptist preacher's dream come true: people begging to be baptized. He could hardly say no. One at a time, he began leading repentant sinners into the dark, cold waters of the lake to be washed of their sins.

Because almost everyone wanted to be baptized just before the rapture, the baptisms went on for over an hour. Finally, Reverend Slaughter's feet and legs were so numb from the cold, he had to come out and warm himself by the fire.

The crowd begged the reverend to please, for God's sake, please, just baptize my children and me. The preacher begged off; it's just too cold in that water. Finally, Reverend Philip Greene, the pastor of the Negro Baptist church down in The Quarters, stepped forward and announced that he would begin baptizing colored people who wished it.

Within seconds, the crowd of Negroes began to hum and shuffle their feet with a rhythm and soul-deep sincerity that white people can only marvel at. The large crowd of Negroes moved down to the lake, and, soon, Reverend Greene was baptizing people left and right. Nobody noticed it at the time, but white people began to mix in with the crowd of Negroes awaiting baptism. It was about two o'clock in the morning when it came the turn of the first white person to be baptized.

"It ain't right for a colored preacher to baptize a white person," Reverend Greene protested.

It was an awkward, uncomfortable moment. Reverend Slaughter had no desire to go back into the lake, so he nodded to Reverend Greene and told him that under the circumstances, it was all right, just this once.

The baptisms went on until almost four o'clock in the morning. The air and the water got colder and colder as the night wore on. Finally, Reverend Greene had to be physically removed from the lake, because he began shaking so violently from the cold people were afraid the elderly minister would have a stroke. Reverend Slaughter took up the slack, again venturing back into the cold water until just before dawn, when the last of the crowd was finally baptized.

By five o'clock, people were beginning to drift off and go home. Reverend Slaughter urged them to stay. He was positive that a just and merciful God had put off the rapture until daybreak, the same time as the Resurrection, to give the faithful just a little more time to bring in lost souls. The crowd sang "Amazing Grace" and "Abide with Me" to keep up their spirits.

When the sun finally rose that morning, it illuminated a cold, wet, and sleepy crowd of people. Daylight, instead of bringing the rapture, revealed a gray, overcast sky that threatened rain.

Harry Byrd's enrapture with the Holy Spirit went away about as quickly as it had come. After dancing around on one foot for some time, Harry became chilled and had to go sit by the fire to try and dry his wet clothes. After drying himself as best he could, Harry Byrd climbed into the back of his car and tried to get some sleep. However, sleep did not come, because the crowd was making too much noise, and he was still very wet and cold. As the sun arose, Harry Byrd was sitting on the running board of his car with his head in his hands. He had now been awake for nearly twenty-four hours and had a splitting headache. He hardly noticed that a little Negro boy was eyeballing his new siren.

"What be dis here thing mister?" the boy asked.

All Harry could do was grunt an answer.

"It's a sii-reen."

"What be a si-scream?" the little boy asked.

"Gawddamnit, you turn that there handle, and it makes a lot of noise," Harry said.

"Dis handle?"

"Yes, that damn handle; now shut your mouth for awhile. I don't feel good."

For a few minutes, the little boy eyed the siren handle fascinated by this mysterious contraption. Harry Byrd climbed back into the back seat of his automobile and rolled up into a ball, shivering from the cold. The little Negro boy looked around at the crowd of adults. They were all gathered around various campfires trying to stay warm. The lone exception was Reverend Slaughter; he was standing down by the lake, peering out over the water, deep in thought.

Timidly, the Negro boy touched the handle and moved it just an inch or two. It surprised him how easily it turned. He discovered that if he continued pushing the handle, it moved even easier. After a couple of revolutions, it was moving faster and faster. Finally, the magical machine began to make a strange noise that enthralled the young boy. The faster he turned, the louder the noise became. In a few minutes, the noise was cutting through the early morning calm, scaring birds and rabbits, and even forcing the two alligators to go under water to avoid the awful noise. The little boy was in hog heaven as his small arm twirled the big handle over and over, causing the siren to squeal louder and louder.

Finally, a soft and gentle white hand landed on the boy's shoulder, which caused him to stop turning the handle. It was Reverend Slaughter. He stared down at the small boy with a look of profound hurt in his eyes. The noise had caused Marshal Byrd to sit up in the back seat of his automobile. The reverend stared at him with a look of utter disgust.

"What is this thing?" he asked the marshal.

"It's a siren," he answered.

"What is it for?"

"It goes on police cars. It is used when you're chasing crooks; it tells other folks to get the hell out of your way."

Reverend Slaughter didn't ask Harry Byrd if he had been blowing the siren the night before, since he already knew the answer to that question. Without saying a word to anyone, Reverend Slaughter turned and began slowly walking up the dirt road toward the parsonage. He was broken hearted and as disappointed as a man could possibly be disappointed. He had wanted desperately to leave this terrible place and go home to heaven.

His five-year-old son had died two years ago of typhoid fever, and both Reverend Slaughter and his wife took it very hard.

Ever since the boy's death, Reverend Slaughter's wife had became more withdrawn and depressed. It is very important for a preacher's wife to be at his side and take part in church activities, but, recently, she had begun to refuse to come to church functions. At first, it was just funerals, which was understandable to most folks because of her loss. Then, it was Wednesday night prayer meetings, eventually Sunday school, and finally even Sunday morning services. She even refused to come to happy events like church socials and weddings. They seemed to make her even more depressed than funerals. Reverend Slaughter tried to explain to his congregation that she was ill, but people were beginning to talk. Whispering gossips were saying that Mrs. Slaughter was not living up to her responsibilities. Others were crueler; they said she was going crazy.

Last year, Reverend Slaughter's wife had begun speaking of her dead son as if he were still alive. At Christmas, he discovered that his wife had spent money ordering toys for her dead son out of mail-order catalogs. In the past few months, her illness began to get worse. She began preparing meals for the dead child and even making him clothes.

Mental illness was a common problem in those days. The South was a hard place, especially for women who sometimes broke down under the strain of hard work, poverty, child bearing, and the premature deaths of those same children.

Dr. King, or no other physician for that matter, knew anything about hormone replacement therapy. High-class white women going through menopause were usually referred to as "being peculiar" or "just that way." Low-class white women and Negroes were not given that much respect; they were just called crazy. Southern women, both black and white, either became tough as nails, invulnerable to the hard times and poverty, or they simply slipped away to a kinder and gentler place, where times were not so hard.

Men did not become "peculiar" or "crazy." They could crawl into a whiskey bottle and become drunks. They could gamble all night and frequent whorehouses, which gave them some relief from their everyday problems. However, women had no such outlets; sometimes the strain was just too much, and something just slipped loose.

As he walked back to the parsonage, Reverend Slaughter's wife came up behind him. She had been with him all night patiently praying and waiting for the rapture. Softly, she asked her husband why the rapture had not happened. He could not answer her, his eyes were filled with tears, and he was all choked up with grief. He had so desperately wanted to meet Jesus and go to heaven with his wife and see his little boy.

There was no church that day, even though it was Sunday morning. Reverend Slaughter just couldn't face anybody. People who showed up at the Baptist church found the door locked, and no one answered at the parsonage. It was over two weeks before anyone saw Reverend Slaughter. Later, he tried to explain the whole thing as "personal problems."

No one in Lake Butler talked much about what had happened down by the lake, not even people like Dr. King who had scoffed at the whole thing. He said it would be cruel and heartless to bring it up. However, everyone seemed to clearly understand that it was a major turning point in their lives, and things would never be the same. A few weeks later, the Lake Butler Town Council abolished the position of constable and closed the jail, throwing Harry Byrd out of work. The same week, Reverend Slaughter resigned as pastor of the Baptist church and moved away from Lake Butler. He never told anyone where he was going. Nobody ever really knew for certain what happened to him after he left, but some people said that he left the ministry and found a factory job in Tennessee, somewhere near where his wife's family lived.

After he lost his job as town marshal, Harry Byrd found a job at the Watertown sawmill over in Columbia County. However, it didn't work out. Harry was too old and out of shape to do the hard work expected of a sawmill hand. He was fired after only two weeks. Harry then became a full-time moonshiner; he used his small farm as a cover and grew nothing but corn, which he turned into pop-skull liquor. He doubled the size of his moonshine still and put all four of his children and his wife to work making shine day and night.

There weren't enough customers for that much moonshine in Lake Butler, so Harry put his shine into glass jars and drove over to Gainesville, where he sold his homemade liquor to college students around the University of Florida. This was to prove to be a serious mistake. The high sheriff in Gainesville was proud that the University of Florida was in his county, and he had vowed to maintain a clean, wholesome Christian atmosphere for the students who went to school there.

One night, Harry was stopped on University Avenue by two deputy sheriffs. They found eighteen quart jars of moonshine in Harry's car. When he went to trial, Harry pleaded that he was only selling to Negroes, but the high sheriff put on witnesses who said they had seen Harry Byrd on the campus selling moonshine to university students from his car.

Harry Byrd drew three years on the chain gang. In those days, there was no prison system in the state of Florida. Convicted criminals were leased out to large pulpwood and turpentine operations for only pennies a day, plus their food and quarters. The convict lease system largely replaced slavery in the South after the Civil War and was actually more profitable, since the people who leased convicts didn't have to buy them the way they did slaves and lost no capital investment if a convict died from maltreatment or disease. There were always an infinite number of drifters, alcoholics, and petty criminals for sympathetic (and often bribed) judges to send to the chain gang.

Harry was sent to a large turpentine firm working the thick pinewoods up on the Florida–Georgia border. He labored in the thick undergrowth of the pine forests extracting raw turpentine from pine trees by cutting a V-shaped notch in the tree and hanging a terra cotta cup under the notch to collect the sap. When the cups were full, the turpentine was poured into large barrels and hauled off to a distillery to be made into paint thinner and other products.

Harry Byrd wore the horizontal black and white striped uniform familiar to southern chain gangs, working up to fourteen hours a day in heavy leg chains. He slept each night in an isolated turpentine camp surrounded by a barb-wire fence that was patrolled by shotgun-toting guards. The windows and doors of the building were secured with the same type of iron slats that once covered the doors of the small jail in Lake Butler.

Harry's wife used his chain-gang sentence as an opportunity to get out of an abusive and loveless marriage. She sought out Dr. King, the only person around Lake Butler who had ever showed her any kindness. He arranged for her to get a quick divorce at the courthouse in Starke. This was fairly easy to do, since Harry Byrd was not there to contest the divorce, and giving divorces to women whose husbands were on the chain gang was pretty much of an automatic thing. Dr. King made it even easier, since he was close friends with the county judge, and he had explained the situation to him.

After the divorce was granted, Dr. King agreed to buy the Byrd farm for more than it was worth. This would allow Harry Byrd's wife and children to have enough money to leave Lake Butler and start all over in a new place. Since Harry's oldest boy and daughter were almost grown and his other two children were teenagers, Dr. King suggested that the family move up north somewhere and find jobs in a factory. With the whole family working, they should make out fine.

The family held a farm auction and managed to get a good price for their plows, planters, mule tack, and house furniture. They also managed to sell every chicken, hog, mule, cow, and hound dog on the farm. They had even managed to secretly sell Harry's big moonshine still to a man of dubious reputation from over in Suwannee County.

Harry's wife was terrified that her ex-husband would follow them to wherever they went. If he ever found them, there would be hell to pay. Harry Byrd had vowed to kill his wife if she ever left him, and everyone knew he would probably do it. Dr. King advised her not to buy her train ticket in Lake Butler, since the old woman who ran the depot had a big mouth and was always tending to other people's business.

Early one cold winter morning, Dr. King loaded the family into his automobile and drove them the sixty miles to the big railroad terminal on Bay Street in Jacksonville. Everything the family had left after the auction, mostly only their clothes, was carefully packed into five cardboard suitcases. Dr. King's wife had packed a large picnic lunch for the family to eat on the train. She had put in three whole fried chickens, a pot of boiled sweet potatoes, turnip greens, and a freshly made and still-warm pecan pie for dessert. They had spent their last night in Lake Butler at Dr. King's big, wood frame house overlooking the town square. Harry's wife and Mrs. King had become very close, and both women wept in each other's arms as they said good-bye.

While Dr. King stood guard, looking out for anyone from Lake Butler who might be in the crowd at the train terminal, Harry's wife bought five one-way tickets to Chicago. Before her train left, she thanked Dr. King for all his help and kissed him good-bye. He wished them all good luck and said he would pray that they would find happiness. For the rest of his life, Dr. King never once dropped a hint as to where they went. He would only say that they were in a place where Harry Byrd could never find them.

Harry Byrd returned to Lake Butler from the chain gang a broken man. He had almost died from pneumonia one winter, and, during one especially hot and humid summer day, he had suffered a heat stroke. Because he was such a poor worker, the turpentine company had arranged with the governor's office to reduce his sentence to only a year and a half.

To everyone's surprise, Harry never asked about his wife and children. Since they had never written him while he was in the chain gang, he really hadn't expected to find them at home when he came back. However, Harry never expected his farm not to be there. He protested strongly, but the high sheriff explained to him that the judge had awarded the farm to his wife during the divorce hearings, and she had legally sold it to Dr. King, so there was nothing he could do.

There was one bright spot for Harry Byrd. His wife could not sell his automobile and siren, since it was in his name. The high sheriff in Gainesville had the automobile up on blocks behind the jail. He told Harry he could come get it anytime he wanted, but Harry never claimed the automobile, and, eventually, the sheriff sold it at an auction for junk. The sheriff drove all the way over to Lake Butler to give Harry the eighty dollars he had gotten for the automobile. Harry didn't even say thank you.

With everything he had gone, Harry quickly became the town drunk, doing odd jobs in exchange for a meal and enough money to buy some moonshine. Dr. King let Harry live in the shack on his old farm and sleep on a pallet thrown on the floor in front of the fireplace.

Most of the old farms around Lake Butler were more valuable as timber-growing land than they were for producing cotton, corn, or tobacco. Dr. King was one of the few people around Lake Butler who had enough brains to realize this, and that was how he got rich. He would buy up old, worn-out farms and plant quick-growing pine trees on the farms. The pine trees would bring in a rich harvest later on, without the backbreaking work and financial risk associated with running a dirt farm.

Harry Byrd used to come to my grandmother's back door begging for work. She would usually let him rake the yard or chop some firewood. She never paid him money, since she knew he would only use it to buy moonshine. She would fix him a nice dinner that he would eat sitting on the back porch steps. She never let him into the house, because she said he was too dirty. My grandmother was so kindhearted she would always fix Harry a little something to take home with him. She also was always giving him old clothes that my grandfather couldn't wear anymore and old blankets so he would be warm.

As time went on, Harry's condition became worse. His drinking became an everyday thing. My grandmother would not give him work if she could smell liquor on his breath. After awhile, he stopped coming to my grandmother's house. Harry would only work for those folks who would give him money to buy shine. He lost weight until he was thin as a rail. At the same time, his face became swollen up and turned beet red. He looked so bloated sometimes that it appeared that if you stuck a pin in him, he would pop like a balloon.

One night, Harry was walking home stone drunk and fell into a ditch next to the railroad tracks. There was only two feet of water in the ditch, but it was enough to drown him. He landed on his face, and he was so drunk he couldn't roll over. It was Dr. King who pronounced him dead and offered to pay the funeral home for the expense of burying him.

Reverend Slaughter's replacement at the Baptist church preached the funeral. Only about half a dozen people came, but that included Dr. King, his wife, and my grandmother who said she came, because she was afraid if she didn't go, nobody would be there. "It is so sad when someone is laid away all alone," she said.

The new preacher had heard stories about Harry's siren and the notorious baptism down by the lake, but he didn't mention it at the funeral. All he said was that Harry was a fully baptized Christian, who he firmly believed was asleep in the Lord. He reminded everyone that Harry was what God made him, and he wasn't that much different than the rest of us. My grandmother said that at the funeral, Dr. King and his wife cried.

Harry was buried in Dukes Cemetery, along the north fence where the town of Lake Butler discretely buried people who didn't have a family plot. A small wooden headstone was put up, but, over the years, it rotted away, and everybody forgot about Harry Byrd.

Everyone has two sets of grandparents, one on the mother's side and the other on the father's side. The grandmother, who told me the story of Harry Byrd, was my mother's mother. I called her Grand Murry, since her name was Murry McElroy Farnell. I spent a lot of time with her when I was growing up, and, from her, I learned every worthwhile value that came out of my twisted and warped childhood.

I asked her if she had been baptized that night by the lake. She said she had accepted the Lord Jesus Christ as her personal savior when she was seven years old and never felt the need to accept him a second time. My grandmother was the most decent, hard-working Christian person I ever met. She was constantly in the kitchen or outside scratching around her flowers. I never saw a yard better tended or a cleaner house. She hated television and thought it would be the ruination of America. She never owned a television and seldom watched one. She didn't even like to listen to the radio.

Her husband, my maternal grandfather, had died in 1935 while serving on jury duty. He probably had a stroke, but nobody could tell for sure. That morning, he told the judge he wasn't feeling well, so he was allowed to go lie down in a house across the street from the courthouse. When somebody went to check on him later that afternoon, he was dead.

At the time of his death, my grandfather was working for the State Road Department and farming one hundred and seventy acres of land. He left my grandmother a small, but adequate, pension, and she earned extra money by leasing out her farm.

My grandmother was an independent woman and used her own money to build herself a small two-bedroom house next door to my aunt. I loved both of them dearly. I spent every summer and every school holiday of my childhood living with my grandmother. If I turned out to be a decent human being, it was because of the moral lessons I learned at my grandmother's knee. During her entire life, she had never taken a drink of whiskey, smoked a cigarette, or walked into a dance hall, saloon, or gambling house. She used to proudly tell me that she would not know what a saloon looked like if she hadn't seen pictures of them in magazines. When my grandfather died, she accepted his death as the will of God, and there was no thought of remarriage, even though she was still a fairly young woman. She had five children that she knew would always take care of her. Grand Murry always told me that my grandfather was waiting on her in heaven. It amazes me to this day how matter of fact she always said it, like there was no doubt in her mind. Her faith in God was absolute.

All my adult life, I have been associated with well-educated intellectuals, the vast majority of which were atheists, agnostics, Unitarians, or some type of "New Age," avant-garde, semi-Buddhist environmental spiritualists. They all have one thing in common. None of them possessed the calm assurance and piece of mind my grandmother more or less took for granted.

My grandmother read her Bible every day, and she never once put food into her mouth without first saying grace. I never will forget one day sitting on the back steps of her house peeling apples. The apples were for a pie, but we talked it over and decided to eat a couple. She sliced up one of the apples, and we each took a piece. However, before she slipped it into her mouth, we both bowed our heads and said a simple blessing that, by the time I was five years old, I had memorized by heart. "Dear Lord, for these and all your blessing, we offer our most humble thanks. Amen."

She never made a big fuss about it. It wasn't something she did for show. It was almost a natural thing to her, like breathing. Before you ate anything, you bowed your head and thanked God for giving it to you.

It didn't surprise me that Grand Murry didn't get baptized that night. She always had secret reservations about the whole thing. She believed that it was every Christians' duty to accept Christ, profess your faith, and be accepted with believer's baptism. However, sometimes she wondered just exactly how much of a change it made in people. It seemed that every good-for-nothing, drunken wife beater and backsliding reprobate she knew had been baptized at some point in his sorry life. She also knew many hardworking, good, and decent people who had never been baptized. She wondered, sometimes, just how much sin it really washed off. It just didn't seem right to her that you could live your life wicked, sinful, and cruel, and, then, people like Harry Byrd got baptized at the last minute and got to go to heaven. She always felt that God would save whomever he wanted to save, regardless of whatever kind of religious ceremony you happened to go through. She always told me that God made up the rules, not the preachers.

# The Scout Hole in Hard Times

Harry Byrd's farm had been located only a mile from Lake Butler on a narrow strip of blistering hot, gray-white Florida sand people called the "Scout Hole Road." The road sliced through fifteen miles of dark pinewoods to where an old twelve-foot-wide, wooden beam bridge crossed the New River. Beyond the wooden bridge was the northernmost part of Alachua County. About ten miles into Alachua County, the dirt road reached the small village of Brooker; from there, the road became paved and led to Gainesville.

Only a half a mile downstream from the bridge was a mysterious place on the river that was shaded by one-hundred-year-old oak trees and covered with thick clusters of Spanish moss that hung like long, gray stalactites over the dark waters of the New River. This was the Scout Hole.

The New River is a winding strip of tea-colored water that is usually so shallow and narrow a person could wade across it without getting their hip pockets wet—that is, except in the spring when the heavy rains came. Then, the New River could became a mile-wide raging torrent of ink-black flood waters, washing away underbrush and leaving a dark band around the sides of trees to show how high the water had been.

Florida is a state cursed by a peculiar geologic phenomenon called the sinkhole. Under the sandy topsoil of Florida lies a vast honeycomb of limestone deposits known as the Ocala aquifer. Limestone is the residue of trillions of tiny, million-year-old marine creatures whose shells have been turned into a soft yellowish stone. Limestone is extremely soluble in water, and, over the course of time, underground waters, seeking their own level, carve out huge subterranean caves in the limestone deposits. Sometimes, these underground caves collapse under the weight of the topsoil, and a sinkhole develops. They form a large V-shaped hole in the ground that seems to eat everything around it and pull in trees, bushes, and sometimes cars and houses. Like some ancient mythological monster, the sinkhole devours all around it, pulling everything deep into the dark bowels of the earth. When something goes into a sinkhole, it is gone forever.

After a time, the sinkhole stabilizes and stops growing. As time passes, the steep banks erode and are covered with wild foliage. The high water table in Florida and heavy rainfall will eventually turn most sinkholes into lakes or small ponds. Finally, after the passage of centuries of time, the once-fearsome monster becomes just another part of the landscape.

The Scout Hole was a sinkhole that had formed along the channel of the New River. Its once-steep banks were now worn down into a wide plain by eons of hard rainfall. The Scout Hole's banks were kept free of the usual thick Florida underbrush by the regular flooding of the river, leaving the ground clear of vegetation, except for the tall cypress and moss-draped oak trees, which always survived the floods with little damage except the dark stain on their bark showing how high the water had been.

The water in the Scout Hole was not stagnant and dead like most sinkholes. The flow of the New River in and out of it kept the water fresh and oxygenated, creating a dark and deep reservoir full of aquatic life that was fed upon by large schools of freshwater fish. The water was made jet black by the tannic acid given off by the millions of leaves that daily fell into the river and decayed.

The Scout Hole was deep, but nobody really knows how deep. People used to say that a man once dropped a hundred-foot rope weighted with a steel plow tip into the Scout Hole, and it never touched bottom. Many old folks claimed that the Scout Hole was bottomless and that people who drowned in it would never be found. Everybody was afraid to swim in the Scout Hole, because the dark waters made it impossible to see the black cottonmouth water moccasins and big bull alligators that populated the waters.

The Scout Hole was the best fishing hole anywhere around Lake Butler. During the winter when farm work was light, yellow flies and mosquitoes were not so bad and the cold weather made the reptile population slow and lethargic, farm families and people who lived in town would hitch up their mule-drawn wagons and ride down to the Scout Hole to camp and fish. Once you passed Harry Byrd's farm, the Scout Hole Road became very low and swampy; it was overhung with giant oaks and flanked by pine forests so thick they blocked out the bright Florida sun, and cloaked the road in dusk-like darkness. In some places, logs had been laid down to bridge the swampy holes. At other places, a hard rain could literally wipe out the road, turning it into a sea of mud and water. Nobody would risk driving an automobile to the Scout Hole; only mules and wagons, or riding horseback, could guarantee that you would not get permanently stuck in the water and mud of the Scout Hole Road.

Since the Scout Hole was a fairly long wagon ride from Lake Butler, a lot of people would camp out on the banks of the river, float fishing and running catfish lines. People liked to clean their fish right after they caught them, bread them with a little flour and cornmeal, and then fry them up in a skillet right next to the river. Many moonshiners plied their trade down by the Scout Hole and sold shine to fishermen. Always, where there is cheap liquor, there is also trouble.

The dirt farms and small towns of north Florida could become very violent places, especially when the price of cotton was low and moonshine was cheap. These people had always been a clannish and provincial people, going back two thousand years to the time of their Celtic ancestors, who once besieged the walls of Rome. Even the poorest dirt farmer demanded the respect he felt was due him. They were quick to fight and liked to boast about their own animal-like prowess as warriors and hunters. As a natural consequence of their ancient ancestry, they always preferred to settle problems among themselves without all the arbitrary rules and procedures of a court of law. As the sons and grandsons of Confederate veterans, they had about as much use for courts as their pre-Christian, Teutonic forefathers, living in the cold and damp woods above the Danube and Rhine Rivers, had for the rule of the Roman Caesars.

Almost all grown men, and most teenage boys, routinely carried pistols and razor-sharp Barlow knives. Fistfights, shootings, and cuttings were common in a region where poverty and hard work blew small things all out of proportion to their real value, and a man's honor demanded that he never back down or accept defeat.

A teeth-jarring fistfight or a bloody killing could take place over a stolen hog, the price of a mule, farm boundaries, unexplained pregnancies, and romantic promises not kept. The so-called "shotgun wedding" was a no-laughing-matter reality in this hard-bitten region of the Old South. Blood feuds once started could go on for generations, being passed from father to son. It didn't help things that the courthouse and sheriff's office were both located in Starke, over twenty miles away, which was a hard day's journey by mule and wagon. Cotton was planted in the spring, cultivated in the summer, and harvested in the fall. It could take anywhere from thirty to one hundred man hours of backbreaking labor just to harvest one acre of cotton. These people worked from before daylight to dusk dark trying to scratch out a living from their cotton farms.

A subpoena to appear in court in Starke could throw a farmer days or weeks behind in his work. However, more importantly, it could mean the loss of a cotton crop if bad weather or some other calamity hit while they were away. A small herd of wild cows not worth the cost of the shotgun shells needed to kill them or a pack of wild hogs could get into your cotton field or vegetable garden and destroy a year's worth of work in hours, rooting up and trampling the plants. Weasels and foxes could kill all your chickens, and a worthless neighbor could steal your hogs and mule.

Fences meant nothing, even if the poor cotton farmers could afford to surround their farms with the expensive creosote-coated posts and galvanized wire. Wild cows had a knack for finding holes in a fence or locating a weak fence post they could push over. Wild hogs were harder to keep out; they could root under fences and gain access to the young plants in the fields. No type of fence could keep out weasels and foxes that would kill and eat everything from baby chickens to shout hogs.

The only absolute protection for a farmer's crops and livestock was a loud barking dog to guard the hen houses and fence lines and a double-barrel shotgun to make short work of the varmints. During the growing season, from early March until late November, a farmer could not afford to take the risk of leaving his farm for any longer than it took to go to church on Sunday, and then he would probably leave his older children at home with chores to do and instructions to watch out for predators.

In 1919, people on the west side of the New River began a petition drive to have the courthouse moved to Lake Butler. People who lived east of the river around Starke and who faced the same basic problems with leaving their farms were angered at the thought of losing their nearby courthouse. It started out as a civil debate between reasonable men, but, like so many things in those harsh times, it soon turned violent. A mob from both counties met on the bridge over the New River, and, before it was over, shots were fired and men laid dead.

Dr. King tried to stay out of the fracas, but it came home to him one night when a local farmer showed up at his office door bleeding badly from a nasty stab wound. The doctor cleaned out the wound and sewed it up. The man refused to answer Dr. King's queries about who had stabbed him. He paid the doctor two dollars for his treatment and left. Just as he stepped out the front door of Dr. King's office, shots rang out and the man fell dead.

Nobody was ever arrested for the murder. The man's wife was a closemouthed as he had been. She had two teenage sons, and she once told Dr. King that both boys knew who killed their father, and, when they reached maturity and the time was right, they would avenge his death.

This killing infuriated Dr. King. He decided what the county needed was its own high sheriff and courthouse. Unless people had a nearby place to peacefully resolve their differences and good law enforcement—not someone like Harry Byrd—the killings and feuding could go on forever.

Dr. King called several of his friends together to try and find out what could be done. The small group decided that forming a new county was the only way to solve things peacefully. Moving the courthouse from Starke to Lake Butler would only aggravate the tensions between the two sides of the New River.

A petition drive, followed by a special election, finally settled the issue. People voted overwhelmingly to create a new county west of the New River. In May of 1921, the Florida Legislature acquiesced to the will of the people and voted to divide the existing county along the flow of the New River. The new county, to be called Union County, would be the smallest in Florida with only one hundred and fifty-six thousand acres or just over two hundred and forty square miles of land. The county seat would be Lake Butler.

The new county went into operation the following October, using the Masonic Hall as the first courthouse. In 1922, a formal courthouse was built in the town square. It was a wooden, two-story building overlooking a tree-shaded open area that was now called the "Courthouse Square." It still served as a gathering place for local citizens who enjoyed picnicking under the oak trees after church on Sundays. Dr. King's wife started a garden club and set about further beautifying the town square with azaleas, gardenia, camellia, and rose bushes. They also set up park benches and oversaw the building of a gazebo where the town band held concerts on Sunday afternoons and the Fourth of July.

The first elected high sheriff of Union County was a man named Walter Mizell. He was a close friend of Dr. King, who had strongly supported his election. Dr. King was anxious that someone like Harry Byrd not be elected high sheriff. Walter Mizell was a church-going, nondrinking man who was a loyal and loving father and husband to his wife and family.

The county charter specified the sheriff be paid a regular monthly salary, instead of being paid by the arrest, as the old town marshal had been.

It was decided that the old jail that had been used by Harry Byrd was not a fit place to incarcerate people. The county managed to get a financial grant from the State of Florida, and a small jail was built behind the courthouse on the extreme northwest corner of the square. Since the sheriff's salary was limited, the bottom floor of the jail would be the sheriff's home and office. Upstairs would be six racially segregated small cells, three for whites and three for Negroes. Later, an annex would be added containing two cells for female prisoners.

The sheriff complained that his biggest headache was intoxicated Negroes on Saturday nights and that Negro women were more violent and hard to deal with than the men when they were all liquored up. Every Sunday morning saw the jail filled with at least a half dozen hung-over Negro men and women, many of them bloody from fights and stabbing the night before.

The sheriff had no cells for white women; he refused to throw a white woman in jail, no matter how drunk or rowdy she was. He would simply take her home or to her kinfolks, and they would deal with her.

Most white men who went to jail were either public drunks or low-class drifters passing through. The sheriff would not tolerate bums or loafers in his county. Sheriff Mizell once formed a local posse and arrested a dozen Gypsies who had camped outside of town. He said they were the most worthless people on earth, who would steal anything not red hot and nailed down. After the county judge fined them heavily, they left Union County and never came back.

Feuds and shootings still happened, and the new sheriff found that there was little he could do about it. He knew he could not afford to get involved in these things and still get reelected. When a murder was blatant, and public, he would be forced to take action, but, most of the time, nobody saw anything and folks were reluctant to testify in court. The general feeling in Union County was: If it was a fair fight, then the guns, knives, or knuckles could decide the issue as well as a bunch of shyster lawyers and a crooked judge.

There were also wild and rowdy juke joints for both blacks and whites scattered around the county. These places openly sold illegal whiskey at the height of the Prohibition Era, but Sheriff Walter Mizell knew his limitations. He did not have a deputy to help him raid the juke joints, and, if he formed a posse, someone would tip them off that the raid was coming. However, more importantly, Sheriff Mizell had the good common sense to know that hardworking folks needed some recreation in life and a release for their frustrations. When the church-going folks complained about a juke joint, he always answered that he wasn't a federal law enforcement officer, and it wasn't his job to enforce the Volstead Act.

The Great Depression hit Union County very hard. There were two small banks in the county in 1930, and they both quickly had to close. Unable to get credit from the bank to buy cottonseed and the heavy loads of fertilizer needed to make their farms productive, many small farmers went bankrupt.

The Great Depression had been accompanied by the arrival of the boll weevil, a disgusting little insect that had seeped northward out of Mexico and was first observed in Texas cotton fields in 1892. Ever since then, it had been migrating steadily eastward toward the lush cotton fields of the Deep South. Finally, in the late 1920s, it reached northern Florida. About a quarter of an inch long, it has a short black snout that bores a hole into the green bolls of the cotton plant. There, the insect lays its eggs that hatch into a larva that destroys the cotton boll.

Sea Island cotton, the kind most people in Union County produced, was particularly susceptible to the boll weevil. Sea Island cotton was first grown on the coastal barrier islands of Georgia and South Carolina, and it quickly became famous all over the world for its extra-long silky fibers. It had been brought to Florida, because the sandy topsoil was similar to that found on the coastal barrier islands.

Florida cotton farmers did very well during the boom days after World War I, planting hundreds of acres of Sea Island cotton that always brought a good price. However, cotton was hard on the land. After a decade of bearing one cotton crop after another, even the heavy loads of fertilizer the farmers applied each year didn't do any good. The cotton plants just couldn't get enough nourishment from the worn-out land to produce bolls, and the land just gave up and went to weeds. When the land went bad, the farmer's only choice was to sell his farm for whatever he could get and move on. The small cotton farms were usually bought up by the large pulp and paper companies who quickly cleared them and planted pine trees.

Farmers who lost their farms in the Dust Bowl region of the Midwest were made famous by the writings of John Steinbeck, and the long trek to California along U.S. Route 66 has become a part of American history and folklore. However, Union County farmers who lost their battle with the boll weevil and their worn-out land during the Great Depression had a far different journey.

Some folks packed up what they could carry and moved to Jacksonville, seeking employment in the shipyards. Others went to Tampa to try and find jobs in the cigar factories. Some were even reduced to becoming migrant farm workers on the truck farms and sugar cane fields around Belle Glade and Okeechobee. However, most of these people never found work and returned to Union County poorer than when they left.

However, most farmers decided not to move away. When you asked them, they would tell you they didn't expect the Depression to last or they were looking to buy a new farm, but everybody knew better than that. The truth was they simply couldn't bear to say good-bye to all their friends and relatives and just move away from the only place they had ever called home.

These people decided to abandon their worn-out farms and try to permanently camp out on the sandy banks of the Scout Hole, aiming to live off the land. They built small shelters scattered above the high water mark on the New River's floodplain and dug shallow pitcher pump wells to get drinking water. These people were only one or two generations removed from the frontier. They felt that they were as good as their grandparents, and, if they could live off the land and make a living, so could they.

They looked to the river for their food source. They ate soft-shell turtles, possums, raccoons, alligators, and swamp cabbage, which is the soft white heart of the palmetto plant. They also began small vegetable gardens and grew mostly root crops, potatoes in the summer, and turnips in the winter. The biggest single item in their diet was catfish, a bottom-dwelling parasite of a fish that could be caught with cane poles or long lines strung across the river on which were hung a dozen or so baited hooks. Since catfish were basically parasites, they would bite at anything, such as bits of animal fat, chicken guts, fish eyes, possum skins, and raccoon's tongues—anything. When the brim and speckled perch were "bedding," laying their eggs in the shallow waters of the river, men would wade into the shallow water with small twenty-two-caliber rifles and shoot the fish. It was nice to have a break from catfish; the flaky white meat of the brim and the speckled perch were considered gourmet delicacies, especially when served up with grits and "hush puppies," delicious bits of corn meal batter that is deep fried in the same grease used to cook the fish. They could also go "frogging," hunting frogs with cane poles tipped with a hand-forged, metal barbed hook. The frog's legs were deep-fried in grease and were very tasty.

Some of the more enterprising farmers pulled the boards and tin roofs off the clapboard shotgun shacks; salvaged the nails; loaded the whole thing on a rusty, dilapidated old farm truck or mule-drawn wagon; and hauled it to the nearest navigable waterway, such as the Suwannee, Santa Fe, or St. Johns Rivers. Others went to large freshwater lakes such as Lochloosa Lake, Orange Lake, or big Lake George on the St. Johns River.

These people spent the Great Depression "on the river," a southern euphemism for living on a ragged-looking, clapboard houseboat floating on a lake or river. Places that had springs were particularly popular houseboat campsites. Salt Springs Run that emptied into Lake George and Manatee Springs Run on the Suwannee River had hundreds of houseboats tied along their banks during the Depression years.

These displaced people were not seeking some kind of romantic wilderness experience. They were trying to survive what country people called "the hard times."

The people who were their neighbors "on the river" were often a lot of help, especially in an emergency, such as an accident, illness, or birth of a child. Houseboats were prone to sink unexpectedly, so they were always tied in shallow water where they could be refloated easily. Refloating a sunken houseboat was a big job that could not be done by one man. Most houseboats used old oil drums for flotation, and it took at least ten men to hoist the boat out of the water and replace the oil drums. If new oil drums could not be found, then cypress logs also provided good flotation. The biggest advantage of cypress logs was they would never spring a leak and sink. However, they also made the houseboat heavy and difficult to move up and down the river. Survival on the river meant being able to move from where the food wasn't to where the food was.

The houseboats were heavy and clumsy, so, when the people wanted to travel by water, they did so in a long and narrow cypress wood boat, which was either paddled by hand or pushed by a small, ten- to twenty-horsepower outboard motor, commonly called "a kicker." The houseboats had only one room, usually less than ten feet square. Here, both the adults and children slept together on the floor. The beds were fashioned from old mattresses brought from home or big canvas bags that had once been used to hold freshly picked cotton, which had been stuffed with pine straw or Spanish moss. Others only had beds made from burlap bags thrown over a pile of pine straw. The roofs of the houseboats were always made from the rusty-red tin salvaged from the roofs of their old farm shacks. Some houseboats also had their sides made of tin, but this made them very cold in the winter, when the cold winds off the river would blow through the nail holes, and cracks in the tin would fill the small room with a bone-shaking wet cold.

People did little more than sleep on the houseboat; food was cooked over a fire onshore. You couldn't risk building a fire aboard a houseboat, because the wood was so old and dry, it would burst into flames easily. Many people, especially the elderly and young children, developed pneumonia from sleeping on the floor of the cold houseboats, only inches above the water of the river. The fact that the houseboat was floating only a few feet offshore meant that the family was not trespassing on anybody's property. Since the government or large timber companies owned most of the land on the river, nothing was ever done to evict the houseboat people. The small campfires on shore seldom caused any notice.

The Great Depression in some strange ways brought out the best in people. The displaced farmers in the houseboats were decent, hardworking folks, who had just come on hard times. If they caused no trouble, local sheriffs left them alone and so did anybody else that knew what was good for them. Hard times did not mean that these people had lost the ability to get violent when pushed.

During a hard rain, the houseboats leaked like sieves. During the summer, when huge thunderstorms and hurricanes crossed the Florida peninsula with regularity, people would tie their houseboats under the spans of large concrete highway bridges in order to get the overhead protection of the roadway. Narrow banked rivers, such as the Ocklawaha in the Ocala National Forest, also gave some protection during times of heavy weather. The tall cypress trees that lined the riverbanks sheltered the houseboats from high winds, but they did little to hold out the rains.

In those days, before the influx of tourists, immigrants and industrial pollution, the rivers of Florida were alive with all kinds of things to eat. There was plenty to eat for those who weren't finicky, such as freshly caught fish, turtles, alligator tail, baked possums and raccoons stuffed with sweet potatoes, as well as rabbits, squirrels, and cabbage palm; even rattlesnake and gophers were eaten by people who were "on the river" during the hard times.

In the winter when the hides were thick and heavy, the men would silently move up and down the river at night in boats hunting deer. They would anchor their small boat opposite spots where the deer were known to come down to the river to drink. When a deer would appear on the riverbank, the men in the boat would turn on a bright spotlight powered by an old car battery. When the spotlight blinded a deer, it would not run away. Instead, it would freeze and refuse to move. Then, it could be easily killed with a rifle or shotgun. Deer meat called "venison" was delicious when cooked properly, and the deer hides could be tanned and sold for spending money. Hunting deer at night with a light is now illegal, but, during the Depression, it was a common practice.

They money raised by selling deer hides allowed the people to obtain things they couldn't find on the river. People would also trap and skin otters, alligators, muskrats, raccoons, and rattlesnakes. They would take the hides by boat to the rough-looking, hard-drinking men who ran the fish camps that were scattered along the lakes and rivers. These isolated pine board and tin buildings, hanging out over the river on cypress docks, were called "fish camps," but, in reality, they were also juke joints, whorehouses, and general stores. The otter, muskrat, rattlesnake, alligator, and deer hides were usually not sold for money, since few people had any money during the Depression; instead, they were traded for shotgun shells, kerosene for lamps, gasoline for outboard motors, or needed groceries, such as salt, flour, sugar, or banking powder. Usually, the fish camp owner would also recharge your battery, fix your cypress boat, or repair an outboard motor for free.

Later, he would sell the hides to traveling buyers who would ship them to sweat shop factories in Cuba and Mexico, where they were turned into expensive handbags, shoes, belts, wallets, and leather coats, which would be sold in expensive Fifth Avenue shops in New York City.

One of the first things people did when they moved to the river was sell their horses and mules. Yellow flies and mosquitoes were so bad along the river, they were known to drive the animals mad with their stinging bites. Untreated insect bites on horses and mules would bleed and attract screwworm flies that would lay their eggs in the open wounds. The eggs would hatch into small maggot larvae that would eat huge chunks out of the animal's flesh, causing them to go crazy with pain.

Being on the river was a hard life, especially for young children. Their little arms and legs were covered with large ugly sores caused by insect bites that had been scratched until they bled and then got infected. Painful red boils filled with ugly white pus often accompanied these sores. Children on the river seldom bathed, and, when they did bathe, it was often in cold water with no soap. This did not kill the bacteria on their skin, and, the slightest cut or scratch, or sometimes just the rubbing of their clothes against the skin, would cause the painful boils to form. When these sores and insect bites healed, they would produce small dark scars that would forever brand these children as "poor white trash" to their more well-to-do neighbors, who slept in nice homes with screened windows and electric fans. Even today, in many parts of the South, a schoolteacher can tell the economic status of their children by the ugly, dark insect bite scars on their arms and legs.

Children were also tormented with an affliction called "sore eyes." It was caused by the small, gray gnats that would swarm in huge black clouds over the riverbanks during the hot summer months. The gnats would fly into the eyes of children and get caught in their eyelashes and the mucous membranes of the cornea. The small gnats would scratch and irritate the surface of the eyeball, and this irritation would become infected, causing the eye to turn red and the eyelid to swell and discolor. Untreated, the sore eyes could sometimes become painful and affect the children's vision. Luckily, most young bodies are strong and heal quickly. The sore eyes would usually clear up and go away in a few weeks with little or no treatment.

Many of the children were bowlegged from a lack of calcium in their diet during infancy. Others had rickets, ringworm, head lice, and intestinal parasites that caused their little bellies to swell out and become bloated. Many small children also died from diarrhea, caused by unsanitary living conditions and polluted drinking water.

In 1934, a cholera epidemic broke out on the Scout Hole. Dr. King and his wife spent weeks camped down by the river treating people suffering from acute vomiting, diarrhea, stomach cramps, and exhaustion. Dr. King realized that the cholera was caused by the fact that these people used the toilet wherever they happened to be when the need occurred. Playing children came in contact with the offal matter, developed cholera, and then passed it to their parents through their diarrhea and vomiting. Dr. King assembled all the men and ordered them to construct sanitary latrine structures, commonly called outhouses, on high ground far away from the campsites where small children would not be playing. He also ordered a general cleanup of the scattered campsites. They were littered with tin cans, scrap wood, cooking grease, and ashes from old campfires. There were also scattered bones, hair, and visceral materials left over from the skinning of animals.

Sheriff Mizell accompanied Dr. King to the Scout Hole, and his badge and gun backed up all of Dr. King's orders. He also poked around and discovered a couple of small, homemade moonshine stills that he busted up with an ax. Sheriff Mizell knew that poorly made moonshine often contained lead salts poison that could cause blindness and death. He also knew that the drinking of moonshine often led to domestic violence and child abuse. Many of the children Dr. King examined at the Scout Hole showed the effects of severe beatings with wide leather belts. Many of the women had split lips and black eyes; this was the result of a drunken husband, driven to frustration and despair by the knowledge that he could not live up to his responsibilities as a man, because he couldn't support his family to a decent standard of living. Poverty is as much a thing of the spirit as the pocketbook.

Black people, for the most part, decided not to fight the Great Depression. The South was hard enough on African Americans even during the best of times, but with the Depression on, many decided it was time to move on to greener pastures. Every morning, Dr. King would see several Negro families standing on the loading platform of the train depot in Lake Butler, clutching their cheap cardboard suitcases, and wearing the best clothes they owned.

The small depot in Lake Butler didn't have a "colored waiting room," so blacks had to stand outside on the loading platform. Should it begin to rain, all they could do was crowd under the eves of the roof overhang and use their umbrellas, if they had any, to ward off the rain.

They were bound for the cramped tenement apartments of their relatives who lived in such northern cities as Chicago, Detroit, St. Louis, Newark, Boston, or New York. Until they could find a job and get an apartment of their own, they would live—probably for some time—with their northern relatives and sleep on couches, cots, and pallets thrown on the floor.

The movement of blacks from the rural South to the large urban areas of the North was one of the greatest migrations of Americans from one area of the nation to another, since the days of the California gold rush. Those who went before would aid their southern relatives to make the long journey to the North, with money, advice, lodgings, and hopefully a job. These poor pilgrims were not fleeing religious persecution, Communism, or the repression of a foreign potentate. Instead, they were fleeing a part of the United States that had, through laws and social customs, separated itself from the rest of America in how it treated part of its own population.

Most blacks heading north knew there would be no pot of gold awaiting them at the end of their long train ride. In the North, they would still have to accept low-paying menial jobs, but the opportunities would be better, and the insults to their personhood would be fewer and subtler.

There has always been a strange relationship between southern black people and trains. Their small homes lined the railroad tracks of the South; they lived so close to the noise and smoke of the big engines that a white person would openly wonder how they could possibly live a normal life. I used to notice that when the train pulled into Lake Butler, white people would back away from the huge monster of a machine, while Negroes would actually draw close, almost as if they wanted to be a part of its rhythm and magic.

To us children in the days before special effects and video games, the big locomotives were the most exciting things to come into our lives. Every kid in Lake Butler knew when the big freights were due to pass through town. We would line the railroad tracks to watch as the big freights roared past. The engineers and conductors would always wave at us, and, if we gave the engineer the high sign, he would blow the big whistle.

We were all fascinated by the noise and smoke of the big trains, but, with the Negro children, it was different. I noticed that they would actually tap their feet in rhythm with the big locomotives. As the cars would whirl past, the Negro children would sway back and forth, like old-time Christians caught up in the Holy Spirit. Years later, when I would listen to the music of Little Richard and Chuck Berry, I could still hear in their music the rhythms of the trains that roared across the southern landscape when I was a small boy.

It has always seemed ironic to me that these two peoples, African Americans and southern whites, were thrown together by the fortunes of history.

The Celtic tribes that populated northern Europe were the ancestors of most southern white people in the days before the mass migration of senior citizens, Cuban refugees, Yankee tourists, and other assorted emigrants from around the world made their way to the South to make a new life in the warm sunshine. The people who farmed the southern Sahara in West Africa were the ancestors of most southern black people. In the days before the beginning of the slave trade by the Portuguese in 1440, the Sahara Desert was only about half the size it is now, and the land on its peripheries was lush with green fields and great cattle herds. The now-extinct African forest elephant—the same beasts Hannibal used to carry his men across the Alps—wandered freely on the plains of the southern Sahara. They shared their habitat with the dark-skinned farmers, who had embraced the monotheistic religion of Islam.

These were a peaceful, kindhearted people, who tended their fields and herds with no thought of conquest and warfare. They were no match for the flint-hearted and well-armed Arab slave traders, who invaded their lands and sold them to the strange-looking white men, who anchored their ships off the Windward and Gold Coasts of West Africa.

The sweat and blood of these longsuffering African people would help forge the American nation and give other European whites the military and economic power to spread colonialism and white supremacy to the far corners of the earth.

The Celtic warriors of northern Europe were a different breed from the West Africans; they were a superstitious and mystical people, who trusted in their Druid priests the same way their descendants would trust in television evangelists. They were a race of storytellers with a special order of priests, the Bards, whose responsibility it was to keep and tell their history in the form of lyrical poems, songs, and fearsome yarns. Mythology was a part of their creed. There wasn't that much difference in a Celtic Bard sitting beside a roaring hearth inside a round Celtic communal house spreading yarns about the great Celtic chieftains who had besieged Rome, and an old man on a courthouse square somewhere in the Deep South, telling a wide-eyed youngster about the exploits of the great General Nathan Bedford Forrest. The South is a land of myths and heroes. No matter if we are talking about Robert E. Lee or Huey P. Long, the creed is the same; superior men proving their superiority.

The Celtic warriors were a fearsome and violent race. To the lettered and law-abiding Romans, these people, whom the Greeks called the *Keltoi*, were the ultimate savages. With their long blond hair spiked with combed-in lime deposits, and their naked bodies covered with the *wode* paint they believed would make them invincible, they swept down on the orderly Roman legions and slayed thousands with their fearsome broad axes and deadly *spatha* or two-edged sword.

The Celts were the people of the dark northern forests, whose only worth to the Romans was that of a hired warrior. They were undisciplined, violent, and prone to boasting, feuding, and excesses in food, alcohol, and sex. Like the Native Americans who lived beyond the great sea that was yet to be crossed, the Celts lived in great tribes such as the Picts, the Goths, and the Vandals. Also, like the Native Americans and unlike the Muslim West Africans, they worshipped the spirits of nature: Thor, the god of the hammer, who brings on the thunder and lightning; Freya, the god who chose the noble dead; and Woden, or Oden, the leader of the gods who would take them to Valhalla, the heavenly place where they would wage war all day and engage in drunken debauchery and feasting all night. They might have later forsaken their pagan beliefs to pacify their converted Christian ruler Charlemagne, but they maintained contact by naming the days of the week Wednesday for Woden, Thursday for Thor, and Friday for Freya in order to give a perpetual honor to the old gods.

In the first century of the Christian era, the Apostle Paul made contact with a small group of Celts who lived in the city of Galatia in Asia Minor. They were probably brought to this remote region of present-day Turkey from their cold northern homeland as mercenaries of the Roman Army. Some heroic early Christian missionary approached the Galatian Celts with the Gospel of Christ, which, probably to his great surprise, they embraced as their own.

The Apostle Paul was a well-educated Jewish intellectual of high birth. To Paul, the Celtic Christians in Galatia were an enigma. In the Book of Galatians in the New Testament, he speaks to them much like a stern schoolmaster would speak to a wayward pupil that wasn't too smart.

"O foolish Galatians! Who has bewitched you?" he asked.

Paul warned the Galatians about succumbing to the desires of the flesh. He warned them against the evils of idolatry, hatred, strife, envy, impurity, licentiousness, idolatry, sorcery, jealousy, anger, selfishness, drunkenness, reveling, and fornication. To understand what Paul was really saying, you must almost read between the lines, and translate his writing into the modern tongue:

Why are you always feuding and brawling among yourselves?

Why are you always over drinking, overeating, and fornicating?

Why must you constantly boast about fairly minor accomplishments?

Why do you continue to decorate your bodies with strange paints and tattoos?

Why do you still clothe yourself in wild animal skins?

Why do you bedeck your homes with the skulls and horns of the wild animals you have slain?

Why, although you profess to be Christians, do you still put your trust in the old sorcery, magic charms, ancient oracles, and superstitions?

Why can't you just accept the suffering of this life, deny yourself, and quit coveting your neighbor's possessions?

It was in the book of Galatians that Paul gave his famous warning: "Be not deceived; God is not mocked: for whatsoever a man soweth, that shall he also reap."

Paul could not understand these strange people. Neither could the Quaker abolitionists of New England, descendants of the more refined Norman-Saxons, who populated southern England. They could not fathom why thousands of poor southern whites who didn't own slaves would march off to war against the Yankee armies who had invaded their land. Neither could the young, Ivy League, civil rights workers, who entered the South in the early 1960s, understand the nature of the white people who stared at them from behind closed windows and over the steering wheels of local police cars.

The southern people they met, both black and white, were genuinely friendly. Southern hospitality is not a myth. However, at the same time, in their zeal to right a serious wrong, they seriously underestimated the cowardly cruelty that southern white people were capable of when they felt threatened.

James Chaney, one of the three civil rights workers murdered in Nashoba County, Mississippi, in 1964, was the only southerner in the car that faithful night. He was also the only black. Chaney tried to convince his two white companions—Micky Schwerner, a Jewish college student with a beatnik-style goatee beard, and Andrew Goodman, a liberal crusader from Queens College in New York City—not to stop, but try to outrun the cars that were following them that dark summer night in rural Mississippi. Unfortunately, the two white boys, raised in an environment of respect for the law and obedience to police officers, refused to listen. They pulled over for the Nashoba County sheriff's deputy's red light and paid for it with their lives.

The warlike Celtic blood still flows in the veins of southern whites. There is something in the heat and humidity of the Deep South that brings out the Barbarian spirit that lies just beneath their white skin and sunburned red necks. You can hear it, in the xenophobia of the Charlie Daniel's Band, and the drunken rowdiness of Hank Williams Jr. The southern rock and roll band Lynyrd Skynyrd would sing to thousands of screaming fans, "This is a bird you cannot change."

Most religions on earth have some form of dietary code it imposes on its believers, food that isn't to be consumed under any circumstances. Jews and Muslims will not eat pork or shellfish. The Hindus and Buddhists will not eat meat. Southern people seem proud of the fact that they have no dietary code and will eat absolutely anything and then brag about it. Southerners eat gophers, ground hogs, raccoons, possums, frog legs, squirrels, rabbits, rattlesnakes, and every part of a hog except the teeth and hair, which, for some strange reason, doesn't taste good to them.

It is a cross-racial thing. Blacks and whites together love a big old possum stuffed with sweet potatoes, which the Yankee people call "yams," because they don't know any better. Southerners take a particular pleasure in telling people, especially outsiders, about their strange dietary habits. They long to see the look of shock and disgust cross the face of some old retired Yankee, just moved to Florida, when they mention casually in passing that they had some really good fried raccoon the other night.

Even Martin Luther King used to amuse himself by inviting wealthy northern patrons and reporters to a meal of chitlins and turnip greens. During the civil rights movement, eating such dishes became kind of a hip, liberal, and with-it thing to do. Traditional southern dishes all of a sudden became "soul food," and Park Avenue limousine liberals would ride up to Harlem to dine on fried chicken, collard greens, cathead biscuits, and sawmill gravy.

It is a uniquely southern form of entertainment, grossing out Yankees. It's twice as much fun when it's done at a dinner table under formal or semiformal conditions. I have attended polite dinner parties, attended by well-educated people, and seen some redneck wannabe mention casually in passing, "Why this tastes just like hogshead cheese," making everyone at the table nauseous at the thought of eating the brains of a hog. It is a type of power that native-born southerners have over outsiders; it is a way of reminding them of their foreigner status and the fact that they are not as strong as you, because of their reluctance to eat possums, hog guts, and raccoons. Being squeamish in the South is a sign of weakness.

Eating these "soul foods," which outsiders usually find totally repugnant, is almost a sacred ritual in the South; it is a way southerners, both black and white, have of reminding themselves of their heritage. They didn't start eating chitlins, hog brains, possums, and coons on large cotton and sugar plantations with magnolia-scented mansions. They started eating these foods on the southern frontier in small cabins when times were hard and food was scarce.

Southerners are the only Americans who appear to revel in hard times. Irish people do not brag about the potato famine. Jews do not like to dwell on the Holocaust, and blacks avoid the thought of slavery. Yet, southerners seem proud of the fact that their women wore homespun dresses during the Civil War, and they will tell you with a great deal of pride how they ate catfish and hog chitlins during the Great Depression.

# Dr. King

There was no man in Union County more respected during the hard times than Dr. J. W. King. By the beginning of the Great Depression, Dr. King had become de facto leader of Union County, although he had never held an elected political office. Almost every person in the county was beholding to him either financially or personally. Dr. King had sewed up thousands of cuts and delivered hundreds of babies. On many cold and rainy nights, he had risen from his bed to attend to a medical emergency, only to be paid in chicken eggs or homemade butter. If he even suspected that the people's small gifts might cause some want or hunger in the family, he would decline them, not with a refusal or patronizing speech, because he knew how prideful these people were, but with a gentle little lie. "Why, Mrs. Thomas, I just bought a dozen eggs this morning."

"My wife just yesterday made a whole tub of homemade butter, and, if I took yours, one would spoil. Why don't you just keep it?"

However, that does not mean Dr. King was a financially naive person. Those who could pay their medical bills did so. Dr. King made sure of that. If these people didn't pay him promptly, then the next medical emergency would cost them double, due in advance.

He was a frugal man, who believed that waste not meant want not. He wore the same old worn and frayed, lightweight gray suit day in and day out. His only jewelry was a reliable pocket watch from Sears and Roebuck and a plain gold wedding band. For years, Dr. King and his wife saved money by living in a small apartment behind his office. He was famous among the children of the town for his high-top, reddish-brown kangaroo shoes. He either had several dozen pairs or they lasted him a lifetime.

His only extravagance was a fine Buick automobile that often served as an ambulance, when people had to be rushed to the hospital in Gainesville. Dr. King felt a good automobile was important. He didn't want someone to bleed to death, because his vehicle was unreliable. Dr. King's greatest headache was dirt roads. Many times, a team of mules would be needed to pull his Buick out of the mud. It really infuriated Dr. King when he lost a patient that he knew he could have saved, if only the roads hadn't been so bad, and he could have gotten there on time.

Early in 1925, Dr. King made several trips to Tallahassee to see friends in the state legislature. Working behind the scenes, he managed to get the funds to pave Highway 100, connecting Lake Butler to Starke. The next year, he also got the road connecting Lake Butler to Lake City, also Highway 100, paved. When the Depression hit, work was under way paving Highway 121, running from Lake Butler through Worthington Springs into Alachua County. The Depression caused the work to stop with the road paved only part way. This disappointed Dr. King bitterly, since this was the road he had to drive over in order to reach Alachua General Hospital in Gainesville, the nearest real hospital to Union County.

Dr. King owed the fortune he would eventually build to his remarkable agricultural foresight. In the early 1920s, he invested in a cotton gin, located on the edge of town near the railroad tracks. Every farmer, whose family was ever tended by Dr. King, felt honor bound to get his or her cottonseeds removed at the gin he owned. For over ten years, the cotton gin brought in more than twice as much income as his medical practice. However, Dr. King realized, even before the boll weevil came, that the days of growing cotton in Union County were coming to an end. In 1925, he invested part of the profit from his cotton gin in a large turpentine still on the Lake City highway.

With the profit he made from his cotton gin and turpentine still operations, Dr. King accelerated his already-established policy of buying up old, worn-out cotton farms and planting pine trees over them. His turpentine still allowed him to process the sap from his own trees at cost, while at the same time processing other tree farmers' pine sap at a profit. Because he had his money invested in land and two businesses, instead of having it socked away in a bank or in stocks and bonds, the coming of the Great Depression only minimally hurt Dr. King. He lost some money when the two banks in Union County went broke, but farmers still had to gin their cotton, and pine sap still needed to be refined into turpentine, so he stayed in business, actually increasing his wealth.

Almost all the Negro farmers who moved to the North sold their small farms to Dr. King. Just as with Harry Byrd's wife, he usually paid more than he needed in order to get the land. However, Dr. King was a decent man, who didn't want it on his conscience that he had cheated anyone. He also knew the sentimental value this land had for many of the blacks heading to the North. Most of them had labored long and hard under the tenant farm system and saved every dollar in order to buy their own land. They had worked even harder to keep the land, raising crops and paying their taxes.

Many of the Negro farmers were selling land that had been in their family since the Civil War. When the Union Army occupied Florida during the Civil War, it began a policy of awarding free land to former slaves. During the Reconstruction Period, this policy was accelerated, despite bitter white opposition. Some of the land was seized from white owners, but most was simply wilderness or farmlands once owned by the Seminole Indians before they were pushed off during the Second Seminole Indian War.

Dr. King had always ignored politics, claiming he was too busy to worry about it. However, all that changed in 1932, when Franklin D. Roosevelt became the Democratic nominee for the White House. He thought Roosevelt was the finest thing to happen to this country since Abraham Lincoln. It had always appalled him how the government just turned its head and ignored the suffering of its citizens. He hated how the Vanderbilts and the Rockefellers lived in regal splendor, while thousands of children lived in squalor and went hungry. It was Dr. King's job to clean up the mess these millionaires made with their reckless greed.

He had long subscribed to socialist literature and left it in the waiting room of his office, but most of his patients were barely literate and only looked at the pictures. Dr. King had always been a moderate on racial matters. The word "moderate" in those days, and right up through the civil rights movement, was a code word for a liberal integrationist. Dr. King maintained a "Colored Only" waiting room at his office, as social custom dictated, but he always considered it a stupid thing to do. As a man who had examined almost everyone in Union County, both inside and out, he knew that there was really no reason why they couldn't sit next to each other. However, he kept his mouth shut about his personal feeling, not wanting to waste his time arguing with idiots.

Dr. King's father, Henry Clayton King, had been born in a small mountain cabin in the Nagoochee Valley of north Georgia. He was an extra bright child who was educated in a one-room schoolhouse in Sautee, Georgia. When the Civil War began, he was a tall, healthy seventeen-year-old boy.

One of the great myths of the Civil War was that everyone who lived in the South was for the Confederacy and that everyone who lived in the North was for the Union. Nothing could be further from the truth. The mountain folks of north Georgia did not own slaves and had little sympathy for the slave-owning, landed gentry of the lowlands and their rebellion against the government of the United States. Henry Clayton King's loyalties were to the Union, and he saw his duty clearly.

He traveled by horseback, train, and riverboat to Cairo, Illinois, where he enlisted in the Union Army. The young Georgia soldier would fight through all four years of the Civil War. He was shot through the calf of the leg at Perryville, Kentucky, on October 8, 1862, and he was hit in the hip by a piece of exploding artillery shell at Chattanooga, Tennessee, a year later. Because of his valor, the young mountain boy was first promoted to sergeant and then to lieutenant, and he was a captain of infantry when the war ended.

He marched through Georgia with General William Tecumseh Sherman and had seen the ocean for the first time on the beaches near Savannah. The infantrymen he commanded led Sherman's destructive crusade through South Carolina, and he watched as the flames destroying the city of Columbia, South Carolina, leaped into the cool night sky. Finally, Captain Henry Clayton King had marched with the Army of the Tennessee when it paraded down Pennsylvania Avenue at the close of the war.

Captain King had done well in the Union Army. Every four months when he reenlisted, he received a sizable bounty paid by both the federal government and the State of Illinois where he had originally enlisted. Unlike most Union soldiers, who drank and gambled away their reenlistment bounties, Captain King saved his money, socking it away for when the war would be over. When he was mustered out of the service in June of 1865, he had thousands of dollars saved.

Henry King returned home to Georgia a well-to-do man with plans for the future. With the money he had saved, he opened a country store in Union County, Georgia, on a well-traveled road leading to Blairsville.

His store was prosperous from the start, and he expanded it several times. His customers, for the most part, were local lumberjacks and sawmill workers that were stripping the north Georgia mountains bare of timber for large eastern corporations, most of which were controlled by the Rockefeller family.

It pained him greatly to see the lovely Georgia mountains laid waste by greedy lumber men, who clear cut the mountains, killed all the undergrowth in the process, and polluted the rivers and mountain streams with the trailings of their timber harvesting. After the trees were gone, the heavy summer rains would cause massive mud slides that washed away the whole sides of mountains and filled rivers with choking silt and mud that killed all the fish.

Henry Clayton King eventually married a local girl, whose father had been killed in the Civil War fighting in the Confederate Army. The couple had only one child, a baby boy, they named after a friend of his father's who had been killed at Stone's River, Tennessee.

James Weldon King, who would always be known as J. W. or "Doctor," had been born on a cold morning in November of 1880. With snow on the ground outside and a fire casting its warm glow over the house, he came into the world in the front bedroom of his father's modest home. He was a healthy and exceptionally bright child, and his mother doted on him. He was to be her only child and the light of her life.

Henry Clayton King died in 1895 of a cerebral hemorrhage; he was only fifty-two years old. His young son sadly mourned his father's premature death and decided to find a career in medicine. The next year, he enrolled in Cumberland University in Lebanon, Tennessee. In 1900, he graduated as a medical doctor. While he was in college, J. W. King had met a refined young southern belle from Macon, Georgia, named Emily Ann Nilson. She immediately fell in love with the tall, lanky youth, and soon the two were a couple. She took the somewhat crude mountain boy under her wing, teaching him the more refined aspects of southern life. They attended formal tea parties, debutante balls, and receptions at the Order of the Eastern Star. They both graduated the same year and were married a few months later.

In 1901, Dr. King opened an office in Blairsville. Business was slow in the small Georgia mountain community that already had two established doctors. The next year, the young doctor was hit by a double tragedy. His mother died after a long bout with pneumonia, and his wife had a miscarriage. Dr. King blamed both tragedies on the cold mountain winters. He decided to move to the warmer climate of Florida.

For two years, he shared a practice with a Jacksonville physician, an old Union Army friend of his father, who had written him describing the mild Florida winters in glowing terms. In 1905, Dr. King broke out on his own and moved to a small town called Lake Butler, sixty miles southeast of Jacksonville, in what was then still part of Bradford County.

Fifteen years later, when the county was divided by the state legislature, Dr. King used his influence to have the new county named Union, after his home county in Georgia and the cause his father fought for during the Civil War.

# The Southern Sot Weed

T he big problem on most people's minds during the Depression was what to grow, now that the boll weevil had wiped out the cotton crop. Other areas of the South had successfully switched to soybeans and peanuts. However, north Florida decided upon another more-sinister crop.

Tobacco is a strange plant. Although it can be successfully grown in almost all parts of the United States, for some reason that is probably as much psychological as it is agricultural, 90 percent of all tobacco is grown in the South. Tobacco, originally called "sot weed," was the first "cash crop" grown in the Virginia Colony, and, without it, the small Jamestown settlement might have faltered, and the whole course of history might have been altered. In colonial America, tobacco was so valuable that it was often used as a medium of exchange. If a man could not pay his debts in cash, then he could always send tobacco.

Tobacco is a member of the deadly nightshade family of plants. It is genetically akin to both the potato and the tomato plants. It comes in two basic varieties: *Nicotina tabacum* and *Nicotina rustica*.

The tobacco grown in Virginia, and later in Kentucky, was a dark reddish-brown burly that was an excellent cigar and pipe smoke. Just before the beginning of the Civil War, two brothers who lived in the sand hills of central North Carolina decided to plant two acres of land in tobacco seeds they had obtained from friends in Virginia. Ignoring warnings from neighbors that the seeds would never grow, the two young men planted the tobacco. What resulted was a shock to both of them and a major new agricultural discovery. The sandy loam soil of North Carolina produced a tobacco plant with a light yellow leaf. What these two young men had accidentally produced was later named "bright leaf" tobacco. While it was not a good leaf for cigars or pipes, it was excellent for the newest tobacco product, the cigarette.

The two young men's discovery would be overshadowed by the coming of the Civil War, and it would be mostly forgotten afterwards by southern farmers anxious to return to the production of cotton. However, in the decades after the Civil War, two things happened; cigarette smoking became more popular, and cotton became harder and harder to grow. The old pre-Civil War practice of abandoning worn-out fields for new land on the frontier could no longer continue in the latter half of the nineteenth century. For awhile, the use of heavy loads of guano fertilizer gave new life to old cotton lands; however, with the coming of the boll weevil in the first decades of the twentieth century, king cotton—the plant that had fueled the slavery debate, brought on the Civil War, and had become synonymous with the South—had to give way.

One of the big advantages of tobacco over cotton was that less land was needed to produce it. Because of the tremendous amount of work involved, even the most hardworking farm families could not produce more than five or six acres of tobacco. A farmer could never plant tobacco on the same ground two years in a row, and the land used had to be extensively prepared with heavy loads of fertilizer, because tobacco plants sap many of the soil's nutrients.

Tobacco begins its life in January or February as tiny black seeds that look very similar to black pepper. In fact, one ounce of tobacco seeds contains the beginnings of over three hundred thousand individual plants. The precious black specks are sprinkled on to a carefully prepared, raised seedbed protected by a layer of delicate cheesecloth. Tradition dictated that the soil in the "tobacco bed" should be "sterile" (that is, free of weeds or any other plant growth) and that the soil should never have before born a cotton or tobacco crop.

Once the seedlings had sprouted, they had to be carefully tended. Inferior plants had to be removed by hand and periodically the beds thinned to give the healthy plants room to grow. The tobacco farmer's worst nightmare was that a small deer or wild cows would get into the tobacco beds and eat the small tinder plants. Many farmers actually slept next to their tobacco beds with a shotgun close at hand.

While the tobacco plants are "in the bed," the farmer must be busy carefully preparing the fields, where the young tobacco plants will be replanted. The field had to be first "disked" or cut up with round blades pulled behind a tractor or team of mules. Then, the fields had to be "turned," with the ground broken and turned back upon itself with a curved plow blade. Finally, the ground had to be "harrowed," to break up the soil and prepare raised furrows to receive the young tobacco plants.

Transplanting tobacco is incredibly hard work. Some farmers used special sleds where a man would sit on a special seat only inches above the ground planting tobacco plants between his legs as he was pulled down the rows by either a tractor or a team of mules. Farmers who could not afford a transplanting sled had to set the tobacco plants out by hand. The whole family, from the youngest child to the oldest grandparent, would go into the fields to do the backbreaking stoop labor of resetting the small, delicate tobacco plants into nice straight rows.

Once the tobacco plants were transplanted, the danger of deer or wild hogs getting into the fields and eating the young plants was great. It was easier to guard the seedlings when they were in the small beds than when they were out in the open fields. Once the plants were more than two feet high, they lost their appeal to deer that found the tobacco plants too tough and bitter to eat. However, wild hogs were still a problem, since a wild hog will eat anything.

For every deer or wild hog the farmer killed during the winter, it meant two things: fresh meat for the table and a reduced threat to his young tobacco crop.

Hunting in Florida is not easy. The woods are full of thick undergrowth, mass tangles of vines, and sharp briars, which tear at the skin and make walking difficult. In the warm months, deer are lethargic and feed late at night. During the heat of the day, they, just like people, find a nice cool spot and seldom move. When the weather turns cold, the deer have to move around to stay warm and have to range far and wide seeking food. This is when hunting is easy. The cold weather also gets rid of the mosquitoes, yellow flies, ticks, and red bugs that torment humans in the woods during the long, hot Florida summer.

The fact that the fall and winter is the deer's mating season makes it all the easier to find and kill them. Deer mark their territory with scent glands, rubs on small trees, and deposits of saliva on the ends of overhanging tree limbs. Unlike deer, hunting wild hogs is outright dangerous. The wiry beasts that populated the Florida woods were descendants of the razorback hogs brought over from Spain by the murderous Spanish conquistador, Hernando de Soto. They were a far cry from the large, fat domesticated animals found wallowing in the mud of foul-smelling pens on farms. Wild hogs are lean and mean, and they are capable of killing or badly injuring either a man or his hunting dogs. Unlike deer, wild hogs will not run away; instead, they will turn and fight. They have razor-sharp tusks that can rip open a dog's belly with one swipe and sharp teeth that can literally tear a man's leg off. Wild hogs are always found near water and mud. They have no sweat glands, so they have to wallow in the wet mud to stay cool. However, early in the morning and late in the afternoon, they range far and wide seeking wild acorns and roots upon which they feed.

Hunting wild hogs requires the use of well-trained dogs to flush them out of the thick undergrowth and muddy swamp areas where they are found. A good hunting dog was worth his weight in fresh meat to a poor farmer and his family. If he was a good watchdog, then he was even more valuable.

Critics of the South often point out that southerners tend to brag about very minor accomplishments, such as catching a big bass or killing an eight-point buck. What they don't understand is that to poor dirt farmers, hunting was about the only recreation available to them. During the years before television, farmers would gather at local stores, barber shops, and courthouse squares to brag about the skill of their hunting dogs and their own prowess as a hunter. Such stories would be listened to with awe by young children who hoped to someday imitate these acts of greatness by bringing home their own eight-point buck deer.

Hunting season was something that farmers looked forward to each year like a kid looks forward to Christmas. It was a break from the grudging hard work of planting, cultivating, and harvesting. The farmer's only luxury was a well-oiled shotgun and a good pair of hunting dogs. He treated both with reverence and a deep abiding love, and he would never sell either unless his situation was just above starvation. Many jokes have been made about southerners who loved their dogs and shotguns more than they loved their wife and kids, but such an analogy was ridiculous. Hunting was a bright point in a life that had few bright points. Farmers always knew that soon hunting season would soon be over, and they would have to return to the hot, dry fields to do backbreaking hard labor to bring in another tobacco crop.

Once the plants were transplanted, and the hot and humid Florida summer arrived, the farmer's work increased. Every day, the farmer and his family would have to be in the fields, carefully hoeing the rows to make sure no weeds grew among the tobacco plants. They also had to pull off the smaller tobacco leaves called "suckers" to make room for the larger leaves to grow.

With tobacco, the product being sold is the leaf of the plant itself; the larger and brighter the leaf, the higher the price. The largest leaves on a tobacco plant grow low to the ground at the very bottom of the plant. They are called "sand lugs," because they actually touched the ground, and the leaves were always coated with fine white grains of Florida sand.

Insecticides cannot be used on tobacco plants, because they either discolor the leaves or affect the taste of the smoke. The biggest pest threat to the tobacco plant is a fat, little white worm called a "cutworm." It gets onto the tobacco plant, cuts a path across the leaf, and eats as it goes. The only sure way to get rid of cutworms is to pick them off by hand; this is a long, slow process that doesn't end until the last leaf is picked for sale. Some farmers put their trust in a foul-smelling homemade concoction they pour around the stem of the plants. Every tobacco farmer has his own recipe, but it is usually a mixture of sour milk, hot peppers, rotten meat, or anything else you might think a cutworm will find disgusting enough to make him turn around and forsake your tobacco plants.

When I was a child, most of us found picking cutworms kind of fun. It was a little like looking for Easter eggs, except you were looking for worms. They didn't bite or sting, and they were fun to play with. Farmers tried to make it fun for their children by handing out cheap penny candy to the child whose bucket was most full of cutworms.

After cutworms are picked off the tobacco plants, there are several ways to get rid of them. The most fun for children is cutting them up into little pieces and watching the pieces crawl around independent of each other. However, most farmers had little time for such nonsense and simply doused the pile of cutworms with kerosene and set them ablaze.

The real hell of tobacco farming came in the blazing heat of mid-July, when the sand luggs reached their maximum size and had to be harvested or "cropped" in the farm-speak of north Florida tobacco production. Everything in tobacco farming up to this point had to be done slowly and carefully. However, cropping tobacco had to be done quickly. Once the sand luggs reached their maximum size, you only had a few days to get them picked before they began to "burn up" in the hot Florida sun. They don't literally "burn up," but the heat in the tobacco fields will make the leaves turn brown and wither on the stalk. Once a leaf has started to "burn," it is useless and has to be thrown out. A whole field of tobacco can "burn" in only one or two days.

Because of the crucial time factor involved, "cropping" was the only time a farmer would hire outside labor. In Union County, that labor came in the form of children home from school for the summer. The men and teenage boys would go out to the fields to harvest the sand luggs. Teenage girls and young boys would "hand tobacco." They would take the picked tobacco out of the wooden sled, where it was put after it was picked, and hand it to the "stick woman," who was usually the mother or grandmother of the family. Tying the tobacco leaves onto the sticks was the most important job done during the harvesting of tobacco, and the responsibility of doing it was seldom entrusted to strangers.

She would sit at a long bench and tie the tobacco onto the square, four-foot-long tobacco sticks. Her hands and fingers were wrapped in black electrical tape, so she could maintain enough manual dexterity to tie the small knots needed to hold the leaves on the stick, while at the same time protecting her hand from being cut to ribbons by the strong string. The leaves were handed to her, four or five to a hand. The leaves had to be perfectly even and about the same size. The stick woman was the boss of the hand table, and anyone who didn't pick out leaves about the same size, and even up to the stems, would get a swift and harsh rebuke from the stick woman. Anyone who gave her any back talk or continued to mess up would be fired. Tying the tobacco on the stick was a critical procedure. If the knots were not secure or one leaf was shorter than the other, it could fall off the stick during cooking and start a fire.

The hand table, usually made from plywood or boards, was always in a shady place either between two trees or under a shed next to the tobacco barn. The stick woman was not expected to do anything except tie the leaves to the stick and supervise the handing. When she finished tying a stick, she would simply say "stick off," and one of the teenagers would take off the full stick and hand her an empty one. Next to the farmer himself, she was the boss, and what she said went.

Cropping sand luggs was very hard work. Only mature teenage boys and young men could do it. The job of driving the tractor or leading the mules that pulled the tobacco sled belonged to the man who owned the field. From his high perch on the tractor seat, he could supervise the cropping and make sure that all the mature leaves were picked and that leaves not fully grown were not picked. The big sled he pulled was a homemade contraption; it was a simple, wooden rectangular box fashioned from plywood or boards; mounted on two skids; and made from squared cypress. It could go anywhere such as over soft mud, loose sand, and wet clay without any danger of getting stuck. It could not move fast, but then it really didn't have to. The sled had to only stay ahead of the croppers in the field, and, when it was full, it made its way to the hand table, where it would be unloaded one handful at a time.

The temperature in the fields in July and August could easily get to over a hundred degrees, and the heavy Florida humidity only made it worse. The worst thing about harvesting the big leaves was that while you were doing it, you were bent over at the waist, and your head was only inches above ground level. To make thing even worse, your head was always stuck up into the tobacco plant, and the leaves were constantly rubbing against your face and head.

The leaves were easy to break off, but then you had to put them under your free arm until the bundle got so large you couldn't hold anymore. Holding the huge bundle of tobacco leaves could be pure torture, but it was a matter of honor not to go to the sled unless you simply couldn't hold anymore. Every time a picker had to go to the tobacco sled, he lost time. A man who only had to go to the sled to deposit his pickings every ten minutes was more productive than a man who had to go every five minutes. When hiring tobacco harvesters, the farmers looked for young boys with long arms and big hands. Young boys who couldn't hold a lot of tobacco were given rows close to the sled so they wouldn't have to walk so far. Each picker had his own row, and, if it had not been cropped properly, the farmer knew whom to blame.

The worst thing about cropping tobacco was getting "bear caught." You spent five to ten minutes bent over, picking sand luggs with your head only a few inches above ground, and then when you finally had to stand up, you might get nauseous and vomit or simply pass out. Getting "bear caught" was almost an initiation rite among tobacco croppers. When you showed up to work, nobody would warn you about the pitfalls of drinking too much water, picking too fast, or coming to work on an empty stomach, both of which would lead to a new tobacco cropper getting "bear caught." Eventually, the young and healthy teenage boys would learn to pace themselves in the field, avoid drinking too much water, keep a full belly, and not get "bear caught."

Allowing it to dry in a shaded place for two to twelve weeks can cure tobacco grown in other parts of the United States. This is called "air curing" or "shade tobacco." It involves the hanging of the entire tobacco plant upside down in a protected enclosure with good ventilation and letting the hot sun and cross ventilation cure the plants. Air curing, or shade tobacco, produces a yellow to tan leaf that is low in sugar and varies in nicotine. However, the high humidity in Florida means that tobacco grown here must be "flue cured." It literally has to be cooked until the green leaves turn the golden yellowish-brown color desired by tobacco buyers. Flue curing results in a darker brown tobacco with a low sugar content that is higher in nicotine than shaded tobacco.

On every tobacco farm in Union County was a tall square structure called a "tobacco barn." They were originally made from logs, but the newer ones were fashioned from boards and insulated with heavy coats of tar paper. A tobacco barn has a dirt floor on which four large cookers rest, whose function it is to heat up the barn during the hottest part of summer until the temperature inside reaches close to one hundred and fifty degrees on the floor to nearly two hundred degrees at the top of the barn.

Once the tobacco crop has been picked, handed and tied onto sticks, then it must be hung in the barn. This job fell to the strong teenage boys who picked the crop. They would form a line and pass the sticks from one to the other. The most experienced boy would be located in the top of the thirty-foot-high tobacco barn, carefully positioning the sticks on wooden supports called "tiers." The sticks had to be exactly four to six inches from each other, and the leaves had to hang straight down in order to cook properly. Even though it was usually over one hundred degrees in the top of the barn, even without the heaters going, this was no time to get in a hurry. One mistake and a tobacco crop, which had begun six hard months before in a covered planting bed, could be completely ruined by a simple thing like improper cooking. Most barns had between four to six layers of tiers holding as many as one hundred sticks of tobacco. The tobacco that was hung on the bottom tier was only one or two feet above the hot kerosene-powered heaters.

The tobacco farmer's greatest nightmare was a fire in the barn. While farmers took every precaution against a fire, every summer at least one tobacco barn would go up in flames. When the green tobacco leaves begin to dry out and shrink in size, if they had not been tied properly, a handful of leaves could work loose and fall off the stick. If the leaves hit the dirt floor of the barn, then there is no problem; however, if they landed on one of the hot cookers, then they would burst into flames. If the flames reached the bottom row of tobacco sticks, then the whole barn would be engulfed within a few minutes. Once a barn is ablaze, there is really nothing the farmer can do to put it out. All he can do is watch the inferno and try to figure out how he and his family will survive without the money from the tobacco crop.

Once the tobacco is cooked, it is carefully taken down, removed from the sticks, and "graded." The leaves are arranged in a circle with the stems pointing inward and the point of the leaves facing the outside of the circle. Slowly, the tobacco will rise from the floor, as one layer of leaves will be placed one on top of the other. There is a certain amount of artistic endeavor involved with grading tobacco. The largest and most perfect leaves have to be placed on the outside and top of the pile, while short or discolored leaves go on the inside, where a tobacco buyer will not be likely to see them. It takes weeks for the family to grade an entire tobacco crop. When they finish they have a three-hundred-pound, carefully positioned bale of tobacco that is carefully wrapped in burlap cloth to hold it together until it is carried to market.

The nearest tobacco warehouses to Union County were located in the western section of Lake City, near the railroad tracks. They were either named after the man who owned them such a Yancy's Warehouse or Sonny's Warehouse or they were given names such as "Top Dollar" or "Big Dollar," implying that the farmer will get a better price at this particular warehouse than any other.

Tobacco warehouses were huge tin-roofed and tin-sided buildings that were only in use a few months of the year. Farmers would pull onto a ramp with their tobacco crop in the rear of the largest farm truck they owned. The bales would be unloaded by strong-backed Negroes who worked for the warehouse, weighted, and then marked with a slip of paper on which was written the farmer's name, the weight of the bale (tobacco is paid for by the pound), and the floor number, where the bale is to be positioned on the warehouse floor. The tobacco bales were placed on the floor in long, straight, and neat rows, so the buyers could quickly walk between them and inspect the bales for signs of improper cooking, cutworm damage, or the smell of a pesticide.

The buyers represented large tobacco companies, such as the American Tobacco Company, R. J. Reynolds, or Philip Morris. The buyers were seasoned professionals who knew their business and were well paid for their expertise. The buyers were always easy to spot. Each wore a snap-brim white or gray Stetson hat. Their pants were a dark khaki, held up with a pair of button suspenders over a stained white shirt. In their shirt pockets was always a freshly opened pack of cigarettes, manufactured by the company they represented. No tobacco buyer would dare aggravate his employer by not smoking his company's brand of cigarettes. They were almost never seen without a cigarette dangling from their lips.

The buyers drove around in big Cadillac automobiles, stayed in the finest hotels in town, ate in the best restaurants, and got roaring drunk every night. No auction ever began before noon, so the late-night, hard-drinking buyers would not be forced to arise too early. A grumpy tobacco buyer is not as likely to pay a very good price.

The buyer's job was to buy the best tobacco available at the cheapest possible price. They looked at the poor tobacco farmers much like a master would look upon a slave. Since they were the only buyers in town, the farmer's future was to be determined by these still half-drunk aristocrats, who swaggered about the big warehouses and decided, often on a whim, how much their Fortune 500 bosses would pay for a farmer's year of hard work. However, the big tobacco companies weren't stupid. They were not about to kill the goose that laid the golden (or bright leaf) egg. Tobacco farmers would never get rich working in their hot fields every summer; most would never even get out of debt, but the tobacco companies were not about to let them starve either. They would need another tobacco crop next year.

A tobacco auction is a fixture of southern folk life. Everyone has seen the image of the fast-talking auctioneer walking swiftly between the neat rows of tobacco bales, followed by a gaggle of buyers, screaming out numbers and making hand signs that only a person who belongs to the elite corps of tobacco buyers and auctioneers would understand.

The auctioneer was the supreme ruler of the warehouse, at least during the auction itself. Usually a former tobacco buyer himself, the auctioneer had attended a special school and spent years practicing to perfect his fast-talking craft. An auctioneer would have to go for hours in his sing-song lyrics, coughing off the heat and tobacco dust inside the big warehouses, without pause. Once an auction began, tradition and the buyers' precious time dictated that it go uninterrupted until it was over. The faster the auctioneer could talk, the faster the auction went, and the more popular he was with the buyers. At the end of the auction, he would be soaking wet with sweat. His first stop would always be a jug of cold water and a cold bottle of beer kept in a refrigerator in the warehouse office just for him.

During the auction, the farmers would line the walls of the warehouse, keeping out of the way of the auctioneer and the group of harried buyers who followed him. They were set apart by their faded blue overalls and sweat-stained floppy hats. Their callused hands, the dirt under their fingernails, and their sunburned, leathery faces told everyone who they were. As soon as the auctioneer and buyers had passed their particular bale of tobacco, the farmer would casually, attempting to hide his nervousness, stride over to check the price on the bale.

No money changed hands. The auctioneer's assistant would scribble the agreed-upon price on the small slip of paper attached to each bale of tobacco, and the buyer would initial the price. The farmer would take his receipt to the warehouse office and would be issued a check for the weight of the bale against the price per pound the buyer offered. Later, the warehouse would receive a check from the tobacco company for all the tobacco they bought during a season, plus a liberal kickback to the owner of the warehouse. The "official fee" for selling at the warehouse was always deducted from the money paid to the farmer. The farmer could reject the price, but few did. The top price per pound was more or less uniform across the state. It was determined by factors nationwide. Only if the buyers found something wrong—burned leafs, the aroma of pesticide, or cutworm damage—would the price be seriously reduced.

During the whole period of time when southern farmers produced cotton, they were deviled by wide swings in cotton prices. One year, the price would be way up, and the next year, it would be way down. The law of supply and demand determined it all. If it was a good crop year and the fields produced a bumper harvest of cotton, then the price would be low. If cold weather, hailstorms, too much rain, not enough rain, or boll weevils restricted the size of the crop, then the price would be high. What all this meant in plain, everyday language is that the cotton farmer just couldn't win.

During the 1930s, the Roosevelt Administration sought to ward off this problem among tobacco farmers by requiring each farmer to obtain a "tobacco allotment" from the U.S. Department of Agriculture. The allotment told each farmer how many acres he could grow, thus controlling the size of the crop, preventing overproduction, and keeping the price up. The paperwork was minimal, and every county seat had an Agricultural Extension Office where local farmers could apply for their yearly allotment. It soon became well known that a healthy tobacco crop would almost guarantee a good market price. This greatly encouraged people to switch from cotton to tobacco.

Most people's allotment was for only two or three acres, which caused little complaint, since that was about all a farm family could handle because of all the work involved. Having only two or three acres of tobacco meant that the farmers could rotate their crops, not planting on the same piece of land year after year. Tobacco, like cotton, was hard on the land; however, by rotating the crops not as much, chemical fertilizer was needed, and the land lasted longer. Most farmers would divide their farms into four sections. They made a practice of going around in a circle planting the northeast section one year, the southeast the next, then the southwest, and finally the northwest. This meant that a particular section of soil would not have to produce a tobacco crop but one year out of four, giving the ground time to renew itself.

The reduced amount of land need to produce tobacco also meant that farmers had land left over for truck crops; corn, beans, peas, cucumbers, and watermelons were grown in the summer. Collards, turnips, strawberries, potatoes, and cabbages were grown in the fall and winter months. Farmers continued to raise hogs, chickens, cattle, and sometimes even horses or mules. The selling of a hog, horse, mule, or cow would buy the children a new suit of clothes to wear to school or help pay off the bank debt.

Tobacco farming didn't mean an end to the Great Depression by any means, but it did mean survival during one of the hardest periods in American history.

The brilliant mind that created the huge market for "bright leaf" tobacco production was a father and son team from North Carolina, the "Duke boys." The father's name was Washington Duke or "Wash" as he was better known, and the son was James Buchanan or "Buck" Duke. Together they formed the company of Duke, Sons, and Company. The product they would make was store-bought, already-rolled-in-the-pack cigarettes made with "bright leaf, flue cured" tobacco. In the 1890s, they changed the name of their corporation to the American Tobacco Company.

The "Duke boys," as they were known in North Carolina, were mass producing and selling the most addictive drug in the world. People who shook cocaine, heroin, and morphine addictions found it impossible to stop smoking. Once someone purchased and began smoking the ready-rolled cigarettes, they were hooked for life. Wash and Buck Duke never saw it that way, and their well-healed descendants still don't today. According to the Duke boys, they were giving poor working people a whole day's worth of relaxing smoking pleasure for only fifteen cents a pack.

Before Buck Duke died in the 1920s, the Duke boys had socialized and did business with the richest men in America and Europe. They were the first, super-rich robber barons to come out of the South. The Duke family also owned textile mills, coal mines, railroads, and banks, and eventually they founded Duke Power, a monopoly that even today controls all the electrical power produced in North Carolina and South Carolina. They were also able to take over the Alcoa Aluminum Company.

The Duke boys—both church-going, devout Methodists—hated the very idea of trade unions and suppressed them with unbelievable brutality. They also fixed prices, coerced rivals, bullied and cheated their workers, and routinely bribed judges, governors, and members of Congress.

The greatest measure of the Duke boy's wealth was the fact that Buck Duke spent over one hundred and fifty million dollars founding Duke University. They hired Frederick Law Olmstead's sons to landscape the grounds and bought entire quarries to get enough stone to build all the buildings.

The southern sot weed had served them well.

# The New Deal

All his adult life, Dr. King had avoided open political campaigning, preferring to work behind the scenes with whoever held political office to get things done. However, in 1932, all that changed. He became a strong supporter of Franklin Delano Roosevelt and the Democratic New Deal ticket. Dr. King had always disdained the election process with its backslapping, hand shaking, and baby kissing. However, with the nomination of Franklin Roosevelt as the Democratic candidate for president, he gave up his medical practice to campaign full time for the Democratic ticket.

After turning his medical practice over to a young intern from Gainesville, Dr. King traveled all over the state of Florida making rousing stump speeches for Franklin D. Roosevelt. His son founded a Young Democrats Club in Union County, and his wife was a Democratic National Committee Woman. Dr. King was a regular feature at swank cocktail parties in Tallahassee, Miami, and Jacksonville. He also made several trips to New York and Washington DC, where he was a favorite after dinner speaker at Democratic fundraisers. Dr. King was in the mold of Huey P. Long, who was equally comfortable speaking at a black tie dinner party at a plush Long Island country club or standing on the back of a pickup truck and quoting Scripture to convince a group of semiliterate farmers of the evils of the Republican Party. If they could vote, or knew someone who could vote, Dr. King was willing to take the time to talk to them.

Dr. King proclaimed, to all who would listen, that the Republican Party didn't give a damn about poor working people. It was the party of millionaires and Wall Street tycoons. The poor dirt farmers to whom he spoke would not know a millionaire or Wall Street tycoon if they saw one, but they did know

Dr. King, who had delivered their babies and tended them when they were sick and in need of help; if he said that the Republicans were only interested in helping millionaires and Wall Street tycoons, then that was good enough for them.

Dr. King's message took roots and grew among the poor dirt farmers and small store merchants of north Florida. In barbershops, gasoline stations, courthouse benches and Garden Club socials, all the talk revolved around one thing, how to get Franklin D. Roosevelt elected president of the United States. Only in Baptist and Methodist churches, where there was a strict rule against talking politics of any kind, were people silent. People weary of the Depression, and Herbert Hoover's lack of action, flocked to the Democratic standard. On Election Day, Dr. King was proud that all of north Florida as well as the state as a whole went for the Roosevelt ticket by an overwhelming majority.

Shortly after Roosevelt took office, Dr. King traveled by train to Washington, where he met with Florida's Senators and Congressmen who were lobbying hard to get New Deal money for Union County. He had not forgotten the poor children he had treated down at the Scout Hole. While in Washington, Dr. King met a man who would become his hero for the rest of his life, Congressman Claude Pepper.

Raised in extreme poverty in rural Alabama, Claude Pepper had gone to law school and then ran for political office on the coat tails of Franklin D. Roosevelt. He was always a friend of the little man, the elderly, the sick, and the young children. Claude Pepper could always be counted on to do his best.

When the New Deal went into effect, in the first hundred days after Franklin D. Roosevelt took office, Dr. King's hard work paid off. Early in 1934, an extensive road-building program was begun in Union County. State Road 121, the road connecting Lake Butler to Worthington Springs, was finally finished, and a new concrete bridge was built over the Santa Fe River at Worthington Springs. This meant that a paved road now existed all the way from Lake Butler to Gainesville, allowing sick and injured people to be quickly transported over paved roads to Alachua General Hospital.

As soon as the Worthington Springs' road was finished, work began on the other end of State Road 121, running northeast from Lake Butler to Raiford. When this road was finished, it would complete a connection with paved roads in Baker County, which meant, for the first time, Union County residents could drive on a hard roadway all the way to Jacksonville.

Dr. King insisted that hiring priority be given to Union County residents in the road-building project. He personally went down to the Scout Hole to recruit men to shovel dirt and drive the big earth-moving machines. Over fifty, able-bodied men were eventually hired to pave the two roads, and another twenty-five men were employed to construct the bridge over the Santa Fe River.

Preference was also given to white men. Originally, the contractor had planned not to hire any Negroes. However, one night, over a fine southern meal of fried chicken and pecan pie, Dr. King convinced the contractor that Negroes were better suited for certain jobs than whites. The contractor was reluctantly forced to agree with Dr. King. The black workers would be relegated to the most menial and low-paying jobs on the road-paving project, but Dr. King was proud that he had managed to get ten black men with families to support the much-coveted work.

By 1936, many of the farmers who had lost their land were able to get a fresh start farming thanks to loans granted by the Farm Credit Administration. With these loans, they were able to buy new farm equipment, seeds, and transplanters, and they were able to make the necessary change from cotton to tobacco and truck farming.

The Agricultural Adjustment Administration that regulated farm prices and issued tobacco allotments further helped farmers. Many chose to put their land in what was called the "Soil Bank," where they were actually paid by the government not to grow crops. Since pine trees were not considered to be a crop by the government, any piece of land placed in the "Soil Bank" would be quickly planted over in timber, using labor from the Civilian Conservation Corps. In ten years, the trees would be large enough to cut for turpentine production, and, in twenty years, they could be harvested for pulpwood.

In 1936, just as the work on building the two roads and the bridge over the Santa Fe River was coming to a close, the Works Projects Administration began construction of a new Union County courthouse. The old wooden courthouse was moved to a new location overlooking the lake, and it became the County Health Clinic and Civic Center; it would also house the Lake Butler Women's Club. The old building has been the sight of many weddings, parties, banquets, receptions, and, in the 1950s and 1960s, teenage rock and roll dances.

The new courthouse was to be a grand structure, a two-story redbrick monument to good government. It would have a large, spacious courtroom; jury deliberation room; and ample office space for judges, clerks, and administrators. Every elected official from the supervisor of elections to the high sheriff himself would have a suite of offices.

In 1938, work was also begun on a new jail facility. Like the old jail, the bottom floor would be the living quarters of the high sheriff. It would be a poured concrete building fronted with red bricks to match the courthouse. Each prisoner would have his own private cell equipped with a flushing toilet and a small sink. The jail's steel-barred cells were divided into white and colored sections, with a special area set aside for female prisoners.

One of Dr. King's pet projects was the paving of the Scout Hole Road. The road through Worthington Springs provided a good paved road all the way to Alachua General Hospital in Gainesville, but it was a long, out-of-the-way route. If the Scout Hole Road was paved, then it could cut a lot of time off the drive to Gainesville. When someone had a heart attack or stroke, that thirty minutes could be crucial. Also, with the work coming to an end on the paving of the road to Raiford, new jobs had to be created or the men would soon find themselves out of work and back down at the Scout Hole again.

However, Dr. King had just about expended all his political clout getting the new courthouse and jail built. His political friends in Tallahassee and Washington tried to explain to the doctor that the number of registered voters in Union County was awfully small for such a large number of high-priced, pork barrel projects and that many other, much larger, counties were feeling slighted.

However, Dr. King just didn't see it that way. To him, it wasn't political pork he was after. The big-shot politicians had never treated children with sore eyes, head lice, and malnutrition. The government projects in Union County were the government doing what the government was supposed to do, help people. He was determined to get as many work projects as he could until the Depression was over. He knew that the more registered voters there were in Union County, the more New Deal money he could get. One night at a Democratic Committee meeting, he proposed that the county's Negroes be registered to vote. The proposition shocked everyone; it was quickly voted down and never mentioned again.

In 1938, Union County had a number of tiny schools scattered all over the county. They were located in such out-of-the-way and unincorporated towns as Worthington Springs, Raiford, Providence, and in very small communities as Johnstown, Liberty, and Midway, which were little more than wide places in the road. There had long been talk of consolidating the schools, but, as long as the Depression lasted, there would be no money for school buses or new construction.

Most children who bothered to go to school had to walk anywhere from two to twelve miles one way just to get there. They wore old and faded blue denim overalls that were always purchased two or three sizes too big, so the children could "grow into them." They carried their lunch in a silver lard bucket that looked like a modern paint can. A sweet potato and a couple of breakfast biscuits with a stale, hard outer crust were inside each can. Before the child's mother would pack up the lunch each morning, she would stick a finger into the biscuits, press out a cavity, and then fill it with homemade cane syrup, creating a syrup sandwich that the children found delicious.

Most of the scattered schools were small, white wood-framed buildings, except for the two-story school at Raiford, which was red brick. Each school had from five to ten classrooms holding grades one through twelve. The hallways and classrooms had pinewood floors, which always smelled of a strange type of oil. These oily pine floors were bad to put ugly splinters into the children's bare feet. Some of the larger schools had a tiny library, but most made do with a single bookshelf in the back of each classroom, where the children had the choice of picking out a well-worn book to take home and read.

A bright silver flagpole, upon which hung the flag of the United States, fronted each school. While everything else in the school might be old and worn out, the flag was always replaced as soon as it showed the slightest sign of wear and tear. The flag was almost a religious relic. It was considered a great honor to be allowed to put it up or take it down. Only very well-behaved students with good grades were allowed to touch the flag. It was put up each morning with great ceremony, and, at the end of each school day, it was slowly lowered and carefully folded. It was carried, being held at chest level with both hands, to the principal's office, where it sat in a place of honor next to his desk. It was never allowed to touch the ground, and nothing could be laid on top of it, except a Bible. Should it begin to rain, someone would always run outside to bring down the flag. It was never allowed to fly in bad weather. Every child knew the pledge of allegiance by heart, and it was recited each school day with deep sincerity as the flag was being raised to the top of the flagpole.

Behind each school was the playground, made up of all kinds of mostly homemade equipment; there were see-saws fashioned from old boards, swings made from old tires hanging from an oak limb, and what the children called "monkey bars" that had been put together from old galvanized pipe; the monkey bars were arranged so children could climb and swing to their heart's content.

No matter how small, each school contained an auditorium, where all the students could gather each day. Both teachers and students always called the auditorium "the chapel." Each school day would begin with a short worship service, complete with Bible reading and recitation of the Lord's Prayer. In the schools of Union County, there were no Catholics, Jews, Muslims, Hindus, Buddhists, agnostics, liberals, humanists, or atheists. Everyone was a Bible-believing Baptist or Methodist, fundamentalist to the core of their being. They read Scripture in class, memorized Bible verses as part of the lessons, and sang hymns and patriotic songs. They also had organized mandatory prayer before lunch each day, and nobody ever though twice about it. In some way, that's impossible to explain to someone who didn't experience it; the whole thing just seemed so natural. Adam and Eve, Noah's flood, the Tower of Babel, the Holy Ghost, the joys of Heaven, and the pains of Hell were as real to the children who populated the small scattered schools of Union County as the morning's sunrise.

It was an innocence I shared as a child and found hard to give up as an adult. I still miss it dearly. The Vietnam War, the University of Florida, the Social Revolution of the 1960s, *Playboy* magazines, intellectual friends, and professors drove all that from me. They squeezed it out of me like you would wring water out of a mop. Now, I am left without the warm glow of the rock-solid faith that so comforted those who came before me. Megabyte computers, cyberspace, cable television, and cellular telephones are a poor substitute for the childlike innocence of an absolute faith in the Lord Jesus Christ.

The largest school in Union County was the Lake Butler Normal School, located at the southern end of Lake Street. It was a coeducational, all white institution that had less than one hundred students in grades one to twelve. It was a rambling, two-story structure with a large bell tower over the main entrance. It had been built sometime before the turn of the century, and, by the end of the Depression, it was showing its age. All the wood in the building was infested with termites. The roof leaked badly, and the foundation had shifted, causing the walls to crack.

It was fast reaching the point where it was actually dangerous for children to attend classes in the crumbing old structure. Everyone agreed that the damage was too much to repair, and the old building would have to be torn down and replaced. Everyone said Union County was lucky, because this could be a new WPA project. However, certain fundamental questions had to be answered. Do; we simply replace the Normal School with another school the same size; or do we build a "consolidated" school"" that will be big enough to educate all the children in Union County?

There was really no debate; the county would consolidate all its far-flung schools. The reason for this momentous decision was simple: sports. As long as the counties' schools were small and scattered all over the place, Union County would never have a decent football, basketball, or baseball team. A group of businessmen and school administrators had put together the Suwannee Conference, where the rural north Florida counties could compete against each other in sporting events, and Union County wanted to make a decent showing.

People in Union County also wanted an indoor gymnasium to play basketball. The 1930 Lake Butler Normal School's boys' basketball team had been so good they had been invited to the state championship tournament in Tampa. Unfortunately, they had lost by default. The team had gotten drunk in their hotel rooms, created a disturbance, and destroyed some property. The manager of the hotel locked them out of their rooms and seized their entire luggage until the damage was paid. On the day of the big basketball tournament, the team's uniforms were still in their suitcases, which were locked up in their hotel rooms. By the time the problem was resolved, and the damages paid for, the tournament was over.

The team had practiced outdoors on a hard clay basketball court behind the Normal School. Union County has always been a sports crazy place, and the performance of the basketball team made everyone swell with pride. The fact that they had all got drunk and blew it just never seemed to come up in conversations. As people used to say, "It just don't amount to much." Most people felt that a state championship could still be possible, if only the team had an indoor gymnasium with a decent hardwood floor to practice on.

Basketball was just one of the many things people used during the Depression to cheer themselves up. In the summer, rousing baseball games were played all over the county. The games were always spirited and enjoyed by all, except when an umpire made an unpopular call and the whole thing ended in a brawling free-for-all. Football had been banned in the early 1920s when a young man was killed during a game. Everyone more or less agreed that the game was too rough and the equipment too poor to allow football to continue. Union County would not have a football team until after World War II.

Movies were always a big thing in Union County. There was no theater in Union County; however, once a week, the man who owned the movie theater in Lake City would come over to Lake Butler, set up a portable screen made from a bed sheet, and show movies in the Normal School auditorium. About once a month, he would also show a movie in Worthington Springs, Providence, or Raiford. Westerns were the favorite, but other people liked musicals and comedy shows. It cost a nickel to see the movies, and that was a lot of money during the Depression, especially if a whole family was going to what the old folks called the "moving pictures."

These grainy, mostly black and white films were more than just entertainment; they were a window to the world that existed beyond Union County. The vast majority of poor, Union County dirt farmers had never been any further from their shotgun shacks than the tobacco market in Lake City or a rare trip to Gainesville to visit someone in the hospital. Movies, radio broadcasts, and Sears and Roebuck catalogs were the only evidence these people had that a place called the United States of America even existed.

Next to the movies, radio was the most popular form of entertainment. Every barbershop, gasoline station, and country store had an RCA or Philco radio that people gathered around to listen to baseball games broadcast from such exotic and faraway places as New York, Chicago, St. Louis, and Boston.

When the poverty of the Great Depression began to lift, one of the first financial splurges most people made was to buy themselves a radio. Since the people who lived in the rural parts of the county did not have electricity in their homes, stores in Lake Butler sold battery-powered radios and recharged the batteries for free.

Besides baseball, people also loved to listen to the country music broadcasts originating from Renfro County, Kentucky, and rebroadcast all over the South every Saturday night. They were fans of the old blue yodel of Jimmie Rodgers, the down-home lyrics of the Carter Family, and the cornball humor of Uncle Dave Macon. While they may listen to baseball games and watch movies that came from far away, when it came to music, they preferred their own.

Late in 1938, work began on the new consolidated school that was to have two long wings, one for elementary students housing grades one through six and another wing for grades seven through twelve. Connecting the two wings would be a large auditorium and a suite of offices for the principal. The high school wing would also house Union County's only library, a typing classroom, and eventually a biology lab. It would be named Union County High School, despite the fact that it housed grades one through twelve.

The school would also have something unheard of only a few years before: a lunchroom. Instead of having the students bring a lard bucket from home, the school would sell hot lunches to students for ten cents, and free lunches would be given out to those who could not pay. This was made possible, because the school system was eligible to receive surplus government commodities. As part of the New Deal, the government agreed to buy up any surplus crops that farmers could not sell at government-regulated prices. This surplus food—wheat made into bread, peanuts made into peanut butter, corn, cheese, butter, milk, beans, and eggs—was all then distributed free of charge to public hospitals and schools.

By 1940, even though Roosevelt was still president, the WPA money for the building of the new school began to dry up, and construction work slowed down dramatically. However, by that time, the entire elementary wing and most of the high school wing were complete and in operation. Before the money completely ran out, the auditorium and office suite were also finished.

Work on the new school would be completely halted during World War II, but would resume quickly thereafter. Construction was done in stages as money became available. The long-waited-for gymnasium was not dedicated until 1950, and the final classrooms would not be added onto the high school wing until late in 1955. That was also when construction was begun on the new "Consolidated School." The 1954, *Brown* vs. *Board of Education* ruling, handed down the year before, had shocked and terrified the entire South. Segregation was the region's most cherished institution, and it was under challenge. Politicians scurried about looking for ways to bolster the ancient doctrine of "separate but equal" and ward off integration. In the decade after the famous Supreme Court decision, southern school districts spent millions of tax dollars building new, ultra-modern schools for black children. Likewise, the white citizens of Union County were taking no chances. They dug deep into their pockets and built a brand new school for Negro children, only a short distance from Union County High School.

The misnomer of "Consolidated School" was hung on this new school as part of a silly semantic game meant to fool no one. Calling it the "Colored School" or the "Negro School" was just too obvious. All over the South, every time a new, all-black school was opened, school boards racked their brains to think up a suitable name to disguise its true purpose. Names such as "Academy," "Institute," "Mechanical," or "Consolidated School" were in wide use.

The building of the new "Consolidated School" was a feeble attempt by the white citizens of Union County to ward off school integration. They sincerely believed that if the new "Consolidated School" was as good as, or in their eyes, even better than the white school (which it wasn't), then blacks would be content to stay "in their place." In their minds, integration was a Communist plot implemented by white agitators and beatnik radicals to destroy the United States.

For decades, Union County's black children had attended pitiful excuses for schools held in Negro churches scattered around the county. They used old textbooks with pages torn out, broken chalkboards, old pencil stubs, and scrap paper "donated" by the white schools. Only about 10 percent of the black children in Union County ever attended school; the rest were needed at home to help with the farm work. Even those who did go to the scattered Negro schools seldom stayed past their twelfth birthday. The schools taught little more than simple arithmetic, reading, and writing. Once a child had learned these most basic of educational skills, there was little reason to stay.

The opening of the "Consolidated School" eased the consciences of many white people, who had the basic human decency to worry about the unfairness of the whole rotten system of "separate but equal." White southerners love myths, and one of the greatest was that they loved the Negroes and the Negroes loved them back. They honestly believed that blacks were treated fairly under the system of segregation and were happy with it. However, they also saw blacks as childlike and easily influenced by outside agitators, so caution must be exercised.

In 1940, with the opening of Union County High School, and the purchase of half a dozen used yellow school buses from Alachua County, the policy of school consolidation was formally begun. The county's three smallest schools located in the isolated communities of Johnstown, Liberty, and Midway were closed, and the county began busing the students to the new school in Lake Butler. Consolidation would slowly continue until 1958, when the last of the scattered rural schools, the redbrick structure at Raiford, was closed.

The most exciting thing that happened in 1940 was the opening of Union County's first movie theater on the west side of Lake Butler. It could hold almost a hundred people and was just like the big theaters in Gainesville and Jacksonville, with a popcorn machine, snack bar, and a segregated balcony reserved for black moviegoers.

The owner was not a native Union County man, so he was hypersensitive to local feelings. No *Our Gang* comedies were shown, because of the integrated cast. Buckwheat it seems was a serious threat to the southern way of life. John Ford's adaptation of John Steinbeck's *The Grapes of Wrath* was also not shown, because it had been labeled as "Socialist" in some of the literature distributed to local ministers. Even after it won the Academy Award for best picture of the year, it was banned in most of the South due to the influence of powerful anti-Communist and anti-Union groups.

However, when the film *Gone With the Wind* opened in Lake Butler, attendance became almost mandatory. Every showing was standing room only. Going to see the movie became a pilgrimage, and offering high praise for it became a patriotic act. To ensure that the children understood their sacred heritage, the superintendent of schools ordered that all Union County school children be taken by their teachers to view the maudlin, three-hour-plus epic of the Old South.

The owner of the theater was upset because he had to turn away paying customers at the box office because the white's only section of the theater was full, while there were still lots of empty seats in the segregated balcony. In a serious breech of social custom, he temporarily closed the balcony to Negroes and offered to seat the overflow of white viewers there. No one took him up on the offer, and most people were offended by it. They were not about to watch the most stirring film made about the glorious "Lost Cause of the Southern Confederacy" while sitting in the "Nigger section" of the movie theater.

It was also in 1940, that a chapter of the FFA was started at the new Union County High School. The organization had been founded in 1928, in the interest of promoting good agricultural practices. The organization worked hard educating young people in sound land management practices. It advocated crop rotation, shallow furrow planting, windbreaks between fields, and the proper management of water runoff to reduce erosion.

Dr. King first heard of the FFA in St. Louis, in 1936, while on a reelection campaign swing for Franklin D. Roosevelt. He was impressed with the organization's message to young people who were considering a career in agriculture. Dr. King knew enough about farming to know that many of the Great Depression's natural calamities such as the Oklahoma Dust Bowl and the horrible flooding in the Tennessee River Valley were basically man-made disasters, which could have been prevented by sound agricultural practices.

Simple, inexpensive things, such as planting rows of trees between fields, could dramatically reduce wind erosion by acting as a windbreak. The old practice of cutting deep furrows dried out the soil and made it easier for it to blow away. Planting crops in strips and plowing parallel to the rise of the earth would catch the rainwater and prevent the topsoil from being washed away during a hard rain.

However, most southern farmers didn't know about these simple rules or felt that to farm scientifically would cost them money. Before the Great Depression, deep row plowing was considered to be a hedge against drought, and farmers were encouraged by the tenant farming system to plant every square inch of land allowing no room for windbreaks, strip farming, or crop rotation. Old-time farmers simply didn't understand that topsoil was not an unlimited resource.

In some regions of the South, thousands of acres of valuable farmland had been lost due to soil erosion. Washouts caused by heavy rains cut deep ruts through the topsoil, growing wider with each hard rain and making it impossible to farm the land. Hundreds of small farmers were forced into bankruptcy by their own foolish practices. In 1917, after years of prodding, Congress finally took some feeble action. It passed the Smith Hughes Act that provided limited funds, and a lot of encouragement, to establish high school courses in vocational agriculture.

The Future Farmers of America was born in the fertile mind of Henry C. Groseclose, who had started an organization called the Future Farmers of Virginia. While he only educated high school students, they carried their knowledge home to their parents, and, within only a few years, the evidence was plainly visible in less soil erosion and increased production.

The first national convention of the FFA was held in Kansas City, Missouri, in the fall of 1928. There were thirty-three official delegates from eighteen states. Ever since the first convention, Kansas City has always been the spiritual home of the FFA. It was also in Kansas City that the first livestock judging was held under the supervision of the American Royal Livestock and Horse Show. African American high school students were not allowed in the

FFA, but they could join another organization called the New Farmers of America or the NFA. It was a strange name, and the letters NFA were easily translated into the "Nigger Farmers of America."

The money received under the Smith Hughes Act did little more than pay the salary of the vocational agriculture teacher. The FFA was dedicated to the principal of learning by doing. Everyone knew that farm boys were not the type to flower in a classroom, working out of a textbook. The chapter needed money for land, farm equipment, and tools. They also needed a barn, a tool shed, a tractor, a pickup, and flatbed truck.

Again, Dr. King was the one who came through. In 1940, he was sixty years old and had been semiretired from the practice of medicine since 1932, when he quit to go on the campaign trail for Franklin D. Roosevelt. Dr. King had been in poor health since he had suffered a mild heart attack in 1939. He did not drink and smoked only an occasional cigar. He knew nothing about cholesterol, and, in 1940, there was no medication to control high blood pressure. Dr. King had treated enough people in the same shape he was now in to know that his time was growing short. He tried to control his high blood pressure with a low salt diet and by losing weight, but it was really too late. A lifetime of eating greasy pork meat, too many eggs, and over-salted vegetables flavored with animal fat had taken its toll. Dr. King's main arteries were clogged with thick cholesterol deposits, and his blood pressure was too high. He was also constantly thirsty; he carried a mason jar full of water with him everywhere he went, indicating that he probably had the first stages of adult-onset diabetes.

However, he was not depressed; he had earned a good living without taking advantage of anybody. He was financially secure, and his wife would be well provided for after his death. All of his children were grown and doing well in life. Hundreds of Union County citizens owed their lives and limbs to his medical skills. He could not go anywhere in Union County without seeing grown men and women he had brought into this world by the light of a kerosene lantern playing with their own children whom he had also delivered under a naked electric light bulb.

Dr. King decided to do one more good thing in life before he died. He would donate fifty acres of land to the Union County chapter of the FFA. He also negotiated with the board of directors of the newly created Farmer's and Merchant's Bank to arrange a loan to the FFA chapter to buy a Farmall tractor with a set of disks and plows.

Dr. King also used his well-known political skills to make a deal with local farmers to donate their used farm equipment to the FFA chapter in exchange for an unofficial, and probably illegal, break on their property taxes with the county tax assessor's office. This kind of deal could never have been worked out in a large county with a snooping newspaper or a lot of political bickering. However, Union County was a small place, folks knew each other, their children and grandchildren were in the FFA chapter, and everybody's income was directly or indirectly tied to agriculture. Besides, no one was getting hurt. Incidentally, the county tax assessor's son was chosen to be the first president of the Union County chapter of the FFA.

One afternoon in the late fall of 1940, Dr. King went out to the small garage behind his modest home on Lake Street. In a far back corner was an old wooden file cabinet that had once sat in the corner of his office. It was one of the first pieces of office equipment he had purchased when he moved to Lake Butler. It had come from a used office furniture store in Jacksonville and had been shipped, along with Dr. King's familiar rolltop desk, to Lake Butler by train. At first, it had held his patient's medical records, but as Dr. King's practice grew, he bought several of the new metal file cabinets and used this old wooden one to store the records of his real estate transactions. When he closed down his medical practice, Dr. King brought only two things home: his old wooden roll top desk that he put in the den and this old file cabinet that he kept in his garage to appease his wife who thought it looked terrible.

Rambling through the old, dust-covered, file cabinet and fingering through forty years of real estate deals, Dr. King was seeking a suitable piece of land to donate to the FFA. It was not going to be easy. Dr. King's property was located all over the county, and most of it had been planted over in pine trees that were producing so much valuable turpentine, it would be financially foolish to turn it back into farmland. However, after searching for several minutes, Dr. King finally sighted what he was looking for. It was a piece of land near the new school site, where the timber had just been harvested and pine trees had not yet been replanted.

Dr. King slowly removed the manila file folder from the cabinet. It was so old the documents inside were brittle to the touch, and the ink had dried to a point where the once dark blue ink was now a light, faded blackish-brown. Dr. King took the folder and moved next to the dirty window of his garage so he could read it better. The deed was dated 1916, and the land transferred was described as the "Byrd Farm." A note on the back reported that the husband was currently in prison, and the wife was now making the transfer of the deed for five thousand dollars and other good and worthwhile considerations.

Seeing the old folder in the dust-filled light of the garage window brought back a lot of memories to the old doctor. He wondered how Harry Byrd's wife and children fared in Chicago. He never heard from them after he last saw them at the train depot in Jacksonville. Tomorrow, he would take the folder down to the Clerk of the Courts office and transfer the land to the Union County chapter of the FFA.

# Camp Blanding Days

On December 7, 1941, bombs fell on a faraway place most people in Union County had never heard of before. It was an American Naval base in Hawaii called Pearl Harbor. An old navy man, who was now the postmaster over in Starke, had been stationed there in the 1920s, and everyone sought him out to find out what kind of place it was. All most people knew about Hawaii was that it was a warm place where the women wore skirts made out of grass. Later, after reading the newspaper, they found out that Hawaii was really a group of islands in the middle of the Pacific Ocean, which was the ocean over by Hollywood, where they made the moving pictures. Pearl Harbor was located on one of the islands spelled Oahu in the newspaper, but no one in Union County knew how to pronounce it. Was it O-ha-U or was it Ou-he-wa or O-wa-hue? Even the guys on the radio couldn't say it the same way twice.

The coming of World War II ended the Great Depression once and for all. Hundreds of Union County boys enlisted in the U.S. Army, Navy, and Marines the first week after Pearl Harbor. This group included Dr. King's oldest son, James Weldon King Jr. Urged on by smooth-talking recruiters, they were filled with a burning patriotism and a desire to prove themselves as men. Just like their nonslave-owning ancestors who died on the battlefields of the Civil War, they wanted to shake off the dust of poverty and backbreaking farm labor to don the uniform of a hero and march off to save the world.

However, not everyone was interested in becoming a hero. There was a select group of Union County young men who felt strongly that their education and career goals should not be interrupted by military service. The local Selective Service Board over in Starke was flooded with letters from doctors certifying that a certain young man was physically unfit for military service. Dozens of young men, who had been patients of Dr. King before his retirement, approached him for what was becoming known as "a 4-F letter." He wrote some letters for young men who were legitimately unfit, but most he refused. It bothered Dr. King that military service was becoming a matter of social class. The boys from poor families went without question, while the sons of Union County's social and financial elite found ways to avoid service. Just like in all wars, it was a rich man's war and a poor man's fight.

The clear skies and flat terrain of north Florida made it an excellent place to train fighter pilots. Early in 1942, the U.S. Navy opened Sprinkle Field, just west of Lake Butler, on a triangular piece of barren pine scrub between the Scout Hole Road and Highway 121 to Worthington Springs. It was little more than a couple of runways and some hangers, but several hundred pilots, mechanics, and support personnel were stationed there. Another, much-larger naval air station training field was opened east of Lake City only twenty miles away. The pilots from Lake City practiced takeoffs and landings at Sprinkle Field.

The navy also built a series of small airfields up and down the east coast of Florida. They housed navy blimps and attack planes that searched for German submarines off shore. The closest of these bases to Union County was located on the banks of the St. Johns River at Green Cove Springs.

However, by far the greatest influence of World War II on Union County came when the U.S. Army decided to build Camp Blanding on the shores of Kingsley Lake, just east of Starke, in Clay County. It was only about thirty miles from Lake Butler, and Camp Blanding drove all the final vestiges of the Great Depression from the region. Construction began in September of 1940, with the hiring of over twenty-two thousand workers. They worked three shifts around the clock paving roads and building mess halls, barracks, firing ranges, and storage and headquarters buildings. By December, the base was ready to receive the first wave of nearly seventy-five thousand infantry replacement recruits, coming from U.S. National Guard units from all over the South.

In 1942, the first German prisoners of war arrived at Camp Blanding. They were crewmen from sunken German submarines that had been fished out of the waters of the Gulf Stream by allied naval vessels. With them were a small group of German civilians taken prisoner in the United States, Guatemala, Costa Rico, Nicaragua, and the Panama Canal Zone. They were confined with the submarine crewmen in a special stockade, which was operated by the U.S. Navy. These U-boat crewmen and civilians tended to be hard-core Nazis, and there were problems, especially when the navy officers foolishly confined a small group of German Jews, which had fled to Panama to escape Nazi persecution, in the same stockade. Later, most of these hard-core Nazis would be transferred to a maximum-security facility on the windswept plains of Oklahoma.

Eventually, Camp Blanding would house over three thousand German prisoners of war. Most of these later groups were part of Erwin Rommel's Africa Corps. These soldiers were separated from the U-boat crewmen in what became known as the "army compound," which was much larger than the navy compound. They were, for the most part, not hard-core Nazis and were allowed to work around Camp Blanding and in twenty labor camps spread around the state of Florida. They were paid eighty cents a day for cutting sugar cane, picking oranges, or other agricultural work. Under the Geneva Convention Rules, only privates could work, they had to be supervised by their own noncommissioned officers, and they could not work in armaments production.

The owner of the movie theater in Starke was allowed to show movies in the army prisoners of war compound at Camp Blanding. This was part of the army's policy of educating German POWs about the "American way of life."

At the height of World War II, over one hundred ten thousand soldiers would be stationed at Camp Blanding. Over one million soldiers passed through Camp Blanding between 1940 and 1945. Nine infantry divisions and one parachute infantry regiment were trained in the sandy scrub of Camp Blanding. One, all-Negro unit was trained at Camp Blanding early in 1941, but was transferred out after some ugly racial incidents occurred between the black soldiers and some white Jacksonville police officers.

There were thousands of civilian jobs on Camp Blanding doing all kinds of things, such as carpentry, roofing, and electrical and plumbing work. There were openings for civilian barbers, cooks, grounds keepers, nurses, pharmacists, and common laborers. For almost the entire four years of World War II, construction work at Camp Blanding never ceased. There were daily job openings posted in all the local newspapers. The army needed civilian workers so bad that they bought a fleet of school buses, painted them the standard army olive drab green color, and set up a transportation network hauling people to and from Camp Blanding from all points on the compass. Workers came down from Jacksonville, up from Daytona, and over from Lake City, Starke, Gainesville, and Lake Butler. The army went so far as to hire professional contractors to recruit workers. Unskilled workers were assigned as partners to trained electricians, plumbers, carpenters, and heavy equipment operators.

Thousands of the workers were women who had stepped out of their traditional female roles to drive trucks, operate bulldozers, hammer nails, and saw lumber. At the time, everyone felt like this was a temporary wartime situation. Few people realized that it was the beginning of a permanent change in the way men and women interacted with each other.

Thousands of African Americans were also hired at Camp Blanding. At first, they were mostly common laborers wielding shovels and doing landscaping work. However, as more and more white men were drafted into the service, blacks were promoted to skilled positions as carpenters, plumbers, and electricians. Northern-born army officers, architects, and engineers gave these southern blacks their first taste of racial equality. Like with the women, this was not to be a temporary wartime situation; at Camp Blanding, the seeds of the civil rights movement were being planted.

When I was a young boy growing up in Lake Butler, adults would never say World War II. Instead, they would say "Camp Blanding days." It was generally a good time, people had lots of money, and everyone who wanted one had a job. However, some people I talked to, like my minister and Sunday school teacher, would wrinkle their noses when you mentioned "Camp Blanding days." They never told me what they didn't like about the "Camp Blanding days," only that they would just change the subject really fast and talk about something else. I learned very early in life who to see if you wanted accurate information. Preachers, parents, schoolteachers, and almost anyone at church either didn't know anything or they weren't saying anything. Luckily, I had relatives, alcoholic relatives, who would wax poetic about the good old "Camp Blanding days" when they were drinking.

Every Friday afternoon, about a third of the seventy-five thousand troops stationed at Camp Blanding got a weekend pass. A private was paid twenty-one dollars a month, without hardly any expenses except for cigarettes and writing paper. That was a lot of money in those days, when America was just coming out of the Great Depression. The soldiers would flood into town looking for excitement. Most went to Jacksonville, but others traveled to smaller places like Starke, Green Cove Springs, and Lake Butler. What these soldiers were looking for was sex and alcohol. Houses of prostitution sprang up all over north Florida. Whole sections of Jacksonville became red-light districts. Even small towns like Starke, St. Augustine, and Green Cove Springs had well-known areas where motels and even private homes were not what they seemed. It was said that every whore from Atlanta to Miami knew when it was payday at Camp Blanding.

The majority of the small counties in north Florida were "dry," which meant that the selling, manufacturing, and possession of alcoholic beverages were against the law. My daddy, who was a hard-drinking man, used to say it was ridiculous for the government to think it could outsmart the collective intelligence of millions of horny soldiers looking for a drink of liquor and a piece of pussy and the millions more who would gladly provide it to them for the right price.

The soldiers' desire for drinking liquor far outstripped the ability of any bootlegger to keep them supplied. The small group of low-production country moonshiners soon found that the liquor they had made and sold for a dollar during the Depression was now going for eight to ten dollars a gallon. That was enough money to make even the hardest, hard-shell Baptist get into the liquor business. Stills sprang up all over the piney woods and cypress swamps of north Florida.

Since it has always been an illegal activity, it's hard to tell for sure, but experts believe that the first moonshine was produced in the American colonies by Scotch–Irish immigrants sometime in the early 1700s. A traveler in Colonial America once wrote that the residents were accomplished distillers and often used homemade liquor as currency. The intrinsic relationship between liquor and taxes created the first constitutional crisis in U.S. history, when farmers in western Pennsylvania began the so-called "Whiskey Rebellion" during the administration of George Washington. Claiming that the whiskey they made was "food" and was thus protected against taxation, they steadfastly refused to pay the excise tax levied against liquor, until George Washington's federal troops were marched into Pennsylvania making short work of the rebellion.

Ever since the Whiskey Rebellion, there has been a running war between whiskey makers and the U.S. government. In a futile effort to disguise what was really in the jug, there are over fifty known synonyms for illegal whiskey. Everything from such well-known euphemisms as white lightning, mountain dew, and corn squeezings to such unknown and seldom used terms as alky, preacher's lye, and stump hole puller.

The difference between legal and illegal whiskey was the payment of taxes levied by local, state, and federal governments. Except for the brief period of Prohibition, there were no federal laws against whiskey production. Federal agents busted up stills, not because they were making liquor, but because no taxes were being paid on the whiskey. Therefore, federal authorities became known as revenue agents or "revenooers" for short.

Prohibition was the golden age of whiskey making. With legal whiskey forbidden, illegal whiskey became the norm. Before the advent of the great social experiment of Prohibition, there was really no such thing in the United States as organized crime as a national entity. There has always been local corruption, and some illegal gambling and prostitution, but nothing that had national prominence. Prohibition changed all that. Italian immigrants made illegal whiskey for Al Capone in their tenement apartments in Chicago's Little Italy, and Appalachian coal miners carved liquor pits out of the sides of mountains to set up their stills far from the prying eyes of government agents. Small-time hoodlums became overnight millionaires by buying judges, police chiefs, and prosecutors just like they bought their flashy new cars, cold steel revolvers, pin-striped suits, and gunmetal gray snap-brim hats.

In the South, whiskey production flourished long after Prohibition ended. Some whole states, such as Mississippi, and the vast majority of small, rural counties decided to remain ""dry" and continued to ban the legal selling of alcoholic beverages. In these out-of-the-way places, the moonshiners and bootleggers still plied their trade, selling to those people who found that living without alcohol was beyond their endurance.

At the beginning of World War I, the U.S. War Department decided to build the majority of its large military training bases in the South, because the warm winter weather permitted year-round training. Places such as Fort Jackson, South Carolina; Fort Benning, Georgia; Fort Bragg, North Carolina; Fort Stewart, Georgia; and Fort Polk, Louisiana, trained thousands of young men during and after World War I.

With the beginning of World War II, these existing training bases were enlarged, and hundreds of new ones, like Camp Blanding, were opened. Because of all the soldiers who flooded into these areas—mostly single men on a weekend pass with a pocket full of money—formerly quiet and peaceful southern towns such as Fayetteville, North Carolina; Phenix City, Alabama; Biloxi, Mississippi; and Augusta, Georgia, suddenly became huge vice dens that rivaled anything found in New York City, Chicago, or Los Angeles. These towns were filled with clip joints, gambling dens, black marketers, penny arcades, and trashy bars filled with loose women, who could pick a soldier's pocket with the skill of a first chair violinist, while making him believe he was on the verge of the best sex of his life.

The nearest "wet" place to Camp Blanding was Jacksonville, which was forty miles away, and, every weekend, thousands of soldiers rode buses and hitched rides to the bars and whorehouses located down on Bay Street and in the LaVilla and Springfield sections of town.

However, other soldiers felt Jacksonville was too far to travel and sought their excitement closer to the base. Located in the deep piney woods of the small rural counties around Camp Blanding, there began to arise cheaply built, pinewood frame buildings that became known as "honky-tonks" to differentiate them from the "juke joints" that catered mostly to blacks.

Inside these honky-tonk bars, there was little except what one would expect to find—a cheaply made pinewood bar usually topped with linoleum that made it easier to wipe up the spilled beer. A brightly colored Wurlitzer jukebox would be turned up as loud as it would go. The honky-tonks were festooned with assorted signs warning against spitting on the floor and cussing in front of women. There were neon signs for Ballentine Ale, which along with 3.2 percent alcohol beer, was legal even in dry counties. Colored tin advertisements for Bull of the Woods chewing tobacco and Camel cigarettes were tacked to the bare pine walls. Most also had gaudy, brightly lit pinball machines and one-armed-bandit slot machines that were as crooked as a mountain road. Each honky-tonk had, by necessity, an enormous dance floor where the soldiers and their newly found dance partners swayed cheek to cheek to the rhythms of the flashy Wurlitzer jukebox.

The music was mostly country, because that was what southerners liked. The lyrics and rhythms of Bill Monroe, Roy Acuff, and Ernest Tubb cut through the dark pine forests surrounding the scattered honky-tonks, often carrying for miles on windless nights. Some of the big city boys preferred the big band music of Glen Miller, Ozzie Nelson, or the Dorsey Brothers. Many young girls were suckers for the crooners such as Frank Sinatra or Bing Crosby, but they were mostly disappointed. In the South, country music predominated. Millions of young men and women from outside the South first heard country music during their military service during World War II. A large number found they liked country music, and American GIs spread it all over the United States, Europe, and Asia during and after World War II. Every weekend, thousands of soldiers and an almost equal number of both prostitutes and marriage-minded local girls descended on these piney woods honky-tonks. These women became known as "Victory Girls," since they were said to be so good for the morale of the troops.

When I was a teenager, I was constantly berated by members of the older, World War II generation about how sex obsessed our "baby boomer" generation was. Any time they saw Elvis on *The Ed Sullivan Show* or found a copy of *Playboy* under my bed, they would moan and cry that America was going to hell in a hand basket, carried by the sex-crazed younger generation. They talked about the time before my birth as if it was some kind of wonderful place where everyone was honest, God-fearing, and hard working people. It was a place where girls were chaste and protected their virginity like the crown jewels. It was also a place that never existed. The America they described to me was as fictional as the Land of Oz.

History sometimes is a hard lesson. At the beginning of the war, most small towns and cities in Florida turned off their streetlights after ten o'clock and didn't turn on the lights in public parks at all as a wartime energy-saving measure. However, prostitution and Victory Girls were so rampant that the street lights had to be left on all night, and new, brighter lights were installed in public parks to prevent what became known at the time as "petting parties."

Many of the scattered honky-tonks had small cabins in the rear that could be rented by the night or the hour. They were advertised in small signs in front of the honky-tonk as a "tourist court." However, everyone knew their real purpose.

On the weekends, the honky-tonks were filled to overflowing with drunken soldiers and happy Victory Girls. The crowd often spilled out into the parking lot, where it became a strange combination of happy partying mixed with an occasional fistfight and rampant sexual activity in the cabins and back seats of automobiles.

The music raged on into the early hours of the morning. When the sun finally broke over the horizon, the honky-tonks were surrounded by passed-out soldiers, empty beer bottles, and scattered mason jars that smelled of the residue of homemade moonshine. Many of the small cabins had been used a dozen times or more during the evenings.

None of these honky-tonks had any kind of liquor license. They were so far out in the woods, the noise and rowdiness didn't bother anybody. Most of the time, the local sheriff was either a part owner of the honky-tonk or had been well bribed to look the other way. Illegal bars are a southern tradition, but the scattered juke joints that existed before World War II were nothing like this. Owners of honky-tonks carried their money home in large empty beer boxes. People who owned legal bars up in Jacksonville could make as much money supplying country honky-tonks as they could sell beer and whiskey to their regular customers. Every day, large trucks filled with beer and bonded, factory-made liquor crossed the boundaries separating wet and dry counties as if there were no such thing.

Honky-tonk owners couldn't enlarge their "tourist courts" fast enough. The war had created a shortage of both building materials and carpenters. They solved this problem by buying small aluminum travel trailers, designed and built to be used on family vacations. They were now cheap, since wartime gas rationing had made family vacations out of the question. These hump-backed trailers were so small they could be pulled behind an ordinary automobile. They made a cramped, but suitable, place for sex. Many of the more well-to-do women bought their own trailers, so they could rent them out to other girls on slow nights and wouldn't have to pay rent to the honky-tonk owners, who charged the girls a fee, even though the soldiers had already paid the "official" rent for the cabin or trailer.

After the end of World War II, Camp Blanding was radically scaled back and the naval air stations in Lake City and Green Cove Springs were eventually closed. For a while, the base at Green Cove Springs housed the navy's mothball fleet, ships no longer in commission, but soon that too was gone. Today, the naval air station at Lake City houses a community college and an aircraft manufacturer. The navy base at Green Cove Springs is an industrial park. The navy auxiliary landing strip called Sprinkle Field near Lake Butler is now a correctional institution. However, Camp Blanding never closed. It was taken over by the Florida National Guard and is the primary site of its major training programs. Although only a shadow of its former self, Camp Blanding, Florida, is still an important part of America's national defense.

# The Golden Age of Moonshine

Walter Mizell had been high sheriff of Union County since the day the county was formed in 1921. Before that, he had been a deputy sheriff in Bradford County for five years. By 1941, that was a total of twenty-five years of service, with very little to show for it.

When he became sheriff, the county awarded him a salary of fifty dollars a month, which was what the entire county could afford to pay. When the Depression hit Union County, the board of county commissioners asked him to take fifteen dollars a month cut in pay. He had little choice but to accept, since this was no time to go off hunting for a new job. When the New Deal came along, the county was reluctant to raise the sheriff's salary until he warned them that he could make more money working on the road-building crew than being high sheriff. Finally, after much deliberation, they restored his salary to the original fifty dollars a month.

Besides being high sheriff, the county also expected him to serve as head jailer with no increase in salary. The only compensation for that duty was the use of a small, cramped two-bedroom apartment on the bottom floor of the jail. That was where Walter Mizell and his family lived for twenty years, with him and his wife occupying one bedroom and his four girls sleeping in the other. Sometimes when there were no prisoners, the girls would go upstairs and sleep in empty cells in the women's section of the jail. In the hot summer months, it was cooler on the second floor than the first, and it afforded the girls a lot more privacy than their cramped bedroom in the sheriff's living quarters. Sheriff Mizell strictly prohibited the girls from entering the men's section of the jail; he did not want his daughters reading the often-obscene graffiti on the walls.

In all his years as high sheriff, Walter Mizell had not had a single day off from work. There wasn't a day that went by when he was not called upon to look for a lost mule, do something about a pack of wild dogs scaring people's cows, referee a family argument, or clean up the mess after a juke joint brawl. There wasn't a single night when he did not have to get out of bed to quiet down some rowdy drunk up in the jail or go help move a cow that had been killed on the highway. Every Friday and Saturday night, there were scores of drunks to put in jail or drive home; on weeknights, there were the usual family arguments, with men beating their wives and wives shooting or stabbing their husbands. There were runaway kids and missing hogs, dead bodies found in the swamps, and crazy old women who were sure someone was in their chicken coop. Walter Mizell had forgotten what it was like to sleep all night or relax on a warm summer afternoon. It was always something. It got to the point where the sound of the telephone ringing or a knock on the door automatically caused his blood pressure to rise.

In the twenty years he had been sheriff, he had watched as his wife Gladys slowly changed from a petite young girl to a heavy-set jail matron. Her long black hair that she used to brush a hundred strokes each night to make it shine was now streaked with gray, pinned up, and tied into a tight bun so it didn't get in the way when she was cooking. His daughters were all overweight, which was the result of a childhood of being fed over-sweetened, too starchy, and grease-soaked food. Even the sheriff himself had changed into a potbellied, balding, middle-aged man. His bones were now brittle, and his muscles had lost their hardness and elasticity. His gun belt almost disappeared within his ever-expanding belly, and his baggy khaki pants were frayed and worn.

Every morning, sick or well, Gladys Mizell had to arise from her bed to prepare the meals for the jail inmates. She spent most of the day in the kitchen baking cornbread, cooking sweet potatoes, stirring big pots of grits, and washing turnip greens. Every Tuesday was washday. Using whatever jail trustees she might have to help her, she had to wash all the sheets and pillowcases and air out all the blankets. On Mondays and Wednesdays, she had to supervise the general cleaning of the jail, mopping the floors and scouring the sinks and toilets in the cells.

Every Friday, weather permitting, she would have all the mattresses taken outside to lay in the sunshine and fresh air, flipping then over around noon, so both sides could air out evenly. Nothing got rid of bedbugs and lice better than good old-fashioned fresh air and sunlight. However, during the summer, she had to keep an eye on the southwestern sky for those pesky Florida thunderstorms that could come on quickly, seemingly out of nowhere. The jail was a source of pride for Mrs. Mizell, and she would not have anyone say it was not clean and sanitary.

She was required by state law to feed the prisoners two meals a day, but she always fixed them a little something for lunch, usually only cornbread and beans, and on Sundays baloney sandwiches, but something.

The Union County jail was famous all over north Florida as a place with good food. Breakfast was a bowl of cheese grits with a couple of slices of toasted white bread and black coffee. Lunch was the meal the prisoners wouldn't get in most other jails, so they never complained about eating cornbread and navy beans. However, everyone looked forward to the six o'clock meal. It was the jail's only meal where a meat dish was served. Mrs. Mizell served up the best fried chicken, chicken and dumplings, sugar-cured ham, pork chops, beef liver, and fried catfish in the state, so bragged the wandering tramps, who knew what they were talking about. The sheriff's family always ate the same food as the jail inmates, thereby expanding the family income by not having to buy weekly groceries.

As the years creaked by, the work became harder and harder on Gladys Mizell. Lately, her legs had started to swell each night, and she had trouble walking in the morning. Also, things were getting hard on the sheriff. When he was a young man, he didn't mind jailing rowdy drunks and chasing lost cows all night, but now he did. He was sick of living in the jail and was ashamed that his kids grew up in the shadow of it. However, he could not afford to live anywhere else, not on his pitiful fifty-dollar-a-month salary.

As they grew older, the sheriff and his wife worried more and more about the future. The day would soon come when they both could no longer do the hard work of running the jail and enforcing the law. Then, the people of Union County would vote Walter Mizell out of office, replacing him with a younger and healthier man.

Walter Mizell had taken his first bribe in 1935 from, of all people, his own sister. The pinewoods of Union County are crossed with numerous narrow dirt roads used by pulpwood and turpentine operators to work their trees and haul out the timber. Moonshiners also used these dirt roads to get to their stills hidden deep in the woods

Moonshine equipment is heavy and bulky, and stills have to be accessible. Nobody wants to carry hundred-pound sacks of corn or five-gallon jugs of moonshine over any longer a distance than necessary. Therefore, moonshine stills had to be located at a place where you could get to them by either a truck or mule and wagon.

Walter Mizell would routinely patrol these isolated dirt roads during the day looking for the telltale signs left by shiners as they hauled their equipment and fixings (the big bags of corn and sugar) into the swampy pinewoods. He would often come back at night to sniff the air, looking for the aroma of smoke or the sour milk smell of corn mash, both a sure sign somebody was making shine in the woods nearby.

The federal boys from up in Jacksonville had airplanes to fly over the north Florida woods and swamps looking for signs of moonshining. Their favorite time was in the winter months when the leaves were off the trees. Seldom was a still itself seen from the air. The shiners had learned to put their stills under stands of holly or pine trees that remained green all year and carefully hide them with overhead arbors covered with freshly cut tree branches. Instead, the agents looked for vehicle tracks cutting through the woods; places where the thick underbrush had been mashed down by the heavy weight of either a truck or mule and wagon. These tracks almost always led to an operating still.

Some operators built themselves small shine sleds, which were crude devices made from pine sapling poles, that could be loaded with fixings or equipment and pulled by two men through the pinewoods staying under the cover of the trees. Shine sled tracks could only be spotted from the ground, and Walter Mizell was constantly on the lookout for the marks they made through the thick underbrush.

Shiners tended to be lazy characters. They didn't like to pull their heavy fixings through the thick underbrush with a shine sled. They preferred to drive their pickup trucks right up to their stills, and some of them came up with some pretty smart ideas of how to hide their vehicle tracks.

Early one morning in 1938, the federal agents were flying around looking for stills when they spotted a farmer on his tractor plowing his field, a common enough sight in Union County. The next day, he was again plowing the same field; a couple of days later, he was back on his tractor, again plowing the same field.

"Why," they asked, "would a farmer be plowing the same field over and over again, always out early in the morning?" The answer was simple. He was covering the tracks made the night before, when he had been hauling sugar and corn to his still. The next day, the agents came on the farm with warrants and found the still only a few feet from the corner of the field.

The best way to fool the federal revenue agents was to build your still in an old tobacco barn, chicken coop, corncrib, or other farm outbuilding. There, tracks would draw no notice, and the still couldn't be seen from the air. Stills this carefully hidden were the hardest to find, but, at the same time, they were very small operations. They provided little more than drinking whiskey for the farmer and his relatives. Walter Mizell and the federal agents really didn't spend a lot of time looking for them. They were much more interested in the large commercial operations that supplied the moonshine sold in the bump houses of Jacksonville and in the scattered juke joints and honky-tonk bars.

Walter Mizell kept a mental inventory of how much use was on the various dirt roads he drove over. When he saw signs of more traffic than normal, it would draw his attention. Usually, Walter would park far off the road behind some bushes and wait to see who would drive by. He was always looking for someone in a pickup truck or fast car that he knew didn't live anywhere near the dirt road.

Late one afternoon, the sheriff spotted a red pickup truck he knew well; his sister's oldest son Robert was driving it. Sticking out of the back of the truck was a shine sled, with the bark still on the pine saplings, indicating that it was a new sled. Dragging a shine sled through the thick underbrush of the Florida woods quickly wears the bark off the pine poles used as runners beneath the sled. Most experienced moonshiners leave their shine sleds in the woods hidden near their still, not wanting to risk having it seen in their truck. His young nephew was being very foolish riding around with a shine sled clearly visible in the back of his truck, but then he was still just a kid, barely sixteen years old. The sheriff could also see several bundles in the back of the truck covered with burlap sacks, probably either fixings or still equipment.

The sheriff could just wait a few minutes and then follow the truck's tracks down the sandy dirt road to the place where the shine sled and the bundles in the back of the pickup truck were unloaded. Then, he would follow the sled tracks to the still. He could then probably have surprised the men at the still and arrested them in the act. He could, but he didn't.

Common sense and a good understanding of the people he was dealing with are what make a successful southern lawman. Sheriff Mizell had learned a long time ago that the fewer people you put in jail, the better. Southerners are funny people. They don't want a corrupt sheriff who allows rampant moonshining to go on. But, at the same time, they don't want to see their friends, neighbors, and especially their relatives have to spend three years on the chain-gang. The people who made moonshine were not your usual criminal lot, especially during the Great Depression when times were hard and farm crops brought little money.

When Sheriff Mizell discovered a still, he would either bust it up when nobody was around or go and warn the people he suspected of running the still that he was on to them. The sheriff had to choose his words carefully. There were many church-going people in Union County, who were always on his case to stamp out moonshining once and for all. If they thought he was cutting the shiners some slack, the preachers would begin railing against him, and all the church-going folks would vote against him in the next election. However, the sheriff knew that if he put one of these good church-going people's relatives on the chain-gang for moonshining, they would hold a grudge against him. They wouldn't say anything. They had a reputation as God-fearing Christians to maintain; they would just vote against him in the next election and urge all their relatives to do the same.

What the sheriff would usually do was go by the house of the suspected moonshiner and simply tell him to "stay out of the woods for the next few days." There was really no need for a long conversation. While the moonshiner was sorry that his still would be busted up, at the same time, he was happy that he wouldn't be going off to jail. This little trick had won Walter Mizell many votes over the years. The sheriff was well known as a reasonable man, who understood how folks were.

That night he went by his nephew's house to give him the word. The boy came to the door in his nightshirt and listened politely as his uncle warned him about spending too much time in the woods. The sheriff winked and said, "The redbugs are too bad this time of year; they will eat you alive." All the boy could say in reply was a polite "yes sir."

Less than an hour after he had gotten back from talking to her son, Walter Mizell was shocked to see his sister standing at the door of the jail wanting to talk to him in private.

The two of them walked out to her car, where they sat and talked quietly. She started off by telling her brother that the still he had found was not her son's, but hers. She pleaded, through tear-filled eyes, for her brother not to bust up the still. Her husband had two bad tobacco crops in a row, and the family was now in danger of losing their farm to the bank.

"We got to make at least a couple of runs of shine," she sobbed. "Every dime we have is tied up in that still apparatus; if we don't get our money back, we will lose the farm."

In the South, the family is a powerful thing. Families were the economic and social safety net before the days of welfare and food stamps. Union County dirt farmers didn't have retirement plans or health or life insurance. They expected their children to take care of them in their old age and their brothers, sisters, aunts, uncles, and cousins to help out until the children were grown. When a farmer became sick and couldn't do his farm work, his brothers would come over and take over the work until he was well. The favor would be returned when and if the situation was reversed. If there was a feud over the sale of a mule, you were expected to take the side of your blood kin, no matter if he was right or wrong. To do otherwise would brand you a traitor to your own kind, a man who couldn't be trusted, an outcast.

Political power in the South was measured by the number of relatives you had to go out and beat the bushes looking for votes in the scattered farms and turpentine camps. Social power was measured the same way. A man with no family was impotent. An atrocity against him could be committed without fear of retaliation. You could steal his hogs or raid his chicken house, and there was nothing he could do. He knew if he retaliated against you, even if he just went to the sheriff and accused you, he would have to fight both you and your whole extended family. He would be starting a blood feud that he knew he could not win, because he was outnumbered.

Sheriff Mizell agreed to let his nephew keep the still and make moonshine until the family got back on their feet. His sister dried her tears and thanked her brother for his kindness. However, before she left, Walter warned her that he had no control over what the federal boys were up to, and they could raid the still at any time. She said that was a chance she would have to take.

Four days later, Walter Mizell awoke early and went out to his 1932 Ford V-8 patrol car. He found a small brown envelope on the front seat. He slowly opened the envelope and found it contained a fresh, crisp five-dollar bill. There was no note, but Walter knew it was from his sister. It was his share of the moonshine run.

Sheriff Walter Mizell knew he should have returned the money and busted up the still after allowing one or two runs, but he didn't. The truth of the matter was the sheriff needed a new hat. His old one was so sweat stained and floppy, he was ashamed to put it on. He had been going bareheaded for the past six months, because he couldn't afford a new hat. This was an embarrassing thing for a man in his position.

That afternoon, the sheriff drove the sixty miles to Gainesville to buy himself a brand new, snap-brim Stetson hat at a well-known gentlemen's store that faced the Alachua County Courthouse.

It's funny sometimes how a simple little thing, such as a new hat, could change the way a man felt about himself. Riding back to Union County, he felt like a new man. As he walked up to his courthouse office, his step had a fresh bounce to it. The old men who always sat in the shade of the oak trees on the courthouse square took notice of the sheriff's new hat and gave him some good-natured ribbing about looking more like a G-Man than a "po-folk's county sheriff."

It's amazing how fast the word gets around. The arrangement between the sheriff and his sister should have been a well-kept secret, but it was no time before everyone knew about it. As the Depression years passed, several dozen other moonshiners came to see the sheriff to ask his permission to make enough shine to get them out of some financial bind. Most of them were telling the truth; times were hard. The price of tobacco and corn was low. Late freezes and spring droughts wiped out tobacco crops, leaving families with no alternative short of whiskey making. The money paid to the sheriff was just a taste of the profits from the shine making, usually around five or ten dollars a run. It really wasn't a bribe, as much as a thank you gift. However, over a period of time, it started to add up. It also seemed that once a still was up and in operation, it stayed in operation. Stills that began as temporary economic measures turned into permanent sources of income.

By 1939, Sheriff Mizell had saved enough money to put a down payment on a modest home just outside of town. He turned his small jail apartment over to his one and only deputy, whose wife agreed to assume the duties of jail matron. The extra cash he obtained from the moonshiners also provided enough money to enroll his oldest daughter in Florida State University, the all-girl's college in Tallahassee, where she was studying to be a teacher. He was proud to be able to do that for her.

As the Depression came to an end, the amount of moonshining in Union County increased. The men who worked on the roads were steady and reliable customers of the shiners. By this time, the sheriff could not say no to anyone. As long as they agreed to the sheriff's rule that the moonshine be high quality and they pay him a cut of the profits each time they made a run, Sheriff Mizell would more or less automatically approve the placement of a still. Very seldom would anyone try and cheat the sheriff, but, when someone did, all Walter Mizell would do was to go out and bust up the still. There was no violence or hard feelings; he just had to teach them that it was cheaper to pay him than to replace all their still apparatuses.

Walter Mizell could never determine when it was that he changed, but he did. By the time Camp Blanding opened, he was wearing pin-striped suits and riding around in his own car, a classy 1940 Ford V-8 automobile with white sidewall tires and fancy hubcaps. Only Dr. King drove a better automobile than the sheriff. He had sold his modest home and moved his family into a much larger house on South Lake Street. He smoked nickel cigars and was well known as a powerful and wealthy man, even though he spent every dime he collected as fast as he got it.

Walter Mizell knew he had sold his soul to the gods of moonshine, but he really didn't care. He now lived in a decent house and drove a decent car, and his children had enough money to go to college. His wife could finally take it easy, sleeping late each morning. He was able to take her to the doctor over in Gainesville, and he had given her medication that made the swelling in her legs go away.

With the opening of Sprinkle Field Air Base just outside of town and Camp Blanding, the demand for moonshine was so great and the stuff was selling for such a high price many farmers abandoned the risky business of growing tobacco for full-time corn production. The whiskey that could be made from the corn was worth more than the price of tobacco. Stills became more numerous with larger and larger production capacity.

Since the end of the Prohibition, the number of federal revenue agents in the Jacksonville area had been sharply cut back by the Roosevelt Administration, which was strongly anti-Prohibition. When World War II started, they were completely neutered. The pilot of their airplane was drafted into the army, and they had to give up their small, two-seat aircraft to be used to train navy pilots. Without their airplane and with only half their force of agents, mostly older men beyond military age, the risk of moonshine still being busted by federal agents was almost nonexistent. These years, when Camp Blanding was in operation and the federal agents didn't have any airplanes, was what my family would call "the golden age of moonshine."

One Sunday, a new minister in the Methodist church down in Worthington Springs preached a rousing hellfire and brimstone sermon against the evils of moonshining. He blasted the sheriff as a corrupt politician and proclaimed that anyone who made moonshine was in danger of hellfire. The next Sunday, over half the congregation did not show up for services, and the collection plate was nearly empty. He never mentioned moonshining again.

Walter Mizell also found that his relationship with the shiners meant that he no longer had to worry about reelection. Charlie Waters was a prosperous Lake Butler businessman, who owned the town's largest hardware and appliance store. He was also head deacon of the Baptist church. The fact that moonshine whiskey was being made all over Union County drove him to despair. After careful prayer and meditation on the issue, he decided to run against Walter Mizell for high sheriff. In his announcement for office, he pledged to rid Union County of moonshiners.

Walter Mizell had political opponents before, but never one this strong. Charlie Waters had enough money to run a well-financed campaign, and he had strong support among the church-going people of Union County. In a fair election, he could beat Walter Mizell. Therefore, Walter Mizell decided that there would not be a fair election. One night, a group of well-known moonshiners went to see Charlie Waters as he was working late in his hardware store. The group included several of his wife's relatives, as well as his cousin. They talked for about an hour, and, the next morning, Charlie Waters withdrew from the race for sheriff. As long as he lived, he never brought up the subject again, and everyone knew enough not to say anything to him about it.

# Jack's Still

For a brief period, I helped a man run a still that was located close to the New River about two miles from my home. Even though the year was 1962, instead of 1942, the running of a moonshine still hadn't changed that much from when Walter Mizell was sheriff. The man was named Jack Taylor, and the still was on his property. He was a close friend of Slim's, and I always suspected that Slim had a part interest in the moonshine operation. That was Slim's way, and, by this time, I had enough sense not to ask Slim certain questions about his business.

Jack was paying me five dollars every night I helped him make a run, which took almost all night, and three dollars when I just showed up to stir the mash and check the fence, which took only a couple of hours. Slim and all my older brothers knew what I was doing, but we took great pains to make sure my mother didn't find out. If she did, she would have had a hissy fit. However, as almost everyone I knew used to say, "What mama don't know won't hurt her."

The first thing you learn about moonshining is that for an illegal activity, there is a lot of damned hard work involved. That's why Slim never messed around with moonshining much. However, Slim often financed moonshine operations and took part of the profits as a silent partner. Jack's still was just such an operation.

A moonshine still has to sit on level ground; so, if the ground isn't level, such as the side of a hill or a creek bank, you have to dig a liquor pit. You shovel out a wedge of dirt, creating a level piece of ground with upright sides. If the ground is full of roots, like it always is in Florida, they have to be cut with an ax before you can dig any further. The whole thing is hot, sweaty work and can take days to finish. It is best to do this in the winter, because, in the summer, the mosquitoes and yellow flies in the woods will eat you alive.

One of the key ingredients in moonshine is water. In the mountains of Tennessee and Kentucky, there are small springs and clear mountain streams that can be easily channeled to a cleverly hidden still in a mountain hollow. That is not the situation in Florida where creeks are filled with black stagnant water, and springs are rare. The water used to make moonshine doesn't have to be crystal clear or even free of bacteria, since it is going to be boiled into steam and then recondensed, but it does have to be free of large pollutants like mud, sticks, leaves, and other assorted trash.

Pumping water out of a creek has two problems associated with it. The first is availability. Sometimes, the creeks are only a trickle; other times, they are a flooded, swollen river. If you build your still too far away, you have the problem of hauling water, usually uphill, to the still site; if you build the still too close to the creek, a spring flood could wash it away.

Some shiners, who had big still operations, would pump water to the still using a gasoline-powered pump and a long section of fire hose. This system had lots of problems. First off, in the dry season, you would have to dam up the creek to create a pool of water, and this would always tip off the lawmen, who could spot even a small dam and reservoir from the air. Secondly, the pump tends to suck up a lot of mud and trash that would clog up the pump. A screen wire over the nozzle of the fire hose could keep out the trash but not the mud. Also, the gasoline-powered pump makes a lot of noise and puts out carbon monoxide gas that could attract attention.

The best way to get shine water in Florida is to dig a shallow well. The water table in Florida is very high, and a good supply of fresh water is only about twenty-five or thirty feet below your feet. To get to it, you can drive a four-inch pipe into the ground using a heavy weight and a rope thrown over a tree limb or an A-frame brace. There were people in Union County who made their living digging these shallow wells for sharecroppers, and, for a little extra, they would come out at night and sink a pipe at your still sight. Once you have the four-inch pipe deep enough, you then put down a two-inch pipe inside of it and attach a hand-operated pitcher pump. You must prime the pump with a couple of quarts of water to get the flow started. For a long time, you will be pumping out more sand and mud than water, but after a few days, a pool of fresh water is created at the bottom of the pipe, and the water is nice and clear.

Many times, a moonshiner didn't even have to dig a shallow well; you could find them already dug out in the woods. When the process of buying up the small dirt farms and planting them over in pine trees began, many of the sharecroppers' shacks were just left in the woods to slowly fall apart.

However, others were torn down for the tin in the roof and the nails in the boards. Others were set on fire and burned so there would be more room for pine seedlings.

Walking through the woods of Union County, a person could always tell when they were coming onto one of these old farms. The trees would change from young slash pines to a much older hardwood variety, mostly oaks or pecan trees, planted by the farm families years ago to provide much-needed shade during the long, hot Florida summers.

Sometimes, the old shacks would still be there, slowly falling apart, and they would be overgrown with wisteria vines and infested with termites so bad the floors would fall through if you tried to walk on them. Other times, there was no trace of the old shack, except for some assorted trash, the old stone foundation blocks, and the single pitcher pump well sticking up out of the ground. The pump used to be next to the back porch of the old farmhouse, close to what was known as the "shaving bench."

The "shaving bench" was the closest thing these old shacks had to a kitchen or bathroom sink. It was here that the farmer would shave every morning and where his wife would wash and cut up the dinner vegetables. The "shaving bench" would always have a broken piece of a mirror hanging on the wall next to it and a small tin pan that everyone called a "face bowl" sitting on top of it or hanging from a rusty nail on one of the back porch posts.

Sometimes, you could find the big cast-iron kettle that the small farmers used to cook their slop before they fed it to their pigs. The kettle would now be covered with brown rust, collecting rainwater and breeding mosquito larvae. It was always left behind when the farm was abandoned, because it was too heavy and bulky to be hauled off with the rest of the household items.

Many times, moonshiners would locate their stills on these old farm sites, using the existing pitcher pump well to provide their water supply. Sometimes, the old, rusty roof tin and assorted boards could be used to hide the still. However, the presence of the oak and pecan trees, isolated in a sea of young pines, were a dead giveaway to the federal agents in their airplanes, especially in the winter when they lost their leaves, and you could spot the still under the bare branches.

The ingredient most associated with moonshining is of course corn. It is the starches within the corn that when combined with yeast and sugar produce the alcohol. There has always been an ongoing debate among veteran moonshiners about which type of corn is best for making shine. Some people swore by yellow corn, and others were determined to use only white corn. Jack was a white corn man, because he always claimed it was sweeter than yellow corn that he often dismissed as chicken feed. Jack had a peculiarity that drove the other moonshiners crazy. He insisted that he would only make his shine from white corn that had first been allowed to sprout. It was an old trick that he had learned from his father who was also a veteran shiner.

Jack got most of his corn from a farmer over in Columbia County that was famous for growing the best sweet corn in north Florida. Most of his corn wound up in the hands of moonshiners who bought it in bulk paying much more than he could get at the farmer's market. The farmer considered Jack to be a pain in the ass, because he insisted that the white corn be sprouted before it was ground up. Probably the only reason he humored Jack was because they had both served in Korea.

Because it was a lot of trouble and extra bother to sprout the corn, Jack always sent me over to his farm to help out. To get the corn to sprout, it had to first be soaked for several days in a big barrel filled with rainwater. It was then spread out on the concrete floor of a pole barn and covered with wet croker sacks. A couple of days later, each little corn kernel would have a tiny white and green spout. Then, the farmer would remove the wet sacks, let the corn dry out, and finally grind it into a course meal in a gasoline-powered mill. The finished product was put into fifty-pound cloth bags, which I hauled back to Union County.

Jack talked a lot about his corn. He said that some moonshiners would use horse feed or yellow corn with shucks and cobs mixed in; however, he produced a quality product, and, when people got their shine from Jack Taylor, they were buying good stuff. Besides paying him top dollar for his corn, Jack always sent his friend a gallon of the first run shine as a gift. The farmer always said that it was the best popskull moonshine he had ever drunk.

While corn was fairly easy to get, sugar was a whole other story. A moonshiner's greatest challenge was to get enough sugar to make his product. The state and federal law enforcement agencies attempting to stomp out moonshine production saw sugar as the Achilles heel of the illegal whiskey business. If they could keep sugar out of the hands of moonshiners, then they could halt the production of illegal whiskey. They closely monitored the big grocery chains and checked their sugar inventories and sales receipts frequently. There were rumors that they even went so far as to put undercover agents in the stores as new employees to report any illegal sales of sugar.

The State of Florida passed a law that no person could buy more than two five-pound bags of sugar at one time. To get these two five-pound bags of sugar, the consumer was required by law to buy at least ten dollars or more of other groceries. As usual, the state legislature screwed it up royally. They left a major loophole in the law, namely that you could buy one five-pound bag of sugar, without buying any other groceries. This is the loophole that all the moonshiners jumped through to get their sugar.

In those days, before the coming of the so-called "convenience stores," there were hundreds of little "mom and pop" grocery stores all over north Florida. Every little settlement and crossroads had at least one. The people who ran these small grocery stores tended to be nice, friendly people who depended upon repeat customers to stay in business.

A group of us teenage boys from Union County, who had an operator's license and access to a car, found a nice and quick way to pick up a little extra cash, what Slim used to call "picture show money." Once or twice a week, usually on a Wednesday or Friday, we would meet at the school and take a direction on the compass and set out to make what we called a "sugar run." We had to make certain that we didn't cross each other's path, and, because we believed a steady customer could get away with it easier than a stranger, we held the same territory for a long time. One of us would head east, taking in Starke and western Clay County. Another would head north, getting all the stores between Lake Butler and Jacksonville. Another would head west toward Lake City and Columbia County.

My route was the most dangerous, because it was the southern route that took me into Alachua County. There was an understanding in the moonshine business that certain counties were safe to operate in and others weren't. I could never prove anything one way or the other, but I trusted other shiners to let me know which sheriffs tolerated things and which sheriffs didn't. I knew for a fact that the sheriff of Alachua County didn't cut anybody any slack. It was because of the damned University of Florida in Gainesville. They didn't want the stuck-up, rich-boy college kids to be corrupted with the evils of strong drink. Parents who sent their children to the University of Florida wanted to be reassured that their little darlings would be in a proper moral atmosphere. So, the sheriff was a real hard ass, and anybody caught shining, gambling, or whoring in Alachua County got the book thrown at them. Of course, we weren't running moonshine, but collecting sugar could be just as dangerous.

I confined my run to the small towns and hamlets in the northern part of Alachua County, avoiding Gainesville like the plague. My first stop would be at the small grocery in Providence and then south down Highway 441 through Ellisville to Alachua and High Springs. Then, I would double back to pass through Brooker before returning to Lake Butler with my load of sugar. That way, I only dipped into Alachua County, staying way to the north of Gainesville.

These small grocery stores, where I purchased my five-pound bags of sugar, are almost all gone now. They have been driven to extinction by the greedy daemons of corporate America. Kangaroo, Jiffy, Suwannee Swiftly, IGA, and 7-Eleven have replaced them all.

These modern glass and steel, in and out, joints with their paved driveways and bright lights and gaudy signs are almost screaming at the customer, "Hurry up. Get finished. Get out of here. You're wasting time." They simply do not have the down-home ambiance of the small stores I stopped at on the sugar run. In those little mom and pop grocery stores, you were expected to stay around awhile and be friendly. They were ad-hoc community centers to wide places in the road where they didn't have a courthouse or city hall. Most of the stores had a front porch, complete with old church benches where the old men could sit around on warm summer days and talk about how their tobacco crop was doing. When it turned cold or was raining, you could go inside to an old potbellied stove surrounded by rocking chairs. You could sit for hours, sip on an RC Cola, munch on a Moon Pie, visit with your neighbors, and be sociable.

I remember how incredibly banal and simple these conversations were. The old men would not talk about politics, sports, religion, or anything else that might get somebody mad; friendship was too important for that. Instead, they restricted their conversations to safe topics that made for good conversation but didn't threaten anyone. They would talk for hours about such things as if it would freeze again this year, or if this winter was colder than last winter, or how long it's been since the last rain, and the most important topic of all, speculation about farm prices for the coming year.

The insides of these stores were usually as neat as a pin in a run-down, well-worn sort of way. They were all well swept out with most of the dust kept off the canned goods. The rows of shelves were straight, and the merchandise and groceries were neatly arranged with the prices clearly marked. In the very back of the store was a long glass-faced meat cooler, backed by a large wooden chopping block. Inside the meat cooler was ground hamburger, steaks, chickens, and pork chops all clearly priced with little plastic tags sticking in the meat with two small steel pins. This area was the domain of the storeowner. He would stand behind the meat cooler wearing a long, white bib apron that was often stained with the blood of the animals that were cut up on the wooden chopping block.

The man behind the meat cooler would always go out of his way to speak to each of his customers inquiring how their tobacco crop and how their children were doing. Although these little mom and pop stores were friendly places, ran by nice folks, good sanitary food-handling practices were something that were still coming to the rural South. I will never forget one day hearing a storeowner yell out the rear door of the meat section to his son in the backyard, "Fuller, quit playing with the dogs and come grind the hamburger."

The owner's wife would always be in the front of the store, guarding the cash register and ringing up the customer's purchases. She never talked about crops or hunting; that was her husband's domain. Instead, she would always inquire from each of the ladies about how they were feeling. Southern women really enjoy having medical problems and talking about them to other women. While ringing up the groceries, she never forgot a name or an ailment. She would listen patiently to a detailed explanation of the customer's aches and pains, then often dish out a little medical advice, and recommend some form of treatment or medicine that would get her customer feeling better in no time.

Most of the these store owners would sell me a single five-pound bag of sugar without comment, while others would look at me funny, and sometimes ask me what a boy with Union County license plates was doing way over here buying sugar. I always had a pat answer that put their concerns to rest. I was a great liar, and, I found that if my story had a little suffering and misery in it, it was much easier for them to believe. I would always say that I was visiting a sick relative or there had been a death in the family. This would usually shut everybody up and get me my sugar. Basically, these were friendly, unsuspicious people who were more or less programmed to always keep their customers happy and coming back.

After I had made my run a couple of times, I had to modify my schedule and bypass the small town of Providence, located in extreme western Union County. Just the name "Providence" had a religious ring to it that made me nervous. To make matters worse, the small grocery in Providence was right next to the Baptist church, and the folks that ran it were, to put it mildly, very religious. Painted on the side of the store was a large red and white sign that said, "Jesus is Lord," with three small black crosses. After I stopped by a couple of times, they added another sign behind the counter, which said, "Read Your Bible Every Day." That got me scared, so I decided that I was pushing my luck by stopping in Providence.

Spindler's grocery in Brooker, which was in Bradford County, was another story altogether. It was the damnedest place I ever saw. It was a large, barn-like building that had been painted white sometime in the far and distant past. However, now the paint was so old that the building would probably have looked better if it had never been painted. The building was totally covered inside and out with decades of dirt and grime that nobody who either worked or shopped at Spindler's grocery seemed to notice. The old, worn-out paint job was hidden behind dozens of large tin signs advertising Royal Crown Cola, Martha White Self-Rising Flour, Wonder Bread, Prince Albert Smoking Tobacco, and Bull of the Woods Chewing Tobacco. Even the ragged, old screen doors on the front had a tin sign advertising Nehi Grape Soda. Years ago, somebody had painted a large sign covering almost the entire tin roof of the building. In big black letters, it said, "SEE ROCK CITY," referring to a well-known tourist spot located on Lookout Mountain near Chattanooga, Tennessee.

Unlike the other little grocery stores that I stopped at, Spindler's grocery was totally filthy. The outside driveway and surrounding area were covered with all kinds of run-over beer cans, cigarette butts, old drink bottles, cardboard boxes, Coca-Cola crates, and every other kind of paper trash you could think of. The walkway to the front door was almost paved with hundreds of soft drink bottle caps smashed into the ground by years of pedestrian traffic.

Spindler's grocery sold more horse feed and fertilizer than it did groceries. The store had that old musty smell that feed stores always have. Inside it was dark and cavernous, with one long counter running down the right-hand side of the store. In the center was a large kerosene-fired stove. There were no rocking chairs, but the customers had fashioned seats out of wooden Coca-Cola crates and milk boxes. The store had only three rows of sparsely stocked shelves, where you could buy canned corn, bags of Dixie-Lily grits, pork and beans, Vienna sausages, sardines, and soda crackers. On the large counter, in big glass jars were pickled eggs, crackers, hot sausages, potato chips, pork rinds, and pickled pig's feet.

When a person eats any or all of these pickled and preserved commodities, especially the pig's feet and pickled eggs, they would get lower bowel gas so bad nobody could stand to stay around them. Nothing on earth smells as bad as a big old fresh fart from somebody who has been eating pickled eggs or pig's feet.

Everything on the shelves in Spindler's grocery was covered with a thick layer of dust. The bread and rolls were so stale they were as hard as a brick. When I picked up my sugar, I had to be very careful that I didn't get a bag that was full of cockroaches, weevils, or old rat shit. Spindler's store was virtually alive with all kinds of vermin, although there were rattraps and roach poison everywhere you looked.

The man who owned Spindler's grocery was a seventy-five-year-old former rodeo cowboy who had grown up tough and wild in the vanishing frontier country of Montana and Nevada. He had met his wife when she was a young, attractive rodeo groupie in Macon, Georgia. They shacked up for a number of years before deciding to get legally married in 1928, only a few months before their first child was born. Mrs. Spindler followed her husband on the rodeo circuit until he became so old and fat that he just couldn't do it anymore. They moved to Florida, because Mrs. Spindler wanted to return to the South to avoid the freezing-cold winters of her husband's native Montana. In 1939, with money he had managed to save from his rodeo days, they purchased a small grocery store just one mile south of Brooker and settled down to live out their remaining years.

In the years since then, they had done well. The store had been enlarged over and over again, until it was a labyrinth of small dark rooms filled with all kinds of animal feed, chicken incubators, and rabbit cages. Mr. Spindler kept buying up local farmland until the family owned over two hundred acres where he raised cattle and quarter horses.

Mr. and Mrs. Spindler had four sons and three daughters, all of which were now grown and married to local spouses. They all had numerous children, only adding onto Mr. Spindler's dynasty. Most of the boys worked for their father either at the store or on the ranch looking after the cattle and horses. Many of the girls' husbands also worked at the store. The children were just about as raw boned and tough as you could get. They tossed around hundred-pound bags of horse feed like they were matchboxes. In my opinion, the girls were just as tough as the boys. They could all ride horses and punch cattle, and, if you wanted a fight, they were as quick to give you one as any man I knew.

Spindler's store was the center of all commerce in Brooker, Florida. While other stores had just as much business, the difference in Spindler's store was that people hung around longer, much longer. All day long, there were all kinds of people coming and going. They bought horse feed and fertilizers, and some even picked up a few groceries. Then, there were the drunks. I never went to Spindler's store when there wasn't at least a half dozen drunks hanging around. They would be passed out on the front steps or sleeping it off on one of the big bags of horse feed that was piled up against the wall.

Spindler's store legally sold beer and illegally sold pint jars of moonshine. They were one of Jack's best customers. Sober people who stopped at Spindler's store just stepped around the passed-out drunks, and Mr. Spindler's boys just went about their daily routine, paying little notice to the foul-smelling men lying on the floor or curled up in the corner.

The main reason people spent so much time at the store was that Mr. Spindler was a raconteur extraordinary, which is a polite way of saying he was a genuine bullshit artist. Since his sons did all the heavy lifting and managing of the store, Mr. Spindler would just sit behind the counter on an old well-padded barstool like a medieval king on his throne holding court. Nobody came or went without first stopping and paying their respects to Mr. Spindler, and, once you did, you might as well as sit back and relax, because, once Mr. Spindler had your ear, he was going to talk it off.

Mr. Spindler was an old-time cowboy, and his dress reflected it. He always wore high-heeled cowboy boots, dirty jeans, and western shirts with white pearl buttons. His shirts and pants looked like they had never been washed or ironed in their long, pitiful existence. He had an enormous belly that almost obscured his western belt and big oval buckle. Although he had long ago gotten too arthritic and old to ride a horse, his dress adequately reflected what he used to be.

Mr. Spindler and I hit it off from the very beginning. He loved to tell stories, and I loved to listen to them. He would sit on his old padded stool and talk for hours about how he used to catch mustang horses out in Nevada and the big bulls he conquered in his rodeo days. It always seemed to me that the younger you were the more pleasure Mr. Spindler got from telling his stories. I would always sit patiently on a stool in front of the big counter sipping a Coca-Cola, listening patiently, and asking intelligent questions, although I had already heard the story before. Mr. Spindler was like an old hound dog; if you scratched his belly by listening to his stories, he would repay the kindness. How I wanted to be repaid was in sugar, and I always got it. State law or no state law, I could always count on getting at least a half dozen bags of sugar whenever I stopped at Spindler's store.

Mr. Spindler was basically a nice old man, but, at the same time, everyone clearly understood that he was not to be trifled with. He always carried a pistol and would use it at the slightest provocation. I never forgot my grandfather shooting the Negro man at his cotton gin. I clearly understood that even though these men were often so old and fat they couldn't walk, they were still dangerous as long as they could pull a trigger. One day, because he liked me so much, Mr. Spindler decided to show me his "nigger toe."

One of the big problems store owners had was getting the customers who bought on credit to pay their bills. These people were hard working, but often mentally slow. They often bought whiskey and beer rather than groceries and shoes for their children. It often seemed to me that the concept of credit was confusing to many of these poor people. To people who have never had anything, getting it on credit was often the same as getting it for free, since many times they couldn't or wouldn't comprehend that they were supposed to pay it back.

This situation often left the merchants between a rock and a hard place. They had to sell on credit or they would lose their customers, but, if word ever got out that they didn't have to pay their bills, the merchant could be out of business in short order. To take legal action was an exercise in futility for what was usually a small amount of money. Also, most of these debts were just verbal agreements or a few numbers written in pencil on the yellow pages of a ledger book. Even if the merchant did go to court, most of the debtors were sharecroppers and had no real property or chattel to take away.

That only left intimidation and violence. Mr. Spindler bragged to me that all he had to do was show his "nigger toe" one time and he could get the money "even if they had to rob their mama to get it." This was not an idle threat at a time when lynchings were still a reality in the South. While a white man might get more respect and time because of the color of his skin, that didn't mean he didn't have to pay his bills. The "nigger toe" was kept in a small baby food jar filled with alcohol and discretely hidden under the counter. Having it sit out on the counter would destroy its shock value. All over the South, having a "nigger toe" under the counter was a tried and true method of getting poor people to pay their bills. I never saw them, but I had heard stories of merchants who had testicles, a penis, fingers, or a whole hand in an alcohol-filled jar under the counter. Again, the "nigger toe" was not an idle threat from what I saw of Mr. Spindler and his muscle-bound sons, and they were perfectly capable of carrying out a threat of violence.

I beheld the amazing effectiveness of the "nigger toe" one cold and windy Friday afternoon. I always came by Spindler's store late on Friday afternoons, making it the last stop on my sugar run, because I had to spend so much time listening to Mr. Spindler's bullshit stories. I usually got there around six o'clock, just as it was getting dusk dark in the wintertime.

That day, I had driven through Brooker, and I saw an elderly black man, who was one of the regular drunks down at Spindler's store. He was standing outside the post office, bundled against the cold, and selling boiled peanuts for ten cents a bag. I almost stopped but instead drove on to Spindler's store to finish my business, because it was very cold and I needed to get home early.

I was sitting at Mr. Spindler's counter listening to him recount again how he used to pan for gold in Colorado, when the little old man came sheepishly through the front door. It was the first time I had really taken a hard look at him. He was at least sixty years old and showed the effects of having stood outside in the cold wind all day selling his peanuts.

Mr. Spindler seemed to be expecting him, because he kept glancing toward the door as we were talking. The old black man had two bags of peanuts left, and he asked me if I would like to buy them. More out of pity than hunger, I reached into my pocket and pulled out twenty cents. He then walked over to Mr. Spindler and dumped his pockets out onto the table. He then began to slowly count out all the nickels and dimes in his pockets. He had been selling peanuts at the post office since it opened at eight-thirty this morning and had managed to accumulate a little less than nine dollars in loose change. After the old black man finished counting his money, Mr. Spindler reached over with a ham-like hand, and, with one massive movement, he swept the collection of nickels and dimes into a Have-A-Tampa cigar box.

The elderly Negro asked if he could have a beer on credit, and Mr. Spindler obliged him. With his hands shaking violently, the old black man gulped down the beer in only one or two swallows. Without being asked, Mr. Spindler went under the counter and took out a half-pint bottle of moonshine, put it in a brown paper bag, and handed it over the counter to the old man.

He quickly slid it into the pocket of the old, ragged, and dirty jacket that he wore over his faded bib overalls. He thanked Mr. Spindler and turned to go home and drink his moonshine. Mr. Spindler reminded him that he would add the price of the beer and the half-pint of shine to his account. The old man just nodded his head and left.

"That there's a good old nigger," Mr. Spindler said, as he used the dull stub of a pencil to scribble down the price of the beer and half-pint of shine into an old greenback ledger book.

"He seems like a nice old man," I replied.

"Yeah, he is," Mr. Spindler smiled and said. "I ain't had to scare him with the 'nigger toe' except for one time."

On Saturday nights, Mr. Spindler would stage cockfights in a twelve-foot-diameter ring, which was called "the pit." It was really little more than a plywood ring built in the center of the old barn behind his store. But, on Saturday nights, hundreds of local people would gather to watch the banty roosters go at each other.

You had to be careful when you walked around Mr. Spindler's barn, because the place was filled with fresh horse shit. It always amazed me how the half-drunk crowd could trample through the horse shit all night without even appearing to notice. Mr. Spindler's boots were always covered in the stuff, and he moved from the barn, to his store, and into his house without slowing to wipe his feet. I guess when you've smelled horse shit all your life, after awhile, you just learn to ignore it.

Mr. Spindler had a special "rooster house" where he raised some of the best fighting cocks in the South. Many times, high rollers would come all the way from Miami or Atlanta to use one of Mr. Spindler's roosters as breeding stock or to negotiate a cockfight. These animals had been carefully bred for their fighting ability, which went all the way back to Ancient China, where cockfighting originated. Mr. Spindler prized his roosters as much for breeding stock as anything else, so he always forbade the use of the inch-long steel spurs attached to the roosters' legs during a fight. The razor-sharp spurs made the fight shorter and bloodier, but, at the same time, it usually killed one rooster and badly injured the other. This messed up Mr. Spindler's plans to pass each winning rooster's belligerent gene pool onto a new generation of fighting cocks.

The cockfights would begin shortly after dark on Saturday night with a single hundred-watt bulb illuminating the pit. In the summer, the barn could get stifling hot, and the light would attract all kinds of bugs and mosquitoes. In the winter, everyone was too drunk or excited to notice the cold. No fires were allowed in the barn, but the gamblers could always warm up at a fire built out in the horse pasture.

The cockfights were almost a surreal, out-of-this-world experience. The crowd was heavily integrated with blacks and whites rubbing arms with each other as they jockeyed to get a good viewing spot of the pit. The fights were done according to strict rules. Cockfights were fairly short affairs, and, within minutes, one rooster or the other would begin to get the upper hand. The fight ended when the owner of the rooster getting the short end of the stick would step into the pit and remove his rooster before it was too badly injured. The rule was one foot in the pit, and the fight was over. If the owner didn't step in to take out the rooster, then one of Mr. Spindler's burly sons would do the job. No rooster was killed in one of Mr. Spindler's fights. Most of the time, there was little to argue about, but sometimes weird things happened.

The person who lorded over the cockfights was Mr. Spindler's huge wife, Lois, backed up by her four beefy sons. The obese woman would sit behind a crude desk made from a pair of sawhorses and a sheet of plywood. She would write down each bet in a Montag Blue Horse Notebook, the same type I used at school. All bets were made through Mrs. Spindler; anybody caught betting on the side was kicked out and forbidden to come back until they had returned to the store and paid her proper homage. She got a percentage, twenty cents on the dollar, of each winner's take. No bet could be enforced unless it was written in her book.

Lois Spindler always looked like some kind of rustic Queen Victoria sitting behind her plywood throne. Her word was law. Those who lost, paid up, and those who won, collected. Nobody dared argue with her, although she sometimes was called upon to make Queen Solomon-like decisions on the worth of a rooster to fight and who won and who lost.

One night, I saw her part a black man's hair with a bullet. He was a tall young man, who had a grease-encrusted, Little Richard-style pompadour hairdo that looked like some kind of greasy black wave about to break on some far and distant beach. He had foolishly made a five-dollar bet on the wrong rooster and lost. He was drunk and couldn't afford to lose that much of his paycheck. He tried to undo his mistake by arguing that Mrs. Spindler had written his bet down in the wrong place in her book, taking advantage of the fact that he couldn't read or write. In the heat of the argument, the Negro man called Mrs. Spindler a "white bitch." This was to be an almost-fatal mistake.

Although she was fat and elderly, Mrs. Spindler was also remarkably still strong, especially in her arms and legs; this was the result of years of hard farm work in her native Georgia. She always carried a leather-covered blackjack in her apron pocket and could whip it out and bring it down on somebody's head with lightning-fast speed. Between her two enormous breasts was a pearl-handled thirty-two-caliber, nickel-plated Smith and Wesson revolver.

When she heard the black man say the words "white bitch," Lois Spindler leaped to her feet, pulled out the pistol, and fired directly at the black man's head. The bullet pierced the man's greasy Little Richard pompadour, causing it to split like a piece of white oak hit with an ax. The two sides of the pompadour parted like the Red Sea, making the top of his head look like it was split in half. The gunshot made everyone in the barn run for cover, except for one of Mrs. Spindler's sons who finished the job by slamming the black man to the ground with a shovel handle across his shoulders. When he tried to stand up, Lois Spindler used her blackjack, knocking the man unconscious.

A couple of weeks later, the black man meekly showed up at Spindler's store. He had nineteen stitches in his head and a broken collarbone, but he knew he was lucky to be alive. If the bullet had been off its mark only an inch one way or the other, it would have went right through his skull. He apologized to Mr. Spindlier and begged to be allowed to return to the cockfights. Mr. Spindler wasn't a vindictive man. He agreed to sell the man beer and moonshine, but he thought it was best if he stayed away from the cockfights until things calmed down. He said his wife was still pretty pissed off. Within two months, the wounded man—his head mostly healed and his pompadour restored—was back betting on the cockfights.

I always returned from my sugar run around eight or nine o'clock and drove straight to Jack's house to deliver my sugar. Most of the time, I had between twenty-five to thirty five-pound bags. I always sold to Jack as part of our deal. The other boys who made sugar runs had their own customers. Jack and I agreed that he would pay the retail price of the sugar plus twenty cents a bag profit. I only made six dollars a run, but that wasn't bad money in those days when gasoline was only thirty cents a gallon, and a loaf of bread cost fifteen cents. Sugar runs were a fairly safe and fun, if not illegal, way to make money.

The bad thing about the sugar run was that everyone liked to made moonshine in the winter when the farm work was slow and the bugs in the woods weren't so bad. It was not wise to stockpile sugar anytime. Being in possession of too much sugar was against the law. Then, there were the logistical problems of where to keep it. The heat and humidity would cause mildew and mold to grow in the sugar, and it was almost impossible to keep cockroaches and rats out of the bags of sugar. Unless you had an expensive upright freezer large enough to hold the sugar, it was best to buy your sugar as you needed it.

Problems arose when amateurs got into the business of making the sugar run. They would cross each other's path, try to pressure the little store owners into selling them more than one bag of sugar, and generally running their mouths too much about what they were up to. It eventually got so bad, that store owners began to put up little blue signs they got from the State Beverage

Agency that said, "We Don't Sell Sugar to Moonshiners." Underneath that ominous warning was a telephone number you could call to report suspected moonshiners.

Of course, Mr. Spindler never put up one of the signs, but the other little stores did, especially the one in Providence. They put up two; one was next to the "Jesus is the Answer" sign, and the other was next to the "Read Your Bible Every Day" sign.

Luckily, the moonshiners had a backup source for sugar. There were large commercial operations that smuggled in good sugar from Cuba and south Florida. When Fidel Castro came to power, that halted the Cuban connection, but this was only a minor setback, since sugar could also be obtained from the Dominican Republic and a host of other Latin American nations.

The sugar smugglers brought in their sugar by boats from the islands and operated their distribution rings out of old warehouses near the Talleyrand docks in Jacksonville. Other sugar distributors moved sugar up by truck from south Florida where it was grown around Lake Okeechobee. They stored their sugar in cold storage warehouses out on West Beaver Street. Jack and I decided that the sugar run was getting too risky and decided to start buying the more expensive sugar from the smugglers up in Jacksonville.

The men who ran the sugar operations in Jacksonville were a mean-looking bunch that appeared to me to be either Cubans or Italians. It was hard to say, since they didn't talk much, and Union County didn't have any people that belonged to these two particular ethnic groups. In other words, I had never seen a Cuban or Italian before except on television. We purchased a single fifty-pound bag of sugar that was the smallest amount they would sell. It was in the back of the building, carefully hidden in a freezing-cold meat locker to keep the cockroaches and rats out of the big bags of sugar. They were really irritated that we were only buying fifty pounds of sugar, and they told Jack they didn't fool with small-time operators. Jack promised that in the future he would get at least 200 pounds that would make thirty pounds of moonshine, which was the capacity of his still.

The sugar cost us twenty-five cents a pound, about twice what it cost at the store. But, with the fifty dollars worth of sugar, we could produce thirty gallons of moonshine, which would sell for between seven to ten dollars a gallon. The corn, even though it was sprouted, only cost us six dollars for a fifty-pound bag, and it only took five 50-pound bags of corn to make a run, since it would swell up during the fermentation process. The general rule was that a one-gallon bucket of corn could be mixed with five one-gallon buckets of water

So, for a total investment of eighty dollars, fifty for the sugar and thirty for the corn, you could make at least two hundred dollars worth of moonshine.

Of course, there was still the yeast, water, and the cost of heating fuel, but Jack used to say that was all chump change; the big money was in the sugar and corn.

Jack Taylor had been a U.S. marine during the Korean War and had been badly wounded in the battle for the Chosin Reservoir. A Communist Chinese bullet had crashed into his helmet while he was laying flat on the ground trying to take cover. It cracked his skull, knocking him unconscious. Because of his head injury, Jack had a three-inch-long metal plate in his head. The bullet also took off the tip of his ear before it stuck his shoulder, smashing his collarbone to bits before moving into his left lung.

Jack was often plagued with violent headaches that left him bedridden sometimes for days at a time. The headaches were so bad—Jack confessed to me—he often thought about suicide just to stop the pain.

Because he was a disabled veteran, Jack could not buy life or hospitalization insurance. Whenever he got sick, he had to drive to the Veteran's Administration Hospital in Lake City. He hated the place and would never go there unless he was really bad off. He said they made you feel like you were some kind of bum. The first thing you had to do was prove to them that you were really sick. They always made Jack wait for hours and then fill out all kinds of paperwork before he could see the doctor. The doctor would spend about ten minutes with him and then tell him to take aspirins when he felt a headache coming on.

He received a check from the VA, but it was for only 50 percent disability. Jack often told me that if he had enough money to hire a lawyer and appeal, he might be able to get more. But, the guy at the VA who handled his casework was a real son of a bitch and screwed Jack over, saying his head wound didn't prevent him from "working and earning an honest living." Jack really took offense at the words "honest living," because it inferred that he was somehow trying to cheat the VA out of the taxpayers' money.

The only work Jack could get was to farm a little and work part time as a barber in Lake Butler. If he made too much money, the VA would cut back his pension check, so he had to be really careful. The money he earned growing his little bit of tobacco was a matter of record, so Jack lied about the money he made barbering, counting only every other customer. In those days, a haircut only cost a dollar and a quarter, and most people paid with cash. Forty percent of what he earned went to the owner of the barber shop, who was nice enough to help Jack out by lying on his tax forms about how much money Jack made. Naturally, the money we made making shine was all undeclared and gravy.

I never felt any guilt about what we were doing, even though it was against the law. The way I saw it, the VA was screwing Jack out of his pension, and we were screwing the federal government out of their whiskey tax money.

When Jack would tell me stories about all the hell he went through in Korea, and the hard time the VA gave him after he got back home, it made me proud to be a moonshiner.

Jack also had a lot of trouble lifting heavy objects because of his shoulder wound. He had a steel pin holding his left collarbone in place, and the path of the bullet into his shoulder had done a lot of muscle damage in his back and left arm. That's why he always needed me when there was any heavy lifting to be done.

Because of high school, I had a lot of trouble getting free during the week, so Jack and I tried to do everything on the weekends. However, this caused problems, since Saturday was always a big day down at the barbershop. On a busy Saturday, Jack might work from eight in the morning until eight or nine at night finishing up customers. Out of a fear of losing business, the man who owned the barbershop never turned anybody away, no matter how late they came in. Anybody sitting in the barbershop at six o'clock when the shop officially closed got their hair cut no matter how long it took. Most of the customers were old-fashioned farmers who only came to town on Saturday. All the businesses in Lake Butler, including the bank, were open at least half a day on Saturday to take care of their needs. Since getting a haircut was one of the least important things they did on a Saturday, the barber tried to be accommodating. When Jack would finally drag himself home on Saturday nights, he would usually have a splitting headache and sleep all day Sunday.

I finally talked Jack into letting me go up to Jacksonville by myself on Saturdays to pick up the sugar. At first, he was reluctant, but, finally, he gave in and gave me my own key to his shine car. It really made me feel like a big shot to walk around school with the key to a shine car in my pocket, especially during civics class, when I would patiently listen to my teacher explain how it was our duty to always to obey the law and be a good little citizen of the United States of America. I had watched Robert Mitchem in *Thunder Road* at least a dozen times, and, to me, it was the total epitome of adventure.

One of the problems of hauling moonshine or sugar was the weight of the whole thing. Every time I would go to Jacksonville, I would pick up at least two hundred pounds of sugar, and that was enough weight to make the rear end of a regular automobile almost drag the pavement.

All over north Florida, there were shade tree mechanics that specialized in installing extra shock absorbers and axle springs to make your automobile look normal, even when you had a heavy load in the truck. These cars were referred to as being "jacked up." Naturally, when the car was empty, the rear end tended to stick up in the air. You could "unjack" your vehicle by having the extra rear axle springs and shocks removed, but that was a lot of work and expense. In the 1960s, a lot of teenage boys drove "jacked-up" cars in imitation of the hot-rod drag racers we all idolized. It was a funny thing; if Jack was driving the "jacked-up" car, he would probably have been pulled over as a suspected moonshiner. But, when I—a teenage boy—was driving, the beverage agents probably figured I was just another punk, hot rodder, so they just let me go. I was never stopped.

The bottom line was that it really wasn't important if they stopped me or not. Because, when a car's rear end is sticking up in the air, it means the car is empty, and there was no law against having your car specially modified so the rear end sticks up in the air.

Beverage agents used to stake out major roadways, like Highway 301 between Starke and Baldwin, looking for automobiles whose rear bumper was too low to the ground. They also looked for other signs, such as something in the back seat of the car covered with a blanket. A pickup truck became suspicious if the items in the bed of the truck were covered with a tarpaulin. The beverage agents called this "banking," because they liked to park high on the ditch bank, so they could look down into the vehicles. Beverage agents were easy to spot; they always drove unmarked, late-model Fords with large engines. For some reason, probably government financial frugality, their vehicles never had white sidewall tires. The biggest giveaway was the long radio antenna sticking up from the back bumper. It was like a little sign saying, "Hey, here we are, your tax dollars at work."

State beverage agents really dressed like dorks. They wore sweat-stained white or plaid shirts with "city britches" type dress pants and Dick Tracy-style, snap-brim hats, pushed far back on their heads. Their hats were not pulled down over their eyes, gangster style.

For some reason, they never wore jeans or overalls, although they spent almost all their time outdoors. Even when they were in the deepest woods or swamps, busting up a still, they still had on their dress pants and snap-brim hats.

When they went to court, beverage agents wore these ugly wide ties that never came down to their belt line. Since the ties never reached their belts, they were like little fat arrows pointing toward their potbellies. If this wasn't bad enough, they often had a large rose, lily, or gardenia flower imprinted on the widest part of their tie.

The agents usually carried snub-nosed, blue steel Colt thirty-eight revolvers, which hung on their belt in a cheap-looking brown leather holster. It had a little brown strap over the trigger guard to keep the pistol from falling out.

You never saw a beverage agent wearing a suit or sport coat, unless they were in court. When you saw them on the road, they had on brown or black windbreaker jackets that they got from the JCPenney Store. Like most adults

I knew when I was growing up, the beverage agents were all either chewing on a cigar or had a cigarette dangling from their mouth.

If a person knew what he was doing, it was possible to drive all the way from Union County to the edges of Jacksonville without once going out onto a paved road, except for very short stretches where you had to cross a road. The woods were honeycombed with miles and miles of old logging roads, which, during the winter months, were usually high and dry and easy to drive.

Jack's shine car was a beautiful, white over powder blue, 1959 Buick. He liked Buick cars, because they had a large trunk and were tough enough to handle the dirt roads.

Since I was not hauling shine or sugar, and therefore not breaking any laws, I usually drove up over the paved roads, avoiding Highway 301 where I knew the beverage agents would be. There was no sense in letting them get a look at me. When I returned, I always waited until after dark, and then I avoided the major highways. I drove on the back roads as much as possible and frequently changed my speed and direction. Sometimes, I would even double back over my own tracks to make sure nobody was following me.

Dealing with beverage agents was different from the highway patrol. If a person is speeding, then they can pull them over. However, especially at night, beverage agents had to follow you for a while before they could decide if you were a potential moonshiner or not. It was harder for them to follow someone at night without being noticed because of the headlights.

It was also easier to shake them. All you had to do was go around a curve, cut off your headlights, and then turn down a dirt road you knew about in advance. Once the agents have passed, don't sit there, because they will be back as soon as they realize you're gone. Just pull out and follow them at a respectful distance. When they turn back, they will just pass you by, because they are in a hurry to get back to the place where they lost your trail.

I wasn't an expert on the old logging roads, so I only took well-traveled dirt roads. I didn't want to get lost or stuck in the mud. A shine car that is loaded is very heavy, and, when it gets stuck, it is really stuck. I might have to walk miles before I found a telephone to call Jack to come with his truck and pull me out.

Once, my car broke down on a lonely dirt road. It was very cold, and I must have walked five or six miles before finding a house. It was just cracking daylight, and the woods were covered in a beautiful white frost that I might have admired, if I wasn't freezing. I was greeted by a pack of dogs that I was afraid would eat me alive, but they only barked and barked and barked. I was scared to death that any minute I would be blasted by a shotgun, by somebody thinking I was an escaped convict. Finally, somebody finally came to the door only to tell me they didn't have a telephone. Luckily, they offered to drive me to a gas station about five miles away in Lawtey, where I could call Jack. I will never forget how good the heater in the man's truck felt as we rode to the gas station.

When I finally got in touch with Jack, he was relieved. He was afraid I was in jail. After this incident, we decided to travel only on an agreed-upon route, so if I wasn't home by a certain time, he could drive the route looking for me.

Jacksonville, Florida, has always been one of my favorite towns. I often went there with my mother on her frequent shopping trips. It was different from Gainesville, Lake City, Starke, or any of the other towns I visited, because it was a seaport. For some reason, I had a fascination with the ocean. I must have read *Treasure Island* a dozen times. To me, a ship on the ocean was the ultimate symbol of freedom. I could get into a ship and forever leave the heat, humidity, bugs, and ignorance of north Florida for those "faraway places with strange-sounding names" that Patty Page sang about on the radio.

Jack had once taken me to a small bar that sat next to the Merchant Marine Hiring Hall on Bay Street in Jacksonville. It was just down from the Maxwell House coffee plant and across the street from the Jacksonville shipyards.

Bay Street in the 1950s and early 1960s was not at all like it is today. The street was peppered with small bars, cheap hotels, penny arcades, and shower and locker rooms where sailors could change from their uniforms into street clothes.

It was also where the Greyhound bus station was located. Every day, the big gray dogs deposited all kinds of people onto the streets of Jacksonville. The street was alive with navy men on shore leave, merchant seamen, shipyard workers, longshoremen, and a large number of single and divorced women, most of whom had come to Jacksonville trying to escape the poverty of some rural county in north Florida or south Georgia. They would find some kind of waitress job to survive and then haunt the bars at night husband hunting. If their quests were unfruitful, they would often be forced to turn to crime or prostitution in order to survive. Many wound up running small-time poker and dice game operations in the cheap hotel rooms above Bay Street. Others engaged in prostitution or ran cheap little hustles, fleecing sailors of other horny men out of their paychecks.

There was a lot of prostitution in Jacksonville in those days. There were regular brothels on Monroe Street and freelance hookers who worked the bars and cheap hotels. When a woman got too old to hustle, she would often as not open and operate her own bar. These women were big and hard. They knew how to throw a drunk out of a bar as good as any man. They also had the social skills to keep customers coming back.

Of course, I was underage, but since all the bartenders knew Jack, they let me hang out while he drank beer. I tried to show them respect by not drinking and sitting next to the back door so I could slip out in case the law came in. Later, when I began making the trip to Jacksonville by myself, I would always drop by and spend a couple of hours at one of these neat little bars before I went to pick up the sugar.

A big Italian woman named Lu ran the bar I stayed in. She always had a big pot of red Italian pasta sauce on behind the bar. It was full of fresh tomatoes, sausages, and tons of garlic. She called it "mama's sauce," because only she knew what was in it. She served it up with homemade pasta and a huge slice of hot garlic bread.

Before me was a panorama of characters better than you would find in any movie theater or Broadway show. There were married men looking for a girlfriend on the side. Married women, whose husbands were far out to sea, were also there looking for a little excitement to pass a lonely night. On the other side, there were horny sailors, with a pocket full of money and all kinds of women willing to take it from them. There were whores, pimps, card sharks, pool hustlers, and con artists, all mixed up with innocent young boys fresh off the boat and timid young girls fresh off the farm.

The merchant seamen, who hung out in these bars, were some of the most interesting people I ever met. They carried their passports and seaman's papers in their back pockets and were always either about to ship out or just got in. They talked about places like Cairo and Singapore, like it was just down the street.

One day a member of the black gang, the part of the crew that worked down in the big engine rooms of the ships, told me about a place called Saigon. I had never heard of it, since we never studied about Vietnam in school; we only studied about London, Paris, Rome, and places like that, where white people lived. He had to actually walk me down to the merchant marine hiring hall and show me where Saigon was on the big world map that hung on the wall.

He told me that Saigon was as hot as the hinges of hell and as bad or worse than Florida during the middle of summer. However, he said the girls were beautiful, and Saigon was a cheap port to have liberty, much cheaper that either Hong Kong or Tokyo. He said that they had American GIs stationed in Saigon, and they all lived in downtown hotels, with fancy French restaurants and ornate bars. He said the best looking girls were the half-French and half-Vietnamese women you found hanging around the Continental and Rex Hotel. I listened with fascination of his tales of sexual conquest and of living together with two women at the same time. He said that any American was big shit in Saigon, where the women would do anything for someone with round eyes and a fat wallet.

I told him that if I couldn't get into the military after I graduated from high school, I was considering going into the merchant marine. He told me that no matter what I did to make sure I went to Saigon. I eventually did make it to Saigon. I went there twice during the Vietnam War and once to Ho Chi Minh City, its new name, in 1993, when I returned for a nostalgic visit.

Bay Street, as I knew it then, is now urban renewed out of existence. The merchant marine hiring hall has been torn down, and all the little bars, arcades, and cheap hotels have been replaced by high-rise office buildings, lawyers' offices, City Hall, and an upscale yuppie shopping and entertainment complex, called "The Landing." The shipyard is now closed, and it is only suited executives and the well-dressed power women, who are climbing the corporate latter, who walk where the old sailors and hookers once tread. It is a crying damn shame.

However, before all this happened, I had to get back to Union County with Jack's sugar.

Once all the ingredients are collected, the next step is the actual making of the moonshine. It involves two distinct processes: fermentation and distillation.

Fermentation is the mixing of the corn, sugar, and yeast and then allowing it to ferment, which is a fancy word for letting it get good and rotten. Fermentation takes place in fifty-five-gallon drums, which are called "boxes," because, in the old days, it was done in long wooden feed troughs. It is one of the ways a still is classified; you could have a five-box still, a ten-box still, and so forth. The mixture that is created in the boxes has a lot of names, but in north Florida it was always called "mash."

Mixing the ingredients to form the mash is a long, nasty job. The corn, sugar, and water spill all over the place, and, pretty soon, the ground around the boxes is swampy with a slimy mixture of the spilled mixings. The ingredients have to be added slowly in even parts and mixed thoroughly to make sure the sugar is dissolved. It is hard work stirring the thick mash mixture. Different moonshiners used different things; some had only an old oak limb. Jack and I had a pair of old boat paddles that did a fairly good job. Jack once told me about a man who tried to use an outboard motor to mix his mash. When he cranked up the outboard motor, the propeller slung the mash so hard it flew fifty feet into the air, showering the whole area with corn and sugar.

After the boxes are full of mash, they are covered with screen wire and old pieces of tin. Every day, somebody had to come and stir the mash, and that was my job. It was nasty work. As the mash began to get ripe, as Jack described it, the smell really got bad. It was kind of a sour milk smell, which is why they call the stuff "sour mash" whiskey. Each day, it was worse, and, when you stirred it, the mash would slosh out of the barrels and run all over the place.

When working the mash, I had to wear knee-high rubber boots, because I was always standing in the mud created by the spilled mixings. I also had a pair of old bib overalls that I hid down by the still. I always changed clothes before going to work. I couldn't go home to my mother smelling like sour mash.

It usually took about four days for the mash to get fermented enough to make into shine. This was a crucial time when eighty dollars worth of sugar and corn could be ruined if things didn't go right.

The first threat, of course, was revenuers. The smell of the rotten mash would often carry for miles through the woods. If your still was anywhere near the highway, you had to be really careful or the smell would attract unwelcome visitors. Some moonshiners burned old tires to cover the smell. Others built their stills next to dairy barns, hog pens, and garbage dumps; some would even kill an old cow and let him swell up and rot close to the still. Jack felt our still was far enough back in the woods that we didn't have to worry. He said he would have to be pretty desperate before he would work all night around a stinking dead cow.

However, the biggest threat to our still was wild hogs. They loved mash, and, if they sniffed out your still, they would get into your boxes and turn them over to get at the corn and sugar mixture. Besides ruining your corn and sugar, the hogs would get drunk as hell from drinking the sour mash. There is nothing like a bunch of drunk hogs wandering out onto the road and getting into people's gardens and flower beds to let everyone in the county know you had a moonshine still.

There were only two ways to prevent this; either have somebody stay at the still all the time or fence off your still, at least the boxes.

Many people don't know this, but there is a special type of fence wire just to keep in, or out, hogs. It is smooth wire put together to form four-inch squares. When properly installed, a hog couldn't go under it, over it, or through it. The neatest thing about "hog wire" is that it is almost free. All over Union County, there were the remnants of old fences, long forgotten, with the posts either rotted away or eaten by termites. The hog wire, although very rusty, was as good as ever. Jack and I found a long section of hog wire about half a mile from his house. It was probably part of an old sharecropper's farm, now grown over with pine trees.

We positioned our box barrels in an area where we could use the pine trees as fence posts. We strung out the wire and installed a makeshift gate. As long as the wire was firmly stapled to the trees and stakes were driven into the ground, there was no danger of wild hogs getting into our mash barrels. However, just to be on the safe side, Jack put up three strands of barbed wire to make sure no deer jumped the fence.

It's amazing sometimes how really dumb people think they are so smart. I would often read in the newspaper where they found a still surrounded by barbed wire "to keep out revenuers." What nonsense, how can a simple wire fence keep out a grown man with a gun and carrying still-busting axes? The damn fence was to keep out hogs.

You could tell when the mash was ready by the crust that formed on the top of the barrels. When ready, it was about four inches thick and made up of the residue of the corn after fermentation.

Before turning the mash into whiskey, it had to be filtered by passing it through a fine wire screen, overlaid with a piece of cheesecloth. Jack said that when he made whiskey with his father, they used to strain the mash through an old felt hat. It took awhile to filter the mash, and it was a smelly, unpleasant job. When it was all over, you had about four boxes of a milky-looking substance that was ready for the next step of moonshine making, which was distillation.

The most expensive part of a moonshine operation was the still itself. In reality, a moonshine still can be slapped to together out of almost anything. Jack used to call these "shit stills," built by amateurs often with deadly results. They used old hot water heaters, water barrels, fuel oil drums, automobile gas tanks, radiators, and rubber hoses to fashion some kind of contraption capable of producing a barley tolerable substance that would get you drunk and maybe kill you.

The great danger is something called lead salts poisoning. In the 1960s, lead or lead-based materials were commonly used to seal containers and hold together pieces of sheet metal. Lead-based paint was often used to color metal objects. These quickly made, slapped-together-out-of-anything moonshine stills were full of materials that could cause lead salts poisoning.

A piece of lead the size of a pinhead can leave a person blind or paralyzed for life or both. A piece of lead the size of a thumbtack could kill a person. The rule with moonshine is: If you don't know who made it, don't drink it.

A decent still is made from pure copper, nothing else. A common thing such as galvanized pipe, which is fine for transporting water, can turn moonshine whiskey into a deadly poison. Even cast-iron pipe can be risky. A good still could be homemade or there were people who earned a fairly good living turning copper sheet metal and pipe into moonshine stills. Jack made his still himself, using skills he had learned from his father and special tools he borrowed from a man who worked at the Jacksonville shipyards.

A still has four parts: the boiler, the retort, the thump keg, and the cooler.

The boiler was the second way moonshine still was measured. You could have a ten-gallon boiler, a twenty-gallon boiler, or, like Jack, a thirty-gallon boiler. It was nothing but a large copper pot where the milky filtered mash would be poured. When it was full, a fire was built under the boiler and the contents brought to a boil.

There were little tricks to boost efficiency. Lining the outside of the boiler with red bricks or caked-on hard clay would help hold in the heat and required less fuel. Most shiners used wood, because there was plenty of it close at hand. However, Jack liked liquid propane gas, because it gave off no smoke and burned very hot. One cylinder would last long enough to run off a boiler full of shine.

On top of the boiler is the retort, a bulbous object that appears to have a funnel attached to the side of it. The retort's job is to collect the steam and force it down the funnel to the cooler.

The cooler's job is to convert the steam back to a liquid by cooling it down. It is nothing more than a coil of copper pipe submerged in a barrel of water. It helps a lot if the water is changed frequently or a flow system is set up. One of the worst things to happen to moonshining was when someone discovered that an old car radiator submerged in a pool of flowing water makes a great cooler. However, if the radiator has ever been repaired with melted lead, it could also be a good source of lead salts poisoning.

Sometimes, you could get what shiners called "puke" into the retort. When the mash is boiling, some of the raw materials could splash up into the retort and slide into the cooler; this would ruin the whiskey. So, between the retort and the cooler, you have a keg with one pipe going in and another going out. It was designed to catch any puke and deposit it on the bottom of the keg. It tended to make a thumping sound as it operated, so some people called it the "thump keg."

The product that comes out of a spigot in the bottom of the cooling barrel looks like crystal-clear water, except that the odor it gives off is unmistakable. This crystal-clear liquid is over one hundred-proof alcohol. If it were allowed to age for seven or eight years in oak barrels, like the commercial brands, the oak in the barrels would make it turn into the familiar brown-yellow color of the commercial brands. However, no one has time for that in the moonshine business. This stuff will be sold and drunk within only a few days.

Jack and I would put the shine in Knox brand glass quart jars, and we would place them carefully back into the cardboard box the empty jars came in. This way we didn't have to worry about the jars breaking when we were hauling them. Some moonshiners put their whiskey in glass jugs. However, when you do this, the jugs have to be carefully wrapped in burlap and stacked just right in the trunk of the car to keep them from breaking. A broken gallon jug was bad news on two fronts. First, you were out seven bucks worth of whiskey. Secondly, your car will smell of moonshine for weeks. A broken five-gallon jug was even worse. Nothing attacks the attention of beverage agents more than moonshine dripping from the trunk of a car.

Jack would always check the bead on the quart jars of moonshine. It was a way shiners had of telling if their product was of high quality. He would hold the jar up to the light, slightly shake it, and tiny bubbles would appear. They would appear to hang in midsuspension; they would not rise to the top, creating something that looked like a tiny sting of pearls, hence the phrase "checking the bead."

In the old days, the whiskey was mixed with gunpowder and sat on fire. A small explosion would tell the whiskey maker his product was good. The term "one hundred proof" meant that an equal amount of whiskey and gunpowder was needed to make the explosion. Ninety or eighty proof meant that more gunpowder than whiskey was needed to make the explosion, indicating a lower level of alcohol in the brew. The strongest alcohol product I ever saw was called "Alcohol Puro," and it was 190 proof.

Jack would always sample his wares. He said he would not sell anything he would not drink himself. Just before he took the first sip of shine he would always make the same toast.

"Between her eyes her beauty lies.

Between her thighs her pussy lies.

Oh, snake shit."

# The Reckoning

Sometimes, I wonder how my mind works. I really don't know if I fell asleep under that azalea bush or if I was just hallucinating because of all the hell I had been through that last night of initiation week. I have no idea why my brain went racing off like that. I have no idea why the sirens somehow triggered in my mind the old story my grandmother told me about Harry Byrd's baptism, the Scout Hole, Dr. King, and all of the rest of it.

Lying there that night on the cold ground under the wet azalea bush, I felt like some kind of a giant weight was on top of me. It was more than just initiation week; it was all of it. It was the South itself, with its fearful history of Indian wars, slavery, segregation, backwardness, and ignorance. It was the old World War II whorehouse behind the rowdy juke joint where I lived. It was Slim, my mother, and this pine tree-covered little corner of nowhere into which I was thrust at birth by my karma.

My fatigue and the pain of my ordeal somehow triggered within me all that had just raced through my mind. If I drew a conclusion from it all, it was that sometimes a person's heritage can become a terrible thing, an oppression, more of a burden and an onus than anything else.

"Young man, come out from in there."

The voice sounded like it was coming from a thousand miles away, like it was a distant echo off the side of an ancient mountain somewhere in a strange and foreign land that I had never studied about in school.

I didn't stir.

"Young man, come out of there this instant; the high sheriff wants to see you."

I looked through the maze of tangled azalea leaves and saw the bottom

293

of a pink housecoat and fuzzy white bedroom slippers. Something about the word "sheriff" and "wants to see you" had gotten my attention.

"Yes mam," was my pitifully weak reply.

Slowly, with great care, I emerged from the azalea bush crawling on my hands and knees. I looked up and saw Mrs. Doric glaring down at me in disgust. In her hand was what appeared to be a woman's housecoat.

"Put this on, and cover yourself," she commanded. "You should be ashamed of yourself, coming around and scaring people out of their wits. I hope the high sheriff throws you in jail."

I wanted very badly to say, "Listen, this whole thing wasn't my idea, and I didn't set out in life to be crawling around naked in your azalea bushes." But, I didn't. To tell the truth, all the fight was out of me. I was so cold, tired, and weak that a small child could boss me around. I reached up and took the housecoat out of her hand. I tried to keep my genitals covered while I remained on my knees and started wrapping it around my waist.

"Don't you dare get my good housecoat dirty. Get up!"

Slowly, I came to my feet and held the housecoat in front of my private parts. Mrs. Doric turned to walk away, and, when she did, I quickly put on the housecoat. It didn't fit. Miss Doric was a small woman, and my arms could barely go through the sleeves. When I finally had it on, the wraparound housecoat needed at least six more inches of terry cloth material before it would cover my genitals. I thought for a minute about asking her for something larger and more masculine, but I decided against it. I did the only thing I could do; I took off the housecoat and quickly wrapped it around my waist and tucked it in like a towel so it wouldn't fall down. When I finished, I saw Miss Doric standing in the light on her back porch glaring at me. She didn't say anything else. She just pointed in the direction of the front of the house, like she was running an old dog out of her yard.

Slowly, I walked through the wet grass toward the awaiting road. I could see the reflections of the bright red lights atop the sheriff's cars flashing in the windows of the houses across the street. As I came around the corner of the house, the sheriff was standing in the headlights of his vehicle talking to a group of about a dozen Sprinkle Field homeowners. I could hear him apologizing for this intrusion into the peace and quiet of their little neighborhood. The sheriff was saying that it was nothing but a bunch of teenagers engaged in silliness and promised he would look into it first thing in the morning.

I did not see any of the other green hands, and I was wondering where they were. The sheriff turned toward me and asked if there was anyone else behind the house. I answered no. He pointed toward his car and told me to get in. I meekly complied, not knowing if I was on my way to jail or not.

The high sheriff's car was one of the flashiest in the county. It was basically an unmarked white Oldsmobile with a high-powered engine and a siren hidden under the hood. Its red light was carefully hidden behind the grillwork over the front bumper. Behind it was the vehicle of the sheriff's one and only deputy. It was a green and white Ford Fairlane with the traditional sheriff's star on both front doors and a bubble-gum-machine-type red light on the roof. Both cars sported long two-way radio antennas, which were spring mounted on the back bumper.

As I approached the sheriff's car, I could see it was full of green hands. There were only eight of us left. We had started the night with ten, but had lost the one guy down at the skating rink when he decided to fight the seniors, and, of course, we had left poor Sidney at the branding barrel. There were four green hands sitting passively in the sheriff's car, not talking, and looking straight ahead. They had a look of shell shock on their faces. I was really relieved to see the other three green hands sitting in the deputy's car. We were all accounted for, and nobody had been shot or killed.

I opened the rear door of the deputy's vehicle and sat down in the back seat just behind the empty driver's seat. All three of the guys had towels wrapped around their waists. I wished I had a towel instead of this ridiculous-looking women's housecoat.

At first, it was as if we were afraid to speak to each other. Sitting in the back seat of a deputy's car can be an intimidating experience for a teenage boy by itself, but sitting in the back of a deputy's car naked with your hands and balls painted green was even worse. Finally, the spell was broken when the boy sitting next to me asked, "Did the sheriff talk to you?"

"No," I replied.

"Are you going to tell them anything if they question you?"

"Fucking-A duke I will."

"You're going to be a snitch?"

"Fuck it, I'm not in the mood for this bullshit anymore."

In reality, I didn't have to tell the sheriff anything. The two boys behind Mr. Rippinger's house had pretty much told the gun-wielding veteran everything about Sidney and the branding barrel, and they later repeated it to the high sheriff. They had not told the sheriff or Mr. Rippinger about anything else that had happened that night.

Personally, I just didn't give a shit. I would have gladly told anybody anything they wanted to know.

The two law enforcement vehicles pulled out of Sprinkle Field with the sheriff driving the lead car and the deputy's vehicle following close behind. On the way, the deputy briefed us on what happened to the boys behind Mr. Rippinger's house. I was kind of glad to be relieved of the burden of not being the first one to talk.

Our first stop was the Ag barns. Nobody was there. The branding barrel had been placed back inside the cinder-block building where it was normally stored; the fire behind the pole barn had been extinguished, and it was dark and quiet, as if nothing had happened. I even saw the fifty-five-gallon oil drum onto which Sidney had been tied neatly positioned around the corner of the building.

We next drove to the Ag building and found everything dark with no sign of life. The sheriff tried to open both doors, but they were locked. We argued that our clothes were inside, but he said he couldn't force the door open without a warrant. The sheriff seemed as if he was getting annoyed with all this nonsense and just wanted to get rid of us so he could go back home.

When we drove up to the jail, I was shocked to see my mother sitting in the parking lot, very impatiently waiting for me to arrive. How did she know I would be there?

When Mrs. Doric saw me in her backyard in the glare of her back porch light, she had slowly turned around and went into her living room. She picked up the phone and calmly called my mother and politely, but firmly, told her that her son was, at that moment, standing naked in her backyard with his hands and private parts apparently painted some type of green color.

My mother went crazy and immediately called the Sheriff's Department. When she finally got through, the lady who worked as the night dispatcher told her that the sheriff was on his way to Sprinkle Field, and the best thing she could do was to come to the jail and wait there for the sheriff to get back.

My mother was not the only parent there. Apparently, as each boy was flushed out of the bushes, the sheriff had relayed their name to the night dispatcher, and she had immediately called their parents. The sheriff had told her to tell the parents to go to the sheriff's office, since he didn't want any more disturbances at Sprinkle Field.

The ride home was filled with my mother lecturing me and asking me all kinds of questions about what happened. I refused to answer. I told her I was sick and only wanted to take a bath and go to sleep. When I got home, all my bothers and sisters were standing and gawking on the front porch. When they saw me drive up, each one had a million questions. I refused to get out of the car until somebody brought me some clothes. In a remarkable display of sensitivity, which was very uncommon for her, my mother told them to leave me alone. She also went into my bedroom and brought me out a clean pair of jeans.

The hot bath I took that night was one of the most pleasurable experiences of my life. Despite the cold shower at the Pure Oil Station, I could still feel and smell the pig shit. It was as if the stuff was up my nose or some other place where I couldn't get at it. I put Merthiolate tincture and hydrogen peroxide on my cuts and burns; it stung like hell, but I didn't mind. I somehow felt as if I was becoming immune to pain. I got into bed sometime around midnight, after spending a considerable amount of time arguing with my mother about why I wouldn't tell her what happened. Slim wasn't at home, and I wanted to get to sleep before he arrived.

I awoke around five in the morning to take a piss. My arm was hurting me so bad I couldn't get back to sleep. Specks had really laid one on me with that oak limb. It throbbed with pain, and it was now stiff, making it hard for me to move my arm. I worried that my shoulder might be broken, but I could move my fingers, so I convinced myself it was just sore and stiff and it would be all right.

I sat on the front porch until past dawn. The dog came up to play with me and I enjoyed his company. There are many crises in life, and this was just one of them and I would have to deal with it. My mother had been talking about me not going to school and wanting to take me to the doctor in Starke, but I would not hear of it. I had to go to school and face the Ag boys and show them I wasn't whipped.

Shortly after daylight, Slim came out on the front porch and sat down beside me. I was glad to see him. He always understood these things better than my mother, who tended to get very crazy and hysterical when confronted by something she didn't understand. And, she totally didn't understand this.

One time, I had gone off to Starke with a group of older boys and got absolutely messed up. I had lived around liquor all my life, and it was inevitable that sooner or later I would have to take a drink.

Back then, teenagers were always looking for a cheap way to get drunk, because we didn't have any extra money to spend on booze. There were all kinds of myths flying around about how to get drunk quickly and cheaply. One of them was to drink beer through a soda straw. If you did, or so the story goes, that one beer was supposed to be enough to get two or three people drunk. Everyone swore it worked, but being a teenage bartender who lived behind a honky-tonk bar, I had my doubts.

However, my opinion carried very little weight. Reality is something nobody wants to hear about or deal with, when that reality interferes with a good time. If you want to get drunk off one beer, and believe you will get drunk off of one beer, you will get drunk off of one beer.

This night, somebody came up with a new idea, mixing whiskey with a milk shake. Somebody had read about it in *Playboy* magazine; it was called a "Brandy Alexander." Since there was no place in Union County that sold milk shakes except the drug store, which closed at five in the afternoon, we drove all the way over to Starke to a late-night hangout called Tuck's Drive

In. There, we purchased a large vanilla milk shake, poured half of it into a second cup, and then filled each cup from a half-pint bottle of Old Grand Dad Whiskey. We passed it around and sipped on the very sweet alcoholic mixture as we drove home.

That night, I prayed to Almighty God to let me die or at least quit vomiting. The guys I rode home with literally dumped me on the front porch of my house, where my mother found me moaning and groaning, covered with puke. I didn't want to tell her I had been drinking, so I said I was sick, probably an appendicitis attack. Of course, Slim knew exactly what was wrong with me, since, many times, he had been in the exact same situation.

To make a long story short, he covered for me, lying through his teeth to my mother, but he never let me forget it. Anytime I walked out the front door to go somewhere, he always warned me not to come back with an appendicitis.

That morning, while sitting on the front porch and watching the sun come up, I told him everything that had happened at the FFA initiations. His emotions went from concern, to anger, and finally to amusement. I could always talk to him and count on him to reign in my mother when she was being totally unreasonable. Luckily, he was the head of the house, and what he said went. My mother awoke that morning with all kinds of bad talk about going to see Mr. Clemmons and demanding an explanation for why her son came home from a school function covered with burns and bruises. All during breakfast, all she talked about was calling the principal, the school board, the superintendent of schools, and on and on. Slim let her blow on for a while and then finally told her to shut up and let him handle it. They were the most beautiful words I had heard since this whole thing started.

Slim drove me to school, and we timed it so I would arrive just as the first bell rang. I didn't want to have to hang around outside facing everybody and answering a lot of dumb-ass questions. The rest of the student body be damned, all I had to face were the Ag boys. I had to show them I wasn't whipped.

The bell had just ceased ringing as I walked up the concrete steps through the double wooden doors into the high school wing of the school. I was walking directly in front of the principal's glass-fronted office when I saw him standing there.

It was Sidney Martin, grinning from ear to ear. He was wearing a pair of cowboy boots, Levi jeans, and a brand-new blue corduroy FFA jacket, with his name neatly stitched over his right breast pocket. Under his name was a small bronze medal.

God almighty damn, he had only been officially in the chapter for less than twelve hours, and he already had a medal?

"What happen to you guys?" the chubby little fuck asked.

"What happened to you?" I asked back.

"We went to the party."

"What fucking party?"

"The party at Harry Stanton's hunt camp out in the woods, just off the Palestine Lake Road. You should have been there; the FHA girls cooked up a great spread—fried chicken, potato salad, and all kinds of cakes and pies. They even let me take a hot water shower in the bunkhouse before they gave me my clothes back. They had you guy's clothes there too, but we didn't know where you went. Specks said that since you ran off like a bunch of little pussies, you didn't deserve no damn party; so I was the only green hand there. After we ate, they had a real nice ceremony, and they presented me with my FFA jacket. Mr. Clemmons said I could be reporter next year, but I needed to start learning the duties now so I would be ready."

I looked at the damned metal on his chest; it read in tiny bronze letters, "Outstanding Green Hand."

"Shit!"

I wanted to beat the shit out of him, but my arm hurt too badly. I couldn't believe that they had made him, the guy who cried like a little baby, the outstanding new chapter member. I was disgusted.

"Did they brand you?" I asked.

"Naw," he laughed, "they just shoved a piece of ice up my asshole. I knew it all along, but I only acted scared to fool you guys."

*Fucking lying asshole!* I thought to myself.

"Where did you get the duds?" I asked, referring to his flashy cowboy boots and Levi jeans. Sidney usually wore typical double-knit nerd clothing.

"My father got them for me," he answered with a big smile. "He said if I was going to be an Ag boy, I would have to look like an Ag boy. He was real proud that I made it into the chapter."

Hurt arm or no hurt arm, this fat bastard and I were going to fight, right now. I started wondering how many licks I could get in before somebody came charging out of the principal's office to break it up.

The ringing of the tardy bell broke my chain of thought. Sidney laughed and said, "Got to go. See you in class." Then, he started to walk off.

He took two steps before he abruptly stopped and turned around. Sidney looked at me and said, "Hey, by the way, Specks is looking for you. We're having a special meeting right after school."

"I won't be there," I replied, letting the tone of my voice show Sidney how thoroughly pissed off I was. He looked a little worried, and then he turned and walked off.

Because of my conversation with Sidney, I was now late for my first period math class and would have to go to the office and get a tardy pass.

When I handed her the tardy pass, my math teacher—who I hated about as much as the subject she taught—had to get in a little bitching about the importance of punctuality before letting me sit down. I didn't want to hear it. As soon as math class was over, I walked out into the hall and hadn't taken ten steps before Specks and Frog immediately accosted me.

"We got to talk to you," Specks said.

"Well, I don't got to talk to you," I said.

I then tried to walk around them, but Frog's hairy hand stopped me cold.

Specks got right up in my face, collared my shirt, and laid it on the line.

"Look, asshole, whatever happened last night is over and done with. You made it; you're in the FFA. It wasn't anything personal; everybody goes through this. This afternoon, we're going to have a special ceremony over at the Ag building just for you chicken shit guys who ran off last night. We're going to give you your clothes back and formally present you with your FFA jacket. We even have some cakes and pies left over from the party last night. All you got to do is show up, keep your mouth shut about what happened, do something about that shit-faced attitude of yours, and you tell your grandchildren you were once an Ag boy."

"I don't want to be an Ag boy anymore."

Specks' face flushed red, and his lip curled menacingly.

"Okay, next year you drop Ag and resign from the chapter, but for right now you're in, and if I hear any more shit out of you, I promise, we will chew you up and spit you out."

Frog stepped forward and stuck a huge finger into my chest. His eyes looked like the headlights of an oncoming freight train.

"I'll take care of it personally," he said. "I'll put an ass whipping on you you'll never forget. Now, gawddamnit be there this afternoon to get your jacket, and you damned better look like you're happy to get it, because if you don't, your next trip to the Ag barns will be one you will never forget."

They weren't bluffing. I remembered the kid from Texas. If I kept being a hard ass, I would wind up like him. I would have to fight every senior in the FFA. I could never be able to go to the movies, the skating rink, or any football game without having to put up with some bullshit hassle from one of the Ag boys trying to prove how tough he was. I didn't want to spend the next four years in one long fistfight, especially since I would probably lose every one of them.

During lunch, I called home and told my mother I would not be on the bus this afternoon. When I told her I had to stay after school for an Ag meeting, she went crazy on the phone. It took me awhile, but I finally calmed her down. I lied and told her that everything was all right and that I would catch a ride home with one of the guys with a car after the meeting.

I hung up the phone feeling really bad. I felt like a gutless coward. I was going along to get along. For the rest of this school year, I would have to put up with two hours of Ag every day, pretending like I liked it. I would have to kiss Specks' ass every day and even suck up to that asshole Mr. Clemmons. I would have to wear the blue corduroy jacket, which I now hated, and carry a blue FFA notebook to class. Even the thought of dating an FHA girl didn't cause me much pleasure. Last night had fundamentally changed me. I just didn't have the heart for it anymore.

Little did I know it at the time, but only a half mile from the school, over at Dukes Cemetery, something had happened that would soon change everything.

One year ago that very day, Mrs. Lillie Mae Townsend's seventy-three-year-old husband had died of a fatal heart attack. Shortly after eight o'clock, about the time that the tardy bell was ringing over at the school, she and her sister Ophelia were driving to Dukes Cemetery to put fresh flowers on her late husband's grave. The two elderly ladies slowly drove their big 1958 Oldsmobile through the cemetery gate and headed up the narrow dirt road toward the Townsend family plot.

In the trunk of their automobile was a twenty-dollar floral display with the words "Husband and Father" emblazoned across a pure silk ribbon. Both ladies had very bad vision that naturally went along with their advanced age, so they really didn't realize that anything was wrong until they got out of the car and approached the late Mr. Townsend's beautiful granite headstone.

They really smelled it before they saw it: an ugly black mark across the top of Mr. Townsend's tombstone.

"Oh my God!" Mrs. Townsend cried out. "Someone has desecrated my husband's grave with animal waste!"

The high sheriff of Union County, Walter Brannon, had been over in Raiford since six o'clock that morning, trying to locate a runaway cow.

He was dead tired. He had not gotten to sleep until after midnight last night thanks to all the silliness at Sprinkle Field, and now he had to get up at the crack of dawn to chase a damned runaway cow. After almost two hours of running through briar patches and broom sedge fields, they finally cornered the brute and managed to get him back into the pasture. The sheriff had been helping the farmer fix the gate that the old cow had kicked down, and he did not hear the first two times the dispatcher at the jail called his signal on the radio.

"Lake Butler S.O. [sheriff's office] to car one [the sheriff's vehicle]," she kept saying. "Lake Butler S.O. to car one, please come in; this is urgent."

When the sheriff finally got to his radio, the dispatcher at the jail was almost hysterical. Her mother was also buried in Dukes Cemetery, and she could hardly contain herself.

"Sheriff," she sobbed into the microphone. "Come quick, this is terrible. Someone has vandalized dozens of graves in Dukes Cemetery."

The sheriff left Raiford and proceeded on Highway 121 toward Lake Butler at emergency speed, with the red light flashing and the siren wailing.

Deputy Sheriff Alfred Witt was the first law enforcement officer to arrive at the cemetery. He had put in a call to Florida Highway Patrolman Charlie Jones for assistance until the high sheriff arrived from Raiford.

Once she had found the excrement on her husband's grave, Mrs. Townsend and her sister Ophelia had immediately drove home and called the sheriff's office, and, as it appeared to Deputy Witt, everybody else in Lake Butler who had a telephone and a relative in Dukes Cemetery.

Before Deputy Witt could get to the cemetery—driving directly from the jail—about half a dozen people had already beaten him there. It took Deputy Witt a long time to clear the people from the cemetery. The women were crying and the men were, to put it mildly, very angry. Deputy Witt only got them to leave by convincing them that they might be trampling on valuable evidence.

The deputy was greatly relieved when he saw the county's only highway patrolman pull up to the cemetery. Now, he would have some help, but he wished the sheriff was there; this whole thing could get very tricky, very fast. The two lawmen got together and quickly worked out a plan of action.

Trooper Charlie Jones pulled his Florida highway patrol cruiser up to block the entrance to the cemetery and posted himself at the gate to keep unauthorized people out of the cemetery. Deputy Witt then quickly surveyed the cemetery and determined that maybe two dozen tombstones had been smeared with a type of animal excrement, which his farm boy childhood told him was from a pig. The worse vandalism was in the family plot of Dr. and Mrs. J. W. King, with every head stone covered with excrement.

*Oh Lord*, the deputy thought to himself.

Back down at the entrance to the cemetery, Trooper Jones was having more and more trouble keeping people out of the cemetery. There were heated words, as people demanded the right to see their family plot to survey the damage. To make matters worse, the crowd was growing at an alarming pace. Within fifteen minutes after the first call went out, over fifty people had gathered at the cemetery, and they were in an ugly mood.

Trooper Jones got on his car radio and briefed the sheriff of the situation as he drove toward Lake Butler. He urged him to get there as soon as possible, because he didn't think he could keep the crowd out much longer by himself. The sheriff reported that he was now nearing Lake Butler and under no circumstances was anybody to be allowed into the cemetery.

Deputy Witt did not hear the conversation on the radio. He had found what he thought was a valuable clue, a set of nearly perfect tire tracks in the road that ran through the cemetery. In the trunk of his car, Deputy Witt carried a Moulage evidence kit. He had purchased it from a police supply house several years ago, and this was his first chance to use it. It consisted of a plastic jug full of tap water, a bag of quick-drying plaster, an adjustable wooden frame, and an aerosol can of hair spray to hold the loose sand in place when the freshly mixed plaster was poured into the frame.

He returned to the cemetery gate, got into his automobile, and drove up the dirt road dissecting the cemetery. He stopped just short of the spot where he had spotted the tire tracks. Deputy Witt then set to work making his tire track impressions. He first sprayed the tracks with the stiff hair spray, and then he carefully positioned the wooden frame to take in as much of the tire tracks as possible. He mixed the water and plaster in a small plastic bucket, and, with a steady hand, he slowly poured the mixture into the frame. As he had been taught in the directions that came with the Moulage kit, he took a small stick and wrote his name and the date and time of the casting in the plaster before it completely dried. Finally finished, he stood up and congratulated himself on a job well done.

It was about this time that Sheriff Brannon arrived at the cemetery. He had cut off his siren as he approached Lake Butler, because he didn't want folks thinking it was the fire siren. Also, in cases like this, it is best not to do anything that will get the people any more upset than they already were.

He didn't like what he saw. The large crowd, which had now swollen to over one hundred people, was ugly and getting uglier. Being the consummate politician, the high sheriff quickly parked his big flashy car and waded into the crowd. He shook every hand and assured the group that evidence was being collected, and he would soon have the perpetrators in jail where they belonged. A small knot of people in the crowd stepped forward to offer the high sheriff a suggestion or theory about who might have done this terrible thing.

"It is those damned beatniks from over in Gainesville," one man confidently proclaimed.

Another man yelled out, "It's them damn integrationists; that's who's behind all this."

One lady was confident that all this was the work of some Satan-worshipping cult operating in this area. Another woman said she had seen some people a few days before she felt sure were gypsies, driving slowly through town as if they might be looking for a cemetery to vandalize. Others said they were positive it had something to do with the Communist Party.

"Communists are bad about doing this sort of thing. They do it to convince the American people that the government can't protect them. I read about it in a book written by J. Edgar Hoover."

The theorists were only a small part of the group. The rest were just very upset and very angry people, who had relatives they loved and cared about buried in the cemetery. Several of the women were crying at the cruelty needed to do such a vile thing. A rumor spread through the crowd that Mrs. Lillie Mae Townsend had been so upset, it was necessary to take her to the hospital. This type of shock could kill a woman of her age.

"Sheriff you better catch whoever did this," was the message Sheriff Brannon received from every man and woman he talked to. "You better catch them before we do."

After giving everyone his personal assurance, the sheriff politely asked everyone to please go home.

The whole crowd in one voice refused. They weren't going anywhere until they had surveyed the damage.

The sheriff didn't know what to do. He remembered clearly the nonsense at Sprinkle Field last night and had a gut feeling that the FFA initiation had something to do with this, not beatniks from Gainesville, integrationists, communists, gypsies, or devil worshippers. His only hope was to get those graves cleaned off as soon as possible, and hope this whole thing blew over.

He walked slowly into the cemetery up the dirt road and carefully examined each of the graves that had pig excrement smeared across the top. The sheriff quickly determined that no damage had been done that a little soap and water would not quickly take care of.

*Heck*, he thought, *the pig manure would make great fertilizer for the grass and flowers around the graves.* However, he wasn't about to go say that to the angry crowd down at the gate.

Sheriff Brannon walked over to talk to Deputy Witt, who was leaning against his police car and waiting for his plaster to dry. Painfully aware that the crowd below was watching their every move closely, Sheriff Brannon ordered his deputy to join him as he walked around the cemetery. It wouldn't do for the crowd to see him loitering around his car, when such a serious crime had taken place.

They walked over to Dr. King's plot, and the sheriff could quickly see that this was where the worse vandalism had taken place. The graves of both Dr. King and his wife were completely smeared with pig shit. However, there was something about the caked and dried excrement on Dr. King's tombstone the sheriff found interesting. He had to stare at it for several minutes before he discovered what it was. The pig shit formed the pattern of a pair of buttocks. It was if someone had smeared pig excrement on their ass and then sat down on the tombstone. *What a weird thing to do,* he thought.

"Look here, sheriff," the deputy said.

Behind the grave of Dr. King, they could clearly see evidence of recent digging. The sheriff bent down and began poking around in the loose dirt with his pocketknife. In a few seconds, he pulled a quarter out of the ground. The sheriff was totally puzzled.

"What the hell is that doing here?" he asked.

The deputy simply shook his head in bewilderment.

The sheriff continued to dig, and, after a couple of minutes, he had retrieved ten quarters. The undisturbed ground under the last quarter showed that there was no more.

The sheriff stood up and slowly fingered the ten quarters in the palm of his hand. Obviously, these ten quarters had some type of significance. He suddenly worried that maybe all of this was not connected to the FFA initiation. He could not imagine them leaving that much money behind in the cemetery. Quickly, he rehashed the evidence in his mind. If somebody was hell bent to do damage, then they would have done a lot worse than simply spreading a little pig crap on the graves and burying ten quarters. It had to be the FFA thing.

Sheriff Brannon and his deputy were not a couple of Barney Fife-type characters. They may have been small-town lawmen, but they weren't stupid, and they certainly weren't cowards. More than once, since he had assumed the office of sheriff after the death of Walter Mizell in 1952, Sheriff Brannon had stared down the barrel of a firearm. Many other times, he had used a combination of good police work and common sense to solve a crime.

Still fingering the ten quarters, the sheriff and Deputy Witt suddenly looked up and beheld a sight that made both their hearts skip a beat. Coming up the dirt road on foot from the entrance to the cemetery was a tall, handsome man with salt and pepper gray hair, wearing an expensive three-piece suit. He took long strides but walked with a slight limp, the result of a land mine explosion in France during World War II

He was State Senator Henry Clayton King, the forty-one-year-old, second oldest son of Dr. and Mrs. J. W. King. He and his brother, J. W. King Jr., were two of the richest and most politically powerful men in Union County. Just the sight of him made Sheriff Brannon almost choke on his own spit. Not even the highway patrol trooper had dared to try and stop Henry King from entering the cemetery. The sheriff immediately began walking toward

Senator King, discretely slipping the sandy quarters into his pocket. They met about halfway to the gate.

"What happened to my parent's graves?" he asked.

"Well," the sheriff said politely, "it's not as bad as it may seem. It is nothing that a little soap and water won't wash off?"

"God damn it. I asked you a question sheriff, and I better get an answer right now, because I don't intend to ask it again!"

The sheriff was totally shocked by Senator King's words and the tone of his voice. Normally, Henry King was a perfect southern gentleman; he was a very soft-spoken man who never took the Lord's name in vain.

Henry King was an honor graduate of the University of Florida with a law degree from Harvard. He had been wounded in World War II as a captain in the U.S. Army and had returned home with the Silver Star and a Purple Heart. In 1952, he was elected to the Florida State Senate, representing both Union County and Bradford County.

Henry King served honorably and proudly in the Senate, and, in 1958, he was chosen to be president of the Senate, a position that also made him chairman of the Florida Democratic Executive Committee. Only a few days before, he had escorted Senator Jack Kennedy of Massachusetts as he toured Florida seeking votes for the upcoming presidential election.

Besides his elected political office, Henry King was also a prosperous lawyer and held extensive timber and real estate interests in Union and Bradford Counties. His brother, J. W. King Jr.—like his father—didn't like politics and concentrated all his energies on his law practice and managing his timber interests. Both men were well known as decent Christian men who neither smoked nor drank. Henry King was chief deacon of the Lake Butler Baptist Church, and I was past grand master of the Lake Butler Masonic Lodge.

Senator King always managed to handle his political interests and business dealings by working hard and treating everyone with honesty and respect. He never flouted his wealth and power; he always preferred to appeal to people's good side and get them to see it his way. However, today was different; this was personal, very personal. Nobody on earth loved his parents more than Henry King, and the thought that someone might have vandalized their graves filled him with a white-hot rage.

"Answer me," he practically screamed at Sheriff Brannon.

"Somebody appears to have smeared animal waste on the top of the tombstones. That's all."

Thomas King turned away in disgust. "That's all? Did you say that's all?"

The sheriff turned white with fear. Never in his life had he seen Senator King this angry.

"I'm sorry senator, bad choice of words."

"Well, you're damned right about that!"

"What I meant was that no permanent damage was done."

"You ignorant shit ass! Somebody smears animal waste on the grave of my mother and father, and you say no permanent damage was done."

The sheriff was now out of words. He just stood there like a delinquent school boy caught playing hooky. He didn't know what to do or say. He thought about mentioning the ten quarters but decided at the last minute not to do so.

"Senator King," he stammered, "I'm sorry; sometimes, the words don't come out right, and I say the wrong thing. I want to assure you that I'm giving this matter my full attention."

"Get out of my way."

With one long stride, Henry King stepped around the sheriff and began walking toward his family plot. As he walked, he thought about his childhood, growing up under the loving guidance of his parents. From his father, he had learned strength and humility. From his mother, he had learned Christian love and charity. They were the two finest people he had ever met, and the low-class scum that desecrated their final resting place would damn sure pay a price for it.

When he arrived at the cemetery plot, Thomas King had to summon up all of his strength to control himself. His eyes misted over, and his fists became tight white balls. The muscles in his jaws became like tight steel bands, but, slowly, his rage turned to quiet sadness. *Who would do this? Who?* he thought.

The sheriff walked up slowly and respectfully, with his hat off.

"Senator King, I think there is something you should know."

"What?"

"I have a suspicion that this might have just been local high school kids messing around. Last night was the last night of the initiations at the high school, and the agriculture boys were all over town doing all kinds of crazy stuff."

Thomas King's voice was calm and steady.

"I don't care if they're little babies in diapers."

"Yes sir, I understand."

"I'm going to send some of my employees over to clean this mess up."

"That won't be necessary," the sheriff said. "I'll take care of it."

Senator King looked straight into the sheriff's eyes.

"You know who did this don't you?"

"Well, not exactly, but I have an idea."

"You, think it might just be kids who didn't realize what they were doing?"

"Yes sir."

Thomas King had now calmed down tremendously compared to only a few minutes ago. The sight of his parent's graves made him think about how they would have handled this. His father had always taught him never to lose his temper, to always maintain control, and never demand a pound of flesh, and that was what he must do now. He knew how kids were, since he had also been kind of wild in his younger days, drinking and gambling much to the distress of his worrying parents. He also had teenage children of his own, two boys and one girl, all passing through the troublesome years of raging hormones and adolescent silliness. Senator King softly apologized to the sheriff for his anger and foul language. The sheriff said that he understood, and there were no hard feelings.

"I want this dealt with properly, do you understand, sheriff?"

"I understand perfectly, senator," the sheriff replied.

Slowly, he turned away from the sheriff and began walking down the dirt road of the cemetery back toward his parked car. As he came to the cemetery gate, he paused to talk to some of the families who had gathered there. He tried to reassure them, telling them that no permanent damage had been done and that the high sheriff had everything under control. Many of the elderly men and women began to cry, and, finally, Henry King broke down and cried with them. The senator was a strong man who had seen combat, but he was not so strong that he could not feel other people's pain. In a few minutes, he regained his composure and spoke to the crowd.

He told them that this was a terribly sad thing, but it was probably done by some misguided person who did not realize what they were doing. He asked the crowd to summon up their Christian faith and follow the example of Christ. He said those headstones were not their loved ones, that their loved ones were in heaven with God, and nothing on earth could change that. He respectfully asked the people to please go home and let the sheriff handle it.

Most of the crowd were older people, who had been patients of Dr. King. The kind old doctor had delivered many of them and had their children delivered by him. They all felt somehow honor bound by a deep debt of gratitude to obey the wishes of his son. Henry King's short speech made everyone feel better. After several minutes of tearfully embracing each other, the crowd slowly began to break up and move toward their cars to go home.

Sheriff Brannon silently watched the scene from a few feet away, and, as he saw the people begin to leave, his only thought was, *Thank God for small favors.*

The sheriff turned and slowly began walking back up the dirt cemetery road toward Deputy Witt with his head down. The high sheriff moved slowly pondering what to do next. There was no way he could cover this up, not with Senator King on his ass. He was determined to find out what happened.

It was at this point that Deputy Witt mentioned the plaster cast. The sheriff thought hard about it. Did he really want evidence that the members of the FFA did this?

The sheriff thought it over for a minute and then turned to his deputy.

"You and the trooper keep things secure here. Don't let anyone into the cemetery."

"Yes sir," the deputy replied.

The sheriff then walked quickly down to his car and drove toward the high school. He glanced at his watch. It was a little after nine o'clock in the morning, and this was going to be a hell of a long day for somebody.

In 1960, Walter T. Thomas was the only superintendent of schools Union County ever had. He had assumed the job in 1921, appointed to the position by the governor. He had been reelected over and over, usually without opposition, ever since. The people of Union County trusted him with their children, and it was a responsibility he took very seriously.

Walter Thomas was born and raised in a nice, two-story house on the courthouse square in Lake Butler. He had been a teenage boy standing in the crowd the night Harry Byrd was baptized. He came from a typically hardworking Christian family, and it was Dr. King who had helped raise the money to send this bright young man to college. Walter Thomas had graduated from the University of Florida in 1917, when the school had less than one thousand students. He was one of the first graduates the College of Education ever produced. It was Dr. Tigert himself who handed him his diploma, and, every time he passed Tigert Hall, the main administration building at the University of Florida, he silently paid his respects to his old teacher.

Walter T. Thomas started out teaching in a one-room elementary school at Midway. Shortly, he became principal of the Lake Butler Normal School. When Union County was created in 1921, he was really the only man qualified for the job of county school superintendent. The governor of Florida at the urgings of Dr. King appointed him to the position.

Over the years, he had guided the school system as it evolved from a small group of one-room schools, scattered all over the county, to the modern U-shaped consolidated school we had in 1960. He had been one of those who, along with Dr. King, had helped convince local citizens for the need for a "Colored School."

In his many years as superintendent of schools, Walter T. Thomas had hired teachers who had remained in the system for over thirty years, and he had fired teachers on the spot who had engaged in improper conduct. There was no doubt in anyone's mind that Walter T. Thomas was the boss, and that was the roll he was playing today.

The tall, razor-thin, and neatly attired superintendent sat behind the principal's desk and stared over his bifocal lens at Sheriff Brannon and the red-headed boy sitting next to him. To his left, Mr. Clemmons and the principal stood nervously. The Ag teacher was pale with fear, his hands were sweating, and he had a nervous twitch in his left eye. He wanted a cigarette more than anything on earth, but he dared not light up or ask to go out for a smoke. His ass was caught in a crack, and he knew it.

"Tell me what happened last night, son?" the superintendent asked Specks in a soft voice.

Specks cleared his throat and answered, "Why nothing unusual sir."

Sheriff Brannon stirred.

Specks glanced nervously at the high sheriff over his left shoulder.

Superintendent Thomas nodded toward the sheriff and said, "Sheriff Brannon, you've had more experience in these types of matters than I have; maybe you need to talk to this young man."

That was what the high sheriff of Union County wanted to hear. He arose from his seat, grabbed Specks by the collar, and jerked him to his feet.

"Now, you listen to me, boy; this is serious business. Nobody's playing with you. Vandalizing a cemetery is a felony in the state of Florida, and, unless you start talking right now and tell me everything that happened last night in the smallest possible detail, so help me God I'm gonna see you on the chain-gang."

If this was only a few years later, Sheriff Brannon would have had to advise Specks of his right to remain silent and to have an attorney, but that wonderful day in America had not yet arrived. On this day, the sheriff of Union County still had the power and legal authority to do what needed to be done.

Because of this boy and his silly bullshit (with some help from a loose cow), the sheriff had had very little sleep in the last twenty-four hours. He had missed his breakfast and was now late for dinner. The sheriff was tired, hungry, and generally pissed off. He thought about the tears in Senator King's eyes and all those old folks down at the cemetery. That made him want to pull out his blackjack and work on Specks' head like he was a punk chicken thief.

"Talk to me, you!"

Specks started talking, and he talked, and he talked, and he talked some more. The FFA code of silence be damned, Specks spilled his guts. He told the sheriff things the sheriff didn't even want to hear. The cigarette butts, the skating rink, the pig shit in the back of the truck, the episode in the cemetery, everything! Specks rattled on, talking and then answering every question put to him by the sheriff and the superintendent of schools. When he finally finished, he was crying like a little boy and begging for mercy.

The sheriff handcuffed Specks and walked him out of the principal's office and into the outer secretary's office and sat him down, directly in front of one of the large glass windows between the principal's office suite and the hallway. The sheriff had timed it perfectly. There was a class change going on between fourth and fifth period, and at least a hundred students passed by the big glass windows of the secretary's office and saw Specks sitting there in handcuffs, balling his eyes out.

When Frog heard about it, he skipped class and fled the campus. It would take until sundown before his family was able to find him, hiding out not far from his home. When Frog found out he was not scheduled for arrest, he was more relieved than embarrassed. That was until he returned to school and had to endure the laughs and jeers of everyone who had heard about his flight from justice. From that day forward, he had a second nickname, "the Fugitive Frog."

The sheriff really hadn't needed to parade Specks out in handcuffs. Everyone knew what was going on from the moment the sheriff and the superintendent of schools walked through the front door of the school about nine-thirty that morning.

The principal had told his secretary. She had told two English teachers. They had told the rest of the faculty, including the home economics teacher, who had told a couple of the FHA girls she knew could keep a secret, and, from there, it spread like wildfire all over the school. Everybody knew certain basic facts. It was about the smearing of pig shit on the graves in Dukes Cemetery. They surmised that Specks and Mr. Clemmons were definitely going to prison and that other people might yet be arrested. When the story finally reached me, I decide to call my mom and tell her I would take her up on that trip to the doctor in Starke. This seemed to be a good time to get out of school, since it was my ass that smeared the pig shit on the grave of Dr. King.

She checked me out of school halfway through fifth period, and I was gone. I spent the rest of the afternoon in the doctor's office in Starke. He X-rayed my arm and found that it was fractured, but not broken. He put it in a cast that I wore for the next six weeks.

I wasn't in school sixth period when the call came over the intercom for all Ag boys to immediately report to the steps in front of the school.

Mr. Clemmons knew the Ag boys didn't pay any more attention to the school intercom than they did to any of the other school rules, so he started running all over the building like a crazy man, pulling everyone with a blue FFA jacket out of class. He had the wild-eyed look of a man possessed by some type of terrible evil spirit. His shirt was soaking wet with sweat, and his hands were visibly trembling. He didn't slow down until he had every Ag boy assembled on the front steps.

He was calling the roll, when Superintendent Thomas and the sheriff came out of the building. Mr. Thomas looked at the frazzled Ag teacher and said, "No freshmen, I don't want any freshmen on this thing."

"Yes sir," the terrified Ag teacher replied. He excused all the freshmen from the gathering, all except Sidney Martin, who said he wanted to go along and help.

After a short briefing from Mr. Clemmons on what was going on, and what they were going to do, the Ag boys scattered all over the school cleaning out every utility closet on campus. They grabbed every can of scouring powder, scrub brush, mop, broom, mop bucket, and water hose they could find. One dumb-ass boy even got a gallon of the white milky stuff they put in the toilets so they don't stink so much. Another brought up a box of those little square things they put in the bottom of the urinals to cover up the piss smell. Mr. Clemmons also collected all the lawn mowers, rakes, shovels, and hoes on campus, and he loaded them into the back of the Ag truck with the other supplies.

Shortly after two o'clock, just as the school buses were pulling out of their loading zone, the two Ag trucks departed from the front of the school and headed for Dukes Cemetery. The entire FFA membership, minus the freshmen, followed the trucks on foot. They looked like a pitiful bunch of blue-jacketed pilgrims on the way to a holy site to do penitence.

They would remain at the cemetery until it was so dark you couldn't see anymore. It was a little after seven-thirty before they were done. Mr. Clemmons stayed on a little while longer working by the light of the truck headlights.

Every tombstone, not just the ones that were smeared with pig shit, were thoroughly scrubbed and cleaned. Gallons of bleach were used to remove all traces of mildew on the headstones. When they ran out of bleach, Mr. Clemmons drove to every grocery store in Lake Butler (both of them) and bought every bottle of bleach they had, using his own money. The grass in the cemetery was cut twice, and every grass clipping was meticulously raked up, put in a bag, and hauled off. When they were finished, not one twig, not one weed, and not one fallen leaf laid on the ground to spoil the view. The cemetery was gleaming spotless.

Most of the Ag boys were not at the football game that night. Once they got home and showered, they just gave out and didn't have the energy to make it to the game.

Once I got back from the doctor's office, I went to my bedroom and slept for over three hours. I showed up at the game during the second quarter with my arm fresh in a cast. I quickly learned what had happened at school and found it all gleefully funny. I spent the rest of the evening hanging out with the other former green hands, flirting with the FHA girls, and speculating if Specks, Frog, and Mr. Clemmons would be sent to jail.

We were standing around the concession stand shooting the bull, when suddenly Sheriff Brannon walked up behind me.

"How you boys doing?" he asked.

"Fine, sheriff," one of the other freshmen answered.

I jumped and spun around speechless. I was afraid I was going to be immediately arrested. However, I quickly saw from the friendly smile on the sheriff's face that he wasn't in an arresting frame of mind.

"Enjoying the game? Think we gonna win?"

"For sure, for sure," we all replied.

This small talk between the sheriff and us went on for another five minutes. I was getting a little nervous wondering when he was going to get to the point. If Specks had ratted out like everyone said he did, then certainly the sheriff knew it was us who actually smeared the pig shit on the tombstones.

"Well, guess I'll be moving along," the sheriff said. "Oh, by the way, I think I got something that belongs to you boys."

He then reached into his pocket and pulled out ten quarters. Without saying a word, he stuck out his beefy arm and handed them to me.

"Don't spend it all in one place," the sheriff laughed and walked off.

We split the loot up among ourselves, and we all immediately purchased a Coca-Cola, a box of Cracker Jacks, and a Baby Ruth bar, all compliments of the Ag boys. We toasted ourselves with the Coke bottles, "Congratulations on a job well done."

At five o'clock the next morning, Mr. Clemmons arose from his slumber with every muscle aching from yesterday's hard work, which he certainly wasn't used to. He walked out into the predawn darkness, climbed into the Ag truck that was parked in his yard, and drove the short distance down to the Ag building. There, Specks and two other seniors were waiting for him with the other truck. Together, the small group drove the two Ag trucks the twenty-five miles to a plant nursery near Maccclenny. They made the journey back and forth six times that morning, each time bringing two truck loads of flowering shrubs and plants to Dukes Cemetery. After lunch, he and the four senior officers, including the now-recaptured "Fugitive Frog," spent all day Saturday setting out the plants.

Mr. Clemmons even made one special trip to Lake City to pick up a load of special high-quality sod, which they carefully put around the plot of Dr. and Mrs. King. After that, they put down fertilizer and grass seed over the rest of the cemetery and watered it in. They didn't finish working at the cemetery until way after dark that evening.

Early Sunday morning, Mr. Clemmons came out to the cemetery by himself and spent all day watering all the newly set-out plants and raking up any dead leaves that may have fallen overnight. He hung around all day, rotating the water sprinklers and making sure everything was in tip-top shape.

Sunday after church is the traditional time in Union County to visit the graves of loved ones. That Sunday, hundreds of people strolled through Dukes Cemetery marveling at how nice it looked. They talked to Mr. Clemmons who was all over the place raking, watering, and sweating like crazy. They had absolute praise for this fine man who would volunteer to give up his weekend to repair the damage the beatnik, communist, integrationist, gypsy vandals from Gainesville had done.

Mr. Clemmons explained to the ladies that as soon as the FFA chapter learned about what had happened, they were outraged and volunteered to clean up the mess and beautify the cemetery. He also said that from now on, the cemetery would be an official FFA project and that they could count on the grounds to always look great. He also said the FFA chapter would be paying for a new fence and locking gate to make sure no more integrationists and beatniks got in after dark.

That was the end of it. It was one of those peculiarly Union County juxtapositions, doublethink, double-talk, duck-your-head-and-run situations. Given a choice between what is true and what suits your personal agenda, people have a natural tendency to believe what they want to believe. The people of Union County made the conscious choice to believe that the desecration of the graves in Dukes Cemetery was the work of beatnik integrationists from Gainesville, rather than the local chapter of the FFA. They couldn't accept that their own children had done this, and it was all a result of childish pranks that just went too far.

That doesn't mean that Mr. Clemmons got off unscathed. He endured one hell of an ass chewing at the hands of the superintendent of schools. Never again would any FFA activity, especially the initiation of green hands, be conducted without adult supervision. For a long time, Mr. Clemmons was forced to accompany us any time we went to the Ag barns, but that didn't last long. He got out of it by protesting that he couldn't be at two places at once. The principal also began to closely monitor the Ag class to make sure Mr. Clemmons was providing all the classroom instruction required by the guidelines for the proper teaching of vocational agriculture. However, that didn't last long either; the principal was a very busy man and could only spend so much time monitoring the Ag class. Generally speaking, by Christmas, things began to cool off, and, by Easter, everything was back to the way it was before initiation week.

To put it mildly, Mr. Clemmons was very angry at the group of freshmen, blaming us for all of his problems. Because he couldn't have his regularly scheduled cigarette breaks, and actually had to teach for a change, he was always very irritable. He often verbalized his displeasure at us during the boring class lectures he was forced to give. He rambled on and on about those who informed on others and once, in a roundabout way, compared us to Judas who betrayed Jesus. The upperclassmen agreed with him, especially the seniors.

Frog and Specks would have loved to kick my ass, but I was saved by two things; first was the cast on my arm. Somewhere in the Union County High School code of macho behavior it said that you couldn't pick a fight with someone with his arm in a cast. Also, the superintendent of schools had given Mr. Clemmons fair warning that he did not want to hear any more bad news from the FFA or he would be job hunting next year. Mr. Clemmons had called in the officers and told them that anybody who got into a fight in Ag class, for any reason, was out of the chapter. When Specks protested, he literally begged them not to start any more stuff with us, saying his job was on the line.

Because he was always in such a bad mood, for a long time none of us freshmen ever bothered to ask him about our jackets. No freshmen except Sidney Martin had the coveted blue corduroy jacket. As the weather turned cold in late November, some of us asked Specks about our jackets. Specks responded by calling us every kind of foul cuss word you could think of and said he hoped to never see any of us wearing the blue FFA jacket.

On the quiet, a group of the freshmen went to the principal and complained. We felt we had endured initiation week and deserved the right to wear the FFA jacket. The principal agreed and told us he would speak to Mr. Clemmons.

The next day, we came to Ag class and saw a large cardboard box sitting on top of one of the tables in the classroom. We didn't know what was in it, so we more or less ignored it.

We tried to stay out of the classroom as much as possible, because we didn't want to cross wires with Mr. Clemmons. We also stayed away from the Ag barns, because that was where the upperclassmen hung out. We kind of staked out our own territory behind the Ag building, under the pole shed where the Ag trucks were parked. We were surprised when Mr. Clemmons came outside later that day and said, "You guys want your jackets or not?" We just sat there and looked at each other. Mr. Clemmons stood there looking back at us with his hands on his hips and disgust on his face.

"If you're waiting for me to bring them out to you, you're going to have a long wait."

"Where are they?" I asked.

"In the damned classroom in the box."

We didn't all just jump up and run inside. We just sat there and tried to look cool. I told him we would get them in a few minutes, and that made Mr. Clemmons' face go flush red with anger.

After he walked off, we just sat there until we couldn't stand it any longer, and then, one at a time, we slowly got up and went inside.

I was the last freshman to go inside. I found one lone jacket lying rumpled in the bottom of the cardboard box. I assumed it was mine. When I pulled it out, I immediately noticed that my name, which should have been stitched in golden yellow thread on the right breast, had been carefully removed by pulling out the thread, a masterful piece of work by some girl in the FHA. A quick check showed that all the other freshmen's names had been likewise removed. Later, Mr. Clemmons would claim they had come from the factory like that, and if we wanted our names on the jacket, we would have to pay for it ourselves, and he didn't know anybody who did that kind of work. Of course, that was a lie, since Sidney Martin's jacket had his name properly sewed on, and there were dozens of FHA girls who were good enough with a sewing machine to put our names on the jackets.

Without the names sewn on the right breast pocket, it was difficult if not impossible to find out whose jacket belonged to whom. The other freshmen had found theirs by the process of trial and error, trying on jacket after jacket, until they found the one that fit. When I tried on the jacket in the bottom of the box, it didn't fit worth a damn. It was so small I couldn't even zip it up. Some of the others jackets looked a little too large, and I thought maybe they might have on my jacket by mistake, but I decided not to say anything about it. I just didn't care anymore.

I stayed in the FFA for the rest of my freshmen year, but I never went to any meetings nor did I attend the FFA's social events not even the FFA–FHA banquet and prom. I flatly refused to be part of the group photo that appeared in the yearbook. The next year, I did not sign up for vocational agriculture, although Specks and Frog had graduated, and I had a right to do so if I so wanted. Well, to be more correct, Specks graduated. Frog was half a credit short. He never came back to school to finish it. The last time I saw him, he was working at a paint and body shop over in Starke. Specks couldn't find a job, so he went into the navy for four years. When he got out of the navy, he went to work at the prison in Raiford. He still works there today.

During junior year in high school, something happened that shocked Union County and filled me with sadness. In September of 1962, Deputy

Sheriff Alfred Witt was shot and killed. The killing was a loss of innocence for Union County, a clear indication that the times were changing forever in the small rural county. Killed with Deputy Witt was one of the sheriff's young nephews. He was only twenty-four years old. Allegedly, the young boy had been made a special deputy; however, in reality, he had only gone along for the ride.

Alfred Witt had arrested the man who killed him, several times in the past for being drunk and disorderly. Other than not being able to hold his liquor, he had no criminal history. Every time the deputy had arrested him in the past, he had more or less gone along peacefully to sleep it off in the jail. Alfred Witt had no idea that this time the man would not go along peacefully.

The night before, he had got drunk and fired a shotgun into a neighbor's house. Apparently, he and his neighbor's wife were hitting it off. The cuckolded neighbor drove into Lake Butler and sworn out a warrant. It was such a routine arrest, the sheriff decided to wait until the next morning before serving the warrant. It was just typical Union County lawman's work.

They next morning, Deputy Witt and the sheriff's nephew drove up to the man's house near Raiford. The sheriff stayed behind in Lake Butler. He had a meeting with the clerk of the Circuit Court to do some paperwork. When Deputy Witt arrived at the house in Raiford, it was a little after eight o'clock in the morning. The air was balmy, and the sky didn't have a cloud in it. The two deputies got out of their vehicle and knocked politely on the old screen door of the small farmhouse. When the man came to the door, they calmly told him they had a warrant for his arrest. Now sober, but badly hung over, he seemed to accept the arrest and asked to go back in his bedroom to put on his shoes. Deputy Witt agreed and stood by the front door waiting for him to return. In a few minutes, the man returned with his shoes on, carrying a twelve-gauge pump shotgun. In the flash of an eye, he fired though the screen door, and Albert Witt fell over dead. The sheriff's young nephew didn't have a chance. Unarmed, he was shot to death as he tried to flee to the deputy's car, the same vehicle I rode in that Thursday night of initiation week.

The man then reached down and took Albert Witt's nickel-plated Smith and Wesson service revolver and walked into his bedroom. He sat on his bed and took a sip of whiskey from a bottle on the night table. He then slowly put the revolver to his chest and pulled the trigger. The bullet went straight through his heart, and he was dead by the time his head hit the mattress.

# The Light on the Edge of Town

I graduated from high school in June of 1964 and immediately began doing the paperwork necessary to join the U.S. Air Force.

I had been pondering this decision for four years, interviewing everyone I knew who had been in the military, and wanting to find out what each branch of the service was like. Jack had convinced me that I didn't want to have anything to do with the Marine Corps. My brother Ace had gone into the navy, and, to be totally honest, I really didn't like the uniform Ace wore home. I wasn't about to go around with my wallet in my mouth, because I didn't have any pockets. I also didn't like that stupid-looking little white hat and fooling around with all those buttons every time I had to take a piss. Charlie had gone into the Army, and he never got any further away from home than Fort Jackson, South Carolina. He had spent most of his enlistment at Fort Benning, Georgia. That was not for me. I wanted to travel and see the world, but not through a four-inch-diameter porthole. By the process of elimination, I decided on the air force. It had a nice-looking uniform, and there were air force bases all over the world.

I couldn't wait to get out of Union County, and I was willing to pay any price to do so. I practically lived at the recruiting station in Gainesville, bugging the staff sergeant behind the desk about what career field I should get into. The air force isn't like the army; they don't just take anybody warm and breathing. I was given a battery of tests that I just knew I flunked, but the recruiter assured me that my grades were "acceptable." I had no mechanical or electronic aptitude, and my test scores in these two areas were so low, even the recruiters' lies couldn't fool me. The test for the general career field was primarily a basic math and reading test, and I did well on that. Little did I know that the general career field included such exotic jobs as landscaping, food service, fire fighting, and what was considered the worst job in the air force—the security police.

When I first went to the induction center at the naval air station in Jacksonville, I flunked my physical because of my weak eyes. I was terrified. If I couldn't get into the air force, then I really didn't have anywhere else to go. I had no money to go to college, and my SAT scores were not high enough to get me in any institution of higher education. It was either the air force or the life of my parents, forever trapped by economic circumstances in Union County, working at some low-wage, dead-end job. I just had to get into the air force.

While I was sweating blood that I wouldn't get into the air force, in August of 1964, something happened on the other side of the world that would fundamentally change my life, and with one bold stroke, forever erase my childhood.

Allegedly, North Vietnamese gunboats had attacked a group of U.S. naval vessels. They were calling it the Gulf of Tonkin incident. However, back in Union County, I paid almost no attention to it. It was just another news story.

Shortly after the Gulf of Tonkin incident, the air force finally decided my eyes weren't that bad after all, and they accepted me. I was ordered to report to the induction station on September 14, 1964. I got there a day early to make sure I wasn't late. The next afternoon, I was sworn in and was gone like a bat out of hell.

A year later, I was at a secret air base near the Thai–Cambodian border, serving as a security policeman, guarding F-4C jet fighter bombers that were flying top-secret missions and bombing North Vietnam and the Ho Chi Minh trail. I now knew why the air force felt that my eyes weren't so bad after all. The air base in Thailand wasn't even supposed to be there, and we weren't supposed to be bombing Vietnam from a supposedly neutral country. So, I guess it was really an asset that I couldn't see too well.

After a brief respite in the States, I returned four months later for another remote Southeast Asian tour. This time, I was stationed at a desolate, unbearably hot and muggy airfield on the coast of Vietnam. Security police duty in Vietnam was pure hell. We slept in old army general-purpose tents, in a place where the temperature soured to over one hundred degrees on a cool day. At night, we pulled twelve-hour shifts. We sat behind M-60 machine guns, peered out into the dark and wet night, tried to stay awake as the night turned cool, and hoped to God that we wouldn't see or hear anything. For a year, I vacillated between a heat stroke in the daytime and pure terror of a violent death at night.

While I was in Vietnam in 1966, Union County High School, in compliance with the 1964 Civil Rights Act, was racially integrated.

It happened with the peace and calm of the changing of the moon. All those people who had vowed to die first, to never give in, and to fight to the death all just rolled over and accepted it without so much as a grumble. It proved to me something I had always suspected. Despite all their macho bullshit, despite their shotguns and stuffed deer heads and despite all their badass talk, underneath they were all a bunch of gutless cowards.

However, despite the calm, the coming of integration marked the end of the initiation week tradition.

The school board declared a state of emergency and canceled all extracurricular activities. There was serious talk for a while of canceling football and basketball. However, cooler heads prevailed. At the urging of the superintendent of schools, the major sports—football, basketball, baseball, and track and field—continued. However, the school board did do away with all club initiations, banquets, proms, school dances, pep buses, and senior trips; even the junior–senior play was canceled because of the fear that a script might call for a black boy and a white girl to hold hands or, heaven forbid, kiss.

The school still offered vocational agriculture as an academic choice, but the FFA chapter was closed down for over four years. All the animals were sold, and the land was allowed to become overgrown with broom sedge and weeds. They kept the farm equipment, but it slowly rusted away from neglect. The Ag program was rewritten to deemphasize farming in favor of vocational education. For the first time, all the woodworking and auto-maintenance equipment, which had been neatly stored and unused in the back of the Ag building, was finally broken out and put to use.

In 1969, Mr. Clemmons retired from teaching on a medical disability, claiming that the stress of integration had given him a heart condition. He must not have been lying, since he died of a heart attack in 1973.

In 1978, a late-night fire broke out in the auditorium section of the redbrick, U-shaped building that had made up Union County High School. Exactly what caused the holocaust has to this day never been determined, but the fire spread with the speed of a blazing locomotive. By the time the first fire trucks arrived, the old pinewood, oil-soaked floors had transmitted the flames to all corners of the building, and the roof was already falling in. When daylight broke the next morning, the building was nothing more than a pile of charred bricks and still-smoldering ashes.

For the first time in its history, Union County parents did not have a place to send their children to school. In a larger school district, another school could have been put on double sessions and classes would go on. However,

Union County had no other school building. The old U-shaped, redbrick structure was all there was. The old "Consolidated School" or "Colored School" had become Lake Butler Elementary School, and all of its classrooms were geared for elementary-aged kids.

In a crisis, people forget their differences and pull together. This was just the type of calamity to bring out the very best in people and prompt a tidal wave of community support. The whole county rallied to help the school system cope with the disaster. Classes were held in every Sunday school building in the county. Both the black and white churches pitched in to help, and both the black and white churches were needed. Every public and fraternal building was also put into use; the Masonic lodge, the Women's Club, the Garden Club, and even the county courthouse offered space for classes. When the crisis had passed, there was a strong feeling of community cooperation between black and white people that had never existed before.

A new Union County High School was quickly built on the land that had once been the Ag barns and the football field. The site of the old high school became the grounds of the new modern Lake Butler Middle School.

Although the Union County school system was now racially integrated and mandatory school attendance laws were being equally enforced for both black and white students, it was still the smallest school system in the state. The entire Union County school system is housed in only three buildings.

In June of 1996, I received a phone call from an old Ag boy, whose voice I had not heard for over thirty years. He was inviting me to our thirty-second-year class reunion. I told him I would have to think about it.

Class reunions can be a scary thing; and, for me, they can be much scarier than for most people. A lot of water had gone under the bridge since 1964, and I really wasn't sure that old home week was such a good idea.

After getting out of the air force in 1968, I had used my GI Bill to attend the University of Florida and discovered that I wasn't as dumb as I thought I was. After six years of higher education, I managed to land a comfortable teaching job in Palatka. My life was moving along really well, and Union County now seemed a long time ago and a far-off place.

The voice on the other end of the phone line told me that the reunion was to be held at the newly built Civic Center in Worthington Springs on a Saturday night in June 1996.

Worthington Springs is a pleasant hour-and-a-half drive from my home in Palatka, and, in many ways, it is a journey back through time. In order to get to the Civic Center in Worthington Springs, I had to drive past many of my old teenage haunts.

The house I grew up in—the remnants of an old World War II whorehouse that Slim had turned into a home—had long been abandoned. It was now so overgrown with weeds and vines that it couldn't even be seen from the road. It is really a sad thing to see your childhood home in such a shape. When people die, we bury them and they are out of sight and mind. However, you have to go through the emotional hell of watching the house you grew up in slowly rot away in the heat and humidity of the Florida summer.

I reached Lake Butler around six o'clock, and since the reunion wasn't scheduled to begin until seven, I still had plenty of time, so I decided to cruise around a bit.

Lake Butler is still a quiet and peaceful town. Most of the old homes are still standing, except that now the occupants have changed. Dr. King's grandson and great-grandson are both prominent attorneys with offices in Lake Butler, Starke, and Lake City. The King and King law firm's main office is in a modern building across the street from the remodeled and enlarged Union County Courthouse.

Several years ago, the old skating rink down by the lake was turned into a seafood restaurant. It seemed really strange to see black children swimming in the lake. When I was in high school, such a thing would have gotten them arrested.

The school looks nothing like it did in 1960. The only building remaining that was there in 1959 is the gymnasium, and it has been extensively remodeled. Even the old Ag building is gone; it was torn down to make room for county administrative offices.

After thinking about it for some time, I decided to go by Dukes Cemetery. My mother lays in eternal repose close to the plot of Dr. King. Every time I visit the cemetery, I always walk over to the King family plot and silently apologize to Dr. and Mrs. King for smearing pig stuff on their headstones.

A few feet from my mother lays Jack, my old ex-marine moonshine partner. He died of a blood clot in 1993. Also in Dukes Cemetery is the grave of Mr. Rippinger, the former paratrooper who one night discovered teenage boys hiding in his bushes. He suffered a fatal heart attack while responding to a fire in 1969. I liked Mr. Rippinger and was sad he died so young. David Richard—the great turkey hunter, whose eagle eyes spotted three convicts in his house—passed away of cancer in 1990. Miss Doric—the irascible librarian who lent me her housecoat that chilly fall night in 1960—died unmarried and unbowed of old-age-related health problems in 1979. Harry Byrd also sleeps there, but the site of his grave is forever lost to time; only the story of his famous siren lives on.

Some of the Ag boys are also in the cemetery. Two never even finished high school; they both died in a violent car crash trying to out run a highway patrolman on Highway 301 between Starke and Waldo. Three have died of heart attacks in their mid-forties; several more have died of various forms of cancer, associated with their lifelong smoking habits. I had given up the noxious sot weed while attending the University of Florida and getting the degrees necessary for a comfortable life teaching.

PFC Sidney Martin, the little fat kid on the branding barrel, was killed in 1969 while serving with the First Infantry Division in Vietnam. Poor old Sidney had volunteered to take over for a forward artillery observer who had gone on R&R to Hong Kong. One dark and wet night, with his nearsighted eyes clouded with sweat in the thick jungle foliage, he misread his coordinates and called in a bee-hive round from a 105 howitzer too close to his own position. The deadly pellets from the artillery shell cut him in half.

His mother and father were devastated. He was their only child. They had planned for him to go on to college and become a doctor or lawyer. Sidney had graduated with honors from Union County High School, and he had already completed two years at Lake City Community College when he received his notice to report for a draft physical. Instead of complaining and trying to get out of it, Sidney dropped out of college, and, without consulting with his family, he immediately joined the U.S. Army. Sidney wanted to be in the Special Forces and wear a green beret, just like he wanted to be an Ag boy and wear the blue corduroy jacket. Sidney though it would make his father so proud of him when he came home in his bloused paratrooper boots and green beret.

The chubby little Sidney never even made it though Jump School. He flunked the physical fitness part of paratrooper training and was denied admission to the Special Forces. However, with the war in Vietnam raging at its zenith, the army still had use for the fat little soldier. Ashamed that he could not get into the Green Berets, Sidney turned down a chance to become a clerk typist and volunteered for combat in the infantry. He was placed in the Big Red One and sent to Vietnam. Before he left, he promised his father that he would win medals in Vietnam, just like he had won medals in the FFA, and so he did. What could be found of PFC Sidney Martin's body lies in the same cemetery where he once hunted for quarters on top of tombstones.

Sidney's father died of cancer in 1992, but his mother is still alive. She lives in a nursing home. I once went by to see her. She told me she is often very sad and lonely and has few visitors. She mentioned to me several times that since Sidney died so young, she didn't have any grandchildren. I really felt sorry for her.

Specks and Frog never went to Vietnam. Specks had a high draft number, and Frog was 4-F because of his speech problem and low IQ scores. Both of them still live in Union County; they are plagued with bad health, living on fixed incomes, and barely getting by.

Standing there in Dukes Cemetery, I suddenly had a strange, almost frightening feeling. I suddenly realized that I could almost relive my entire life just by walking around that cemetery. It reminded me of something Slim used to say. "You can tell you're getting old, when you know more dead people than live ones."

There are a number of fears one must deal with at a class reunion. The first is that your old classmates will all be rich and hugely successful, while you're just some pea-dunk schoolteacher. Before I went into the Civic Center in Worthington Springs, I had circled the parking lot several times looking at the automobiles. If I had seen a single Mercedes Benz, I was simply going to turn around and go home and pretend that this night never happened. However, what greeted me was a typical collection of fairly cheap automobiles and a large number of pickup trucks. This gave me the courage to go inside.

High school graduation is a funny thing; it is almost like having another birthday, a milestone by which you measure your life and progress. Some of the people you graduate with, you will never see again as long as you live. They will simply walk out of that auditorium that night and out of your life forever. Others, you will promise to keep in touch with, and you will, for a while. However, time will move along, and the two of you will drift apart as life offers up new friends and challenges. Fate might cast you together with others from time to time, and still others may become a life partner.

At first, I felt as much like a stranger. Who were these people? I didn't recognize anyone. I picked up a copy of the yearbook lying on the table by the sign-in desk and tried to match up names and faces. Slowly, the mists of time parted, and they once again became familiar faces.

Most of these people I had not seen since the night in 1964 when I walked across the stage of the old high school auditorium. They were all now in their early fifties, and, to my pleasant surprise, they looked fairly good. My second greatest fear was that I would encounter a room full of geriatric cases in wheelchairs with oxygen tanks, a morbid prequel to my own final years of mortality.

I was surprised how many of them had never left Union County, continuing in the tradition of their parents, and mine, to live their entire lives within only a few miles of where they were raised. At Union County High School, they had learned the important lesson about staying with your own kind.

To most of them, life had been a real bitch with divorces, alcoholism, debts, drugs, layoffs, problem kids, and all the other assorted pressures of modern living. They had survived. They lived from paycheck to paycheck, paid their bills, and raised their children.

They were basically a blue-collar bunch of people working at various local manufacturing plants in the north Florida area. They had survived for decades putting together flashlight batteries and sewed clothing at an apparel factory that eventually closed and moved to a cheaper labor market in Honduras. Others drove rock trucks, and still others cut sheet metal and did paint and body work. Some worked for the post office, and others worked for the telephone company. The class boasted one doctor, but he didn't come. Several had taken over their father's farms, stores, and pulpwood business, carrying on the family's traditional southern professions.

However, most of my old classmates had worked for the Florida Department of Corrections in one capacity or the other. The Department of Corrections is now the county's largest single employer. The sons and daughters of pulpwood workers and poor dirt farmers wear the omnipresent brown-on-brown uniform of the Florida Department of Corrections.

Others, like me, had become educators, serving on the front lines of America's war on ignorance.

While I was at the reunion, I struck up a conversation with an old classmate, Verba Jean Kelly. I had only known her from a distance in high school. She was one of those girls you only dream about. She had been a cheerleader and vice president of the senior class. She had the bad luck to have been chosen homecoming queen at the Friday night football game the same day John F. Kennedy had been shot in Dallas. The assassination cast a damp, cold pallor over what would have normally been a festive occasion, and it left Verba Jean with bittersweet memories.

After high school, she had gone to Florida State University and graduated from the College of Education. She had returned to Union County to teach and wound up marrying the football coach. She still lives in the house of her late mother and father and has three children and four grandchildren.

Since Verba Jean and I were both veteran schoolteachers, we immediately struck up a conversation and swapped war stories about how bad kids are today. We both insisted that today's kids say and do things we would never have even dreamed of doing when we were their age. Of course, I knew all that was total bullshit, but I played along, because I wanted a favor from her. I wanted her to arrange for me to take the fifty-cent tour of the new Union County High School.

Verba Jean was cooperative, and the whole thing was arranged at the reunion in June. I returned the next fall to have my first look at the new Union County High School.

It is a modern facility, with a lot of glass, artificial wood wainscoting, and highly polished terrazzo floors. There is none of the heaviness and remote scent of pine oil found in the old building. Everything seems much more light and airy. Like most ultramodern institutions, this one also left me with a feeling of cold, almost antiseptic, impersonality. Somehow, the dark wood wainscoting and heaviness of the old school gave me a feeling of walking in the footsteps of the ancient ones. The remote scent of pine oil told me that everything was being taken care of, and all was in good order.

In Union County, they still pledge allegiance to the flag, read a verse of scripture, and recite the Lord's Prayer over the intercom. In a small school district, you can get away with things you couldn't normally get away with in a larger district. To this day, there are no Jews and only a handful of Catholics in Union County. It is still a place where it doesn't pay to cause trouble or question the way things are done.

Each classroom was ultramodern with aluminum and plastic desks. The chalkboard is now green instead of black, except that most teachers use an overhead projector, which casts bright, black and white images on a specially designed screen. Each classroom is equipped with banks of computers, and each has a television set hung from the walls on metal perches. The wide main hallway is flanked on both sides with one long, glass-fronted trophy case after another. Union County's football team is better than ever. The school had even risen to state champions in their division. It was something, by the way, that never happened before integration gave them the services of black players.

Across the street from the high school on land that used to be wooded stands a modern brick building with a large sign in front that says, "Vocational Agriculture." I told Verba Jean that I especially wanted to see the Ag building. She was a little puzzled at this request, because she knew I was a history teacher and thought I would naturally want to see the social studies department first.

As we stepped into one of the agriculture classrooms, I immediately saw that it was all still there: the great seal, the owl, the ear of corn, and the rising sun. The classroom was even arranged as it had been in the early sixties, except that now plastic and aluminum desks replaced the old wooden tables.

However, I would soon learn that the arrangement of the classroom didn't mean that everything was the same. I immediately noticed a total absence of cigarette smoke or chewing tobacco stains. The Ag teacher stepped out of his computer-equipped office to speak to Verba Jean and me.

His name was Chuck (short for Charles) Tyler. He was a young man with dark eyes and sandy hair. I could tell at a glance he was not another Mr. Clemmons. He was wearing a typically yuppie, pullover Izod's knit shirt and Duck Head tan trousers. The tired eyes behind his metal-rimmed glasses told me that he had spent many hours behind a computer screen and between the pages of college textbooks.

Chuck told me he had graduated in 1982 from Clemson at the top of his class. His father had been one of the largest cotton growers in South Carolina and was very proud of his son's accomplishment. Chuck decided to go for his Master's degree in Agriculture at the University of Florida, primarily so he could put a little distance between himself and his parents for a while. He had spent four spring breaks in Daytona and Fort Lauderdale and found that he truly loved the balmy Florida beaches and the beautiful, tan college girls he discovered on them.

While lying on the snow white sand of Crescent Beach one warm spring afternoon, he had made the acquaintance of a beautiful young Liberal Arts major, who lived only a few blocks from his fraternity house in Gainesville. They went out on a date the next weekend, began dating steady after that, eventually fell in love, and were married at her parent's home in Tampa two years later.

Chuck told me that he was only teaching in Union County until his wife finished her PhD in Art Education. He was thinking about going for a PhD in Agricultural Economics so he could teach on the college level. However, he wasn't really sure of his future plans. His father was starting to talk about retirement, and he fully expected to have to go home one day and take over the family's extensive agricultural interests.

Chuck was a physically fit young man who did not smoke or drink. I noted from the pictures and trophies in his office that he played tennis, golf, and was a five-kilometer marathon runner.

"Is this your only classroom?" I asked.

"Oh no," he replied. "We have this room and my office, but most of our students are in the agriculture computer lab."

"The Ag boys are in the computer lab?"

"Ag boys?" he asked me, with a look of total puzzlement on his face.

"Excuse me," I answered politely. "But, you see, I teach in a middle school, and we do not have vocational agriculture per se, and it has been a long time since I took it in high school. I am trying to determine how much things have changed. Do you still have an FFA chapter in Union County?"

"Why certainly," he answered. "I'll introduce you to Cindy our chapter president."

The president of the FFA chapter, the successor of Specks and Frog, was named Cindy!

As it turned out, Cindy wasn't just a young woman; she was an African American young woman. She was a beautiful girl with high, Indian-style cheek bones that made her look like a highly paid fashion model on the cover of *Vogue*. Cindy was also vice president of the senior class, a member of the basket ball team, and a varsity cheerleader. As soon as we entered the agriculture computer lab, she arose from her work station and greeted us. Chuck explained who I was and asked Cindy to show me around.

With the sophistication and professionalism of a college instructor, Cindy began to carefully explain to me the current projects that the FFA chapter was involved in. As she spoke, I immediately realized why the teacher had been so puzzled at my use of the term "Ag boys." There were just as many young ladies in the computer lab wearing the familiar blue corduroy jacket as there were boys. There were African American, Caucasian, Hispanic, and one Asian face staring into the rows of computer screens.

Union County had changed demographically since I had left, becoming somewhat more racially diverse. It still isn't a melting pot by any stretch of the imagination, but some foreigners have managed to move in and survive.

I learned from Chuck that the young Asian boy was Filipino and that his father was a doctor at the Lake Butler Reception and Medical Center, part of the ever-growing prison system in Union County.

The Hispanic children were mostly the children of the migrant farm workers who flooded into Union County each year to help harvest the tobacco crop. Some had stayed on, finding full-time jobs doing one thing or the other. It was usually some type of low-paying menial farm work, but it was the first step on the pathway to the American dream. These brave people were willing to take the shit jobs that nobody else wanted just so their children and grandchildren could have something better. They were treading down the same path that so many other immigrant groups had trodden over the centuries. The only difference was that the Irish Catholics, Poles, Jews, and Italians had always somehow managed to avoid Union County, but these people had not.

The black children had moved up significantly in life; most of their parents either worked with the prison system, making the same salary as their white counterparts, or farmed their own land, growing tobacco and corn. One young black boy's father had a fleet of fifteen pulpwood trucks, all hauling pine logs to the paper mill over in Palatka. Their dress reflected their new affluence. Almost all the black children sported high-priced Nike sneakers and two-hundred dollar jackets adorned with prominent NFL logos.

I saw deep within the eyes of the white children in the room faint echoes of the provincialism and xenophobia I knew as a teenager. However, the outright racism was mostly gone; they viewed the African American, Asian, and Hispanic children sitting in the classroom with them as their friends and classmates. The only deep divisions within the school today are between those who wore the garnet and gold colors of the Florida State Seminoles and the orange and blue of the Florida Gators.

Cindy began to explain to me how the students used computers to solve agricultural problems.

"Are you Microsoft or Macintosh?" she asked.

"I'm a die-hard Mac man," I answered, proud of my newly found computer literacy.

"That's good. So are we basically; however, we have now began to use Microsoft so our students will be familiar with both systems."

I couldn't help but try and imagine that ignorant bunch of Ag boys I remembered trying to operate a computer. Driving a stick-shift pickup truck used to confuse them all to hell.

"What system are you currently using?"

"I have a 6200c Mac, and I love it."

"That's a very good system. Many of our students are still forced to use the old Apple IIe's, but we are upgrading as fast as possible. It's very expensive to keep up with the fast-paced technology of computers."

All I could do was stand there and politely nod my head in agreement.

Cindy slowly began to walk around the room stopping at each computer work station and explaining what was going on.

Her first stop was at the computer terminal of a young Hispanic girl, who had the delightfully beautiful name of Lizamina Cruz. Lizamina was putting together a database to keep track of all the farm animals, reflecting their genders, birthing information, weight gain, vaccinations, and feeding schedules. Each time an animal was fed, vaccinated or wormed, it was recorded. When the animal was finally sold, there would be a detailed record of all expenses that could be subtracted from the final selling price of the animal, thus clearly indicating the profit margin.

The next student was a chunky white boy, who was using a spreadsheet to determine all the farm expenses and profit margins from the sale of crops and livestock. He explained that one of the biggest causes of farm bankruptcy was the failure of farmers to keep an accurate record of their expenses and profits. With this spreadsheet technology, every farmer can tell on a day-to-day basis how they are doing and either make cost cutbacks or spend extra money depending on what the data showed.

The next student, a tall, light-skinned, African American girl was using a high-speed modem to access the Internet. She was collecting data on current weather trends to determine the optimum time to plant next spring's crops.

"We have data on the date of the last frost going back almost fifty years," she explained. "With this information we can determine the earliest date that sensitive crops can be planted with no danger of frost damage. On the other end of the season, these data tell us how late in the year crops can be planted without danger of freeze damage. It is an excellent program for citrus farmers."

One of the things that most surprised me was how many students were working on problems dealing with ornamental horticulture, rather than the growing of corn, beans, cotton, or tobacco. Chuck Tyler explained that north Florida was becoming a major area for the production of ornamental house and garden plants. There were several huge nurseries and ferneries within only a short distance from Lake Butler. Ornamental plants require a lot more careful planning than truck crops. Each one has its own special needs in the use of fertilizers and pesticides. It is a multimillion dollar industry that the FFA needs to tap into.

"We try to avoid the over use of fertilizers and pesticides," Chuck explained. "When we are forced to use them, we try to only use those that are biodegradable to protect the environment and use only the bare minimum required to keep our expenses down. Computers help us keep track of how much pesticide or fertilizer we need per acre to get the job done, and no more."

This was a far cry from the philosophy of Mr. Clemmons who was always preaching that the more fertilizers and pesticides you used, the better.

"Do you have any Ag barns?" I asked.

The puzzled look on Chuck's face told me I had to explain further.

"You know, someplace where the kids can get hands-on experience feeding animals, plowing, that sort of thing."

Chuck smiled and said, "We don't have that kind of place on campus, but we have an arrangement with local farmers, and we also have the use of the agricultural substations run by the Institute of Food and Agricultural Sciences at the University of Florida.

Chuck gently reminded me that most jobs in the field of agriculture today are not driving-a-tractor-type farming jobs, but rather things like timber management for large paper companies and ornamental horticulture at the big nurseries, not to mention research and development positions with the University of Florida.

"We also have an excellent wildlife management program, for students who might be interested in finding jobs working in resource management with the U.S. Forest Service or the National Park Service."

We left the computer lab and walked outside to a large greenhouse where a group of students were growing orchids. Again, I was flabbergasted and amazed that these kids had the agricultural sophistication to grow orchids. All we ever grew was corn and beans. These young people with their computer data banks and spreadsheets are so much smarter than we were, it isn't even funny. Vocational agriculture is no longer a joke class for boys too stupid to pass anything else. It is also no longer a refuse for the Neanderthals of the school system. These kids work hard for the grades they get and take what they are doing very seriously.

Cindy spoke up as we exited the greenhouse. "Did you watch those horrible images on television of the famine in Ethiopia?"

When I nodded my head, she continued, "So did I; that's why I decided to follow a career in agriculture. After I finish high school, I have a full scholarship to go to Florida A&M University in Tallahassee. I hope to travel to Africa and work with the Peace Corps or the United Nations. I will do whatever I can to make sure I never again have to look at any other children with bloated bellies. What a lot of people just don't seem to understand is that what we're doing in this county is feeding the whole world. The new types of corn we develop here in Florida and the freeze- and insect-resistant crops we produce could someday prevent a famine in Africa or food riots in India. A well-fed world is a peaceful world."

Chuck stepped in to finish the conversation with a zinger. "When you make fun of farmers, or criticize agriculture," he warned stern faced and serious, "don't talk with your mouth full."

Returning to the main school building from the green house, I caught sight of two pickup trucks in the back parking lot that appeared to be the familiar FFA blue.

"Are those your trucks?" I asked Chuck.

"They belong to the FFA chapter; we had to buy them with our own funds. They come in handy for moving things around."

"Do the kids ever pile in the back to go somewhere?"

"Heavens no," he shot back, looking more puzzled than ever at my question.

"The insurance company would skin us alive if we allowed students to ride in the back of an open pickup truck. If we need to go someplace, we use a school bus."

"Makes sense to me," I answered walking toward the trucks.

I had been a schoolteacher long enough to know how stupid my question was. The public schools have become the number-one target of every shyster lawyer, disgruntled parent, and lying student out to make a fast buck.

The trucks were painted the traditional FFA blue and had the great seal on the cab doors, just like the one I rode in to the skating rink back in … I paused and did a quick math problem in my head. My God, it was thirty-six years ago!

I stared at the trucks for a long time. There was something fundamentally different about them, but it took my brain a few minutes to figure it out. Then, it hit me; both trucks were Japanese-made Nissans.

"Better gas mileage," I said.

"What?" Chuck asked.

"Never mind," I said. "I was just kind of thinking to myself out loud."

Riding home from the new Union County High School, I wasn't disappointed. I didn't feel old, out of date, or depressed about my age. I liked this new world. I was happy about all the changes I had seen. The good old days are a myth, if not an outright lie.

However, I wasn't naive either. I knew that Union County is still a very small, and in many ways, and still a very backward place.

It is also still a very poor place, except that now the mobile home has replaced the shotgun shack as the domicile of the have-nots. The American welfare state is alive and well in Union County. A very high percentage of Union County families, both black and white, survive on welfare checks and aid to dependent children. All the grocery stores of Union County have prominent signs near the front door saying, "We accept food stamps."

Union County still doesn't have a hospital where children can be born. Strangely enough, it does have a hand surgery clinic operated by a doctor with a name that indicates he is either from Pakistan or India. Union County children are still being born in hospitals in Gainesville or Jacksonville, just like they were back in 1945. And, I suppose, they still have the same old rule about who can and can't claim to have been "born and 'reared' in Union County."

Many of the adults of the baby boomer generation had passed along their bad habits to their children. Teenage drinking and tobacco use are widespread in Union County. Also, from what I have observed, teenage hooliganism hasn't gone away either. It seemed to me that every road sign I passed was full of bullet holes and shotgun pellets.

There are no more moonshine stills in the woods of Union County. They have been replaced by marijuana patches, scattered throughout the remote pinewoods where the old stills used to sit. Union County's small sheriff's department and its out-of-the-way location mean that some of the large cow pastures and remote paved roads of the county often double as midnight landing strips for drug-filled, light aircraft.

There are no Wal-Marts, K-Marts, Burger Kings, or McDonalds in Union County. However, I some how feel that this might be a good thing. It means that locally owned, family-operated stores can still exist. In Union County, you can still buy real french fries, made from real potatoes. A hamburger can still be found made from fresh ground beef, rather than that hard-frozen, soybean-based, whatever it is they dish up in the fast-food, burger-in-a-box joints. Corporate America has yet to take over Union County and turn it into a carbon copy of plastic America. The existence of a Wal-Mart or a McDonalds in a town is a piss-poor way to measure progress.

Union County is also free of multiplex movie theaters, outlet malls, interstate highways, and all the assorted tourist trap and junk shop development that go with them. The lake is calm and peaceful, free of the loud and obnoxious jet skis that have spread across Florida like maggots on a dead cow, turning once-peaceful waterways into something that resembles a wet motorcycle track.

The state prison at Raiford is no longer the tiny institution I knew as a child. It is now a full-sized city with thousands of prisoners crowded into various "correctional institutions" located within sight of each other. What exists on paper as separate institutions is in reality one huge prison complex employing most of Union County's residents.

There have also been several new prisons built within easy commuting distance of Union County. Each newly built prison immediately begins to expand with new building and more inmates as soon as it is opened. While larger, more urban areas of Florida protest plans to build a new prison in their backyard, Union County welcomes each one warmly as a source of new jobs and business for local merchants. It seems that Union County is determined to be the major profiteer in America's war on crime.

In some ways, it is a depressing thought to realize that your home county is worth nothing more than to serve as a dumping ground for the human refuge of the state of Florida. The building of all the many prisons has only served to make Union County even more xenophobic and fearful than ever. The hundreds of reporters, lawyers, ministers, sociologists, death-row groupies, liberal do-gooder activists, priests, nuns, politicians, media pigs, and just plain assholes that flood into Raiford each time there is a well-publicized execution only tend to make the area even more distrustful of anyone from outside the county. Perhaps, for good reason, tabloid-style, trash-TV reporters and so-called "real crime authors" have depicted both the prison and surrounding area as a backward and ignorant place where nothing important ever takes place, except executions. Hundreds of times, smooth-talking reporters have betrayed friendships and the hospitality of Union County citizens to portray them as stereotypical ignorant southern hicks, rather than as real people. People who live in Union County have learned to have a healthy skepticism of reporters in particular and outsiders in general. Like many movie stars and politicians, these basically simple people have learned the hard way not to trust anyone and to keep their mouth shut. Therefore, newcomers should not expect to find a warm welcome and a friendly handshake in Union County. It just isn't that type of place, and it probably never will be.

A few weeks after my visit to the new Union County High School, a friend of mine and I were sitting on the tree-shaded outdoor patio of a popular restaurant in St. Augustine. From our black metal chairs, we could see the old Spanish fort, the Castillo de San Marcos—a brooding, squat, and gray structure—overlooking the beautiful blue-green waters of Matanzas Bay.

We were both basking in the beauty of the place and watching the shrimp boats entering the bay and coming to anchor off the old fort. They were patiently waiting for the Bridge of Lions to raise its drawbridge. Overhead, noisy sea gulls and brown pelicans circled waiting for the shrimp boats to begin cleaning their decks of all the dead fish and other sea refuge that had accumulated on their decks during the day.

The guy who sat across from me, drinking a cold Margarita, was named John, and he was a strange choice of friend for me. John was an English Literature major at Flagler College, a twenty-something, pretentious little asshole totally obsessed with his Rolex watch, designer jeans, and hundred-dollar shirts.

However, for some weird reason, we both enjoyed each other's company. John had brains and was a good conversationalist, and we both shared an irreverent, black sense of humor. But, I think what really drew us together was the fact that we were both trying to live down our past and become something we were not.

I was a fifty-something loud mouth of ignorant, po-white-trash ancestry. He was a spoiled-rotten military brat. John's father was a career-obsessed army officer; he was a hard-assed Green Beret colonel, who couldn't seem to understand that John was his son, not just another private. However, because of his father's rank, John had always had the best of everything, including an upper middle class, tennis court and swimming pool, education at Flagler College.

We were discussing southern writers, and he mentioned Thomas Wolf's brilliant novel, *You Can't Go Home Again.* John liked Thomas Wolf, because the famous writer was from North Carolina. John had spent most of his teenage years getting into all kinds of trouble in and around Fort Bragg and Fayetteville, which he called "Fayette-Nam," because it was such a vice-ridden, get-your-ass-whipped-in-a-minute army town. Of course, his father—the senior-ranking Green Beret colonel at Fort Bragg—always got him out of every scrape he got into.

John had graduated from Flagler College the previous June, and the real world scared the shit out of him. He was about to leave the beaches and outdoor patio bars of St. Augustine to take a job in Chicago working for a large insurance firm.

John had found that a Liberal Arts degree from Flagler College really didn't open a lot of doors on Wall Street, so he had to call upon his daddy, who was now retired out in Arizona. John wanted a position in either Los Angeles or New York, but his father didn't have any old army buddies in these places. So, John had to settle on an insurance adjuster's job, for what he though was poverty wages, in a suburb of Chicago.

John hated the thought of the bitterly cold winters he would have to endure in the Windy City. He also hated the thought of being in the real world, away from the warm womb of college and the protection of his daddy. Although his supervisor would be an old army buddy of his father, John would be working for a Fortune 500 company, and they demanded self-discipline and most of all production. John was not a very self-disciplined guy, and the thought of working hard in the insurance industry really didn't excite him. From what I knew of John, I really didn't think he would last long. He just wasn't a workaholic, go-getter type of guy.

I told him that if things didn't work out he could always come back. At this suggestion, John rolled his eyes back in his head and waxed poetic about the writings of Thomas Wolfe and the music of Bruce Springsteen.

"You can never go home again," he said. "Within every one of us is the darkness on the edge of town. You cross it when you graduate from college and move out into the world. You never return from that cold darkness. You never again have the protection of your parents or the camaraderie of your friends. Sooner or later, the darkness on the edge of town will engulf us all, and we must all move out into it, just as we must all some day move out into the cold darkness of death."

I sat back and let him run with his thoughts; he was on a roll.

"You can never go home again, because when you return home, it is no longer there. It is gone forever. Entering the darkness on the edge of town is like death; it is forever."

He paused, deep in thought as we both watched an overweight tourist struggle to get up the hill leading to the sally-port gate of the Castillo de San Marcos.

"It is a one-way trip; you can't go home again," John lamented again.

The way I had maintained my friendship with John was to let him run with his thoughts. I always avoided antagonizing him when he was in one of his deep philosophical moods. I never told him he was as full of shit as a constipated elephant. He imagined himself as some type of William Faulkner type of guy, a refugee in his own land.

I looked him straight in the eye and said, "To you there is a darkness on the edge of town, but, to me, it was a bright and glorious light at the end of a very dark and sinister childhood."

He looked at me with bewilderment. I could tell that I hadn't gotten through that thick head of his.

I had told John many times about what my life had been like growing up in Union County. However, it was like trying to explain nuclear fusion to a third grader. John could never seem to understand what I was talking about. To him dirt roads, segregated schools, hookworms, fleas, ticks, sore eyes, and grinding poverty were just something created in the mind of an imaginative Hollywood writer to give him amusement.

He had grown up with the *Dukes of Hazzard* and the *Beverly Hillbillies*. He had read Erskine Caldwell and thought *Tobacco Road* was hilarious, just like the crowds who watched the Broadway play and later the movie. They laughed their heads off at the antics of Jeter Lester. The South is the only place where poverty is funny, assuming of course that the poor people are white.

John never got the real message that Caldwell was trying to convey in *Tobacco Road*. Finally, I decided that I might as well spell it out for him.

"Of course, I can never go home again," I said; "but personally, I've never wanted to."

# The End